Frederick Marryat

The King's Own and the Pirate

Frederick Marryat

The King's Own and the Pirate

ISBN/EAN: 9783337182793

Printed in Europe, USA, Canada, Australia, Japan

Cover: Foto ©Andreas Hilbeck / pixelio.de

More available books at **www.hansebooks.com**

THE KING'S OWN

AND

THE PIRATE

BY

CAPTAIN MARRYAT

VOL. I.

LONDON
J. M. DENT AND CO.
BOSTON: LITTLE, BROWN AND CO.
MDCCCXCVI

Contents

VOLUME 1

THE KING'S OWN

Contents

List of Etchings

VOLUME I

THE KING'S OWN

Drawn by D. DOWNING.
Etched by W. WRIGHT-NOOTH.

capable of self-denial when his stomach was concerned, and I record it accordingly. (*Par parenthese*) it is well known that monkeys will take the smallpox, measles, and (I believe) the scarlet fever; but this poor fellow, when the ship's company were dying of cholera, took that disease, went through all its gradations, and died apparently in great agony."

It seems probable that *The King's Own*, though not actually published till a year after *The Naval Officer*, was Marryat's earliest work of fiction; and we are told that it was written in nine months. Further details concerning the manner of its composition are at hand. In Chapter xxii. the author delays the narrative by a graphic description of his own circumstances :—" I am seated in the after-cabin of a vessel endowed with as liberal a share of motion as any in his Majesty's service : whilst I write I am holding on by the table, my legs entwined in the lashings underneath, and I can barely manage to keep my position before my manuscript. The sea is high, the gale fresh, the sky dirty, and threatening a continuance of what our transatlantic descendants would term a pretty-considerable-tarnation-strong blast of wind. . . . The main-deck is afloat : and, from the careless fitting of the half-ports at the dock-yard, and neglect of caulking in the cants, my fore-cabin is in the same predicament. . . . I have just been summoned from my task, in consequence of one of the battens which secured my little library having given way to the immoderate weight of learning that pressed upon it : and as my books have been washed to and fro, I have snatched them from their first attempts at natation. . . . . My bones are sore with rocking. Horace says, that he had a soul of brass who first ventured to sea ; I think a body of iron very necessary to the outfit. My cot is swinging and jerking up to the beams, as if the lively scoundrel was some metamorphosed imp mocking at me." He touches, in more serious mood, on the same subject, at the close of Chapter xxix. " Reader, let us look at home. Shall I, now thoughtlessly riding upon the agitated billow, with but one thin plank between me and death, and yet so busy with this futile work, be permitted to bring it to a

close ?   The hand which guides the flowing pen may
to-morrow be stiff, the head now teeming with its subject
may be past all thought ere to-morrow's sun is set—ay
sooner ! and you, reader, who so far have had the courage
to proceed in the volumes without throwing them away,
shall you be permitted to finish your more trifling task ?—
or, before its close, be hurried from this transitory scene,
where fiction ends, and the spirit, re-endowed, will be
enabled to raise its eyes upon the lightning beam of
unveiled truth."   In Chapter xxxvii. he declares that he
has quite " *sprained* his imagination—for you must know
that this is all *fiction*, every word of it," and he proceeds
to indite an entirely irrelevant chapter about the ants in
his cabin, his grandmother, and a " wether sheep " who
learnt to " chew tobacco and drink grog "; all of which
has " nothing to do with the novel," but " a great deal to
do with *making a book*—for I have completed a whole
chapter out of nothing."

In the first chapter of *Newton Forster* it is written :—

"I remember when the 'King's Own' was finished, I was as happy as
a pedestrian who had accomplished his thousand miles in a thousand hours.
My voluntary slavery was over, and I was emancipated. Where was I then?
I recollect ; within two days' sail of the Lizard, returning home, after a six
weeks' cruise to discover a rock in the Atlantic, which never existed except
in the terrified or intoxicated noddle of some master of a merchant vessel.
It was about half-past five in the evening, and I was alone in my after-cabin,
quite alone, as the captain of a man-of-war must be, even in presence
of his ship's company. . . .

"I could not send for any one to whom I could impart the intelligence—
there was no one whom I could expect to sympathise with me, or to whom
I could pour out the abundance of my joy; for that the service prohibited.
What could I do? Why, I could dance; so I sprang from my chair, and
singing the tune, commenced a quadrille movement,—Tal de ral la, tal de
ral la, lity, lity, lity, liddle-um, tal de ral la, tal——

"'Three bells, sir,' cried the first lieutenant, who had opened my door
unperceived by me, and showed evident surprise at my motions; 'shall we
beat to quarters?'

"'Certainly, Mr B——,' replied I, and he disappeared. But this interruption only produced a temporary cessation: I was in the height of
'Cavalier seul,' when his head popped into the cabin—

"'All present, and sober, sir,' reported he, with a demure smile.

"'Except the captain, I presume you are thinking,' replied I.

"'Oh ! no, indeed, sir ; I observed you were very merry.'

> " ' I am, Mr B——, but not with wine; mine is a sort of intellectual intoxication not provided for in the Articles of War.'
> " ' A what! sir ? '
> " ' Oh! something that you'll never get drunk upon, as you never look into a book—beat a retreat.'
> " ' Ay, ay, sir,' replied the first lieutenant ; and he disappeared.
> " And I also beat a retreat to my sofa ; and as I threw myself upon it, mentally vowed that, for a month at least, I never would take up my pen."

The book is full of digressions; on the profession of authorship and the conduct of reviews—chap. xxviii., on courage, on Sunday at sea, on smuggling, on theology and natural history. There is also an interesting auto-biographical note, which may perhaps be partially credited, concerning Marryat's reasons for going to sea. " It was not," he declares, " to escape the drudgery and confinement of a school, or the admonitions received at home." But, after the battle of Trafalgar, "when I returned home, I witnessed the funeral profession of Lord Nelson; and, as the triumphal car, upon which his earthly remains were borne, disappeared from my aching eye, I felt that death could have no terrors if followed by such a funeral; and I determined that I would be buried in the same manner."

Yet the *King's Own* has a more consecutive plot than most of Marryat's novels, and moves with a fair degree of precision along its appointed lines. Its main interest, however, centres around its vivid pictures of sea life, and no one can resist justifying the author's prophecy by " finding out who the characters are meant for, notwithstanding his assertion" that they are purely fictitious. Captain M., like Captain Savage in *Peter Simple*, is certainly drawn from Cochrane, and the most famous passage in the book, the fight and shipwreck described in chapters li.-liv., is worked up from historical material, viz. :—the furious combat during a heavy gale between *The Indefatigable*, under Edward Pellew, Viscount Exmouth, *The Amazon*, and a French 74-gun ship *Droits de l'Homme*, which took place the 13th of January 1797. *The Amazon* and her French opponent both struck on the rocks on the morning of the 14th. Captain Capperbar was probably, as Mr Hannay suggests, a reminiscence of an officer who roused the wrath of Cochrane in Corfu, by granting passes to neutral and hostile vessels for trading with the island.

The novel stands among Marryat's greatest performances, though it will never be so popular as *Peter Simple* or *Midshipman Easy*, and does not quite deserve the honour. It has none of the disagreeable characteristics of *Frank Mildmay*, and is on the whole superior to that work, whether or no it was written before it. One is not surprised to find that its surpassing freshness and vigour were at once recognised by the reviews.

The King's Own is here reprinted from the first edition in 3 volumes, Henry Colburn and Richard Bentley, 1830; several mistakes about names and other details being corrected.

The Pirate is reprinted from the sumptuous first edition, A. Fullarton and Co., MDCCCXLV., with illustrations by Clarkson Stanfield, Esq., R.A.; when it was bound in one volume with *The Three Cutters*.

R. B. J.

The King's Own

—◆—

Chapter I

However boldly their warm blood was spilt,
Their life was shame, their epitaph was guilt ;
And this they knew and felt, at least the one,
The leader of the band he had undone,—
Who, born for better things, had madly set
His life upon a *cast*, which lingered yet.

BYRON.

THERE is perhaps no event in the annals of our history
which excited more alarm at the time of its occurrence, or
has since been the subject of more general interest, than
the Mutiny at the Nore, in the year 1797. Forty thousand
men, to whom the nation looked for defence from its surrounding enemies, and in stedfast reliance upon whose
bravery it lay down every night in tranquillity,—men who
had dared everything for their king and country, and in
whose breasts patriotism, although suppressed for the
time, could never be extinguished,—irritated by ungrateful neglect on the one hand, and by seditious advisers on
the other, turned the guns which they had so often manned
in defence of the English flag against their own countrymen and their own home, and, with all the acrimony of
feeling ever attending family quarrels, seemed determined
to sacrifice the nation and themselves, rather than listen to
the dictates of reason and of conscience.

Doubtless there is a point at which endurance of
oppression ceases to be a virtue, and rebellion can no
longer be considered as a crime : but it is a dangerous
and intricate problem, the solution of which had better not

be attempted.   It must, however, be acknowledged, that
the seamen, on the occasion of the first mutiny, had just
grounds of complaint, and that they did not proceed to
acts of violence until repeated and humble remonstrance
had been made in vain.

Whether we act in a body or individually, such is the
infirmity and selfishness of human nature, that we often
surrender to importunity that which we refuse to the
dictates of gratitude,—yielding, for our own comfort, to
the demands of turbulence, while quiet, unpretending
merit is overlooked and oppressed, until, roused by
neglect, it demands, as a right, what policy alone should
have granted as a favour.

Such was the behaviour, on the part of government,
which produced the mutiny at the Nore.

What mechanism is more complex than the mind of
man ?   And as, in all machinery, there are wheels and
springs of action not apparent without close examination of
the interior, so pride, ambition, avarice, love, play alternately or conjointly upon the human mind, which, under
their influences, is whirled round like the weathercock in
the hurricane, only pointing for a short time in one direction, but for that time stedfastly.   How difficult, then, to
analyse the motives and inducements which actuated the
several ringleaders in this dreadful crisis !

Let us, therefore, confine ourselves to what we do really
know to have been the origin of discontent in one of these
men, whose unfortunate career is intimately connected
with this history.

Edward Peters was a man of talent and education.   He
had entered on board the —— in a fit of desperation, to
obtain the bounty for a present support, and his pay as a
future provision, for his wife, and an only child, the fruit
of a hasty and unfortunate marriage.   He was soon distinguished as a person of superior attainments ; and instead
of being employed, as a landsman usually is, in the after-
guard, or waist, of the ship, he was placed under the
orders of the purser and captain's clerk as an amanuensis.

In this capacity he remained two or three years, approved
of and treated with unusual respect by the officers, for his
gentlemanlike appearance and behaviour : but unfortunately
a theft had been committed,—a watch, of trifling value,
had been purloined from the purser's cabin ; and, as he
was the only person, with the exception of the servant,
who had free ingress and egress, suspicion fell upon him—
the more so as, after every search that could be made had
proved ineffectual, it was supposed that the purloined
property had been sent on shore to be disposed of by his
wife, who, with his child, had frequently been permitted
to visit him on board.

Summoned on the quarter-deck—cross-examined, and
harshly interrogated—called a scoundrel by the captain
before conviction—the proud blood mantled in the cheeks
of one who, at that period, was incapable of crime.   The
blush of virtuous indignation was construed into presumptive evidence of guilt.   The captain—a superficial, pre-
suming, pompous, yet cowardly creature, whose conduct
assisted in no small degree to excite the mutiny on board
of his own ship—declared himself quite convinced of
Peters' guilt, because he blushed at the bare idea of being
suspected ; and punishment ensued, with all the degradation allotted to an offence which is never forgiven on board
of a man-of-war.

There is, perhaps, no crime that is attended with such
serious consequences on board a ship as theft.   A succes-
sion of thefts undiscovered will disintegrate a ship's
company, break up the messes, destroy all confidence
and harmony, and occasion those who have been the
dearest friends to become the greatest enemies : for whom
can a person suspect, when he has lost his property, in
so confined a space, but those who were acquainted with
its being in his possession, and with the place in which
it was deposited ?—and who are these but his own messmates, or those in whom he most confided ?   After positive
conviction, no punishment can be too severe for a crime
that produces such mischief; but to degrade a man by

corporal punishment, to ruin his character, and render him an object of abhorrence and contempt in the absence of even bare presumptive evidence, was an act of cruelty and injustice, which could excite but one feeling; and, from that day, the man who would have gloried in dying for his country, became a discontented, gloomy, and dangerous subject.

The above effect would have been produced in any man; but to Peters, whose previous history we have yet to narrate, death itself would have been preferable. His heart did not break, but it swelled with contending passions, till it was burst and riven with wounds never to be cicatrised. Suffering under the most painful burthen that can oppress a man who values reputation, writhing with the injustice of accusation when innocent, of conviction without proof, and of punishment unmerited, it is not to be wondered at that Peters took the earliest opportunity of deserting from the ship.

There is a particular feeling pervading animal nature, from which man himself is not exempt. Indeed, with all his boasted reason, man still inherits too many of the propensities of the brute creation. I refer to that disposition which not only inclines us to feel satisfaction at finding we have companions in misfortune, but too often stimulates us to increase the number by our own exertions. From the stupendous elephant, down to the smallest of the feathered tribe, all will act as a decoy to their own species, when in captivity themselves; and, in all compulsory service, which may be considered a species of captivity, man proves that he is embued with the same propensity. Seamen that have been pressed themselves into the navy, are invariably the most active in pressing others; and both soldiers and sailors have a secret pleasure in recapturing a deserter, even at the very time when they are watching an opportunity to desert themselves.

The bonds of friendship seem destroyed when this powerful and brutal feeling is called into action; and, as has frequently occurred in the service, before and since, the man who was selected by Peters as his most intimate friend, the man with whom he had consulted, and to whom he had confided his plans for desertion, gave information of the retreat of his wife and child, from which place Peters was not likely to be very distant; and thus, with the assistance of this, his dearest friend, the master-at-arms and party in quest of him succeeded in his capture.

It so happened, that on the very day on which Peters was brought on board and put into irons, the purser's servant was discovered to have in his possession the watch that had been lost. Thus far the character of Peters was reinstated; and as he had declared at the time of his capture, that the unjust punishment which he had received had been the motive of his disertion, the captain was strongly urged by the officers to overlook an offence which had everything to be offered in extenuation. But Captain A——was fond of courts-martial; he imagined that they added to his consequence, which certainly required to be upheld by adventitious aid. Moreover, the feeling, too often pervading little minds, that of a dislike taken to a person because you have injured him, and the preferring to accumulate injustice rather than to acknowledge error, had more than due weight with this weak man. A court-martial was held, and Peters was sentenced to death; but, in consideration of circumstances, the sentence was mitigated to that of being " flogged round the fleet."

Mitigated! Strange vanity in men, that they should imagine their own feelings to be more sensible and acute than those of others: that they should consider *that a mitigation* in favour of the prisoner, which, had they been placed in his situation, they would have declared an *accumulation* of the punishment. Not a captain who sat upon that court-martial but would have considered, as Peters did, that death was by far the more lenient sentence of the two. Yet they meant well — they felt kindly towards him, and acknowledged his provocations; but they fell into the too common error of supposing that the finer feelings, which induce a man to prefer death to dishonour, are only to be recognised among the higher classes ; and that, because circumstances may have placed a man before the mast, he will undergo punishment, however severe, however degrading,—in short, every " ill that flesh is heir to,"—in preference to death.

As the reader may not perhaps be acquainted with the nature of the punishment to which Peters was sentenced, and the ceremonies by which it is attended, I shall enter into a short description of it.

A man sentenced to be flogged round the fleet receives an equal part of the whole number of lashes awarded alongside each ship composing that fleet. For instance if sentenced to three hundred lashes, in a fleet composed of ten sail, he will receive thirty alongside of each ship.

A launch is fitted up with a platform and shears. It is occupied by the unfortunate individual, the provost-marshal, the boatswain, and his mates, with their implements of office, and armed marines stationed at the bow and stern. When the signal is made for punishment, all the ships in the fleet send one or two boats each, with crews cleanly dressed, the officers in full uniform, and marines under arms. These boats collect at the side of the ship where the launch is lying, the hands are turned up, and the ship's company are ordered to mount the rigging, to witness that portion of the whole punishment which, after the sentence has been read, is inflicted upon the prisoner. When he has received the allotted number of lashes, he is, for the time, released, and permitted to sit down, with a blanket over his shoulders, while the boats, which attend the execution of the sentence, make fast to the launch, and tow it to the next ship in the fleet, where the same number of lashes are inflicted with corresponding ceremonies ;—and thus he is towed from one ship to the other until he has received the whole of his punishment.

The severity of this punishment consists not only in

the number of lashes, but in the peculiar manner in which they are inflicted ; as, after the unfortunate wretch has received the first part of his sentence alongside of one ship, the blood is allowed to congeal, and the wounds partially to close, during the interval which takes place previously to his arrival alongside of the next, when the cat again subjects him to renewed and increased torture. During the latter part of the punishment, the suffering is dreadful ; and a man who has undergone this sentence is generally broken down in constitution, if not in spirits, for the remainder of his life.

Such was the punishment inflicted upon the unfortunate Peters ; and it would be difficult to decide, at the moment when it was completed, and the blanket thrown over his shoulders, whether the heart or the back of the fainting man were the more lacerated of the two.

Time can heal the wounds of the body, over which it holds its empire ; but those of the soul, like the soul itself, spurn his transitory sway.

Peters, from that moment, was a desperate man. A short time after he had undergone his sentence, the news of the mutiny at Spithead was communicated ; and the vacillation and apprehensions of the Admiralty, and of the nation at large, were not to be concealed. This mutiny was apparently quelled by conciliation ; but conciliation is but a half-measure, and ineffectual when offered from superiors to inferiors.

In this world, I know not why, there seems to be but one seal binding in all contracts of magnitude—and that seal is *blood*. Without referring to the Jewish types, proclaiming that " all things were purified by blood, and without shedding of blood there was no remission,"— without referring to that sublime mystery by which these types have been fulfilled,—it appears as if, in all ages and all countries, blood had been the only seal of security.

Examine the records of history, the revolution of opinion, the public tumults, the warfare for religious ascendancy—it will be found that without this seal, these were only lulled for the moment, and invariably recommenced until *blood* had made its appearance as witness to "the act and deed."

Chapter II

This is a long description, but applies
To scarce five minutes past before the eyes;
But yet *what* minutes! Moments like to these
Rend men's lives into immortalities.

BYRON.

THE mutiny at Spithead was soon followed up by that at the Nore; and the ringleader, Parker, like a meteor darting through the firmament, sprung from nothing, coruscated, dazzled, and disappeared. The Texel fleet joined, except a few ships, which the courage and conduct of the gallant old Admiral Duncan preserved from the contagion. Let me here digress a little, to introduce to my readers the speech made by this officer to his ship's company on the first symptoms of disaffection. It is supposed that sailors are not eloquent. I assert that, with the exception of the North American Indians, who have to perfection the art of saying much in few words, there are few people more eloquent than sailors. The general object looked for in this world is to obtain the greatest possible effect with the smallest power; if so, the more simple the language, the more matter is condensed, the nearer we approach to perfection. Flourishes and flowers of rhetoric may be compared to extra wheels applied to a carriage, increasing the rattling and complexity of the machine, without adding to either the strength of its fabric or the rapidity of its course.

It was on the 6th of June that the fleet at the Nore was joined by the *Agamemnon*, *Leopard*, *Ardent*, and other ships, which had separated from Admiral Duncan's

fleet. When the admiral found himself deserted by part
of his own fleet, he called his own ship's crew together,
and addressed them in the following speech :—

"My lads! I once more call you together with a
sorrowful heart, owing to what I have lately seen, the
disaffection of the fleets; I call it disaffection, for the
crews have no grievances. To be deserted by my fleet,
in the face of the enemy, is a disgrace which, I believe,
never before happened to a British admiral; nor could
I have supposed it possible. My greatest comfort under
God is, that I have been supported by the officers, seamen,
and marines of this ship, for which, with a heart over-
flowing with gratitude, I request you to accept my sincere
thanks. I flatter myself much good may result from your
example, by bringing those deluded people to a sense of
the duty which they owe, not only to their king and
country, but to themselves.

"The British navy has ever been the support of that
liberty which has been handed down to us by our ancestors,
and which I trust we shall maintain to the latest posterity
—and that can only be done by unanimity and obedience.
This ship's company, and others, who have distinguished
themselves by loyalty and good order, deserve to be, and
doubtless will be, the favourites of a grateful nation. They
will also have, from their inward feeling, a comfort which
will be lasting, and not like the floating and false confidence of those who have swerved from their duty.

"It has often been my pride with you to look into the
Texel, and see a foe which dreaded coming out to meet
us. My pride is now humbled indeed! our cup has over-
flown, and made us wanton—the Allwise Providence has
given us this check as a warning, and I hope we shall
improve by it. On Him then let us trust where our only
security is to be found. I find there are many good men
among us; for my own part, I have had full confidence
of all in this ship; and once more I beg to express my
approbation of your conduct.

"May God, who has thus far conducted you, continue

to do so ; and may the British navy, the glory and support
of our country, be restored to its wonted splendour, and be
not only the bulwark of Britain, but the terror of the world.

" But this can only be effected by a strict adherence to
our duty and obedience ; and let us pray that the Almighty
God may keep us in the right way of thinking.

" God bless you all."

At an address so unassuming, and so calculated, from
its simplicity and truth, to touch the human heart, the
whole ship's crew were melted into tears, and declared
their resolution to adhere to their admiral in life or death.
Had all the ships in the fleet been commanded by such
men as Admiral Duncan, the mutiny at Spithead would
not have been succeeded by that at the Nore ; but the seamen had no confidence, either in their officers, or in those
who presided at the Board of Admiralty ; and distrust of
their promises, which were considered to be given merely
to gain time, was the occasion of the second and more
alarming rebellion of the two.

The irritated mind of Peters was stimulated to join the
disaffected parties. His pride, his superior education, and
the acknowledgment among his shipmates that he was an
injured man, all conspired to place him in the dangerous
situation of ringleader on board of his own ship, the crew
of which, although it had not actually joined in the mutiny,
now showed open signs of discontent.

But the mine was soon exploded by the behaviour of
the captain. Alarmed at the mutinous condition of the
other ships which were anchored near to him, and the
symptoms of dissatisfaction in his own, he proceeded to
an act of unjustifiable severity, evidently impelled by fear
and not by resolution. He ordered several of the petty
officers and leading men of the ship to be thrown into
irons, because they were seen to be earnestly talking together on the forecastle,—and recollecting that his conduct
towards Peters had been such as to warrant disaffection,
he added him to the number. The effect of this injudicious
step was immediate. The men came aft in a body on the

quarter-deck, and requested to know the grounds upon which Peters and the other men had been placed in confinement; and perceiving alarm in the countenance of the captain, notwithstanding the resolute bearing of the officers, they insisted upon the immediate release of their shipmates. Thus the first overt act of mutiny was brought on by the misconduct of the captain.

The officers expostulated and threatened in vain. Three cheers were called for by a voice in the crowd, and three cheers were immediately given. The marines, who still remained true to their allegiance, had been ordered under arms; the first lieutenant of the ship—for the captain, trembling and confused, stood a mere cypher—gave the order for the ship's company to go below, threatening to fire upon them if the order was not instantaneously obeyed. The captain of marines brought his men to the " make ready," and they were about to present, when the first lieutenant waved his hand to stop the decided measure, until he had first ascertained how far the mutiny was general. He stepped a few paces forward, and requested that every "blue jacket" who was inclined to remain faithful to his king and country, would walk over from that side of the quarter-deck upon which the ship's company were assembled, to the one which was occupied by the officers and marines.

A pause and silence ensued—when, after some pushing and elbowing through the crowd, William Adams, an elderly quartermaster, made his appearance in the front, and passed over to the side where the officers stood, while the hisses of the rest of the ship's company expressed their disapprobation of his conduct. The old man just reached the other side of the deck, when turning round like a lion at bay, with one foot on the *comings* of the hatchway, and his arm raised in the air to command attention, he addressed them in these few words :—

"My lads, I have fought for my king five-and-thirty years, and have been too long in his service to turn a rebel in my old age."

Would it be credited that, after the mutiny had been quelled, no representation of this conduct was made to government by his captain? Yet such was the case, and such was the gratitude of Captain A——.

The example shown by Adams was not followed :—the ship's crew again cheered, and ran down the hatchways, leaving the officers and marines on deck. They first disarmed the sentry under the half-deck, and released the prisoners, and then went forward to consult upon further operations.

They were not long in deciding. A boatswain's mate, who was one of the ringleaders, piped, "Stand by hammocks!" The men ran on deck, each seizing a hammock, and jumping with it down below on the main deck. The object of this manœuvre not being comprehended, they were suffered to execute it without interruption. In a few minutes they sent up the marine, whom they had disarmed when sentry over the prisoners, to state that they wished to speak with the captain and officers, who, after some discussion, agreed that they would descend and hear the proposals which the ship's company should make. Indeed, even with the aid of the marines, many of whom were wavering, resistance would now have been useless, and could only have cost them their lives; for they were surrounded by other ships who had hoisted the flag of insubordination, and whose guns were trained ready to pour in a destructive fire on the least sign of an attempt to purchase their anchor. To the main-deck they consequently repaired.

The scene which here presented itself was as striking as it was novel. The after-part of the main-deck was occupied by the captain and officers, who had come down with the few marines who still continued stedfast to their duty, and one sailor only, Adams, who had so nobly stated his determination on the quarter-deck. The foremost part of the deck was tenanted by a noisy and tumultuous throng of seamen, whose heads only appeared above a barricade of hammocks, which they had formed across the deck, and out of which at two embrasures, admirably constructed, two long twenty-four pounders, loaded up to the muzzle with grape and canister shot, were pointed aft in the direction where the officers and marines were standing —a man at the breech of each gun, with a match in his hand (which he occasionally blew, that the priming powder might be more rapidly ignited), stood ready for the signal to fire.

The captain, aghast at the sight, would have retreated, but the officers, formed of sterner materials, persuaded him to stay, although he showed such evident signs of fear and perturbation, as seriously to injure a cause, in which resolution and presence of mind alone could avail. The mutineers, at the suggestion of Peters, had already sent aft their preliminary proposals, which were, that the officers and marines should surrender up their arms, and consider themselves under an arrest—intimating, at the same time, that the first step in advance made by any one of their party would be the signal for applying the match to the touch-holes of the guns.

There was a pause and dead silence, as if it were a calm, although every passion was roused and on the alert; every bosom heaved tumultuously, and every pulse was trebled in its action. The same feeling which so powerfully affects the truant schoolboy—who, aware of his offence, and dreading the punishment in perspective, can scarce enjoy the rapture of momentary emancipation—acted upon the mutineers, in an increased ratio, proportioned to the magnitude of their stake. Some hearts beat with remembrance of injuries and hopes of vengeance and retaliation; others with ambition, long dormant, bursting from its concealed recess; and many were actuated by that restlessness which induced them to consider any change to be preferable to the monotony of existence in compulsory servitude.

Among the officers, some were oppressed with anxious forebodings of evil—those peculiar sensations which, when death approaches nearly to the outward senses, alarm the heart; others experienced no feeling but that of manly fortitude and determination to die, if necessary, like men; in others, alas!—in which party, small as it was, the captain was pre-eminent—fear and trepidation amounted almost to the loss of reason.

Such was the state of the main-deck of the ship, at the moment in which we are now describing it to the reader.

And yet, in the very centre of all this tumult, there was one who, although not indifferent to the scene around him, felt interested without being anxious; astonished without being alarmed. Between the contending and divided parties, stood a little boy, about six years old. He was the perfection of childish beauty; chestnut hair waved in curls on his forehead, health glowed on his rosy cheeks, dimples sported over his face as he altered the expression of his countenance, and his large dark eyes flashed with intelligence and animation. He was dressed in mimic imitation of a man-of-war's man—loose trousers, tightened at the hips, to preclude the necessity of suspenders—and a white duck frock, with long sleeves and blue collar—while a knife, attached to a lanyard, was suspended round his neck: a light and narrow-brimmed straw hat on his head completed his attire. At times he looked aft at the officers and marines; at others he turned his eyes forward to the hammocks, behind which the ship's company were assembled. The sight was new to him, but he was already accustomed to reflect much, and to ask few questions. Go to the officers he did not, for the presence of the captain restrained him. Go to the ship's company he could not, for the barricade of hammocks prevented him. There he stood, in wonderment, but not in fear.

There was something beautiful and affecting in the situation of the boy; calm, when all around him was anxious tumult; thoughtless, when the brains of others were oppressed with the accumulation of ideas; contented, where all was discontent; peaceful, where each party that he stood between was thirsting for each other's blood:—

there he stood, the only happy, the only innocent one, amongst hundreds swayed by jarring interests and contending passions.

And yet he was in keeping, although in such strong contrast, with the rest of the picture; for where is the instance of the human mind being so thoroughly depraved as not to have one good feeling left? Nothing exists so base and vile as not to have one redeeming quality. There is no poison without some antidote—no precipice, however barren, without some trace of verdure—no desert, however vast, without some spring to refresh the parched traveller, some oasis, some green spot, which, from its situation, in comparison with surrounding objects, appears almost heavenly; and thus did the boy look almost angelic, standing as he did between the angry exasperated parties on the main-deck of the disorganised ship.

After some little time, he walked forward, and leaned against one of the twenty-four pounders that was pointed out of the embrasure, the muzzle of which was on a level with, and intercepted by, his little head.

Adams, the quarter-master, observing the dangerous situation of the child, stepped forward. This was against the stipulations laid down by the mutineers, and Peters cried out to him — "Heave-to, Adams, or we fire!" Adams waved his hand in expostulation, and continued to advance. "Keep back," again cried Peters, "or by——, we fire!"

"Not upon one old man, Peters, and he unarmed," replied Adams; "I'm not worth so much powder and shot." The man at the gun blew his match. "For God's sake, for your own sake, as you value your happiness and peace of mind, do not fire, Peters!" cried Adams, with energy, "or you'll never forgive yourself."

"Hold fast the match," said Peters; "we need not fear one man;" and as he said this, Adams had come up to the muzzle of the gun, and seized the boy, whom he snatched up in his arms.

"I only came forward, Peters, to save your own boy,

whose head would have been blown to atoms if you had chanced to have fired the gun," said Adams, turning short round, and walking aft with the boy in his arms.

" God in heaven bless you, Adams ! " cried Peters, with a faltering voice, and casting a look of fond affection at the child. The heart of the mutineer was at that moment softened by parental feelings, and he blew the priming off the touch-hole of the gun, lest an accidental spark should risk the life of his child, who was now aft with the officers and their party.

Reader, this little boy will be the hero of our tale.

Chapter III

Roused discipline alone proclaims their cause,
And injured navies urge their broken laws.
Pursue we in his track the mutineer.

BYRON.

MAN, like all other animals of a gregarious nature, is more inclined to follow than to lead. There are few who are endued with that impetus of soul which prompts them to stand foremost as leaders in the storming of the breach, whether it be of a fortress of stone, or the more dangerous one of public opinion, when failure in the one case may precipitate them on the sword, and in the other consign them to the scaffold.

In this mutiny there were but few of the rare class referred to above :—in the ship whose movements we have been describing, not one, perhaps, except Peters. There were many boisterous, many threatening, but no one, except him, who was equal to the command, or to whom the command could have been confided. He was, on board of his own ship, the very life and soul of the mutiny. At the moment described at the end of the last chapter, all the better feelings of his still virtuous heart were in action; and, by a captain possessing resolution and a knowledge of human nature, the mutiny might have been suppressed; but Captain A——, who perceived the anxiety of Peters, thought the child a prize of no small value, and, as Adams brought him aft, snatched the boy from his arms, and desired two of the party of marines to turn their loaded muskets at his young heart — thus intimating to the mutineers that he would shoot the child at the first sign of hostility on their part.

The two marines who had received this order looked at each other in silence, and did not obey. It was repeated by the captain, who considered that he had hit upon a masterpiece of diplomacy. The officers expostulated; the officer commanding the party of marines turned away in disgust; but in vain: the brutal order was reiterated with threats. The whole party of marines now murmured, and consulted together in a low tone.

Willy Peters was the idol and plaything of the whole crew. He had always been accustomed to remain on board with his father, and there was not a man in the ship who would not have risked his life to have saved that of the child. The effect of this impolitic and cruel order was decisive. The marines, with the sergeant at their head, and little Willy placed in security in the centre, their bayonets directed on the defensive towards the captain and officers, retreated to the mutineers, whom they joined with three cheers, as the child was lifted over the barricade of hammocks, and received into his father's arms.

" We must not submit to their terms, sir," said the first lieutenant.

" Any terms, any terms," answered the terrified captain: " tell them so, for God's sake, or they will fire. Adams, go forward, and tell them we submit."

This order was, however, unnecessary; for the mutineers, aware of the impossibility of any further resistance, had thrown down the barricade of hammocks, and, with Peters at their head, were coming aft.

" You consent, gentlemen, to consider yourselves under an arrest?" inquired Peters of the first lieu-

K. I. B

tenant and officers, without paying any attention to the captain.

"We do, we do," cried Captain A——. "I hope you will not stain your hands with blood. Mr Peters, I meant the child no harm."

"If you had murdered him, Captain A——, you could not have injured him so much as you have injured his father," retorted Peters; "but fear not for your life, sir; that is safe; and you will meet all the respect and attention to your wants that circumstances will permit. We war not with individuals."

It was a proud moment for Peters to see this man cringing before him, and receiving with thanks the promise of his life from one whom he had so cruelly treated. There was a glorious revenge in it, the full force of which could only be felt by the granting, not the receiving party: for it could only be appreciated by one who possessed those fine and honourable feelings, of which Captain A—— was wholly destitute.

If the reader will consult the various records of the times which we are now describing, he will find that every respect was personally paid to the officers, although they were deprived of their arms. Some of the most obnoxious were sent on shore, and the intemperate conduct of others produced effects for which they had only to thank themselves; but, on the whole, the remark made by Peters was strictly correct: "They warred not with individuals"—they demanded justice from an ungrateful country.

It is true that the demands in this mutiny were not so reasonable as in the preceding; but where is the *man* who can confine himself to the exact balance of justice when his own feelings are unwittingly thrown into the scale?

As I before stated, it is not my intention to follow up the details of this national disgrace, but merely to confine myself to that part which is connected with the present history. Peters, as delegate from his ship, met the others, who were daily assembled, by Parker's directions, on board of the *Queen Charlotte*, and took a leading and decided part in the arrangements of the disaffected fleet.

But Parker, the ringleader, although a man of talent, was not equal to the task he had undertaken. He lost sight of several important features necessary to insure success in all civil commotions; such as rapidity and decision of action, constant employment being found, and continual excitement being kept up, amongst his followers, to afford no time for reflection. Those who serve under an established government know exactly their present weight in the scale of worldly rank, and the extent of their future expectations; they have accustomed themselves to bound their ambition accordingly; and feeling conscious that passive obedience is the surest road to advancement, are led quietly, here or there, to be slaughtered at the will and caprice of their superiors. But the leader of the disaffected against an established government has a difficult task. He has nothing to offer to his followers but promises. There is nothing on hand—all is expectation. If allowed time for reflection, they soon perceive that they are acting an humble part in a dangerous game; and that even though it be attended with success, in all probability they will receive no share of the advantages, although certain of incurring a large proportion of the risk. The leader of a connected force of the above description rises to a dangerous height when borne up by the excitement of the time; but let it once be permitted to subside, and, like the aëronaut in his balloon, from which the gas escapes while it is soaring in the clouds, he is precipitated from his lofty station, and gravitates to his own destruction.

He must be a wonderful man who can collect all the resources of a popular commotion, and bring it to a successful issue. The reason is obvious—everything depends upon the leader alone. His followers are but as the stones composing the arch of the bridge by which the gulf is to be crossed between them and their nominal superiors; he is the keystone, upon which the whole depends—if completely fitted, rendering the arch durable and capable of bearing any pressure; but if too small in dimensions, or imperfect in conformation, rendering the whole labour futile, and occasioning all the fabric previously raised to be precipitated by its own weight, and dispersed in ruin and confusion.

This latter was the fate of the mutiny at the Nore. The insurrection was quelled, and the ringleaders were doomed to undergo the utmost penalty of martial law. Among the rest, Peters was sentenced to death.

In the foremost part of the main-deck of a line-of-battle ship, in a square room, strongly bulkheaded, and receiving light from one of the ports, as firmly secured with an iron grating—with no other furniture than a long wooden form —his legs in shackles, that ran upon a heavy iron bar lying on the deck—sat the unfortunate prisoner, in company with three other individuals—his wife, his child, and old Adams, the quarter-master. Peters was seated on the deck, supporting himself by leaning against the bulkhead. His wife was lying beside him, with her face hidden in his lap. Adams occupied the form, and the child stood between his knees. All were silent, and the eyes of the three were directed towards one of the sad company, who appeared more wretched and disconsolate than the rest.

"My dear, dear Ellen!" said Peters mournfully, as a fresh burst of grief convulsed her attenuated frame.

"Why, then, refuse my solicitations, Edward? If not for yourself, listen to me for the sake of your wife and child. Irritated as your father still may be, his dormant affection will be awakened, when he is acquainted with the dreadful situation of his only son; nay, his family pride will never permit that you should perish by so ignominious a death; and your assumed name will enable him, without blushing, to exert his interest, and obtain your reprieve."

"Do not put me to the pain of again refusing you, my dearest Ellen. I desire to die, and my fate must be a warning to others. When I reflect what dreadful conse-quences might have ensued to the country from our rebellious proceedings, I am thankful, truly thankful, to

God, that we did not succeed. I know what you would urge—my wrongs, my undeserved stripes. I, too, would urge them ; and when my conscience has pressed me hard, have urged them in palliation ; but I feel that it is only in palliation, not in justification, that they can be brought forward. They are no more in comparison with my crime than the happiness of one individual is to that of the nation which I assisted to endanger, because one constituting a part of it had, unauthorised, oppressed me. No, no, Ellen, I should not be happy if I were not to atone for my faults ; and this wretched life is the only atonement I can offer. But for you, and that poor child, my dearest and kindest, I should go to the scaffold rejoicing ; but the thoughts—O God, strengthen and support me ! " cried the unhappy man, hiding his face in his hands.

" Fear not for me, Edward. I feel here," said Ellen, laying her hand on her heart, " a conviction that we shall soon meet again. I will urge you no more, love. But the boy—the boy—Oh, Edward, what will become of that dear boy, when we are both gone ? "

" Please God to spare my life, he'll never want a father," said old Adams, as the tears found a devious passage down the furrows of his weather-beaten face.

" What will become of him ? " cried Peters with energy. " Why, he shall retrieve his father's fault—wash out the stains in his father's character. He shall prove as liege a subject as I have been a rebellious one. He shall as faithfully serve his country as I have shamefully deserted it. He shall be as honest as I have been false ; and oh, may he be as prosperous as I have been unfortunate—as happy as I have been miserable. Come hither, boy. By the fond hopes I entertain of pardon and peace above—by the Almighty, in whose presence I must shortly tremble, I here devote thee to thy country—serve her bravely and faithfully. Tell me, Willy, do you understand me, and will you promise me this ? "

The boy laid his head upon his father's shoulder, and answered in a low tone—" I will ; " and then after a short pause, added, " but what are they going to do with you, father ? "

" I am going to die for my country's good, my child. If God wills it, may you do the same, but in a more honourable manner."

The boy seemed lost in thought, and, after a short time, quitted his father's side, and sat down on the deck by his mother, without speaking.

Adams rose, and taking him up, said, " Mayhap you have that to talk of which wants no listeners. I will take Willy with me, and give him a little air before I put him in his hammock. It's but a close hole this. Good-night to you both, though I'm afeard that's but a wish."

But a wish indeed!—and it was the last that was ever to close upon the unhappy Peters. The next morning was appointed for his execution. There are scenes of such consummate misery, that they cannot be portrayed without harrowing up the feelings of the reader,—and of these the climax may be found in a fond wife, lying at the feet of her husband during the last twelve hours of his mortal career. We must draw the curtain.

And now, reader, the title of this work, which may have puzzled you, will be explained ; for, intelligible as it may be to our profession, it may be a mystery to those who are not in his Majesty's service. The broad-headed arrow was a mark assumed at the time of the Edwards (when it was considered the most powerful weapon of attack), as distinguishing the property of the King; and this mark has been continued down to the present day. Every article supplied to his Majesty's service from the arsenals and dockyards is thickly studded with this mark ; and to be found in possession of any property so marked is a capital offence, as it designates that property to be the *King's own.*

When Adams left the condemned cell with Willy, he thought upon what had passed, and as Peters had devoted the boy to his King and country, he felt an irresistible desire to mark him. The practice of tattooing is very common in the navy; and you will see a sailor's arm covered with emblems from the shoulder to the wrist; his own initials, that of his sweetheart, the crucifix, Neptune, and mermaids being huddled together, as if mythology and scripture were one and the same thing. Adams was not long in deciding, and telling our little hero that his father wished it—he easily persuaded him to undergo the pain of the operation, which was performed on the forecastle, by pricking the shape of the figure required with the points of needles, and rubbing the bleeding parts with wet gunpowder and ink. By these simple means the form of a broad-headed arrow, or the King's mark, was, in the course of an hour, indelibly engraved upon the left shoulder of little Willy, who was then consigned to his hammock.

Chapter IV

The strife was o'er, the vanquished had their doom ;
The mutineers were crush'd, dispersed, or ta'en,
Or lived to deem the happiest were the slain.

BYRON.

THE day broke serenely but brightly, and poured in a stream of light through the iron grating of the cell where Peters and his wife lay clasped in each other's arms, not asleep, but torpid, and worn out with extreme suffering. Peters was the first to break the silence, and gently moved Ellen, as he called her by her name. She had not for some time lifted up her head, which was buried in his bosom; and she was not aware that the darkness had been dispelled. She raised her head at his summons, and as the dazzling light burst upon her sunken eyes, so did the recollection that this was the fatal morning flash upon her memory.

With a shriek, she again buried her face in the bosom of her husband. "Ellen, as you love me," said Peters, "do not distress me in my last hour. I have yet much to

do before I die, and require your assistance and support.
Rise, my love, and let me write to my father; I must not
neglect the interest of our child."

She rose tremblingly, and, turning back from her face
her beautiful hair, which had been for so many days
neglected, and was now moistened with her tears, reached
the materials required by her husband, who, drawing
towards him the wooden form to serve him as a table,
wrote the following letter, while his wife sat by him with
a countenance of idiotic apathy and despair :—

"DEAR FATHER,—Yes, still *dear* father,—Before you
cast your eyes upon these characters, you will be childless.
—Your eldest boy perished nobly in the field of honour :
your youngest and last will this morning meet an ignominious, but deserved death on the scaffold.   Thus will
you be childless ; but if your son does meet the fate of a
traitor, still the secret is confined to you alone, and none
will imagine that the unhappy Peters, ringleader of a
mutinous ship, was the scion of a race who have so long
preserved an unblemished name.   Fain would I have
spared you this shock to your feelings, and have allowed
you to remain in ignorance of my disgrace ; but I have an
act of duty to perform to you and to my child—towards
you, that your estates may not be claimed, and pass away
to distant and collateral branches ;—towards my child, that
he may eventually reclaim his rights.   Father, I forgive
you, I might say—but no—let all now be buried in
oblivion ; and as you peruse these lines, and think on my
unhappy fate, shed a tear in memory of the once happy
child you fondled on your knee, and say to your heart, ' I
forgive him.'

"I have dedicated my boy to his king and country.
If you forgive me, and mean to protect your grandchild,
do not change the career in life marked out for him :—
it is a solemn compact between my God and me ; and
you must fulfil this last earnest request of a dying man,
as you hope for future pardon and bliss.

"His distracted mother sits by me; I would entreat you to extend your kindness towards her, but I fear she will soon require no earthly aid. Still, soothe her last moments with a promise to protect the orphan, and may God bless you for your kindness.

"Your affectionate son,
"EDWARD."

Peters had scarcely finished this letter when Adams, with the boy in his arms, was admitted. "I come for final orders, Peters, and to tell you what I did last night to this boy. He is real stuff,—never winced. You said he was to be the King's, and I thought you would like that he should be marked as such. There is no mistaking this mark, Peters," continued Adams, baring the boy's shoulder, and showing the impression of the broad-headed arrow, which now appeared angry and inflamed, as it always is for some days after the operation. "I did not mention that I was going to do it, because Ellen then might not have liked it: but I hope you do."

"Many, many thanks," answered Peters; and opening his letter, which was folded, but not sealed, he added a postscript, pointing out the mark by which the boy would be identified. "You could not have done me a greater favour, Adams; and now you must promise me once more, which is to look after my poor Ellen, when——"

"I understand, my good fellow, and I will," replied Adams. "There is the chaplain outside, who is all ready for service if you would like to see him," continued the old man, passing his hands over his humid eyes.

"Ask him to come in, Adams; he is a good man, and an honour to his profession. I shall be glad to see him."

Adams went to the door, and soon returned with the chaplain. He saluted Peters, who respectfully bowed to him, and said: "I have long made my peace with God and man, sir, and am as well prepared to die as sinful mortal can be—in faith and charity with all men. Many thanks to you, sir, for your kindness; but, sir, you may

be of use here yet.   Can you "—and his voice faltered,—
" can you, sir, help that poor young woman ?   Cannot
you reason her into some kind of tranquillity, some degree
of submission to God's will ?   Oh, do that, sir, and you
will confer a favour on me indeed."

The chaplain approached Ellen, who lay on the deck
in a state of mental stupefaction, and, addressing her in
mild accents, persuaded her to rise and take a seat on the
form ; he kindly contrived to bring it forward to the iron-
grated port, so that she could not witness the motions of
Peters, and, with a low, yet energetic and persuasive
voice, attempted to reason her into patience and resignation.   His efforts were in vain.   She occasionally looked
upon him with a vacant stare, but her thoughts were
elsewhere.   During the period, Peters had time to shave
himself, and dress in clean attire, preparatory to being
summoned to his fate.

The time was approaching fast ; one bell after eight
o'clock, designating the half-hour, had struck ; at two
bells (nine o'clock) he was to be summoned to his doom.
The clergyman rose from his useless endeavours—" Let
us pray," said he, and sank upon his knees,—Peters,
Adams, and the child, followed his example ; and last
of all, poor Ellen, who seemed to recover her recollection,
sank on her knees, but, unable to keep her position, fell
towards the clergyman, who, as he supported her in his
arms, poured forth a fervent and eloquent appeal in behalf
of the one who was about to appear in the presence of
his Maker, and of those who were left in tribulation
behind.   It was scarcely over when the door opened, and
the provost-marshal claimed his prisoner.

The prayer of the chaplain seemed to ring in Ellen's
ears, and she remained supported by the worthy man,
muttering parts of it at intervals, during which time the
limbs of her husband were freed from the shackles.   All
was ready ; and Peters, straining the child to his bosom
in silence, and casting one look at his dear Ellen, who
still remained in a state of stupefaction, denied himself

a last embrace (though the effort wrung his heart) rather than awaken her to her misery. He quitted the cell, and the chaplain, quietly placing Ellen in the arms of Adams, followed, that he might attend and support Peters in his last moments.

The prisoner was conducted on the quarter-deck previously to being sent forward to execution. His sentence was read by Captain A——; and the remark may perhaps be considered uncharitable, but there certainly appeared to be an ill-concealed satisfaction in his countenance as he came to that part where it stated that the prisoner was to "suffer death." Peters heard it read with firmness, and asked permission to address the ship's company. This was at first refused by the captain; but, at the request of the officers, and the assurance of the chaplain that he would vouch for the language of Peters being such as would have a proper tendency to future subordination on the part of the ship's company, it was assented to. Bowing first to the captain and officers, Peters turned to the ship's company, who had assembled on the booms and gangway, and addressed them as follows :—

"Shipmates, the time may come when our country shall be at peace, and your services no longer be required. Then, when you narrate to your children the events of this unhappy mutiny, do not forget to add instruction to amusement, by pointing out to them that it ended in the disgrace and death of the ringleaders. Tell them that, in your presence, one of them acknowledged on the quarter-deck the justice of his sentence, and returned thanks to his Majesty for his kindness in pardoning others who had been led into the same error. Tell them to do their duty, to fight nobly for their King and country, and warn them by our example——"

At this moment Willy, who had eluded the vigilance of old Adams, who was occupied in supporting the inanimate Ellen, pushed his way between the legs of the marines, who were drawn up in ranks on the quarter-deck, and, running

to his father, laid hold of the loose sailor's trousers in which
he was attired, and looked anxiously and inquisitively in his
face. Peters's voice faltered; he attempted to continue his
address to the men, but could not; and waving his hand,
and pointing to the child, in mute explanation of the cause,
after struggling in vain against the overflowings of a father's
heart, he bent over the boy and burst into tears.

The effect was electrical. The shock was communicated
to all; not an eye but was dimmed; sobs were heard in
the crowd; the oldest officers turned away to conceal their
emotions; the younger, and more fresh in heart, covered
their faces, and leant against the bulwarks; the marines
forgot their discipline, and raised their hands from their
sides to wipe their eyes. Many a source, long supposed to
be hermetically sealed, was re-opened,—many a spring long
dry reflowed rapidly; even Captain A—— was moved.

By a singular coincidence, the grouping of the parties at
this moment was nearly the same as when we first introduced our little hero to the reader—the officers and marines
on the after part of the deck, the ship's company forward,
and little Willy standing between the two. Again he
appears in the same position;—but what a change of feeling had taken place! As if he had been a little spirit of
good, waving his fairy talisman, evil passions, which in the
former scene were let loose, had retired to their darkest
recesses, and all the better feelings of humanity were called
forth, and displayed in one universal, spontaneous, and
unfeigned tribute to the melancholy and affecting scene.

The silence was first broken by Willy—" Where are you
going, father; and why do you wear that night-cap?"

" I am going to sleep, child,—to an eternal sleep! God
bless and protect you," said Peters, taking him up and kissing him. " And now, sir, I am ready," continued Peters,
who had recovered his self-possession; " Captain A——,
I forgive you, as I trust to be forgiven myself. Mr——,"
said he, addressing the first lieutenant, " take this child by
the hand, and do not permit him to come forward—
remember he is the ' King's Own.'" Then, bowing to the

chaplain, who had scarcely recovered from the effects that the scene had produced upon him, and looking significantly at the provost-marshal, Peters bent his steps forward by the gangway—the noose was fastened—the gun fired, and, in a moment, all was over.

Loud as was the report of the gun, those who were appointed to the unpleasant duty of running aft with the rope on the main-deck, which swung Peters to the yard-arm, heard a shriek that even that deafening noise could not overpower. It was the soul of Ellen joining that of her husband—and, before the day closed, their bodies were consigned to the same grave—

" Where the wicked cease from troubling, and the weary are at rest.'

Chapter V

Lord of himself, that heritage of woe.

BYRON.

OUR novel may, to a certain degree, be compared to one of the pantomimes which rival theatres annually bring forth for the amusement of the holiday children. We open with dark and solemn scenes, introducing occasionally a bright image, which appears with the greater lustre from the contrast around it; and thus we proceed, until Harlequin is fairly provided with his wand, and despatched to seek his adventures by land and by sea. To complete the parallel, the whole should wind up with a blaze of light and beauty, till our dazzled eyes are relieved, and the illusion disappears, at the fall of the green curtain, which, like the " FINIS" at the end of the third volume, tells us that all is over.

We must, however, be allowed to recapitulate a little in this chapter, previously to launching our hero upon the uncertain and boisterous sea of human life. It will be necessary, for the correct development of the piece, that the attention of the reader should be called to the history of the grandfather of our hero.

Admiral De Courcy was the lineal descendant of an ancient and wealthy family, of high aristocratic connection. He had the misfortune, at an early age, to lose his father, to be an only child, and to have a very weak and doting mother. Add to all these, that he was the heir to a large entailed property, and the reader will acknowledge that even the best disposed child stood a fair chance of being spoiled.

But young De Courcy was not a well-disposed child : he was of a violent, headstrong, and selfish disposition, and was not easily to be checked by the firmest hand. He advanced to man's estate, the cruel tyrant of a fond and foolish mother, and the dislike of all around him. His restless disposition, backed by the persuasions of his mother to the contrary, induced him to enter into the naval service. At the time we are now describing, the name of the boy often appeared on the books of a man-of-war, when the boy himself was at school or at home with his friends ; if there were any regulations to the contrary, they were easily surmounted by interest. The consequence was, that,—without any knowledge of his profession, without having commenced his career by learning to obey before he was permitted to command,—at the early age of eighteen years, young De Courcy was appointed captain of a fine frigate ; and, as the power of a captain of a man-of-war was at that time almost without limit, and his conduct without scrutiny, he had but too favourable an opportunity of indulging his tyrannical propensities. His caprice and violence were unbounded, his cruelty odious, and his ship was designated by the sobriquet of " The Hell Afloat."

There are, however, limits to the longest tether ; and as no officer would remain in the ship, and the desertion of the men became so extensive, that a fine frigate lay useless and unmanned, the government at last perceived the absolute necessity of depriving of command one who could not command himself. The ship was paid off, and even the interest of Captain De Courcy, powerful as it was, could not obtain further employment for him. Having for some time been in possession of his large property, Captain De Courcy retired to the hall of his ancestors, with feelings of anger against the government, which his vindictive temper prompted him to indulge by the annoyance of all round him : and, instead of diffusing joy and comfort by the expenditure of his wealth, he rendered himself odious by avarice,—a vice the more contemptible, as it was unexpected at so early an age.

But, much as he was an object of abhorrence, he was more an object of pity. With a handsome exterior, and with fascinating manners, of high birth and connections, with a splendid fortune,—in short, with every supposed advantage that the world could give, he was, through the injudicious conduct of a fond mother, whose heart he had broken, the most miserable of beings. He was without society, for he was shunned by the resident gentlemen in the neighbourhood. Even match-making mothers, with hearts indurated by interest, and with a string of tall daughters to provide for, thought the sacrifice too great, and shuddered at an alliance with Captain De Courcy. Avoided by the tenants of his large estates, whose misfortunes met with no compassion, and whose inability to answer the demands of the rent-day were followed up with immediate distress and seizure,—abhorred by his own household, who, if their services were not required, vanished at his approach, or, if summoned, entered the door of his room trembling,—he was an isolated and unhappy being, a torment to himself and to others. Wise, indeed, was Solomon, when he wrote, that " he who spared the rod spoiled the child."

The monotony of a life whose sole negative enjoyment consisted in the persecution of others, induced Captain De Courcy to make occasional excursions to the different watering-places ; and whether that, to a certain degree, he was schooled by banishment from society at home, or that he had no opportunity of displaying his diabolical temper, his prepossessing appearance and well-known riches made him a great favourite in these marts for beauty. An

amiable girl was unfortunate enough to fix his attention;
and a hasty proposal was as hastily accepted by her friends,
and quietly acquiesced in by herself. She married, and
was miserable, until released from her heedless engagement by death.

There are those who excuse a violent temper in a man,
and consider it no obstacle to happiness in the marriage
life. Alas, may they never discover the fatal error in
their own union! Even with the best hearted and most
fondly attached, with those who will lavish every endearment, acknowledge their fault and make every subsequent
effort to compensate for the irritation of the moment,
violence of temper must prove the bane of marriage bliss.
Bitter and insulting expressions have escaped, unheeded at
the time, and forgotten by the offending party; but,
although forgiven, never to be forgotten by the other.
Like barbed arrows, they have entered into the heart of
her whom he had promised before God to love and to
cherish; and remain there they must, for they cannot be
extracted. Affection may pour balm into the wounds, and
soothe them for the time; and, while love fans them with
his soft wings, the heat and pain may be unperceived; but
passion again asserts his empire, and upon his rude attack
these ministering angels are forced from their office of
charity, and woman, kind, devoted woman, looks inwardly
with despair upon her wounded and festering heart.

Hurried as she was to an early tomb, the unfortunate
wife of Captain De Courcy had still time to present him
with two fine boys, whose infantine endearments soothed
his violence; and, as long as they showed no spirit of
resistance, they were alternately fondled and frightened.
But children are not blind; and the scenes which continually occurred between their parents,—the tears of their
mother, and the remarks made in their presence by the
domestics,—soon taught them to view their father with
dread. Captain De Courcy perceived that he was shunned
by his children, the only beings whom he had endeavoured
(as far as his temper would permit) to attach to him.

They were dismissed to school at a very early age, and were soon treated by their father in the same harsh manner as all those who had the misfortune to be under his baneful protection.   They returned home at holiday time with regret ; and the recommencement of their scholastic duties was a source of delight.   The mother died, and all at home was desolate.   The violence of their father seemed to increase from indulgence ; and the youths, who were verging into manhood, proved that no small portion of the parent's fiery disposition had been transmitted to them, and showed a spirit of resistance which ended in their ruin.

William, the eldest of the boys, was, as it were, by birthright, the first to fall a victim to his father's temper. Struck senseless and bleeding to the ground for some trifling indiscretion, as he lay confined to his bed for many subsequent days, he formed the resolution of seeking his own fortune, rather than submit to hourly degradation. At the period at which this occurred, many years previously to the one of which we are now writing, the East India Company had but a short time received its charter, and its directors were not the proud rulers which they have since become.   It never was calculated that a company, originally consisting of a few enterprising merchants, could ever have established themselves (even by the most successful of mischievous arts) the controllers of an immense empire, independent of, and anomalous to, the constitution of England ; or that privileges, granted to stimulate the enterprise of individuals, would have been the ground of a monopoly, which, like an enormous incubus, should oppress the nation from the throne to the cottage.   They gladly accepted the offers of all adventurers ; and at that period, there was as much eagerness on their part to secure the services of individuals, as there now is on the part of applicants to be enrolled on the books of the Company.

William, without acquainting his father, entered into an engagement with the Company, signed it, and was shipped

K.   I.   C

off, with many others, who, less fortunate, had been nefariously kidnapped for the same destination. He arrived in India, rose to the rank of captain, and fell in one of the actions that were fought at this time. The letter which William left on the table, directed to his father, informing him of the step he had been induced to take, was torn to atoms, and stamped upon with rage; and the bitter malediction of the parent was launched with dreadful vehemence upon the truant son, in the presence of the one who remained.

And yet there was one man, before whom this haughty and vindictive spirit quailed, and who had the power to soften, although not wholly to curb, his impetuosity,— one, who dared to tell him the truth, expose to him the folly and wickedness of his conduct, and meet the angry flash of his eye with composure,—one whose character and office secured him from insult, and who was neither to be frightened nor diverted from his purpose of doing good. It was the vicar of the parish, who, much as he disliked the admiral (for Captain De Courcy had latterly obtained the rank by seniority on the list), continued his visits to the hall, that he might appeal for the unfortunate. The admiral would willingly have shaken him off, but his attempts were in vain. The vicar was firm at his post, and often successfully pleaded the cause of his parishioners, who were most of them tenants of the admiral. He was unassisted in his parochial duties by the curate, a worthy, but infirm and elderly man, fast sinking into his grave, and whom, out of Christian charity, he would not remove from his situation, as it would have deprived him of the means of support.

Edward, the younger brother, naturally sought that happiness abroad which was denied him at home. The house of the curate was one of his most favourite resorts, for the old man had a beautiful and only daughter,—poor Ellen, whose fate we have just recorded. It is sufficient for the present narrative to state, that these two young people loved, and plighted their troth; that for two years they met with joy, and parted with regret, until the approaching dissolution of the old curate opened their eyes to the dangerous position in which they were placed. He died; and Edward, who beheld her whom he loved thrown unprotected and penniless on the world, mustered up the courage of desperation, to state to his father the wishes of his heart.

A peremptory order to leave the house, or abandon Ellen, was the immediate result; and the indignant young man quitted the roof, and persuaded the unhappy and fond girl to unite herself to him by indissoluble ties, in a neighbouring parish, before the vicar had possession of the facts, or the opportunity to dissuade him from so imprudent a step. He immediately proceeded to the hall, with a faint hope of appeasing the irritated parent; but his endeavours were fruitless, and the admiral poured forth his anathema against his only child.

Edward now took his wife to a village some miles distant, where, by their mutual exertions, they contrived for some time to live upon their earnings; but the birth of their first child, the hero of this tale, and the expenses attending her sickness, forced him at last (when all appeals to his father proved in vain) to accept the high bounty that was offered for men to enter into his Majesty's service,—which he did under the assumed name of Edward Peters.

Chapter VI

———I disclaim all my paternal care,
Propinquity and property of blood.
The barbarous Scythian,
Or he that makes his generation messes
To gorge his appetite, shall to my bosom
Be as well neighbour'd, pitied, and relieved,
As him.
                                        SHAKESPEARE.

IN a lofty room, the wainscotting of which was of dark oak, with a high mantel-piece, elaborately carved in the same wood, with groups of dead game and flowers, and a few choice pictures let into the panels,—upon an easy chair, that once had been splendid with morocco and gold—sat a man of about fifty years of age ; but his hair was grey, and his face was indented with deep lines and furrows. He was listening with impatience to the expostulations of one who stood before him, and shifted his position from time to time, when more than usually annoyed with the subject. It was Admiral De Courcy, and the vicar of the parish, who was persuading him to be merciful.

The subject of this discourse was, however, dismissed by the entrance of a servant, who presented to the admiral, upon a large and massive salver, a letter, brought, as he stated, by a seafaring man. The admiral lifted up his glasses to examine the superscription.—" From my worthless vagabond of a son ! " exclaimed he, and he jerked the letter into the fire without breaking the seal.

" Surely, sir," rejoined the vicar, " it would be but justice to hear what he has to offer in extenuation of a fault, too severely punished already. He is your only son, sir, and why not forgive one rash act ? Recollect, sir, that he is the heir to this property, which, being entailed, must of necessity devolve upon him."

" Curses on the bare thought," answered the admiral with vehemence. " I hope to starve him first."

" May the Almighty show more mercy to you, sir, when you are called to your account, than you have shown to an imprudent and hasty child. We are told that we are to forgive, if we hope to be forgiven. Admiral De Courcy, it is my duty to ask you, do you expect (and if so, upon what grounds) to be forgiven yourself ? "

The admiral looked towards the window, and made no reply.

The letter, which had been thrown into the grate, was not yet consumed. It had lit upon a mass of not yet ignited coal, and lay there blackening in the smoke. The vicar perceived it, and, walking to the fire-place, recovered the letter from its perilous situation.

"If you do not choose to read it yourself, admiral—if you refuse to listen to the solicitations of an only child, have you any objection that I should open the letter, and be acquainted with the present condition of a young man, who, as you know, was always dear to me?"

"None, none," replied the admiral, sarcastically. "You may read it, and keep it too, if you please."

The vicar, without any answer to this remark, opened the letter, which, as the reader may probably imagine, was the one written by Edward Peters on the morning of his execution.

"Merciful Heaven!" exclaimed the man of religion, as he sat down to recover from the shock he had received— "Unfortunate boy!"

The admiral turned round, astonished at the demeanour of the clergyman, and (it would appear) as if his conscience had pressed him hard, and that he was fearful that his cruel wish, expressed but a few minutes before, had been realised. He turned pale, but asked no questions. After a short time, the vicar rose, and, with a countenance of more indignation than the admiral or others had ever seen, thus addressed him :—

"The time may come, sir,—nay, I prophesy that it *will* come, when the contents of this letter will cause you bitterly to repent your cruel and unnatural conduct to your son. The letter itself, sir, I cannot entrust you with. In justice to others, it must not be put into your hands; and after your attempt to commit it to the flames, and your observation that I might read and *keep it too*, I feel justified in retaining it. A copy of it, if you please, I will send you, sir."

"I want neither copy nor original, nor shall I read them if you send them, good sir," answered the admiral, pale with anger.

"Fare you well, then, sir. May God turn your heart!"

So saying, the vicar left the room with a determination not to enter it again. His first inquiry was for the person who had brought the letter, and he was informed that he

still waited in the hall. It was old Adams, who had
obtained leave of absence for a few days, that he might
fulfil the last request of Peters. The clergyman here
received a second shock, from the news of the death of
poor Ellen, and listened with the deepest interest to
Adams's straightforward account of the whole catastrophe.

The first plan that occurred to the vicar was to send for
the child, and take charge of him himself; but this was
negatived, not only by Peters's letter, but also by old
Adams, who stated his determination to retain the child
until claimed by legal authority. After mature delibera-
tion, he considered that the child would be as much under
an All-seeing Eye on the water as on the land, and that,
at so early an age, he was probably as well under the
charge of a trustworthy old man like Adams, as he would be
elsewhere. He therefore requested Adams to let him
have constant accounts of the boy's welfare, and to apply
to him for any funds that he might require for his main-
tenance; and, wishing the old man farewell, he set off for
the vicarage, communing with himself as to the propriety
of keeping the circumstance of the boy's birth a secret, or
divulging it to his grandfather, in the hopes of eventually
inducing him to acknowledge and to protect him.

Chapter VII

To the seas presentlye went our lord admiral,
    With knights couragious, and captains full good;
The brave Earl of Essex, a prosperous general,
    With him prepared to pass the salt flood.

At Plymouth speedilye took they ship valiantlye,
    Braver ships never were seen under sayle,
With their fair colours spread, and streamers o'er their head
    Now, bragging foemen, take heed of your tayle.

Old Ballad, 1596.

MANY and various were the questions that were put by our
little hero to Adams and others, relative to the fate of his

parents. That they were both dead was all the information that he could obtain; for, to the honour of human nature, there was not one man in a ship's company composed of several hundred, who had the cruelty to tell the child that his father had been hanged. It may, at first, appear strange to the reader, that the child himself was not aware of the fact, from what he had witnessed on the morning of execution; but it must be recollected that he had never seen an execution before, and had therefore nothing from which to draw such an inference. All he knew was, that his father was on the quarter-deck, with a night-cap on, and that he told him that he was going to sleep. The death of his mother, whose body he was not permitted to see, was quite as unintelligible, and the mystery which enveloped the whole transaction added no little to the bereavement of the child, who, as I have before stated, from his natural talent and peculiar education, was far more reflective and advanced than children usually are.

Adams returned to his little charge with pleasure: he had now a right to adopt the child, and consider him as his own. In the ship, the boy was such an object of general sympathy, that not only many of the men, but some of the officers, would gladly have taken him, and have brought him up. The name of his father was, by general consent, never mentioned, especially as Adams informed the officers and men that Peters had been a "*purser's name*," adopted by the child's father, and that, although the clergyman had stated this, he had not entrusted him with the real name that the child was entitled to bear. As, therefore, our little hero was not only without parents, but without name, he was rechristened by Adams by the cognomen of the "King's Own," and by that title, or his christian name, Willy, was ever afterwards addressed, both by officers and men.

There is an elasticity supplied to the human mind by unerring Wisdom, that enables us, however broken down by the pressure of misfortune, to recover our cheerfulness after a while, and resign ourselves to the decrees of

Heaven. It consoles the widow—it supports the bereaved lover, who had long dwelt upon anticipated bliss—it almost reconciles to her lot the fond and forsaken girl, whose heart is breaking.

Unusually oppressed as Willy was, with the loss of those to whom he had so fondly clung from his birth, in a few months he recovered his wonted spirits, and his cheeks again played with dimples, as his flashing eye beamed from under his long eyelashes. He attached himself to the old quarter-master, and seldom quitted him—he slept in his hammock, he stood by his side when he was on deck, at his duty, steering the ship, and he listened to the stories of the good old man, who soon taught him to read and write. For three years thus passed his life, at the end of which period he had arrived at the age of nine years.

After a long monotony of blockade service, the ship was ordered to hoist the flag of a commodore, who was appointed to the command of an expedition against the western coast of France, to create a diversion in favour of the Vendean chiefs. Captain A——, whether it was that he did not like to receive a superior officer on board of his ship, or that he did not admire the service upon which she was to be employed, obtained permission to leave his ship for a few months, for the restoration of his health, to the great joy of the officers and crew ; and an acting captain, of well-known merit, was appointed in his stead.

The squadron of men-of-war and transports was collected, the commodore's flag hoisted, and the expedition sailed with *most secret* orders, which, as usual, were as well known to the enemy, and everybody in England, as they were to those by whom they were given. It is the characteristic of our nation, that we scorn to take any unfair advantage, or reap any benefit, by keeping our intentions a secret. We imitate the conduct of that English tar, who, having entered a fort, and meeting a Spanish officer without his sword, being providently supplied with two cutlasses himself, immediately offered him one, that they might engage on fair terms.

The idea is generous, but not wise. But I rather imagine that this want of secrecy arises from all matters of importance being arranged by cabinet councils. In the multitude of councillors there may be wisdom, but there certainly is not secrecy. Twenty men have probably twenty wives, and it is therefore twenty to one but the secret transpires through that channel. Further, twenty men have twenty tongues ; and, much as we complain of women not keeping secrets, I suspect that men deserve the odium of the charge quite as much, if not more, than women do. On the whole, it is forty to one against secrecy, which, it must be acknowledged, are long odds.

On the arrival of the squadron at the point of attack, a few more days were thrown away,—probably upon the same generous principle of allowing the enemy sufficient time for preparation. Troops had been embarked, with the intention of landing them, to make a simultaneous attack with the shipping. Combined expeditions are invariably attended with delay, if not with disagreement. An officer commanding troops, who, if once landed, would be as decided in his movements as Lord Wellington himself, does not display the same decision when out of his own element. From his peculiar situation on board,—his officers and men distributed in different ships,—the apparent difficulties of debarkation, easily remedied, and despised by sailors, but magnified by landsmen,—from the great responsibility naturally felt in a situation where he must trust to the resources of others, and where his own, however great, cannot be called into action,—he will not decide without much demur upon the steps to be taken ; although it generally happens, that the advice originally offered by the naval commandant has been acceded to. Unless the military force required is very large, marines should invariably be employed, and placed under the direction of the naval commander.

After three or four days of *pros* and *cons*, the enemy had completed his last battery, and as there was then no rational excuse left for longer delay, the debarkation took place, without any serious loss on our side, except that of one launch, full of the——regiment, which was cut in halves by the enemy's shot. The soldiers, as they sank in the water, obeyed the orders of the sergeant, and held up their cartouch-boxes, that they might not be wetted two seconds sooner than necessary,—held fast their muskets, —and, without stirring from the gunnels of the boat, round which they had been stationed, went down in as good order as could be expected, each man at his post, with his bayonet fixed. The sailors, not being either so heavily caparisoned or so well drilled, were guilty of a *sauve qui peut*, and were picked up by other boats. The officer of the regiment stuck to his men, and it is to be hoped that he marched the whole of his brave detachment to heaven, as he often had before to church. But we must leave the troops to form on the beach as well as they can, and the enemy's shot will permit, and retire on board.

The Commodore's arrangement had been punctually complied with. The ships that were directed to cover the landing of the troops, knocked down many of the enemy, and not a great many more of our own men. The stations of the other ships were taken with a precision deserving of the highest encomiums; and there is no doubt, that, had not the enemy had the advantage of stone walls, they must have had the worst of it, and would have been well beaten.

The commodore himself, of course, took the post of honour. Anchored with springs on his cables, he alternately engaged a heavy battery on his starboard bows, a much heavier, backed by a citadel throwing shells, on his beam, and a masked battery on his quarter, which he had not reckoned upon. The latter was rather annoying, and the citadel threw shells with most disagreeable precision. He had almost as much to do as Lord Exmouth at Algiers, although the result was not so fortunate.

A ship engaging at anchor, with very little wind, and that wind lulled by the percussion of the air from the report of the guns, as it always is, has the disadvantage of not being able to disengage herself of the smoke, which rapidly accumulates and stagnates as it were between the decks.   Under these circumstances you repeatedly hear the order passed upon the main and lower deck of a line-of-battle ship, to point the guns two points abaft the beam, point-blank, and so on.   In fact, they are as much in the dark as to the external objects, as if they were blindfolded; and the only comfort to be derived from this serious inconvenience, is, that every man is so isolated from his neighbour that he is not put in mind of his own danger by witnessing the death of those around him, for they may fall three or four feet from him without his perceiving it :—so they continue to fire as directed, until they are either sent down to the cock-pit themselves, or have a momentary respite from their exertions, when, choked with smoke and gunpowder, they go aft to the scuttle-butt, to remove their parching thirst.   So much for the lower and main-deck.   We will now ascend to the quarter-deck, where we shall find old Adams at the conn, and little Willy standing behind him.

The smoke is not so thick here, but that you may perceive the commodore on the poop, walking a step or two to starboard, and then turning short round to port.   He is looking anxiously through his glass at the position of the troops, who are ashore to storm the batteries, hoping to see a diversion in our favour made by them, as the affair becomes serious.   By a singular coincidence, the commandant of the troops on shore is, with his telescope, looking anxiously at the shipping, hoping the same thing from the exertions of the navy.   The captain of marines lies dead upon the poop; both his legs have been shot off by a spent shot—he is left there, as no surgeon can help him; and there are two signal-men lying dead alongside him.

On the hammock-nettings of the quarter-deck stands the acting captain of the ship, erect, and proud in bearing, with an eye of defiance and scorn as he turns towards the enemy. His advice was disregarded; but he does his duty proudly and cheerfully.   He is as cool and unconcerned as if he

were watching the flying-fish as they rise from the bows
of the ship, when running down the tropics, instead of the
enemy's shot, as they splash in the water alongside, or tear
open the timbers of the vessel, and the bodies of his crew.
The men still ply their half-manned guns; but they are
exhausted with fatigue, and the bloody deck proves that
many have been dismissed from their duty. The first
lieutenant is missing; you will find him in the cock-pit—
they have just finished taking up the arteries of his right
arm, which has been amputated; and the Scotch surgeon's
assistant, who for many months bewailed the want of
practice, and who, for having openly expressed his wishes
on that subject, had received a sound thrashing from the
exasperated midshipmen, is now complimenting the fainting
man upon the excellent stump that they have made for him:
while fifty others, dying or wounded, with as much variety
as Homer's heroes, whose blood, trickling from them in
several rivulets, pours into one general lake at the lowest
level of the deck, are anxiously waiting their turn, and
distract the purser's steward by their loud calls, in every
direction at the same time, for the tin-pot of water, with
which he is relieving their agonising thirst.

A large shark is under the counter; he is so gorged with
human flesh, that he can scarcely move his tail in the tinged
water; and he now hears the sullen plunges of the bodies,
as they are launched through the lower-deck port, with
perfect indifference. "Oh! what a glorious thing's a
battle!"

But to return to our particular narrative. As we mentioned before, the citadel threw shells with remarkable
precision, and every man who had been killed on the
quarter-deck of the commodore's ship, towards which the
attention of the enemy was particularly directed, had been
laid low by these horrible engines of modern warfare.
The action still continued, although the fire on both sides
had evidently slackened, and the commodore's glass had at
several intervals been fruitlessly directed towards the
troops on shore, when accident brought about a change in

favour of our countrymen. Through some unknown cause, the magazine of the enemy's largest battery exploded, and buried the fabric with its tenants in one mass of ruin. The enemy were panic-struck with their misfortune—our troops and sailors inspired with fresh courage—and the fire was recommenced with three cheers and redoubled vigour. The troops pushed on, and succeeded in taking possession of the masked battery, which had so long and so effectually raked the commodore.

A few minutes after this had occurred, the citadel recommenced its fire, and a shell, descending with that terrific hissing peculiar to itself alone, struck the main-bitts on the quarter-deck, and, rolling aft, exploded. Its fragments scattered death around, and one piece took the hat off the head of little Willy, who was standing before Adams, and then buried itself in the old man's side. He staggered forward, and fell on the coils of rope, near the companion-hatch, and when the men came to assist him below, the pain of moving was so intense, that he requested to be left where he was, that he might quietly breathe his last.

Willy sat down beside his old friend, holding his hand. —" A little water, boy—quick, quick ! " It was soon procured by the active and affectionate child ; who, indifferent to the scene around him, thought only of administering to the wants, and alleviating the misfortune, of his dearest friend. Adams, after he had drunk, turned his head round, apparently revived, and said, in a low and catching voice, as if his powers were fast escaping, " Willy, your father's name was not Peters—I do not know what it was ; but there is a person who does, and who takes an interest in your welfare—he lives in——"

At this moment another shell bounded through the rigging, and fell within a few feet of the spot where Willy and old Adams were speaking. Willy, who was seated on a coil of rope, supporting the head of his benefactor, no sooner perceived the shell as it rolled towards the side, with its fuse pouring out a volume of smoke, than, recollecting the effects of the former explosion, rather than the danger of the attempt, he ran towards it, and not being able to lift it, sank down on his knees, and, with astonishing agility, succeeded in rolling it overboard, out of the larboard entering-port, to which it was near. The shell plunged in the water, and, before it had descended many feet, exploded with a concussion that was communicated to the ship fore and aft. Our hero then resumed his station by the side of Adams, who had witnessed what had taken place.

"You have begun well, my boy," said the old man, faintly. "There's ne'er a man in the ship would have done it. Kiss me, boy."

The child leaned over the old man, and kissed his cheek, clammy with the dews of death. Adams turned a little on one side, uttered a low groan, and expired.

Chapter VIII

Now dash'd upon the billow,
    Our opening timbers creak,
Each fears a watery pillow.
.   .   .   .   .   .
To cling to slippery shrouds
Each breathless seaman crowds,
    As she lay
    Till the day
In the Bay of Biscay O.

Sea Song.

As it will only detain the narrative, without being at all necessary for its development, I shall not dwell upon the results of the engagement, which was soon after decided, with very indifferent success on our side. The soldiers were re-embarked, the ships hauled out of reach of the enemy's guns, and a council of war summoned— on which it was agreed, *nem. con.*, that no more was to be done. The despatches were sent home—they certainly differed a little, but that was of no consequence. The sum total of killed and wounded was excessively gratifying to the nation, as it proved that there had been hard fighting. By-the-bye, John Bull is rather annoying in this respect: he imagines that no action can be well fought unless there is a considerable loss. Having no other method of judging of the merits of an action, he appreciates it according to the list of killed and wounded. A merchant *in toto*, he computes the value of an object by what it has cost him, and imagines that what is easily and cheaply obtained cannot be of much value. The knowledge of this peculiar mode of reasoning on his part, has very often induced officers to put down very trifling *contusions*, such as a prize-fighter would despise, to swell up the sum total of the loss to the aggregate of the honest man's expectations.

To proceed. As usual in cases of defeat, a small degree of accusation and recrimination took place. The army thought that the navy might have beaten down stone ramparts, ten feet thick; and the navy wondered why the army had not walked up the same ramparts, which were thirty feet perpendicular. Some of the ships accused others of not having had a sufficient number of men killed and wounded; and the boats' crews, whenever they met on shore, fought each other desperately, as if it were absolutely necessary, for the honour of the country, that more blood should be spilt. But this only lasted three weeks, when a more successful attempt made them all shake hands, and wonder what they had been squabbling about.

There was, however, one circumstance, which occurred during the action, that had not been forgotten. It had been witnessed by the acting captain of the ship, and had been the theme of much comment and admiration among the officers and men. This was the daring feat of our little hero, in rolling the shell over the side. Captain M——(the new commander) as soon as his more important avocations would permit, made inquiries among the officers (being himself a stranger in the ship), relative to Willy. His short but melancholy history was soon told; and the disconsolate boy was summoned from under the half-deck, where he sat by the body of Adams, which, with many more, lay sewed up in its hammock, and covered over with the union-jack, waiting for the evening, to receive the rites of Christian burial, before being committed to the deep.

Knowing that Adams had been his only protector, a feeling of compassion for the bereaved and orphan boy, and admiration of his early tokens of bravery, induced Captain M——, who never formed a resolution in haste, or abandoned it if once formed, to take the boy under his own protection, and to place him as an officer on that quarter-deck upon which he had so distinguished himself. Willy, in obedience to orders received, stood by the captain, with his hat in his hand.

"What is your name, my boy?" said the captain, passing a scrutinising glance over his upright and well-proportioned figure.

"Willy, sir."

"And what's your other name?"

"King's Own, sir."

This part of the boy's history was now explained by the second lieutenant, who was in command, in consequence of the first lieutenant being wounded.

"He must have a name," replied the captain. "William King's Own will not do. Is he on the books?"

"No, sir, he is not; shall I put him down as William Jones, or William Smith?"

"No, no, those are too common. The boy has neither father, mother, nor name, that we know of: as we may, therefore, have a choice of the latter for him, let it be a good one. I have known a good name make a man's fortune with a novel-reading girl. There is a romance in the boy's history; let him have a name somewhat romantic also."

"Ay, ay, sir," replied the lieutenant—"here, marine, tell my boy to bring up one of the volumes of the novel in my cabin."

The book made its appearance on the quarter-deck. "Perhaps, sir, we may find one here," said the lieutenant, presenting the book to the captain.

The captain smiled as he took the book. "Let us see," said he, turning over the leaves—"'Delamere!' that's too puppyish. 'Fortescue!' don't like that. 'Seymour!' Yes, that will do. It's not too fine, yet aristocratic and pretty. Desire Mr Hinchen, the clerk, to enter him on the books as Mr William Seymour, midshipman. And now, youngster, I will pay for your outfit, and first year's mess: after which I hope your pay and prize-money will be sufficient to enable you to support yourself. Be that as it may, as long as you do credit to my patronage, I shall not forget you."

Willy, with his straw hat in one hand, and a supererogatory touch of his curly hair with the other, made a scrape with his left leg, after the manner and custom of seafaring people—in short, he made the best bow that he could, observing the receipt that had been given him by his departed friend Adams. D'Egville might have turned up his nose at it; but Captain —— was perfectly satisfied: for, if not an elegant, it certainly was a grateful bow.

Our young officer was not sent down to mess in the berth of the midshipmen. His kind and considerate captain was aware, that a lad who creeps in at the hawse-holes, *i.e.*, is promoted from before the mast, was not likely to be favourably received in the midshipmen's mess, especially by that part of the community who, from their obscure parentage, would have had least reason to complain. He was therefore consigned to the charge of the gunner.

Sincere as were the congratulations of the officers and men, Willy was so much affected with the loss of his fond guardian, that he received them with apathy, and listened to the applause bestowed upon his courage with tears that flowed from the remembrance of the cause which had stimulated him to the deed. At the close of the day, he saw the body of his old friend committed to the deep, with quivering lips and aching brow,—and, as it plunged into

K I. D

the clear wave, felt as if he was left alone in the world, and had no one to love and to cling to.

We do not give children credit for the feelings which they possess, because they have not, at their early age, acquired the power of language to express them correctly. Treat a child as you would an equal, and, in a few months, you will find that the reason of his having until then remained childish, was because he had heretofore been treated as a being of inferior capacity and feelings. True it is, that at an early age the feelings of children are called forth by what we consider as trifles; but we must recollect, in humility, that our own pursuits are as vain, as trifling, and as selfish—" We are but children of a larger growth."

The squadron continued to hover on the French coast, with a view of alarming the enemy, and of making a more fortunate attempt, if opportunity occurred. Early in the morning of the fourth day after Willy had been promoted to the quarter-deck, a large convoy of *chasse-marées* (small coasting vessels, lugger-rigged) were discovered rounding a low point, not three miles from the squadron. A general signal to chase was immediately thrown out, and in half-an-hour the English men-of-war were in the midst of them pouring broadside after broadside upon the devoted vessels, whose sails were lowered in every direction, in token of submission. The English men-of-war reminded you of so many hawks, pouncing upon a flight of small birds; and the vessels, with their lowered sails just flapping with the breeze, seemed like so many victims of their rapacity, who lay fluttering on the ground, disabled, or paralysed with terror. Many escaped into shoal water, others ran ashore, some were sunk, and about twenty taken possession of by the ships of the squadron. They proved to be part of a convoy, laden with wine, and bound to the Garonne.

One of the *chasse-marées*, being a larger vessel than the rest, and laden with wine of a better quality, was directed by the commodore to be sent to England; the casks of wine on board of the others were hoisted into the different ships, and distributed occasionally to the crews. Captain

M—— thought that the departure of the prize to England would be a favourable opportunity to send our hero to receive his outfit, as he could not well appear on the quarter-deck as an officer without his uniform. He therefore directed the master's mate, to whose charge the prize was about to be confided, to take William with him, and wrote to his friends at Portsmouth, whither the vessel was directed to proceed, to fit him out with the requisite articles, and send him back by the first ship that was directed to join the squadron. The prize was victualled, the officer received his written orders, was put on board with our hero and three men, and parted company with the squadron.

The master's mate, who was directed to take the vessel to Portsmouth, was the spurious progeny of the first lieutenant of a line-of-battle ship, and a young woman who attended the bumboat, which supplied the ship's company with necessaries, and luxuries, if they could afford to pay for them. The class of people who obtain their livelihood by these means, and who are entirely dependent upon the navy for their subsistence, are naturally anxious to secure the good-will of the commanding officers of the ships, and usually contrive to have on their establishment a pretty-looking girl, who, although very reserved to the junior officers of the ship, is all smiles to the first lieutenant, and will not stand upon trifles for the benefit of her employer. Beauty for men— gold for women! Such are the glittering baits employed, in this world, to entice either sex from the paths of duty or discretion.

The service was indebted to this species of bribery for the officer in question. The interest of his supposed father was sufficient to put him on the quarter-deck; and the profits of his mother, who, having duly served her apprenticeship, had arrived to the dignity of bumboat woman herself, and was a fat, comely matron, of about forty years of age, were more than sufficient to support him in his inferior rank. His education and natural abilities were not, however, of that class to procure him either friends or advancement; and he remained in the capacity of master's mate, and was likely long to continue so, unless some such event as a general action should include him in a promotion which would be regulated by seniority. He was a mean-looking, vulgar little man, with a sharp face and nose—the latter very red, from the constant potations of not only his own allowance, but of that of every youngster in the ship whom he could bully or cajole.

His greatest pride and his constant study was "slang," in which he was no mean proficient. He always carried in his pocket a colt (*i.e.* a foot and a half of rope, knotted at one end, and whipped at the other,) for the benefit of the youngsters, to whom he was a most inordinate tyrant. He could *fudge* a day's work, which he sent in with the rest of the midshipmen, and which proofs of theoretical knowledge of their profession were in those days little attended to ; but he was very ignorant, and quite unfit to take charge of any vessel. Captain M——, who, as we before stated, had joined the ship as acting captain, and had not had time to ascertain the merits or demerits of the officers, had given the prize to his charge because he was the senior mate of the ship.

The prize had scarcely trimmed her sails and shaped her course, when Mr Bullock, the master's mate, called our hero to him, and addressed him in the following elegant phraseology :—

"Now, you rebellious spawn—touch your hat, you young whelp"—(knocking off poor Willy's only hat, which flew to leeward, and went overboard)—"mind what I say, for I mean to be as good as a father to you. You're not an officer yet—and if you were, it would be all the same—so no capers, no airs. You see I've only three men in the vessel besides myself; they are in three watches ; so your duty will be to attend to me in the cabin. You'll mull my claret—I always drinks a noggin every half hour to keep the wind out, and if it an't ready and an't good,

—do you see this? "—(taking the colt out of his pocket).
—"Stop, you'd better feel it at once, and then, when
you knows what the taste of it is, you'll take care how
you're slack in stays." So saying, he administered three
or four hearty cuts on the back and shoulders of our hero,
who had been sufficiently drilled into the manners and
customs of a man-of-war, to know the value of the proverb,
"The least said, the soonest mended."

A spigot had been already inserted into one of the casks
of claret which were lashed on deck; and, as the small
vessel was very uneasy in the heavy swell of the Bay of
Biscay, our hero had sufficient employment in watching the
pot of claret, and preventing it from being upset by the
motion of the vessel, as it was constantly heating on the
stove in the cabin. This potation was regularly presented
by Willy every half hour, as directed, to his commanding
officer, who, if it was too sweet, or not sweet enough,
or if he could not drink the whole, invariably, and much
to the annoyance of our hero, threw the remainder into
his face, telling him that was his share of it.

This arrangement continued in full force for three days
and three nights—for Willy was roused up five or six
times every night to administer the doses of mulled claret
which Mr Bullock had prescribed for himself, who seemed,
thin and meagre as he was, to be somewhat like a bamboo
in his structure (*i.e.* hollow from top to bottom), as if to
enable him to carry the quantity of fluid that he poured
down his throat during the twenty-four hours. As for
intoxicating him, that appeared to be impossible; from
long habit, he seemed to be like a stiff ship that careened
to her bearings, and would sooner part company with her
masts than heel any farther.

On the fourth day, a strong gale sprang up from the
northwest, and the sea ran very high. The *chasse-marée*,
never intended to encounter the huge waves of the Bay
of Biscay, but to crawl along the coast and seek protection
from them on the first indication of their fury,—labouring
with a heavy cargo, not only stowed below, but on the

decks,—was not sufficiently buoyant to rise on the summits
of the waves, which made a clean breach over her, and
the men became exhausted with the wet and the in-
clemency of the season. On the third day of the gale,
and seventh since they had parted company with the
fleet, a squall brought the mainmast by the board; the
foresail was lowered to close-reef, when a heavy sea
struck the vessel, and pouring a torrent over her decks,
swept overboard the three men who were forward reefing
the sail. Mr Bullock, the master's mate, was at the
helm—Willy, as usual, down below, attending the mulled
claret, which had been more than ever in request since
the bad weather had come on.

The mate quitted the helm, and ran forward to throw
a rope to the seamen who were struggling in the water
with the wreck to leeward. He threw one, which was
seized by two of them (the other had sunk); and as soon
as they had hold of it, and it became *taut* from their
holding on, he perceived to his dismay that he had stood
in the remaining part of the coil, and that it had encircled
itself several times round his body, so that the men
were hauling him overboard. "Let go, let go, or I'm
overboard!" was a useless exclamation to drowning men;
they held on, and the mate too held on by the rigging
for his life,—the efforts of the drowning men dragging
him at last from off his legs, and keeping his body in
a horizontal position, as they hauled at his feet, and he
clung in desperation to the lee-shrouds. "Willy, Willy,
a knife—quick, quick!" roared the mate in his agony.
Willy, who, hearing his name called, and followed up
by the "quick, quick," had no idea that anything but
the mulled claret could demand such unusual haste, stopped
a few seconds to throw in the sugar and stir it round
before he answered the summons. He then started up
the hatchway with the pot in his hand.

But these few seconds had decided the fate of Mr
Bullock, and as Willy's head appeared up the hatchway,
so did that of Mr Bullock disappear as he sank into

a grave so dissonant to his habits. He had been unable
to resist any longer the united force of the drowning
men, and Willy was just in time to witness his submersion,
and find himself more destitute than ever. Holding on
by the shroud with one hand, with the pot of mulled
claret in the other, Willy long fixed his eyes on the
spot where his tyrannical shipmate had disappeared from
his sight, and, forgetting his persecution, felt nothing
but sorrow for his loss. Another sea, which poured over
the decks of the unguided vessel, roused him from his
melancholy reverie, and he let go the pot, to cling with
both hands to the rigging as the water washed over his
knees,—then, seizing a favourable opportunity, he succeeded in regaining the cabin of the vessel, where he
sat down and wept bitterly — bitterly for the loss of
the master's mate and men, for he had an affectionate
and kind heart—bitterly for his own forlorn and destitute
situation. Old Adams had not forgotten to teach him
to say his prayers, and Willy had been accustomed to
read the Bible, which the old man explained to the best
of his ability. The vessel laboured and groaned as she
was buffeted by the waves—the wind howled, and the
sea struck her trembling sides and poured over her decks.
In the midst of this wild discord of the elements, the
small voice of the kneeling child, isolated from the rest
of the world, and threatened soon to be removed from
it, was not unheard or unheeded by an omniscient and
omnipotent God, who has said that not a sparrow should
fall to the ground without his knowledge, and has
pointed out of how much more value are we than many
sparrows.

Willy ended his devotions and his tears ; and, feeling
wet and cold, recollected that what would warm his
departed friend the mate, would probably have the same
effect upon him. He crawled up the companion-hatch
with another tin-pot, and having succeeded in obtaining
some wine from the cask, returned to the cabin. Having
warmed it over the fire, and sugared it according to the

well-practised receipt of Mr Bullock, he drank more of
it than, perhaps, in any other situation, he would have
done, and lying down in the standing bed-place at the
side of the cabin, soon fell into a sound sleep.

Chapter IX

And there he went ashore without delay,
 Having no custom-house nor quarantine
To ask him awkward questions on the way,
 About the time and place where he had been:
He left his ship to be hove down next day.

Don Juan.

THE prize vessel, at the time when she carried away her
masts, had gained considerably to the northward of Ushant,
although the master's mate, from his ignorance of his profession, was not aware of the fact. The wind, which now
blew strongly from the N.W., drove the shattered bark up
the Channel, at the same time gradually nearing her to the
French coast. After twenty-four hours' driving before the
storm, during which Willy never once awoke from his
torpor, the vessel was not many leagues from the port of
Cherbourg. It was broad daylight when our hero awoke;
and, after some little time necessary to chase away the
vivid effects of a dream, in which he fancied himself to be
on shore, walking in the fields with his dear mother, he
recollected where he was, and how he was situated. He
ascended the companion-ladder, and looked around him.
The wind had nearly spent its fury, and was subsiding
fast; but the prospect was cheerless—a dark wintry sky
and rolling sea, and nothing living in view except the sea-
bird that screamed as it skimmed over the white tops of
the waves. The mizen of the vessel was still hoisted up,
but the sheet had disengaged itself from the belaying-pin,
and the sail had been rent from the bolt-rope by the storm.
Part of it was blown away, and the rest, jagged and
tattered at its extremities, from constant buffeting, flapped
"mournfully to and fro" with the heavy rolling of the
vessel.

Willy, holding on by the companion-hatch, scanned the horizon in every point of the compass, in hopes of succour, but for a long while in vain.   At last his keen eye detected a small vessel, under a single close-reefed sail, now rising on the tops of the waves, now disappearing in the deep trough of the sea.   She was sloop-rigged, and running down towards him.

In a quarter of an hour she had neared to within a mile, and Willy perceived, with delight, that the people were on deck, and occasionally pointing towards him.   He ran down below, and opening the chest of Mr Bullock, which was not locked, took a liberty which he would never have dared to contemplate during that worthy officer's lifetime, viz., that of pulling forth one of his two best white shirts, reserved for special occasions.   This he took on deck, made it fast to a boat-hook staff, and hoisted as a signal of distress.   He did also mechanically lift his hand to his head with the intention of waving his hat, but he was reminded, by not finding it there, that it had been the first votive offering which had been made to appease the implacable deities presiding over the winds and waves.   The vessel closed with him, hove-to to windward, and, after some demur, a small boat, capable of holding three persons, was hoisted over the gunnel, and two hands, jumping into her, rowed under the stern of the wreck.

"You must jump, my lad—there's no going alongside a craft, without any sail to steady her, in such a sea as this. Don't be afraid.   We'll pick you up."

Willy, who had little fear in his composition, although he could not swim, leaped from the taffrail of the vessel into the boiling surge, and immediately that he rose to the surface was rescued by the men, who, seizing him by the waistband of the trousers, hauled him into the boat, and threw him down in the bottom under the thwarts.   Then, without speaking, they resumed their oars, and pulled to the other vessel, on board of which they succeeded in establishing our hero and themselves, although the boat was stove in the attempt, and cast adrift as useless.

Willy's teeth chattered, and his whole frame trembled with the cold, as he went aft to the captain of the sloop, who was sitting on deck wrapped up in a rough white great-coat, with his pipe in his mouth. The captain was a middle-sized, slightly made young man, apparently not more than twenty-five years old. His face was oval, with a remarkably pleasing expression ; his eye small and brilliant ; and, notwithstanding the roughness of his outward attire, there was a degree of precision in the arrangement of his hair and whiskers, which proved that with him neatness was habitual. He had a worsted mitten on his left hand; the right, which held his pipe, was bare, and remarkably white and small. Perceiving the situation of the boy, he called to one of the men—"Here, Phillips, take this poor devil down, and put something dry on him, and give him a glass of brandy; when he's all right again, we'll find out from him how he happened to be adrift all by himself, like a bear in a washing-tub. There, go along with Phillips, boy."

"He's of the right sort," said one of the men who had brought him on board, casting his eyes in the direction of our hero, who was descending the companion ;—"I thought so when I see'd him have his wits about him to hoist the signal. He made no more of jumping overboard than a Newfoundland dog—never stopped two seconds to think on't."

"We shall soon see what he is made of," replied the captain, relighting his pipe, which had been allowed to go out during the time that they were rescuing Willy and the men from the boat when she returned.

Willy was soon provided with more comfortable clothing ; and, whether it was or was not from a whim of Phillips's, who had been commissioned to rig him out, he appeared on deck the very picture of the animal which he had been compared to by the sailor. Thick woollen stockings, which were longer than both his legs and thighs, a pair of fisherman's well-greased boots, a dark Guernsey frock that reached below his knees, and a rough pea-jacket that de-

scended to his heels, made him appear much broader than he was high.   A red woollen night-cap completed his attire, which, although anything but elegant, was admirably calculated to assist the brandy in restoring the circulation.

"Here he is, captain, *all a-tanto*, but not very neat," said Phillips, shoving Willy up the hatchway, for he was so encumbered with the weight of his new apparel that he never could have ascended without assistance—"I have stowed away some spirits in his hold, and he no longer beats the devil's tattoo with his grinders."

"Now, my lad," said the captain, taking his pipe out of his mouth, "tell me what's your name, what you are, and how you came to be adrift in that barky?   Tell me the truth—be honest, always be honest, it's the best policy."

Now, it rather unfortunately happened for Willy, that these first two questions were rather difficult for him to answer.   He told his story with considerable hesitation,— *believed* his name was Seymour—*believed* he was a midshipman.   He was listened to without interruption by the captain and crew of the vessel, who had gathered round to hear him "spin his yarn."   When he had finished, the captain, looking Willy very hard in the face, thus addressed him:—"My little friend, excuse me, but I have some slight knowledge of the world, and I therefore wish that you had not forgotten the little advice I gave you, as a caution, before you commenced your narrative.   Did not I say, *be honest?*   You *believe* you are an officer, *believe* your name to be Seymour.   I tell you, my lad, in return, that I don't believe a word that you say; but, however, that's of no consequence.   It requires reflection to tell a lie, and I have no objection to a little invention, or a little caution with strangers.   All that about the battle was very clever —but still, depend upon it, honesty's the best policy. When we are better acquainted, I suppose we shall have the truth from you.   I see the land on the lee-bow—we shall be into Cherbourg in an hour, when I expect we shall come to a better understanding."

The *Sainte Vierge*, for such was the name of the vessel,

which smelt most insufferably of gin, and, as our readers
may probably have anticipated, was a smuggler, running
between Cherbourg and the English coast, soon entered
the port, and, having been boarded by the officers of the
douane (who made a very proper distinction between
smuggling from and to their own territories), came to an
anchor close to the mole. As soon as the vessel was
secured, the captain went below, and in a few minutes re-
appearing, dressed in much better taste than one-half of the
saunterers in Bond Street, went on shore to the cabaret
where he usually took up his quarters, taking with him
our hero, whose strange attire, so peculiarly contrasted
with that of the captain's, was a source of great amusement
to the sailors and other people, who were assembled on
the quay.

"*Ah, mon capitaine, charmé de vous revoir. Buvons un
coup, n'est-ce pas?*" said the proprietor of the cabaret,
presenting a bottle of prime French brandy, and a liquor
glass, to the captain, as he entered.

"*Heureux voyage, n'est-ce pas, Monsieur?*"

"*Ca va bien,*" replied the captain, throwing the glass of
liquor down his throat. "My apartments, if you please,
and a bed for this lad. Tell Mr Beaujou, the slopseller,
to come here directly with some clothes for him. Is
Captain Debriseau here?"

"He is, sir,—lost all his last cargo—obliged to throw
over in deep water."

"Never mind: he ran the two before—he can afford it."

"Ah, but Captain Debriseau is in a very bad humour,
nevertheless. He called me an old cheat this morning—
c'est incroyable."

"Well, present my compliments to him, and say that I
request the honour of his company, if he is not otherwise
engaged. Come, youngster."

The landlord of the cabaret ushered the captain of the
sloop and our hero, with many profound bows, into a low
dark room, with only one window, the light from which
was intercepted by a high wall, not four feet distant. The

floor was paved with tiles, the table was deal, not very clean, and the white-washed walls were hung around with stiff drawings of several smuggling vessels, whose superior sailing and consequent good fortune had rendered them celebrated in the port of Cherbourg. The straw had been lighted under some logs of wood on the hearth, which as yet emitted more smoke than flame ; a few chairs, an old battered sofa, and an upright press, completed the furniture.

"I knew your beautiful sloop long before she came in— there's no mistaking her ; and I ordered the apartment *de Monsieur* to be prepared. *C'est un joli appartement, n'est-ce pas, Monsieur?* so retired ! " With some forbearance, but with great judgment, the beauty of the prospect was not expatiated upon by the obsequious landlord.

"It will do to smoke and eat in, Mons. Picardon, and that is all that I require. Now bring pipes and tobacco, and take my message to Captain Debriseau."

The latter gentleman and the pipes were ushered in at the same moment.

"M'Elvina, my dear fellow, I am glad to see that you have had better luck than I have had this last trip. Curses on the cutter, *Sacristie*," continued Captain Debriseau, who was a native of Guernsey, "the wind favoured her three points after we were about, or I should have doubled him —ay, and have doubled the weight of the leathern bag too. *Sacré nom de Dieu*," continued he, grinding his teeth, and pulling a handful of hair out of his rough head, which could have spared as much as Absalom used to pull—"*Que ça me fait bisquer.*"

"*Bah! laissez aller, mon ami*—sit down and take a pipe," rejoined our captain. "This is but pettifogging work at the best ; it won't pay for the means of resistance. My lugger will be ready in May, and then I'll see what a revenue cutter is made of. I was at Ostend last Christmas, and saw her. By Jove, she's a beauty ! She was planked above the watermark then, and must be nearly ready for launching by this time. I'll pass through the Race but

once more; then adieu to dark nights and south-west gales
—and huzza for a row of teeth, with the will, as well as
the power, to bite.   Sixteen long nines, my boy!"

"Quick returns though, quick returns, messmate,"
answered Debriseau, referring to the Cherbourg system of
smuggling, which, being his own means of livelihood, he
did not like to hear disparaged.

For the benefit of those who have no objection to unite
a little information with amusement, I shall here enter into
a few remarks relative to the smuggling carried on between
the port of Cherbourg and our own coast,—premising that
my readers have my entire approbation to skip over a page
or two, if they are not anxious to know anything about these
nefarious transactions.

The port of Cherbourg, from its central situation, is
better adapted than any other in France, for carrying on
this trade with the southern coast of England.   The nearest
port to it, and at which, therefore, the smuggling is
principally carried on, is the Bill of Portland, near to the
fashionable watering-place of Weymouth.

The vessels employed in this contraband trade, of which
gin is the staple commodity, are generally small luggers or
sloops, from forty to sixty tons burthen.   In fine summer
weather, row-boats are occasionally employed; but as the
run is only of twenty-four hours' duration, the dark nights
and south-west gales are what are chiefly depended upon.

These vessels are not armed with an intention to resist;
if they are perceived by the cruisers or revenue vessels
before they arrive on the English coast, and are pursued,
they are obliged (if not able to escape, from superior sailing)
to throw over their cargo in "deep water," and it is lost.
The cargo is thrown overboard, to avoid the penalty and
imprisonment to which it would subject the crew, as well
as the confiscation of the vessel and cargo.   If they reach
the English coast, and are chased by the revenue vessels,
or have notice, by signals from their agents on shore, that
they are discovered, and cannot land their cargoes, they
take the exact bearings and distances of several points of

land, and with heavy stones sink their tubs of spirits, which are always strung upon a hawser like a row of beads. There the cargo is left, until they have an opportunity of going off in boats to creep for it, which is by dragging large hooks at the bottom until they catch the hawsers, and regain possession of their tubs. Such is the precision with which their marks are taken, and their dexterity from continual practice, that they seldom fail to recover their cargo. The profits of this contraband trade are so great, that if two cargoes are lost a third safely landed will indemnify the owners.

I must now observe, much to the discredit of the parties who are concerned, that this contraband trade is not carried on by individuals, but by a company; one hundred pound shares are taken of " *a speculation*," the profits of which are divided yearly : and many individuals residing on the coast, who would be thought incapable of lending themselves to such transactions, are known to be deeply interested.

The smuggling from Havre and Ostend, etc., is confined to the coast of Ireland and the northern shores of England ; the cargoes are assorted and of great value; and as the voyage and risk are greater, they are generally fast-sailing vessels, well manned and armed, to enable them to offer resistance, when the disparity of force is not too great on their side.

Captain M'Elvina had taken up the smuggling trade between Cherbourg and Portland to keep himself employed until a fine lugger of sixteen guns, the command of which had been promised to him, and which was intended to run between Havre and the coast of Ireland, should be ready ; whereas Captain Debriseau had been all his life employed in the Cherbourg trade, and had no intention of quitting it.

" But what have you got there, Mac ? " said Debriseau, pointing with his pipe to our hero, who sat on the leathern sofa, rolled up in his uncouth attire; "is it a bear, or a boy ? "

" A boy, that I picked up from a wreck. I am thinking what I shall do with him—he is a smart bold lad."

"By Jupiter," rejoined Debriseau, "I'll make him my Ganymede, till he grows older."

Had Willy been as learned in mythology as Captain Debriseau, he might have informed him, that he had served in that capacity in his last situation under Mr Bullock; but although the names, as appertaining to a ship, were not unknown to him, yet the attributes of the respective parties were a part of his education that old Adams had omitted.

"He will be fit for anything," rejoined our captain, "if he will only be honest."

"M'Elvina," said Debriseau, "you always have these words in your mouth, ' be honest.' Now, as, between ourselves, I do not think that either you or I are leading very honest lives, allow me to ask you why you continually harp upon honesty when we are alone? I can easily understand the propriety of shamming a little before the world."

"Debriseau, had any other man said half as much, I would have started my grog in his face. It's no humbug on my part. I mean it sincerely; and, to prove it, I will now give you a short sketch of my life; and after you have heard it, I have no doubt but that you will acknowledge, with me, the truth of the old adage, that ' Honesty is the best policy.' "

But Captain M'Elvina must have a chapter to himself.

Chapter X

He hath as fine a hand at picking a pocket as a woman, and is as nimble-fingered as a juggler. If an unlucky session does not cut the rope of his life, I pronounce he will be a great man in history.

Beggar's Opera.

"IT is an old proverb that ' one half the world do not know *how* the other half live.' Add to it, nor *where* they live, and it will be as true. There is a class of people, of whose existence the public are too well aware; but of whose resorts, and manners, and customs, among their own fraternity, they are quite as ignorant now as they were one hundred years back. Like the Chinese and the castes of the East, they never change their profession, but bequeath it from father to son, as an entailed estate from which they are to derive their subsistence. The class to which I refer consists of those members of the community at large, who gain their livelihood by inserting their hands into the pockets of other people,—not but that all the world are doing the same thing, and have, since the creation; but then it is only as *amateurs;*—the class I refer to, do it *professionally*, which, you must observe, makes a wide difference. From this class I am lineally descended; and, at an early age, was duly initiated into all the mysteries of my profession. I could filch a handkerchief as soon as I was high enough to reach a pocket, and was declared to be a most promising child.

"I must do my father and mother the justice to acknowledge, that while they initiated me in the mysteries of my future profession, they did not attempt to conceal that there were certain disagreeable penalties attached to 'greatness;' but, when prepared from our earliest years, we look forward to our fate with resignation: and, as I was invariably told, after my return from some daring feat, that my life would be a short and a merry one, I was not dismayed at the words of my prophetic mother, who observed, 'Patrick, my boy, if you don't wish to bring my grey hairs with sorrow to the grave, promise me to confine yourself to picking pockets; you will then only be transported: but if you try your hand at higher work, you'll be hung before you're twenty.' My father, when I returned with a full assorted cargo, and emptied my pockets into his hands, with as much rapidity as I had transferred the contents of others into my own, used to look at me with a smile of pride and satisfaction, and, shaking his head, would exclaim—'Pat, you'll certainly be hung.'

" Accustomed, therefore, from my infancy, to consider twenty summers, instead of threescore years and ten, as the allotted space of my existence, I looked forward to my exit from this world, by the new drop, with the same placidity as the nobleman awaits the time appointed for the entrance of his body into the vault containing the dust of his ancestors. At the age of eleven years, I considered myself a full-grown man, dared all that man could do, and was a constant, but unwilling, attendant upon the police office, where my youth, and the promises of my mother that I should be reformed, assisted by showers of tears on her part, and by apparent ingenuousness on mine, frequently pleaded in my favour with the prosecutors.

"I often lamented, when at that early age, that my want of education prevented me from attempting the higher walks of our profession; but this object of my ambition was gained at last. I had taken a pocket-book from a worthy Quaker, and, unfortunately, was perceived by a man at a shop window, who came out, collared, and delivered me into the hands of the prim gentleman. Having first secured his property, he then walked with me and a police officer to Bow Street. My innocent face, and my tears, induced the old gentleman, who was a member of the Philanthropic Society, not only not to prefer the charge against me, but to send me to the institution at Blackfriars Road.

"I made rapid progress under their tuition, and after three years' close application on my part, and continual inculcation, on the part of my instructors, of the distinction between *meum* and *tuum*, I was considered not only a very clever boy, but a reformed character. The Quaker gentleman, who had placed me in the institution, and who was delighted with the successful results of his own penetration, selected me as his servant, and took me home."

"Well, I'm glad you were so soon reformed," said Debriseau. "Where the devil's my handkerchief?"

"Oh, I've not got it," answered M'Elvina, laughing. "But you are as much mistaken now as the Quaker was at that time. A wild beast may be tamed, and will remain so, provided he be not permitted again to taste blood. Then all his ferocious propensities will reappear, and prove that his education has been thrown away. So it was with me. At first, I felt no desire to return to my old employment; and had not my master trusted me too much, I might have remained honest. You often hear masters exclaiming against the dishonesty of servants. I know it to be a fact, that most of them have been made dishonest by the carelessness of their employers, in having allowed temptations to lie in their way, which were too strong to be resisted. My master used to send me up to his bureau, for small sums which he required, out of a yellow canvas bag, full of gold and silver. I am convinced that he frequently used to give me the key, when in company with his friends, in order that, after I had left the room, he might tell my history, and prove the beneficial effects of the Society. One day the yellow bag and I both disappeared.

"I threw off the modest grey coat in which I was equipped, and soon procured more fashionable attire. I looked in the glass, and scarcely knew myself; I had, therefore, no fear of being recognised by my former master. Not wishing to be idle, I hired myself out as tiger and valet to a young nobleman, who was spending ten thousand pounds a year upon an allowance of seven hundred. He was a complete *roué*, and I must gratefully own, that I learnt a great deal from him, independently of the secret of tying my neck-cloth correctly;—but we soon parted."

"How was that?" said Debriseau, knocking the ashes out of his pipe.

"Why, he had several diamond rings, and as he only wore two or three at a time, I sported the others at our parties. A malicious fellow, who was envious of the dash I cut, observed, in my hearing, that it was impossible to tell real stones from good paste. I took the hint, and one by one, the diamonds vanished, and paste usurped their places. Shortly after, the creditors, not being able to touch my master's money or his person, seized his effects, and the diamond rings were almost the only articles which escaped. My master, who always looked out for a rainy day, had collected these rings as a sort of stand-by, to 'raise the wind' when required. By ill luck, he took them to the same jeweller who had been employed by me to substitute the paste, and to whom I had sold the real stones. He came home in a great rage, accused me of dishonesty, and sent for a constable. I told him that I did not consider his conduct to be that of a gentleman, and wished him good morning. I had indeed intended to quit him, as he was *done up*, and only waited his return to tell him so. I had moved my trunks, accordingly, before he was out of bed. I believe a few of his suits, and some of his linen, were put in with mine, in my extreme haste; but then he owed me wages.

"When I wished his lordship good morning, I certainly imagined that I had little more to learn; but I must acknowledge that I was mistaken. I knew that there was a club established for servants out of place, and had been a subscriber for two years,—as there were many advantages arising from it, independently of economy. I was now a member by right, which, as long as I was in place, I was not. To this club I repaired, and I soon found that I, who fancied myself perfect, was but a *tyro* in the profession. It was a grand school certainly, and well organised. We had our president, vice-president, auditors of accounts, corresponding members, and our secretary. Our seal was a bunch of green poplar rods, with ' *Service is no inheritance* ' as a motto.

"But not to weary you with a life of adventures which would fill volumes, I shall merely state, that I was in place, out of place, following up my profession in every way, with great credit among our fraternity, until, one day, I found myself, after a tedious confinement in Newgate, decorated with a yellow jacket, and pair of fetters, on board of a vessel of three hundred tons burthen, bound to New South Wales. We sailed for Sidney, where I had been recommended, by the gentleman in a large wig, to remain seven years for change of air. The same night that the vessel came into the cove, having more liberty than the rest of my shipmates (from my good behaviour during the passage), I evaded the sentry, and slipping down by the cable into the water, swam to a ship lying near, which, I had been informed, was to sail on the ensuing day for India.

"The captain being very short of hands, headed me up in a cask; and, although the vessel was not permitted to sail until very strict search had been made for me, I was not discovered, and it was supposed that I had been drowned in making the attempt. Aware that it would not be good for my health to return previously to the expiration of the seven years, I determined to learn a new *profession*—that of a sailor, for which I always had a predilection; besides, it quieted my conscience as to the impropriety of not submitting to the just punishment of the law, as you will acknowledge that seven years at sea, and seven years' transportation, are one and the same thing. From Batavia I went to Calcutta, and worked before the mast in the country vessels to Bombay and the Persian Gulf, for four years, when I thought myself capable of taking higher rank in the service, if I could get it; especially as I had picked up sufficient navigation to be able to work the ship's reckoning.

"At Calcutta, I obtained a situation as second mate of a fast-sailing schooner employed in the smuggling of opium into China, and after three voyages, rose to the office of chief mate. Had I remained another voyage I should have been captain of the vessel; but my seven years were out, and I was anxious to return to England, and look the *Robin Red Breasts* boldly in the face. I had saved enough money to pay my passage, and was determined to go home like a gentleman, if I had not exactly gone *out* in that character. What little cash remained after my passage was paid, I lost at play to an army officer, who was returning in the same ship.

"When I landed at Portsmouth, I retained a suit of 'long togs,' as we call them, and, disposing of all the rest of my stock to the Jews, I started for London. On my arrival I found that my father and mother were both dead, and I was meditating upon my future course of *life*, when an accident determined me. I picked up a pocket-book "—(here Captain Debriseau eyed him hard)—"I know what you mean," continued M'Elvina; "but it *was* on the pavement, and not *in a pocket*, as you would imply by your looks. It was full of slips and scraps of paper of all sorts, which I did not take the trouble to read. The only available articles it contained, were three one-pound notes. The owner's name and address were written on the first blank leaf. I cannot tell what possessed me, but I had an irresistible desire to be honest once in my life, and the temptation to be otherwise not being very great, I took the pocket-book to the address, and arrived at the house just as the old gentleman to whom it belonged was giving *directions* to have it advertised. He was in evident perturbation at his loss—and I came just at the fortunate moment. He seized his book with rapture, examined all the papers, and counted over the bills and notes.

"'Honesty is a scarce commodity, young man,' said he, as he passed the leathern tongue of the book through the strap. 'You have brought me my book, without waiting till a reward was offered. I desired my clerk to offer twenty guineas in the advertisement—I will now give you a larger sum.' He sat down, opened a cheque-book, and wrote me a draft on his banker. It was for one hundred pounds! I was profuse in my acknowledgments, while he replaced his book in his inside pocket, and buttoned up his coat. 'Honesty is a scarce commodity, young man,' repeated he; 'call here to-morrow at one o'clock, and I will see if I can be of any further service to you.'

"I returned to my lodgings in a very thoughtful mood. I was astonished at the old man's generosity, and still more at my having honestly obtained so large a sum. I went to bed, and reflected on what had passed. The words of the old gentleman still rang in my ears—

'Honesty is a scarce commodity.' I communed with myself. Here have I been, nearly all my life, exercising all my talents, exerting all my energies in dishonest practices, and when did I, even at the most successful hit, obtain as much money as I have by an honest act? I recalled the many days of anxious waiting that I had found necessary to accomplish a scheme of fraud—the doubtful success—the necessity of satisfying my associates—the inability of turning into ready money the articles purloined until the hue and cry was over—the trifling sum which I was obliged to take from the purchasers of stolen articles, who knew that I was at their mercy—the destitute condition I occasionally was in—and the life of constant anxiety that I had led. These reflections forced the truth upon my mind, that there was more, in the end, to be gained by honesty than by roguery.

"Once convinced, I determined to lead a new life, and from that moment I assumed as my motto, 'Honesty is the best policy.' Do you hear, youngster?—'always be honest.'"

Chapter XI

Through tattered clothes small vices do appear;
Robes and furred gowns hide all.

Lear.

WILLY, who was tired out with the extreme mental and bodily exertion that he had undergone, gave no answer to M'Elvina's injunction, except a loud snore, which satisfied the captain that his caution in this instance was not heard.

"Well," said Debriseau, after a short pause, "How long did this honest fit last?"

"What do you mean?—How long did it last? Why, it has lasted,—Captain Debriseau,—it has lasted until now; and shall last, too, as long as this frame of mine shall hold together. But to proceed. The next morning I called upon the old gentleman according to his request. He again told me, 'honesty was a scarce commodity.' I could have informed him that it had always been so with me, but I kept my own counsel. He then asked me what were my profession and pursuits? Now, as I had two professions to choose between, and as my last was considered to be just as abundant in the commodity he prized so much, as my former one was known to be deficient, I replied that I was a sea-faring man. 'Then I may find some employment for you,' replied the old gentleman; and having put several questions to me as to the nature of the service I had seen, he desired me to take a walk till three o'clock, when he would be happy to see me at dinner;—'We'll then be able to have a little conversation together, without being overheard.'

"I was exact to my appointment, and my old friend, who was punctuality itself, did not allow me to remain in the parlour two minutes before dinner was on the table. As soon as it was over, he dismissed the servant girl who attended, and turned the key in the door. After sounding me on many points, during a rapid discussion of the first bottle of port, he proceeded to inform me, that a *friend* of his wanted a smart fellow as captain of a vessel, if I would like the employment. This suited me; and he then observed, that I must have some notion of how officers were managed, as I had been in the China trade, and that he *thought* that the vessel was to be employed in the contraband trade on the English coast.

" This startled me a little, for I was afraid that the old gentleman was laying a trap for my newly-acquired commodity; and I was about to refuse with some slight show of indignation, when I perceived a change in his countenance, indicative of disappointment—so I only demurred until he had sufficient time to prove that there was no dishonesty in the transaction, when, being convinced that he was in earnest, I consented. Before the second bottle was finished, I found out that it was not for a *friend*, but for himself, and for one of his own vessels, that he was anxious to procure a smart captain; and that he had a large capital embarked in the concern, which was very profitable. The pocket-book which I had returned was of no little importance; had it fallen into other hands, it might have told tales.

"I have now been three years in the old gentleman's employ, and a generous good master he has been; and his daughter is a sweet pretty girl. I lost my last vessel, but not until she had cleared him £10,000; and now the old gentleman is building me another at Havre. Not to be quite idle, I have in the meantime taken command of one of their sloops: for the old gentleman has a good many shares in the *speculation*, and his recommendations are always attended to."

" *Voici Monsieur Beaujou, avec les habits,*" said the maître d'auberge, opening the door, and ushering in the marchand des modes *maritimes,* with a huge bundle.

" Now, then, boy, rouse out," said M'Elvina, shaking our hero for a long while, without any symptoms of recovering him from his lethargy.

" Try him on the other tack," said the captain, lifting him off the sofa, and placing him upright on his legs.

" There's no sugar in it yet," said Willy, who was dreaming that he was supplying the mulled claret to the old master's-mate.

" Ah," said Debriseau, laughing, " he thinks his mamma is giving him his tea."

" The lying little rascal told me this morning he had no mother. Come, Mr William Seymour, *I believe*"— (mimicking) " officer, *I believe*—Oh, you're a nice honest boy. Have you a mother, or do you tell fibs in your sleep as well as awake? ' Be honest.' "

The last words, that Willy had heard repeated so often during the day, not only unsealed his eyes, but recalled to his recollection where he was.

" Now, my youngster, let us rig you out; you recollect you stated that you were going home for your outfit, and now I'll give you one, that you may have one fib less on your conscience."

By the generosity of M'Elvina, Willy was soon fitted with two suits of clothes, requiring little alteration, and Mr Beaujou, having received a further order for a supply of shirts, and other articles necessary to complete, made his bow and disappeared.

The two captains resumed their chairs, and our hero again coiled himself on the sofa, and in one minute was as sound asleep as before.

"And now, M'Elvina," resumed Debriseau, "I should like to know by what arguments your employer contrived to reconcile your present vocation with your punctilious regard for honesty? For I must confess, for my own part, that although I have followed smuggling as a livelihood, I have never defended it as an honest calling, and have looked forward with occasional impatience to the time when I should be able to leave it off."

"Defend it! Why I'll just repeat to you the arguments used by the old gentleman. They convinced me. As I said before, I am always open to conviction. Captain Debriseau, you will acknowledge, I trust, that laws are made for the benefit of all parties, high and low, rich and poor?"

"Granted."

"You'll allow also, that law-makers should not be law-breakers; and that if they are so, they cannot expect that others will regard what they disregard themselves."

"Granted also."

"Once more—by the laws of our country, the receiver is as bad as the thief, and they who instigate others to commit an offence, are equally guilty with the offending party."

"It cannot be denied," replied Debriseau.

"Then you have acceded to all the propositions that I wish, and we shall come to an undeniable and mathematical conclusion. Observe, law-makers should not be

law-breakers.   Who enacted these laws ?—the aristocracy
of the nation, seated in their respective houses, the Lords
and the Commons.   Go, any night you please, to the
Opera, or any other place of public resort, in which you
can have a view of their wives and daughters.   I'll stake
my existence that every female there shall be dizened out
in some contraband article of dress—not one but shall
prove to be a receiver of smuggled goods, and therefore,
as bad as those whom they have instigated to *infringe* the
laws of their country.   If there were no demand there
would be no supply."

"Surely they don't *all* drink gin ?" replied Debriseau.

"Drink gin!   You're thinking of your d—d Cherbourg
trade — your ideas are confined.   Is there nothing
smuggled besides gin ?   Now, if the husbands and fathers
of these ladies,—those who have themselves enacted the
laws,—wink at their *infringement*, why should not others
do so ?   The only distinction between the equally offending parties is, that those who are in power,—who possess
all the comforts and luxuries which this world can afford,
—who offend the laws from vanity and caprice, and
entice the needy to administer to their love of display,
are protected and unpunished; while the adventurous
seaman, whose means of supporting his family depend
upon his administering to their wishes, or the poor devil
who is unfortunately detected with a gallon of spirits, is
thrown into gaol as if he were a *felon*.   There cannot
be one law for the rich and another for the poor, Debriseau.
When I hear that the wives of the aristocracy have been
seized by the revenue officers, and the contraband articles
which they wear have been taken off their backs, and
that they have been sentenced to twelve months' imprisonment, by a committal from the magistrate, then—and
not till then—will I acknowledge our profession to be
dishonest."

"Very true," said Debriseau ; "it shows the folly of
men attempting to make laws for their *masters*."

"Is it not shocking," continued M'Elvina, "to reflect

upon the conduct of the magistrate, who has just sentenced perhaps four or five unhappy wretches to a dungeon for an offence against these laws? He leaves the seat of Justice, and returns to the bosom of his family. Hear his wife,"—(mimicking)—"'Well, my dear, you're come at last—dinner has been put back this half hour. I thought you would never have finished with those odious smugglers.' 'Why, my love, it was a very difficult case to prove; but we managed it at last, and I have signed the warrant for their committal to the county gaol. They're sad troublesome fellows, these smugglers.'— Now look at the lady: 'What dress is that you put on to greet your husband?' 'Gros de Naples de Lyon.'— 'The lace it is trimmed with?' 'Valenciennes.'—'Your gloves, madam?' 'Fabrique de Paris.'—'Your ribands, your shoes, your handkerchief?' All, all contraband.— Worthy magistrate, if you would hold the scales of Justice with an even hand, make out *one more* mittimus before you sit down to table. Send your wife to languish a twelvemonth in company with the poor smugglers, and then ' to dinner with what appetite you may.' And now, Debriseau, have I convinced you that I may follow my present calling, and still say—' *be honest?* '"

"Why, yes, I think we both may; but would not this evil be removed by free trade?"

"Heaven forbid!" replied M'Elvina, laughing; "then there would be no *smuggling.*"

Chapter XII

Love me, love my dog.

Proverb.

IT is the misfortune of those who have been in constant habits of deceit, that they always imagine others are attempting the same dishonest practices. For some time, M'Elvina felt convinced that our little hero had swerved from truth in the account which he gave of himself; and it was not until after repeated catechisings, in which he found that, strange and improbable as the narrative appeared, Willy never altered from or contradicted his original statement, that he believed the boy to be as honest and ingenuous as might have been inferred from his prepossessing countenance.

To this conviction, however, did he arrive at last; and our hero—who seemed no sooner to have lost one protector than to have the good fortune to find another—became the favourite and companion of his new captain, instead of his domestic, as had been originally contemplated. A lad of Willy's age, who is treated with kindness and consideration, is soon attached, and becomes reconciled to any change of circumstances. It was a matter of indifference to our hero, whether he was on the quarter-deck of a man-of-war, or in the cabin of a smuggling sloop. Contented with his present lot,—with the happy thoughtlessness of youth, he never permitted the future to disturb his repose, or affect his digestion.

Willy had been nearly a month at Cherbourg when M'Elvina's sloop took in another cargo. "Willy," said M'Elvina, one evening as they sat together in the apartment at the cabaret, "to-morrow I shall, in all probability, sail for the English coast. I have been thinking what I shall do with you. I do not much like parting with you; but, on reflection, I think it will be better that I should leave you behind. You can be of no use, and may be in the way if we should be obliged to take to our boat."

Willy pleaded hard against this arrangement. "I never have a friend but I lose him directly," said the boy, and the tears started into his eyes.

"I trust you will not lose me, my dear fellow," replied M'Elvina, moved at this proof of affection; "but I must explain to you why I leave you. In the first place," added he, laughing, "with that mark on your shoulder, it would be felony without benefit of clergy for you to be found in my possession; but of that I would run the risk. My serious reasons are as follow:—If this trip proves fortunate, I shall not return to Cherbourg. I have business of importance in London, which may require my presence for some weeks in that metropolis and its vicinity. I told you before, that I am about to take the command of a very different vessel from this paltry sloop, and upon a more dangerous service. In four or five months she will be ready to sail, and during that time I shall be constantly on the move, and shall hardly know what to do with you. Now, Willy, you are not aware of the advantages of education — I am: and as mine was given to me by strangers, so will I in return bestow as much upon you as I can afford. You must, therefore, go to school until my return. You will at least acquire the French language, and you will find that of no little use to you hereafter."

Willy, accustomed to discipline and to breathe the air of passive obedience, submitted without raising any more objections. Debriseau joined, and they all three sallied forth to make arrangements for placing our hero "*en pension*," where they had been recommended. Having effected this, they agreed to lounge on the *Place d'Armes* till sunset, when they took possession of one of the benches. M'Elvina and Debriseau lighted their cigars, and puffed away in silence, while Willy amused himself with watching the promenaders as they passed in review before him.

They had not remained there many minutes when a poodle-dog, *bien tondu*, and white as a sheep from the river before the day of shearing, walked up to them with an air of sagacious curiosity, and looked M'Elvina stedfastly in the face. M'Elvina, taking his cigar from his mouth, held it to the dog, who ran up to it, as if to smell it; the lighted end coming in contact with his cold nose, induced the animal to set up a loud yell, and retreat to his master much faster than he came, passing first one fore-paw and then the other over his nose, to wipe away the pain, in such a ridiculous manner as to excite loud merriment, not only from our party on the bench, but also from others who had witnessed the scene.

"So much for curiosity," said M'Elvina, continuing his mirth. The proprietor of the dog, a young Frenchman, dressed very much "*en calicot*," did not, however, seem quite so much amused with this practical joke; he cocked his hat fiercely on one side, raised his figure to the utmost of his height, and walking up, *en grand militaire*, addressed M'Elvina, with "*Comment, monsieur, vous avez fait une grande bêtise là—vous m'insultez—*"

"I think I had better not understand French," said M'Elvina, aside to Debriseau; then turning to the French-man, with a grave face, and air of incomprehension,— "What did you say, Sir?"

"Ah! you are Inglishman. You not speak French?" —M'Elvina shook his head, and began to puff away his cigar.

"Den, sare, if you not speak de French language, I speak de Inglis like von natif, and I tell you, sare, *que vous m'avez insulté*. Got for dam!—you burnt my dog nose; vat you mean, sare?"

"The dog burnt his own nose," answered M'Elvina, mildly.

"Vat you mean? de dog burn his own nose! How is a dog cap-able to burn his own nose? Sare, you put de cigar to my dog nose. I must have de *satisfaction* or de apology *tout de suite*."

"But, sir, I have not insulted *you*."

"Sare, you insult my dog—he is von and de same ting —*mon chien est un chien de sentiment*. He feel de affront all de same vid me—I feel de affront all de same vid him. *Vous n'avez qu'à choisir, monsieur*."

"Between you and your dog," answered M'Elvina— "Well, then, I'd rather fight the dog."

"Bah! fight de dog—de dog cannot fight, sare: *mais je suis son maître et son ami*, and I vill fight for him."

"Well then, monsieur, I did insult your dog, I must

acknowledge, and I will give him the satisfaction which you require."

" And how vill you give de satisfaction to de dog ? "

" Why, sir, you said just now that he was *un chien de beaucoup de sentiment :*—if he is so, he will accept and properly appreciate my apology."

" Ah, sare," replied the Frenchman, relaxing the stern wrinkles of his brow, "*c'est bien dit*; you will make de apology to de dog. *Sans doute*, he is de principal, I am only de second. *C'est une affaire arrangée. Moustache, viens ici, Moustache*" (the dog came up to his master.) " *Monsieur est très-fâché de t'avoir brûlé le nez.*"

" Monsieur Moustache," said M'Elvina, taking off his hat with mock gravity to the dog, who seemed determined to keep at a respectful distance, "*je vous demande mille excuses.*"

" *Ah ! que c'est charmant !* " cried some of the fair sex, who, as well as the men, had been attracted by, and were listening to the dispute. " *Que monsieur l'Anglais est drôle ! et voyez Moustache, comme il a l'air content !—vraiment c'est un chien d'esprit.*" " *Allez, Moustache,*" said his master, who was now all smiles, " *donnez la patte à monsieur—donnez donc.* Ah, sare, he forgive you, I am very sure—*il n'a pas de malice*; but he is afraid of de cigar. De burnt shild dred de *vater*, as your great Shakespeare say."

" *C'est un chien de talent : il a beaucoup de sentiment. Je suis bien fâché de l'avoir blessé, monsieur.*"

" *Et monsieur parle français ?* "

"I should esteem myself fortunate, if I spoke your language as well as you do mine," replied M'Elvina, in French.

This compliment, before so many bystanders, completely won the heart of the vain and choleric Frenchman.

" Ah, sare, you are too complaisant. I hope I shall have de pleasure to make your acquaintance. *Je m'appelle monsieur Auguste de Poivre. J'ai l'honneur de vous présenter une carte d'adresse.* I live on de top of my mother's,—*sur*

l'entresol. My mother live on de ground—*rez-de-chaussée.*
Madame *ma mère* will be delighted to receive a monsieur of
so much vit and adresse." So saying, away went monsieur
Auguste de Poivre, followed by Moustache, who was " *all
von and de same ting.*"

" Well, we live and learn," said M'Elvina, laughing, as
soon as the Frenchman was at a little distance ; " I never
thought that I should have made an apology to a dog."

" Oh, but," replied Debriseau, " you forget that he was
un chien de sentiment."

" You may imagine, from my behaviour, that I consider
him a wiser puppy than his master, for he ran away from
fire, whereas his master tried all he could to get into it.
Some of our countrymen would have humoured him, and
turned a comedy into a tragedy—I set a proper value on my
life, and do not choose to risk it about trifles."

" There has been more than one valuable life thrown
away about a dog, in my remembrance," said Debriseau.
" I think you behaved in a sensible manner to get rid of the
affair as you did ; but you would have done better not to
have burnt the dog's nose."

" Granted," replied M'Elvina ; " the more so, as I have
often remarked, that there is no object in the world, except
your children or your own self, in which the *meum* is so
powerful, and the *tuum* so weak. You caress your own
dog, and kick a strange one ; you are pleased with the
clamorous barking of your own cur, and you curse the
same noise from another. The feeling is as powerful,
almost, as that of a mother, who thinks her own ugly cub
a cherub compared to others, and its squallings the music
of the spheres. It is because there is no being that
administers so much to the self-love of his master. He
submits, with humility, to the blow inflicted in the moment
of irritation, and licks the hand that corrects. He bears no
revengeful feelings, and is ready to fondle and caress you
the moment that your good-humour returns. He is, what
man looks in vain for among his kind, a faithful friend, without contradiction—the *very perfection of a slave.* The abject

submission on his part, which would induce you to despise him, becomes a merit, when you consider his courage, his fidelity, and his gratitude. I cannot think what Mahomet was about when he pronounced his fiat against them, as *unclean*."

" Well," said Debriseau, " I agree with Mahomet that they are *not clean*, especially puppies. There's that little beast at Monsieur Picardon's, I declare——"

" Pooh," interrupted M'Elvina, laughing. " I don't mean it in that sense—I mean that, in a despotic country, the conduct of a dog towards his master should be held up as an example for imitation ; and I think that the banner of the Moslem should have borne the dog, instead of the crescent, as an emblem of blind fidelity and tacit submission."

" That's very true," said Debriseau ; " but, nevertheless, I wish mademoiselle's puppy were either taught manners or thrown over the quay."

" *Ce n'est pas un chien de sentiment*," replied M'Elvina, laughing. " But it is nearly dark. *Allons au cabaret*."

They returned to the inn ; and the wind, on the ensuing morning, blowing strong from a favourable quarter, Willy and Debriseau accompanied M'Elvina down to the mole, from whence he embarked on board of the sloop, which was already under way, and in the course of an hour was out of sight.

On the following day, Captain Debriseau accompanied Willy to the *pension*, where our hero remained nearly five months, occasionally visited by the Guernsey captain, when he returned from his smuggling trips, and more rarely receiving a letter from M'Elvina, who had safely landed his cargo, and was latterly at Havre, superintending the fitting out of his new vessel. Our hero made good progress during the few months that he remained at the *pension*, and when M'Elvina returned to take him away, not only could speak the French language with fluency, but had also made considerable progress in what Sir W. C. used to designate in his toast, as "the tree R's," — *viz.*, "Reading, 'Riting, and 'Rithmetic."

The lugger which had been built for M'Elvina by his employer was now ready, and, bidding farewell to Debriseau, who continued in the Cherbourg trade, our hero and his protector journeyed *en diligence* to Havre.

Chapter XIII

Through the haze of the night a bright flash now appearing,
  "Oh, ho!" cried Will Watch, "the Philistines bear down;
Bear a hand, my tight lads, ere we think about sheering,
One broadside pour in, should we swim, boys, or drown."
Sea Song.

"Now, Willy, what do you think of *La Belle Suzanne*?" said M'Elvina, as they stood on the pier about a stone's throw from the vessel, which lay with her broadside towards them. Not that M'Elvina had any opinion of Willy's judgment, but, from the affectionate feeling which every sailor imbibes for his own ship, he expected gratification even in the admiration of a child. The lugger was certainly as beautiful a model of that description of vessel as had ever been launched from a slip. At the distance of a mile, with the sea running, it was but occasionally that you could perceive her long black hull, —so low was she in the water, and so completely were her bulwarks pared down; yet her breadth of beam was very great, and her tonnage considerable, as may be inferred when it is stated that she mounted sixteen long brass nine-pounders, and was manned with one hundred and thirty men. But now that she was lying at anchor in smooth water, you had an opportunity of examining, with the severest scrutiny, the beautiful run of the vessel, as she sat graceful as a diver, and appeared, like that aquatic bird, ready to plunge in a moment, and disappear under the wave cleft by her sharp forefoot, and rippling under her bows.

"When shall we sail?" inquired Willy, after bestowing more judicious encomiums upon the vessel than might be expected.

" To-morrow night, if the wind holds to the southward. We took in our powder this morning. Where were you stationed at quarters on board the—— ? "

" Nowhere. I was not on the ship's books until a day or two before I left her."

" Then you must be a powder-monkey with me; you can hand powder up, if you can do nothing else."

" I can do more," replied Willy, proudly; " I can roll shells overboard."

" Ay, ay, so you can; I forgot that. I suppose I must put you on the quarter-deck, and make an officer of you, as Captain M—— intended to do."

" I mean to stand by you when we fight," said Willy, taking M'Elvina's hand.

" Thank you—that may not be so lucky. I'm rather superstitious; and, if I recollect right, your old friend Adams had that honour when he was killed."

The name of old Adams being mentioned, made Willy silent and unhappy. M'Elvina perceived it; the conversation was dropped; and they returned home.

A few days afterwards, *La Belle Suzanne* sailed, amidst the shouts and *vivas* of the multitude collected on the pier, and a thousand wishes for "*succès*," and "*bon voyage*"—the builder clapping his hands, and skipping with all the simial ecstasy of a Frenchman, at the encomiums lavished upon his vessel, as she cleaved through the water with the undeviating rapidity of a barracouta. But the *vivas*, and the shouts, and the builder, and the pier that he capered on, were soon out of sight; and our hero was once more confiding in the trackless and treacherous ocean.

" Well, she *does* walk," said Phillips, who had followed the fortunes of his captain, and was now looking over the quarter of the vessel. "She must be a clipper as catches us with the tacks on board! Right in the wind's eye too; clean full. By the powers, I believe if you were to lift her, she would lay a point on the other side of the wind."

" Get another pull of the fore-halyards, my lads," cried M'Elvina. " These few ropes stretch most confoundedly. There, belay all that ; take a *severe* turn, and don't come up an inch."

The breeze freshened, and the lugger flew through the water, dashing the white spray from her bows into the air, where it formed little rainbows, as it was pierced by the beams of the setting sun.

" We shall have a fine night, and light weather towards the morning, I think," said the first mate, addressing M'Elvina.

" I think so too. Turn the hands up to muster by the quarter-bill. We'll load the guns as soon as the lights are out ; let the gunner fill forty rounds, and desire the carpenter to nail up the hatchway-screens. Let them be rolled up and stopped. We'll keep them up for a *full due*, till we return to Havre."

The crew of the lugger were now summoned on deck by the call of the boatswain, and having been addressed by Captain M'Elvina upon the absolute necessity of activity and preparation, in a service of such peculiar risk, they loaded the guns, and secured them for the night.

The crew consisted of about eighty or ninety English-men, out of the full complement of one hundred and thirty men ; the remainder was composed of Frenchmen, and other continental adventurers. Although the respective countries were at variance, the subjects of each had shaken hands, that they might assist each other in violating the laws. The quiet and subordination of a king's ship were not to be expected here :—loud and obstreperous mirth, occasional quarrelling, as one party, by accident or inten-tion, wounded the national pride of the other ; French, English, and Irish spoken alternately, or at the same

moment—created a degree of confusion, which proved that
the reins of government were held lightly by the captain
in matters of small importance ; but although there was
a general freedom of manner, and independence of address,
still his authority was acknowledged, and his orders
implicitly obeyed.   It was a ship's company which *pulled
every way*, as the saying is, when there was nothing to
demand union ; but let difficulty or danger appear, and all
their squabbling was forgotten, or reserved for a more
seasonable opportunity : then they all *pulled together*, those
of each nation vying in taking the lead and setting an
example to the other.

Such was the crew of the lugger which M'Elvina commanded, all of whom were picked men, remarkable for
their strength and activity.

As the first mate had predicted, the wind fell light
after midnight, and at dawn of day the lugger was gliding
through the smooth water, at the rate of three or four
miles an hour, shrouded in a thick fog.   The sun rose,
and had gained about twenty degrees of altitude, when
M'Elvina beat to quarters, that he might accustom his men
to the exercise of the guns.   The rays of the sun had not
power to pierce through the fog ; and, shorn of his beams,
he had more the appearance of an overgrown moon, or
was, as Phillips quaintly observed, " like a man disguised
in woman's attire."

The exercise of the guns had not long continued, when
the breeze freshened up, and the fog began partially to
disperse.   Willy, who was perched on the round-house
abaft, observed a dark mass looming through the mist
on the weather beam.   " Is that a vessel ? " said Willy,
pointing it out to the first mate, who was standing near
M'Elvina.

" Indeed it is, my boy," replied the mate ; " you've a
sharp eye of your own."

M'Elvina's glass was already on the object.   " A cutter,
right before the wind, coming down to us ; a government
vessel, of some sort or another, I'll swear.   I trust she's a

revenue cruiser—I have an account to settle with those gentlemen. Stay at your quarters, my lads—hand up shot, and open the magazine!"

The powerful rays of the sun, assisted by the increasing wind, now rolled away the fog from around the vessels, which had a perfect view of each other. They were distant about two miles, and the blue water was strongly rippled by the breeze which had sprung up. The lugger continued her course on a wind, while the cutter bore down towards her, with all the sail that she could throw out. The fog continued to clear away, until there was an open space of about three or four miles in diameter. But it still remained folded up in deep masses, forming a wall on every side, which obscured the horizon from their sight. It appeared as if nature had gratuitously cleared away a sufficient portion of the mist, and had thus arranged a little amphitheatre for the approaching combat between the two vessels.

"His colours are up, sir. Revenue stripes, by the Lord!" cried Phillips.

"Then all's right," replied M'Elvina.

The cutter had now run down within half a mile of the lugger, who had continued her course with the most perfect nonchalance—when she rounded-to. The commander of the vessel, aware, at the first discovery of the lugger, that she could be no other than an enemy, who would most probably give him some trouble, had made every preparation for the engagement.

"Shall we hoist any colours, sir?" said the first mate to M'Elvina.

"No—if we hoist English, he will not commence action until he has made the private signal, and all manner of parleying, which is quite unnecessary. He knows what we are well enough."

"Shall we hoist a French ensign, sir?"

"No; I'll fight under no other colours than those of old England, even when I resist her authority."

A long column of white smoke now rolled along the

surface of the water, as the cutter, who had waited in vain
for the colours being hoisted, fired the first gun at her
antagonist.   The shot whizzed between the masts of the
lugger, and plunged into the water a quarter of a mile to
leeward.

"*A vous, monsieur !*" roared out a French quarter-master
on board of the lugger, in imitation of the compliments
which take place previously to an *assaut d'armes*, at the
same time taking off his hat, and bowing to the
cutter.

"Too high, too high, good Mr Searcher," said M'Elvina,
laughing; "depress your guns to her water-line, my lads,
and do not fire until I order you."

The remainder of the cutter's broadside was now
discharged at the lugger, but the elevation being too great,
the shot whizzed over, without any injury to her crew;
the main-halyards were, however, shot away, and the yard
and sail fell thundering down on the deck.

"Be smart, my lads, and bend on again; it's quite long
enough.   Up with the sail, and we'll return the compliment."

In less than a minute, the tie of the halyards, which had
been divided close to the yard, was hitched round it, and
the sail again expanded to the breeze, "Now, my lads,
remember, don't throw a shot away—fire when you're
ready."

The broadside of the lugger was poured into the cutter,
with what effect upon the crew could not be ascertained;
but the main-boom was cut in half, and the outer part of
it fell over the cutter's quarter, and was dragged astern by
the clew of the sail.

"It's all over with her already," said the first mate to
M'Elvina; and, as the cutter payed off before the wind
another broadside from her well-manned antagonist raked
her fore and aft.   The cutter hauled down her jib, eased
off her fore-sheet, and succeeded in again bringing her
broadside to bear.   The action was now maintained with
spirit, but much to the disadvantage of the cutter, who was

not only inferior in force, but completely disabled, from the loss of her main-boom.

After an exchange of a dozen broadsides, M'Elvina shot the lugger ahead, and, tacking under his adversary's bows, raked him a second time. The commander of the revenue vessel, to avoid a repetition of a similar disaster, payed his vessel off before the wind, and returned the fire as they came abreast of each other; but in these manœuvres, the lugger obtained the weather-gage. It was, however, a point of little consequence as matters then stood. In a few more broadsides the cutter was a complete wreck, and unable to return the fire of her opponent. Her fore-stay and halyards had been cut away, her fore-sail was down on deck, and her jib lying overboard, under her bows.

"I think that will do," said M'Elvina to the first mate. "We had better be off now, for our guns will be sure to bring down some of the cruisers; and if she surrendered, I could not take possession of her. Let's give her a parting broadside and three cheers."

M'Elvina's orders were obeyed; but not one gun was returned by the cutter—"Starboard a little; keep her away now, and we'll close and stand ahead of her, that she may read our name on the stern. It's a pity they should not know to whom they are indebted. They'll not forget *La Belle Suzanne*."

The cutter had not been left a mile astern before the breeze freshened, and the fog began rapidly to disperse; and Phillips, who continued at the conn, perceived, through the haze, a large vessel bearing down towards them.

"High time that we were off, indeed, captain: for there's a cruiser if I mistake not. A gun here is the same to the cruiser, as a splash in the water is to the ground sharks at Antigua;—up they all come to see what's to be had. We shall have a dozen of them above the horizon before two hours are above our heads."

M'Elvina, who had his glass fixed upon the vessel, soon made her out to be a frigate, coming down under a press of sail, attracted, as Phillips had remarked, by the reports of the guns. What made the affair more serious was, that she was evidently bringing down a strong breeze, which the lugger, although steering large, had not yet obtained. Moreover, the fog had dispersed in all directions, and the frigate neared them fast.

"B——t the cutter!" said the first mate; "we shall pay dearly for our 'lark.'"

"This is confoundedly unlucky," replied M'Elvina; "she brings the wind down with her, and won't part with a breath of it. However, 'faint heart never won fair lady.' Keep her away two points more. Clap everything on her. We'll *weather* her yet."

The breeze that ran along the water in advance of the frigate, now began to be felt by the lugger, who again dashed the foaming water from her bows, as she darted through the wave; but it was a point of sailing at which a frigate has always an advantage over a small vessel; and M'Elvina having gradually edged away so as to bring the three masts of his pursuer apparently into one, perceived that the frigate was rapidly closing with him.

The crew of the lugger, who had been all merriment at the successful termination of the late combat (for not one man had been killed or severely wounded), now paced the deck, or looked over the bulwark with serious and foreboding aspects; the foreigners particularly began to curse their fate, and considered their voyage and anticipated profits at an end. M'Elvina, perceiving their discontent, ordered the men aft, and addressed them :—

"My lads, I have often been in a worse scrape, and have weathered it; nor do I know, but what we may yet manage to get out of this, if you will pay strict attention to my orders, and behave in that cool and brave manner which I have reason to expect from you. Much, if not all, depends upon whether the captain of that frigate is a '*new hand*' or not:—if he is an old Channel groper, we shall have some difficulty; but, however, we will try for it, and if we do not succeed, at least we shall have the satisfaction of knowing that we did our best both for ourselves and our employers."

M'Elvina then proceeded to explain to his crew the manœuvre that he intended to practise, to obtain the weather-gage of the frigate, upon which their only chance of escape would depend, and the men returned to their stations, if not contented, at least with increased confidence in their captain, and strong hopes of success.

As the day closed, the frigate was within a mile of the lugger, and coming up with him hand over hand. The breeze was strong, and the water was no longer in ripples, but curled over in short waves to the influence of the blast. The frigate yawed a little—the smoke from her bow-chaser was followed by an instantaneous report, and the shot dashed into the water close under the stern of the lugger. "Sit down under the bulwarks; sit down, my lads, and keep all fast," said M'Elvina. "He'll soon be tired of that; he has lost more than a cable's length already." M'Elvina was correct in his supposition; the commander of the frigate perceived that he had lost too much ground by deviating from his course, and the evening was closing in. He fired no more. Both vessels continued their course,—the smuggler particularly attentive in keeping the three masts of her pursuer in one, to prevent her from firing into her, or to oblige her to drop astern if she did.

Half an hour more, and as the sun's lower limb touched the horizon, the frigate was within musket-shot of the lugger, and the marines, who had been ordered forward, commenced a heavy fire upon her, to induce her to lower her sails and surrender;—but in vain; by the directions of their captain, the men sheltered themselves under the bulwarks, and the vessel continued her course, with all her sails expanded to the breeze.

A few minutes more and she was right under the bows of the frigate, who now prepared to round-to, and pour a broadside into her for her temerity. M'Elvina watched their motions attentively, and as the frigate yawed to with all her sails set, he gave the order to lower away; and the sails of the lugger were in an instant down on the deck, in token of submission.

"Helm hard a lee, now—keep a little bit of the mizen up, Phillips—they won't observe it."

"Marines, cease firing,—hands, shorten sail, and clear away the first cutter," were the orders given on board the frigate, and distinctly heard by the smugglers; but the heavy press of sail that the frigate was obliged to carry to come up with the chase, was not so soon to be reduced as that of a small vessel—and, as she rounded-to with studding-sails below and aloft, she shot past the lugger, and left her on her quarter.

"Now's your time, my men.   Hoist away the jib-sheet to windward."—The lugger payed off as the wind caught the sail.—"All's right.   Up with the lugs."

The order was obeyed as an order generally is by men working for their escape from what they most dreaded, poverty and imprisonment; and, before the frigate could reduce her sails, which were more than she could carry on a wind, the lugger had shot away on her weather quarter, and was a quarter of a mile in advance.   The frigate tacked after her, firing gun after gun, but without success. Fortune favoured M'Elvina; and the shades of night soon hid the lugger from the sight of her irritated and disappointed pursuers.   A long career was before *La Belle Suzanne:* she was not to be taken that time.

Chapter XIV

A fisherman he had been in his youth ;
But other speculations were, in sooth,
Added to his connexion with the sea,
Perhaps not so respectable, in truth,

. . . . . .
He had an only daughter.

Don Juan.

NOT possessing a prompter's whistle, we must use, as a

substitute, the boatswain's call, and, at his shrill pipe, we change the scene to a back parlour in one of the most confined streets at the east end of England's proud and wealthy metropolis. The *dramatis personæ* are an elderly and corpulent personage, with as little of fashion in his appearance as in his residence; and a young female of about twenty years of age, with expressive and beautiful features, but wanting "the damask on the cheek," the true value of which the fair sex so well appreciate, that, if not indebted for it to nature, they are too apt to resort to art for an unworthy imitation.

The first mentioned of these two personages was busy examining, through his spectacles, some papers which lay on the table before him,—occasionally diverted from his task by the pertinacity of some flies, which seemed to have taken a particular fancy to his bald forehead and scalp, which, in spite of his constant brushing off, they thought proper to consider as a pleasant and smooth sort of coursing-plain, placed there (probably in their ideas) solely for their amusement. Part of a decanter of wine, and the remains of a dessert, crowded the small table at which he sat, and added to the general air of confinement which pervaded the whole.

"It's very hot, my dear. Open the window, and let us have a little air."

"Oh, father," replied the young woman, who rose to throw up the sash, "you don't know how I pine for fresh air. How long do you intend to continue this life of constant toil and privation?"

"How long, my dear? Why, I presume you do not wish to starve—you would not be very well pleased if, when you applied for money, as you do every week *at least*, I were to tell you that the bag was empty."

"Oh, nonsense, I know better, father—don't think so poorly of me as to attempt to deceive me in that way."

"And pray, Miss Susan, what do you know?" said the old gentleman, looking up at her through his spectacles, as she stood by the side of his chair.

"I know what you have taught me, sir. Do you recollect explaining to me the nature of the funds—what was the meaning of the national debt—all the varieties of stock, and what interest they all bore?"

"Well, and what then?"

"Why, then, father, I have often seen the amount of the dividends which you have received every half-year, and have heard your orders to Wilmott, to re-invest in the funds. Now your last half-year's dividend in the three per cents was—let me see—oh, £841, 14s. 6d. which, you know, doubled, makes itself an income of——"

"And pray, Miss Susan, what business have you with all this?" retorted her father, half pleased, half angry.

"Why, father, you taught me yourself, and thought me very stupid because I did not comprehend it as soon as you expected," answered Susan, leaning over and kissing him; "and now you ask me what business I have to know it."

"Well, well, girl, it's very true," said the old man, smiling; "but allowing that you are correct, what then?"

"Why then, father, don't be angry if I say that it appears to me that you have more money now than you can spend while you live, or know to whom to leave when you die. What, then, is the use of confining yourself in a dirty narrow street, and toiling all day for no earthly advantage?"

"But how do you know that I have nobody to leave my money to, Susan?"

"Have you not repeatedly said that you have no relations or kin, that you are aware of, except me; that you were once a sailor before the mast—an orphan, bound apprentice by the parish? Whom, then, have you except *me?*—and if you continue here much longer, father, I feel convinced that you will not have *me*—you will have no one. If you knew how tired I am of looking out at this horrid brick wall—how I long for the country, to be running among the violets and primroses—how I pine for relief from this little dungeon. Oh! what would

I give to be flying before the breeze in the lugger with M'Elvina."

"Indeed, miss!" replied old Hornblow, whom the reader may recognise as the patron of our smuggling captain.

"Well, father, there's no harm in saying so. I want freedom. I feel as if I could not be too free—I should like to be blown about in a balloon. Oh, why don't you give up business, go down to the seaside, take a pretty little cottage, and make yourself and me happy; I fancy the sea-breeze is blowing in my face, and all my ringlets out of curl. I shall die if I stay here much longer—I shall indeed, father."

Repeated attacks of this nature had already sapped the foundation; and a lovely and only daughter had the influence over her father's heart, to which she was entitled.

"Well, well, Susan—let M'Elvina wind up the accounts of this vessel, and then I will do as you wish; but I cannot turn him adrift, you know."

"Turn Captain M'Elvina adrift! No—if you did, father——"

"I presume that you would be very much inclined to take him in tow—Eh, miss?"

"I shall never act without attending to your advice, and consulting your wishes, my dear father," answered Susan, the suffusion of her unusually pale cheeks proving that she required but colour to be perfectly beautiful.

And here the conversation dropped. Old Hornblow had long perceived the growing attachment between his daughter and M'Elvina; and the faithful and valuable services of the latter, added to the high opinion which the old man had of his honesty,—which, to do M'Elvina justice, had been most scrupulous,—had determined him to let things take their own course. Indeed, there was no one with whom old Hornblow was acquainted, to whom he would have entrusted his daughter's happiness with so much confidence as to our reformed captain.

A sharp double tap at the street door announced the post, and in a few minutes after this conversation, the clerk appeared with a letter for old Hornblow, who, pursuant to the prudent custom of those days, had his counting-house on the ground-floor of his own residence, which enabled him to go to his dinner, and return to his business in the evening. Now-a-days we are all above our business, and live above our means (which is in itself sufficient to account for the general distress that is complained of); and the counting-house is deserted before dusk, that we may arrive at our residences in Russel Square, or the Regent's Park, in time to dress for a turtle dinner at six o'clock, instead of a mutton chop, or single joint *en famille*, at two.

But to return. Old Hornblow put on his spectacles (which were on the table since they had been removed from his nose by Susan when she kissed him), and examined the post-mark, seal, and superscription, as if he wished to tax his ingenuity with a guess previously to opening the letter, which would have saved him all that trouble, and have decided the point of scrutiny, viz., from whom it came.

" M'Elvina, I rather think," said he, musing; " but the post-mark is Plymouth. How the deuce !—" The two first lines of the letter were read, and the old man's countenance fell. Susan, who had been all alive at the mention of M'Elvina's name, perceived the alteration in her father's looks.

" No bad news, I hope, my dear father ?"

" Bad enough," replied the old man, with a deep sigh; "the lugger is taken by a frigate, and sent into Plymouth."

" And Captain M'Elvina—he's not hurt, I hope ?"

" No, I presume not, as he has written the letter, and says nothing about it."

Satisfied upon this point, Susan, who recollected her father's promise, was undutiful enough, we are sorry to say, to allow her heart to bound with joy at the circumstance. All her fond hopes were about to be realised, and she could hardly refrain from carolling the words of Ariel,

"Where the bee sucks, there lurk I," but fortunately she remembered that other parties might not exactly participate in her delight. Out of respect for her father's feelings, she therefore put on a grave countenance, in sad contrast with her eyes, which joy had brilliantly lighted up.

"Well, it's a bad business," continued old Hornblow. "Wilmott!" (The clerk heard his master's voice, and came in.) "Bring me the ledger. Let me see—*Belle Suzanne*—I wonder why the fool called her by that name, as if I had not one already to take money out of my pocket. Oh! here it is—folio 59 continued, folio 100, 129, 147,—not balanced since April last year. Be quick, and strike me out a rough balance-sheet of the lugger."

"But what does Captain M'Elvina say, father?"

"What does he say? Why, that he is taken. Haven't I told you so already, girl?" replied old Hornblow, in evident ill humour.

"Yes, but the particulars, my dear father?"

"Oh, there's only the fact, without particulars—says he will write more fully in a day or two."

"I'll answer for him, that it was not his fault, father— he has always done you justice."

"I did not say that he had not; I'm only afraid that success has made him careless—it's always the case."

"Yes," replied Susan, taking up the right cue; "as you say, father, he has been very successful."

"He has," replied the old man, recovering his serenity a little, "very successful indeed. I dare say it was not his fault."

The clerk soon made his appearance with the rough balance-sheet required. It did more to restore the good humour of the old man, than even the soothing of his daughter.

"Oh! here we are—*La Belle Suzanne*—Dr. to——, Total, £14,864, 14s. 3d. Contra—Cr. £27,986, 16s. 8d. Balance to profit and loss, £13,122, 2s. 5d. Well, that's not so very bad in less than three years. I think I may afford to lose her."

K. I.   G

" Why, father," replied Susan, leaning over his shoulder, and looking archly at him, " 'tis a fortune in itself, to a contented person."

But as, independently of M'Elvina's letter not being sufficiently explicit, there are other circumstances connected with his capture, that are important to our history, we shall ourselves narrate the particulars.

For more than two years, M'Elvina, by his dexterity and courage, and the fast sailing of his vessel, had escaped all his pursuers, and regularly landed his cargoes. During this time, Willy had made rapid progress under his instruction, not only in his general education, but also in that of his profession. One morning the lugger was off Cape Clear, on the coast of Ireland, when she discovered a frigate to windward,—the wind, weather, and relative situations of the two vessels being much the same as on the former occasion, when M'Elvina, by his daring and judicious manœuvre, had effected his escape. The frigate chased, and soon closed to within a quarter-of-a-mile of the lugger, when she rounded-to, and poured in a broadside of grape, which brought her fore-yard down on deck. From that moment such an incessant fire of musketry was poured in from the frigate, that every man on board of M'Elvina's vessel, who endeavoured to repair the mischief, was immediately struck down. Any attempt at escape was now hopeless. When within two cables' lengths, the frigate hove-to the wind, keeping the lugger under her lee, and continued a fire of grape and musketry into her, until the rest of her sails were lowered down.

The crew of the smuggler, perceiving all chance in their favour to be over, ran down below to avoid the fire, and secure their own effects. The boats of the frigate were soon on board of the lugger, and despatched back to her with M'Elvina and the chief officers. Willy jumped into the boat, and was taken on board with his patron.

The captain of the frigate was on the quarter-deck; and as he turned round, it occurred to Willy, that he had seen his face before, but when or where he could not exactly call to mind; and he continued to scrutinise him, as he paced up and down the quarter-deck, revolving in his mind where it was that he had encountered that peculiar countenance.

His eye, so fixed upon the captain that it followed him up and down as he moved, at last was met by that of the latter, who, surprised at finding so small a lad among the prisoners, walked over to the lee-side of the quarter-deck, and addressed him with—"You're but a young smuggler, my lad; are you the captain's son?"

The voice immediately recalled to Willy's recollection every circumstance attending their last meeting, and who the captain was. He answered in the negative, with a smile.

"You've a light heart, youngster. Pray, what's your name?"

"*You* said that my name was to be Seymour, sir," replied Willy, touching his hat.

"Said his name was to be Seymour! What does the boy mean?—Good Heavens! I recollect," observed Captain M——, for it was he. "Are you the boy that I sent home in the *chasse-marée*, to be fitted out for the quarter-deck?"

"Yes, sir."

"And how long have you been on this praiseworthy service?"

"Ever since, sir," replied our hero, who had little idea of its impropriety.

La Belle Suzanne was as renowned for her fast sailing, and repeated escapes from the cruisers, as Captain M'Elvina and his crew were for their courage and success. The capture of the vessel had long been a desideratum of the English government; and Captain M——, although gratified at her falling into his hands, was not very well pleased to find that a lad, whom he had intended to bring forward in the service, should, as he supposed, have voluntarily joined a party, who had so long bid defiance to the laws and naval force of the country. His countenance assumed an air of displeasure, and he was about to turn away, without any further remarks, when M'Elvina, who perceived how matters stood, and felt aware that Willy's future prospects were at stake, stepped forward, and respectfully addressing the captain, narrated in few words the rescue of Willy from the wreck, and added, that the boy had been detained by him, and had had no opportunity of leaving the vessel, which had never anchored but in the French port of Havre. He also stated, what was indeed true, that he had always evaded explaining to the boy the real nature of the service upon which the lugger was employed: from which it may be inferred that, notwithstanding M'Elvina's defence of smuggling in our former chapters, he was not quite so well convinced, in his own mind, of its propriety as he would have induced Debriseau to suppose.

The assertions of M'Elvina turned the scale again in Willy's favour ; and, after he had answered the interrogatories of the captain, relative to the fate of Mr Bullock and the rest of the men in the prize, Captain M——, who, although severe, was not only just, but kind-hearted, determined that his former good intentions relative to our hero should still remain in force.

"Well, Mr Seymour, you have seen a little service, and your captain gives you a high character, as an active and clever lad. As you have been detained against your will, I think we may recover your time and pay. I trust, however, that you will, in future, be employed in a more honourable manner. We shall, in all probability, be soon in port, and till then you must remain as you are, for I cannot trust you again in a prize."

As our hero was in a new ship, the officers and ship's company of which were not acquainted with his history, except that he had been promoted, for an act of gallantry, by Captain M——, he was favourably received by his messmates. The crew of the lugger were detained as prisoners on board of the frigate, and the vessel, in charge of one of the officers, was ordered to keep company,

Captain M—— having determined to return into port, and not wishing to lose sight of his valuable prize.

"You have a very fine ship's company, Captain M'Elvina," observed Captain M——. "How many of them are English?"

"About eighty; and as good seamen as ever walked a plank."

Captain M—— ordered the crew of the lugger aft on the quarter-deck, and put the question to them whether they would not prefer entering into his Majesty's service to the confinement of a prison; but, at the moment, they felt too indignant at having been captured by the frigate to listen to the proposal, and refused to a man. Captain M—— turned away disappointed, surveying the fine body of men with a covetous eye, as they were ranged in a line on his quarter-deck. He felt what a prize they would be to him, if he could have added them to his own ship's company; for at that time it was almost impossible to man the number of ships which were employed, in an effective manner.

"Will you allow me to try what I can do for you, sir?" said M'Elvina, as the men disappeared from the quarter-deck, to their former station as prisoners. Having received the nod of assent on the part of Captain M——, M'Elvina went down to the men, who gathered round him. He forcibly pointed out to them the advantages of the proposal, and the good chance they had of enriching themselves, by the prize-money they would make in a frigate which could capture such a fast-sailing vessel as the lugger. He also dwelt upon the misery of the prison which awaited them: but what decided them was the observation that, in all probability, they would not be permitted (now that seamen were in such request) to remain in prison, but would be drafted into several ships, and be separated; whereas, by now entering for Captain M——, they would all remain shipmates as before.

Having obtained their unanimous consent, M'Elvina, with a pleased countenance, came aft, followed by his

men, and informed Captain M—— that they had agreed
to enter for his ship. "Allow me to congratulate you,
sir, on your good fortune, as you will yourself acknowledge
it to be, when you find out what an addition they will
be to your ship's company."

"I am indebted to you for your interference, sir,"
replied Captain M——, "and shall not prove ungrateful.
Your conduct in this affair makes me inclined to ask
another favour. I believe you can give me some valuable
information, if you choose. Whether you are inclined to
do so, I am not yet sure; but I now think that you
will."

"You will find me an Englishman, body and soul,
sir; and although I have, in defence of my profession,
been occasionally necessitated to choose between capture
and resistance, I can most conscientiously say, that every
shot I have fired against my own countrymen has smitten
me to the heart;" (and this assertion was true, although
we have no time to analyse M'Elvina's feelings at present).
"I am not bound by honour, nor have I the least inclination, to conceal any information I may have obtained,
when in the French ports. I went there to serve my
purposes, and they allowed me to do so to serve their
own. I never would (although repeatedly offered bribes)
bring them any information relative to the proceedings
of our own country, and I shall most cheerfully answer
your questions; indeed, I have information which I would
have given you before now, had I not felt that it might
be supposed I was actuated more by a view of serving
myself than my country. I only wish, Captain M——,
that you may fall in with a French frigate before I leave
your ship, that I may prove to you that I can fight as
well for old England as I have done in defence of
property entrusted to my charge."

"Then do me the favour to step down into the cabin,"
said Captain M——.

Captain M—— and M'Elvina were shut up in the after-
cabin for some time; and the information received by

Captain M—— was so important, that he determined not to anchor. He put all the French prisoners on board of the lugger at the entrance of the Sound, and, sending in a boat to take out the major part of the men who had charge of her, he retained M'Elvina on board of the frigate, and made all sail for the French coast.

Chapter XV

That which should accompany old age,
As honour, love, obedience, troops of friends
I must not look to have !

SHAKESPEARE.

BUT we must return on shore, that we may not lose sight of the grandfather of our hero, who had no idea that there was a being in existence who was so nearly connected with him.

The time had come when that information was to be given ; for, about six weeks previously to the action we have described, in which Adams the quarter-master was killed, Admiral De Courcy was attacked by a painful and mortal disease. As long as he was able to move about, his irritability of temper, increased by suffering, rendered him more insupportable than ever ; but he was soon confined to his room, and the progress of the disease became so rapid, that the medical attendants considered it their duty to apprise him that all hopes of recovery must now be abandoned, and that he must prepare himself for the worst.

The admiral received the intelligence with apparent composure, and bowed his head to the physicians as they quitted his room. He was alone, and left to his own reflections, which were not of the most enviable nature. He was seated, propped up in an easy chair, opposite the large French window, which commanded a view of the park. The sun was setting, and the long extended shadows of the magnificent trees which adorned his extensive domain were in beautiful contrast with the gleams of radiant light, darting in long streaks between them on the luxuriant herbage. The cattle, quietly standing in the lake, were refreshing themselves after the heat of the day, and the deer lay in groups under the shade, or crouched in their lairs, partly concealed by the underwood and fern. All was in repose and beauty, and the dying man watched the sun, as it fast descended to the horizon, as emblematical of his race, so shortly to be sped. He surveyed the groups before him—he envied even the beasts of the field, and the reclaimed tenants of the forest, for they at least had of their kind, with whom they could associate ; but he, their lord and master, was alone—alone in the world, without one who loved or cared for him, without one to sympathise in his sufferings and administer to his wants, except from interested motives—without one to soothe his anguish, and soften the pillow of affliction and disease—without one to close his eyes, or shed a tear, now that he was dying.

His thoughts naturally reverted to his wife and children. He knew that two of these individuals, out of three, were in the cold grave—and where was the other? The certain approach of death had already humanised and softened his flinty heart. The veil, that had been drawn by passion between his conscience and his guilt, was torn away. The past rushed upon his memory with dreadful rapidity and truth, and horrible conviction flashed upon his soul, as he unwillingly acknowledged himself to be the murderer of his wife and child. Remorse, as usual, followed, treading upon the heels of conviction—such remorse, that, in a short space, the agony became insupportable.

After an ineffectual struggle of pride, he seized the line which was attached to the bell-rope, and, when his summons was obeyed, desired that the vicar might be immediately requested to come to him.

Acquainted with the admiral's situation, the vicar had anxiously waited the summons which he was but too well aware would come, for he knew the human heart, and the cry for aid which the sinner in his fear sends forth. He was soon in the presence of the admiral, for the first time since the day that he quitted the house with the letter of the unfortunate Peters in his possession. The conversation which ensued, between the agitated man, who had existed only for this world, and the placid teacher, who had considered it (as he inculcated) as only a preparation for a better, was too long to be here inserted. It will be sufficient to say, that the humbled and terrified wretch, the sufferer from disease, and greater sufferer from remorse, never could have been identified with the once proud and overbearing mortal, who had so long spurned at the precepts of religion, and turned a deaf ear to the mild persuasions of its apostle.

"But that letter!" continued the admiral in a faltering voice—"what was it? I have yet one child alive—Oh, send immediately for him, and let me implore his forgiveness for my cruelty."

"That letter, sir, was written but one hour previously to his death."

"His death!" cried the admiral, turning his eyes up to the ceiling. "God have mercy on me! then I have murdered him also. And how did he die? Did he starve, as I expressed in my horrid—horrid wish?"

"No, sir: his life was forfeited to the offended laws of his country."

"Good God, sir!" hastily replied the admiral, whose ruling passion, pride, returned for the moment; "you do not mean to say that he was hanged?"

"Even so; but here is the letter which he wrote—read it."

The admiral seized the letter in his tremulous hand, and devoured every word as he perused it. He let it fall on his knees, and said, in a subdued voice—"My God—my God!—and he asked forgiveness, and forgives me!" Then, with frantic exclamation, he continued, "Wretch that I am,—would that I had died for thee, my son—my son!" and clasping his hands over his head, he fell back in a state of insensibility.

The vicar, much affected with the scene, rang the bell

for assistance, which was obtained ; but the wretched man had received a shock which hastened his dissolution. He was too much exhausted to sit upright, and they were obliged to carry him to the bed, from which he never rose again.   As soon as he was sufficiently recovered to be able to converse, he waved the servants from the room, and resumed, in a faltering voice—

"But, sir, he mentions his child—*my grandchild*. Where is he ? Can I see him ? "

"I am afraid not, sir," replied the vicar, who then entered into a recital of the arrangements which had taken place, and the name of the ship on board of which our hero had been permitted to remain, under the charge of Adams, the quarter-master.

The admiral listened to the recital of the vicar without interruption ; and, as soon as it was finished, to the great joy of the worthy pastor, expressed the most anxious wish to make every reparation in his power.   Aware that difficulties might arise from the circumstance of our hero's existence not being suspected by his collateral heirs, who had for some time considered as certain their ultimate possession of his large entailed property, he directed a will to be immediately drawn up, acknowledging his grandchild, and leaving to him all his personal property, which was very considerable ; and praying the vicar to take upon himself the office of guardian to the boy,—a request which was cheerfully complied with.   The admiral would not listen to the repeated requests of the vicar, to take the repose which his excited and sinking frame required, until the necessary document had been drawn out, signed, and duly witnessed.   When all was complete, he fell back on the pillow, in such a state of exhaustion as threatened immediately to terminate his career.   It was late when the vicar took his leave, after having administered some little consolation to the repentant and dying man, and promised to call upon him early on the ensuing morning.

But the vicar had other duties to perform, which induced him to defer his visit until the following noon.   Others were sick, others were dying, and needed spiritual consolation; and he made no distinction between the rich and the poor.   The physicians had expressed their opinion that the admiral might linger for many days, and the vicar thought that advantage might be derived from his being left for a short time to his own reflections, and to recover from the state of exhaustion arising from the communications of the preceding evening.   When he arrived at the hall, the windows were closed—Admiral De Courcy was no more.

Reader, you shall hear how he died.   It was about two o'clock in the morning that he awoke from an uneasy slumber, and felt his end approaching.   The old crone who had been hired as a nurse to watch at night, was fast asleep in her chair.   The rushlight had burned low down in the socket, and, through the interstices of its pierced shade, threw a feeble and alternate light and shadow over the room.   The mouth of the dying man was glued together from internal heat, and he suffered from agonising thirst.   He murmured for relief, but no one answered. Again and again he attempted to make his careless attendant acquainted with his wants, but in vain.   He stretched out his arm and moved the curtains of the bed, that the noise of the curtain-rings upon the iron rods might have the effect, and then fell back with exhaustion, arising from the effort which he had made.

The old beldam, who, for money, was willing to undertake the most revolting offices, and who, without remuneration, was so hardened, by her constant familiarity with disease and death, that she was callous and insensible to the most earnest supplication, woke up at the noise which the curtain-rings had made, and opened the curtain to ascertain what was required.   Long experience told her at once that all would soon be over, and she was convinced that her charge would never rise or speak again.

This was true; but the suffering man (his arm lying outside of the bed-clothes, and his elbow bent upwards) still pointed with his finger to his parched mouth, with a look of entreaty from his sinking eyes. The old fiend shut the curtains, and the admiral waited with impatience for them to reopen with a drop of water "to cool his parched tongue"—but in vain. Leaving him to his fate, she hobbled about the room to secure a golden harvest, before others should make their appearance, and share it with her. His purse was on the table : she removed the gold which it contained, and left the silver; she chose that which she imagined to be the most valuable of the three rings on the dressing table; she detached one seal from the chain of his watch. She then repaired to the wardrobe, and examined its contents. One of her capacious pockets were soon filled with the finest cambric handkerchiefs, all of which she first took the precaution to open, and hold up to the light rejecting those which were not of the finest texture. The silk stockings were the next articles that were coveted; they were unfolded one by one, and her skinny arm passed up, that the feet might be extended by her shrivelled hands, to ascertain whether they were darned or not—if so, they were rejected.

The wardrobe was on the opposite side of the bed; and on that side the curtains had not been closed. The dying man had still enough sight left to perceive the employment of his attendant. What must have been his feelings! He uttered a deep groan, which startled the old hag, and she repaired to the bed-side, to examine the state of her charge.

Again he pointed with his finger to his mouth—and again she returned to her employment, without having rendered the assistance which he required. His eyes followed—and his finger still pointed. Having ransacked every drawer, and secured all that she dared take, or that her pockets could contain, she rang the bell for the servants of the house; then pulling out her handkerchief, ready to put to her eyes in token of sympathy, she sat down on her easy chair, to await their coming.

In the meanwhile, the eyes of the unfortunate man gradually turned upward; his vision was gone, but his agonising thirst continued to the last; and when the retainers of the family came in, he was found dead, with his finger still pointing in the same direction.

With ordinary minds, there is something so terrible in death, something so awful in the dissolution of the elements of our frame, something so horrible in the leap into the dark abyss, that it requires all the powers of a fortified spirit, all the encouragement of a good conscience, and all the consolations of religion and of faith, to enable us to muster any degree of resolution for the awful change. But if aught can smooth the pillow,—can chase away from the terrified spirit the doubt and depression by which it is overwhelmed, it is the being surrounded and attended by those who are devoted and endeared to us. When love, and duty, and charity, and sympathy hover round the couch of the departing, fainting hope is supported by their presence, and the fleeting spirit, directed by them, looks upward to the realms from which these heaven-born passions have been permitted to descend on earth, to cheer us through our weary pilgrimage.

What then had Admiral De Courcy to support him in his last moments ?—A good conscience ?—faith ?—hope ? —love ?—duty ?—or even sympathy ?—Wanting all, he breathed his last. But, let us

> " Forbear to judge, for we are sinners all ;
> Close up his eyes, and draw the curtains close,
> And let us all to meditation."

The vicar affixed seals upon the drawers, to secure the remainder of the property (for the example of the old nurse had been followed by many others), and, having given directions for the funeral, returned to his own home.

The second day after the admiral's death, a carriage and four drove furiously up the avenue, and stopped at the entrance door. The occupants descended, and rang the bell with an air of authority ; the summons was answered by several of the male domestics, who were anxiously looking out for the new proprietor of the domain. A tall man, of very gentlemanlike appearance, followed by a mean-looking personage in black, walked in, the latter, as he followed, proclaiming the other to the servants as the heir-at-law, and present owner of the property. By this time the whole household were assembled, lining the hall for the visitors to pass, and bowing and curtseying to the ground. The vicar, who had expected the appearance of these parties, had left directions that he might be immediately acquainted with their arrival. On receipt of the information, he proceeded to the hall, and was ushered into the library, where he found them anxiously awaiting his arrival, that the seals might be withdrawn which had been placed upon the drawers.

"Whom have I the honour of addressing, sir?" said the vicar to the taller of the two, whom he presumed, by his appearance, to be the superior.

"Sir," replied the little man, in a pompous manner, "you are speaking to Mr Rainscourt, the heir-at-law of this entailed property."

"I am sorry, truly sorry, sir," replied the vicar, "that from not having been well informed, you should be subjected to such severe disappointment. I am afraid, sir, that the grandchild of Admiral De Courcy will have a prior claim."

The two parties started from their chairs, and looked at each other in amazement.

"The grandchild!" replied the little man—"never even heard that there was such a person."

"Very probably, sir; but I have long known it, and so did Admiral De Courcy, as you will perceive when you read his will, which is in my possession, as guardian to the child—and upon the strength of which office I have put seals upon the property."

The parties looked aghast.

"We must inquire into this," replied the legal adviser, for such he was.

"I am ready to give you any information you may require," replied the vicar. "I have here copies of the marriage certificate of the parents, and the register of baptism of the child, the originals of which you will find in the parish church of——, not five miles distant; and I can most satisfactorily prove his identity, should that be necessary."

" And where is the grandchild?"

" At sea, on board a man-of-war, at the dying request of his father, who determined that he should be brought up for the service. Would you like to see the late admiral's will?"

The tall gentleman bowed assent, and it was read. Having been carefully examined by the lawyer, as well as the other documents in the vicar's possession, all appeared so clear and conclusive, that he unwillingly acknowledged to his employer, in a whisper, that there was no chance of setting the will aside. Pallid with the revulsion of feelings from hope to despair, the pretender to the estates ordered the horses to be brought out, and, on their being announced, with a slight bow to the vicar, retired from the library.

But outside, the state of affairs was altered, by the servants having overheard the conversation. No one was attentive enough to open the door to let out those whom they had so obsequiously admitted: and one of the postilions was obliged to dismount, to shut up the chaise after they had entered it. Such is the deference shown respectively to those who are, or are not, the real heirs-at-law.

Chapter XVI

On deck five hundred men did dance,
The stoutest they could find in France.
We with two hundred did advance,
   On board of the *Arethusa.*
Our captain hailed the Frenchman " ho ! "
The Frenchman then cried out " hallo ! "
   " Bear down, d'ye see,
   To our Admiral's lee ; "
" No, no," said the Frenchman, " that can't be ; "
" Then I must lug you along with me,"
   Says the saucy *Arethusa.*

               Sea Song.

THE information received from M'Elvina, which induced Captain M—— not to anchor, was relative to a French frigate of the largest class, that he had great hopes of falling in with. She was lying in the harbour of Brest, waiting for a detachment of troops which had been ordered to embark, when she was to sail for Rochefort, to join a squadron intended to make a descent upon some of our colonies. Previously to M'Elvina's sailing from the port of Havre, the prefect of that arrondissement had issued directions for certain detachments to march on a stated day to complete the number of troops ordered on board.

M'Elvina had sure data from which to calculate as to the exact period of embarkation, and was also aware that the frigate had orders to sail to the port of rendezvous the first favourable wind after the embarkation had taken place. In two days the *Aspasia*, for that was the name of the frigate commanded by Captain M——, was off Ushant, and the captain, taking the precaution to keep well off the land during the day time, only running in to make the lights after dark, retained his position off that island until the wind shifted to the northward: he then shaped a course so as to fall in with the French coast about thirty miles to the southward of the harbour of Brest. It was still dark, when Captain M——, having run his distance, shortened sail, and hove-to in the cruising ground which M'Elvina had recommended; and so correct was the calculation, as well as the information of the captain of the smugglers, that at daybreak, as the frigate lay with her head inshore, with the wind at N.N.W., a large vessel was descried under the land, a little on her weatherbow. After severely scrutinising the stranger for some minutes with his glass, which he now handed to M'Elvina—

"That's she, indeed, I believe," said Captain M——.

"A large frigate, with studding-sails set, standing across our bows," cried out the first lieutenant, from the mast-head.

"She'll try for the Passage du Raz; we must cut her off, if we can. Hands, make sail."

The hands were summoned up by the shrill pipe of the

boatswain and his mates; but it was quite unnecessary, as the men had already crowded on deck upon the first report which had been communicated below, and were in clusters on the forecastle and gangways.

"Topmen, aloft! loose top-gallant sails and royals— clear away the flying-jib," were orders that were hardly out of the mouth of the first lieutenant, breathless with his rapid descent from aloft, when the gaskets were off, and the sails hung fluttering from the yards. In another minute the sheets were home, the sails hoisted and trimmed, and the *Aspasia* darted through the yielding waves, as if the eagerness of pursuit which quickened the pulses of her crew had been communicated from them like an electric shock to her own frame, and she were conscious that her country demanded her best exertions.

"Pipe the hammocks up, Mr Hardy," said Captain M—— to the first lieutenant; "when they are stowed we will beat to quarters."

"Ay, ay, sir. Shall we order the fire out in the galley?"

"When the cocoa is ready, not before—there will be plenty of time for the people to get their breakfast. How does the land bear, Mr Pearce?"

"Saint Island about S.E. by S. eight or nine miles, sir," replied the master.

"If so, I think we shall cut him off, and then 'fight he must.'"

Both frigates had hoisted their colours in defiance, and as they were steering for the same point, they neared each other fast. The French vessel, with his starboard studding-sails, running for the entrance of the narrow passage, which he hoped to gain, and the *Aspasia* close-hauled to intercept him, and at the same time to avoid the dangerous rocks to leeward, far extending from Saint Island, whose name they bore.

"Have the men had their breakfasts, Mr Hardy?" said the captain.

"The cocoa was in the tub, sir," answered the first

lieutenant, "ready for serving out; but they started it all in the lee-scuppers. They wanted the tub to fill it with shot."

Captain M—— smiled at the enthusiasm of his crew; but the smile was suddenly checked, as he reflected that probably many of the fine fellows would never breakfast again.

"If not contrary to your regulations, Captain M——," said M'Elvina, "as the crew of the *Suzanne* have not yet been incorporated with your ship's company, may I request that they may be stationed together, and that I may be permitted to be with them?"

" Your suggestion is good," replied the captain, " and I am obliged to you for the offer. They shall assist to work the quarter-deck carronades, and act as boarders and sail trimmers. Mr Hardy, let the new men be provided with cutlasses, and fill up any vacancies in the main-deck quarters, from some of our own men who are at present stationed at the quarter-deck guns."

The frigates were now within gunshot of each other, and it was impossible to say which vessel would first attain the desired goal. The foremost guns of the respective ships which had been trained forward were reported to bear upon the enemy, and both commanders were aware that " knocking away a stick," *i.e.*, the shots striking the masts or yards of her opponent, so as to occasion them to fall, would decide the point. At the very time that captain M—— was giving directions to fire the main-deck guns as they would bear, the first shot from his antagonist whizzed over his head, and the action commenced, each party attempting to cripple his opponent by firing high at his masts and rigging. The frigates continued to engage, until they had closed-to within half a mile of each other, when the main-top-mast of the Frenchman fell over the side.

This decided the point as to his escape through the passage, which he had made his utmost exertions to effect, in pursuance of the peremptory orders which he had received. He now hauled his wind on the same tack as the *Aspasia* pouring in his starboard broadside as he rounded-to. The manœuvre was good, as he thereby retained his weather-gage—and the wreck of his top-mast having fallen over his larboard side, he had his starboard broadside, which was all clear, and directed towards his opponent; moreover, he forced the *Aspasia* to follow him into the bay formed between the Bec du Raz and the Bec du Chèvre, where she would in all probability receive considerable damage from the batteries which lined the coast.

Captain M—— was aware of all this; but his only fear was that his enemy should run on shore, and prevent his carrying him into port. The *Aspasia* was soon abreast of her opponent, and their broadsides were exchanged, when Captain M——, who wished to bring the action to a speedy conclusion, shot his vessel ahead, which he was enabled to do, from his superiority of sailing, after the main-top-mast of the French frigate had been shot away. It was his intention not to have tacked until he could have fetched his antagonist, but the galling fire of the batteries, which now hulled him every time, induced him to go about, and, as he was in stays, a raking shot entered the cabin windows, and, in its passage along the main-deck, added ten men to his list of killed and wounded.

Again the frigates, on opposite tacks, poured in their broadsides—the fore-yard of the Frenchman was divided in the slings, and fell, hanging by the topsail-sheets and lifts, and tearing the sails, which fell over the forecastle guns, and caught fire, as they were discharged at the same moment. Nor did the *Aspasia* suffer less, for her mizen-top-mast was shot through, and her starboard anchor, cut from her bows, fell under her bottom and tore away the cable (a short range of which Captain M—— had had the precaution to have on deck, as they fought so close in-shore). This threw the men at the guns into confusion, and brought the ship up in the wind. The cable was at last separated, and flew out of the hawse-hole after the anchor, which plunged to the bottom ; but this was not effected, until, like an enormous serpent, it had enfolded in its embraces three or four hapless men, who were carried with dreadful velocity to the hawse-hole, where their crushed bodies for a time stopped it from running out, and gave their shipmates an opportunity of dividing it with their axes.

Order was eventually restored, and the *Aspasia*, who had been raked by her active opponent during the time that she was thrown up in the wind, continued her course, and as she passed stern of the French frigate, luffed up and returned the compliment. The latter, anxious in his crippled state for the support of the batteries, which had already seriously injured his opponent, continued to forge in-shore.

" We shall weather her now ;—'bout ship, Mr Pearce. Recollect, my lads," said Captain M——, when the ship was about, " you'll reserve your fire till we touch her sides ; then all hands to board."

The *Aspasia* ranged up on the weather quarter of her antagonist—Pearce, the master, conning her by the captain's directions, so that the fore-chains of the French vessel should be hooked by the spare anchor of the *Aspasia*. The enemy, who, in his disabled state, was not in a situation to choose whether he would be boarded or not, poured in a double-shotted and destructive broadside, and it was well for Captain M—— that his ship's company had received the reinforcement which they had from the *Suzanne*, for the French frigate was crowded with men, and being now within pistol-shot, the troops, who were so thick on deck as to impede the motions of each other, kept up an incessant fire of musketry, cutting the *Aspasia's* running rigging, riddling her sails, and disabling her men.

" Hard-a-port now ! " cried Pearce, and the vessels came in collision, the spare anchor in the *Aspasia's* fore-chains catching and tearing away the backstays and lanyards of the enemy's fore-rigging, and, with a violent jerk, bringing down the fore top-mast to windward. At this

moment the reserved broadside of the *Aspasia* was discharged, and the two frigates heeled over opposite ways, from the violent concussion of the air in the confined space between them. While yet enveloped in the smoke, the men flew up on deck, as they had been previously directed by Captain M——, who leaped upon the quarter-deck hammocks of his own frigate, and, holding with one hand by the mizen top-mast backstay, with his sword in the other, waving to encourage his men, waited a second or two for the closing of the after-parts of the vessels, before he led on his boarders.

The smoke rolled away through the masts of the French frigate, and discovered her captain, with equal disregard to his safety, in nearly a similar position on the hammock rails of his own vessel. The rival commanders were not six feet apart, when the main-chains of the two vessels crashed as they came in collision. The French captain drew a pistol from his belt and levelled it at Captain M——, whose fate appeared to be certain; when, at the critical moment, a hat, thrown from the quarter-deck of the *Aspasia*, right into the face of the Frenchman, blinded him for a moment, and his pistol went off without taking effect.

"Capital shot, that, Willy!" cried M'Elvina, as he sprang from the hammocks with his sword, " giving point" in advance, and, while still darting through the air with the impetus of his spring, passing it through the body of the French captain, who fell back on his own quarter-deck, while M'Elvina, fortunately for himself, dropped into the chains, for, had he a hundred lives, they would have fallen a sacrifice to the exasperated Frenchmen : but the smugglers had followed M'Elvina, and Captain M——, with the rest of his ship's company, were thronging, like bees, in the rigging, hammocks, and chains of their opponent. From the destructive fire of the French troops, many an English seaman fell dead, or severely wounded, was reserved for a worse fate—that of falling overboard between the ships, and, at the heave of the sea, being crushed between their sides. Many a gallant spirit was separated from its body by this horrid death as the strife continued.

Possession was at length gained of the quarter-deck; but the carnage was not to cease. The French troops stationed in the boats of the booms, formed a sort of pyramid, vomiting incessant fire; and the commandant had had the sagacity to draw up three lines of his men, with their bayonets fixed, from one side of the vessel to the other, abreast of the gangways, forming a barrier, behind which the crew of the French frigate had retreated, and which was impenetrable to the gallant crew of the *Aspasia*, who were only provided with short cutlasses.

Captain M——, as he saw his men falling on every side, and every attempt to force a passage unsuccessful, although accompanied with heavy loss of lives, found himself, as it were, in a trap. To force his way through appeared impossible—to retreat was against his nature. M'Elvina, who had been fighting by his side, perceived the awkward and dangerous predicament they were in, and his ready talent suggested a remedy. Calling out loudly, " *Suzannes!* away there!—follow me! " an order instantly obeyed by his men, he disappeared with them over the hammocks, leaping back upon the quarter-deck of the *Aspasia*.

" Curses on the smuggler, he has run for it. At them again, my Britons, never mind," cried the first lieutenant, leading on the men against the phalanx of bayonets.—But it was not as the first-lieutenant had supposed; for before the cutlasses of the seaman had time again to strike fire upon the steel points which opposed their passage, M'Elvina re-appeared in the fore-rigging of the French vessel, followed by his smugglers, who attacked the French troops in the rear, with a loud yell, and an impetuosity that was irresistible. The diversion was announced by a cheer from Captain M—— and his party abaft, who, rushing upon the bayonets of the Frenchmen, already in confusion from the attack of M'Elvina, forced them down on the main-deck, and in a few minutes the hatches were secured over the remainder of the crew, and the tricolored ensign disappeared from the gaff, and announced to the spectators in the batteries on shore, that " *Britannia ruled the waves.*"

Chapter XVII

Brave hearts! to Britain's pride
Once so faithful and so true,
On the deck of fame that died
With the gallant, good Riou,—
Soft sigh the winds of Heaven o'er their grave,
While the billow mournful rolls,
And the mermaid's song condoles,
Singing glory to the souls
Of the brave!

CAMPBELL.

HASTY congratulations between the survivors of the victorious party were exchanged as they proceeded to obey the orders which were issued by Captain M——, who directed their attention to the relief of the wounded, lying in heaps upon the deck, in many instances nearly smothered with the dead bodies which had fallen upon them, and which their own exhausted powers would not permit them to remove. The task of separation of those who were past all mortal aid from those who might still derive benefit from surgical assistance, was as tedious as it was afflicting. No distinction was made between the rival sufferers, but, as they came to hand, English or French, they were carefully conveyed to the half-decks of the respective ships, the surgeons of which were in readiness to receive them, their shirt-sleeves turned up to the elbows, and hands and arms stained with blood, proving that they had already been actively employed in the duties of their profession.

On the foremost part of the larboard side of the French frigate's quarter-deck, where Captain M—— and his crew had boarded, the dead and dying lay in a heap, the summit of which was level with the tops of the carronades that they were between; and an occasional low groan from under the mass, intimated that some were there who were dying more from the pressure of the other bodies, than from the extent of their own wounds.

Captain M——, although he had lost much blood, and was still bleeding profusely, would not leave the deck until he had collected a party to separate the pile; and many were relieved, who, in a few minutes more, would have been suffocated.

At the bottom of the heap was the body of the gallant French captain; and Captain M—— was giving directions to the first lieutenant to have it carried below, when Willy, who was earnestly looking about the deck, brushed up against the latter, who said to him—

"Come, youngster, out of the way, you're no use here."

"Has any one seen my hat?" interrogated the boy, as he obeyed the order, and removed to a short distance.

"Here it is, my bantam," said one of the boatswain's mates, who had discovered it as they removed the body of the French captain, under which it had lain, jammed as flat as a pancake.

"Then it was to you that I was indebted for that well-timed assistance," said Captain M——, taking the hat from the boatswain's mate, and restoring it as well as he could to its former shape before he put it on Willy's head.

Willy looked up in the captain's face, and smiled assent as he walked away.

"A good turn is never lost," observed Captain M——; "and the old fable of the mouse and the lion is constantly recurring to make us humble. If I had not put that boy on the quarter-deck, I should in all probability have made a vacancy. It was remarkable presence of mind on his part."

We have not broken in upon our narrative to state, that, during the scene we have described, Mr Pearce, the master, had succeeded in putting both vessels before the wind, although they still were hugged in each other's embraces, as if they had always been the best friends in the world, and they were now out of the reach of the enemy's batteries, which (as soon as they perceived the unfavourable result of the action) had commenced firing with red-hot balls, emblematical of their wrath.

When the wounded had been carried below, and placed in comparative comfort on board of their respective ships, the dead bodies were next examined. Those of the French (with the exception of that of the captain) were launched overboard; while those of the English were carried to their own frigate, the only instance in which any difference was shown between the rival sufferers. The hatches were then removed, and the French officers, having delivered up their swords, were permitted to remain on deck upon parole, while the men were secured down below in the fore and main holds of the *Aspasia*, the hatchways being covered over with a strong splinter-netting, that they might not be deprived of fresh air in their crowded situation. The charge of the prize having been confided to the first lieutenant and fifty men, the two ships were separated, and laid to, to repair the damages sustained in the conflict.

Captain M——, whose wounds were not serious, had descended for a short time to have them washed and dressed. His anxiety to put his ship in an efficient state, and get clear of the bay, previously to bad weather coming on, had induced him to return on deck as soon as he had taken a little refreshment.

M'Elvina had also cleansed himself from the gore with which he had been begrimed, and, having applied to the surgeon to assuage the pain of a severe cut which he had received on his shoulder, came upon the quarter-deck with his arm in a sling, dressed with his usual precision and neatness. He touched his hat to Captain M——, with whom he had not communicated since he had quitted him on the quarter-deck of the French frigate, to create the fortunate diversion in favour of the boarders.

"Captain M'Elvina," said Captain M——, taking his hand and shaking it warmly, "I can hardly express how much I am obliged to you for your conduct this day. You may be assured that, upon my return, I shall not fail to make a proper representation of it to government. I only wish that there was any situation in my ship that could induce you to remain."

"Thank you, Captain M——," replied M'Elvina, smiling; "but, although on a smaller scale, I have long been accustomed to command; and I should be very sorry that a vacancy should occur in the only situation that I would accept."

"I expected an answer to that effect," replied Captain M——. "However, you have this day nobly redeemed your character, and silenced any imputations of hostility to your country that might be thrown upon you in consequence of your late employment; and I sincerely congratulate you."

"Captain M——, as you are kind enough to express friendly feelings towards me, may I request they may be shown by the interest you take in young Seymour? I cannot but approve his following the honourable career marked out for him, and my regret at parting with one who has so entwined himself round my heart, will be considerably lessened by the assurance that you will be his friend and protector. Any expenses——"

"Not one word upon that score," replied Captain M—— : "the boy saved my life this day by his unusual presence of mind, and I shall watch over him as if he were my own child."

"His education?"

"Shall be attended to. I pledge you my honour to do him every justice."

M'Elvina bowed, and walked away to the other side of the quarter-deck; the idea of parting with Willy was always painful to him, and, weak with the loss of blood, he was afraid that the emotion would be perceived, which he now felt less able to control.

Thus it is with proud man. He struggles to conceal effects arising from feelings which do honour to his nature; but feels no shame when he disgraces himself by allowing his passions to get the better of his reason —and all because he would not be thought *womanish!* I'm particularly fond of crying myself.

The list of killed and wounded was brought up by the second lieutenant (the duty of the first, who was in charge of the prize, having devolved upon him)—the former having been ascertained by mustering the ship's company, the latter from the report of the surgeon.

A deep sigh escaped from the breast of the captain as he looked down at the total. " Forty-four killed— sixty-seven wounded! This is heavy indeed. Poor Stevenson, I thought he was only wounded "

" Since dead, sir," replied the second lieutenant ; " we have lost a pleasant messmate."

" And his Majesty a valuable officer," replied the captain. " I am afraid his mother will feel it in more ways than one—he supported her, I think."

" He did, sir : will you not give an acting order to one of the young gentlemen ? " (It was the third lieu- tenant over whom they were lamenting.)

" Yes, make it out for Mr Robertson."

" He's in the list, sir."

" What ! killed ! So he is, poor fellow ! Well then, —Mr Wheatly,—let it be made out for him."

" Ay, ay, sir."

It was not until the ensuing day that the loss of the enemy could be ascertained. Crowded as were her decks with troops, it was enormous. Not only the first and second captains, second lieutenant, and seven junior officers of the frigate had fallen, but eleven officers of the detachment of soldiers sent on board of her. The total loss appeared to be one hundred and forty-seven killed, and one hundred and eighty-four wounded, out of an aggregate of nearly nine hundred men.

In a few days the *Aspasia* and her prize arrived at

Plymouth, the English colours proudly waving over the tricolored flag of her late opponent, and both vessels ran into Hamoaze, amidst the cheers of thousands of spectators, assembled upon Mount Wise and Mount Edgecomb to greet their gallant and successful defenders. Captain M—— immediately proceeded to London, where the representation which he made of M'Elvina's conduct was followed by an order for his immediate release, and M'Elvina, taking an affectionate leave of Willy, with a parting injunction to "*be honest,*" set off to report to old Hornblow, and his daughter Susan, all the circumstances attending the capture of his lugger, and the events which had subsequently ensued.

Chapter XVIII

So: poverty at home, and debts abroad ;
My present fortune had ; my hopes yet worse !
What will become of me ?

SOUTHERON's *Isabella.*

THE gentleman who had supposed himself the next heir to the entailed property, vacant by the demise of Admiral De Courcy, and whose hasty visit and departure from—— Hall we have mentioned in a previous chapter, was a third cousin of the deceased. His history is short. He had squandered away the personal property left him by his father; and his family estate, which was of greater extent than value, was mortgaged for even more than it was worth. He had latterly subsisted by borrowing large sums of money at exorbitant interest, upon the expectancy of succeeding to the property of Admiral De Courcy. The result of his visit to the Hall was, therefore, unsatisfactory in more ways than one; and before he had arrived at his own residence, his obsequious little friend in black had reminded him of certain bonds which were in his possession, and assumed a tone and demeanour towards his client very different from that in which he had addressed the supposed inheritor of the large property of D——; intimating, in very plain terms, that some speedy arrangements must be made.

Rainscourt, who had nothing left except the old castle on his property in Galway, his manorial rights, and the unbounded attachment and devotion of the wild tenants, who looked upon him as their feudal chieftain, felt convinced that he had no resource but to escape from his numerous creditors, who would not hesitate to put him in durance, and whose impatience had been with difficulty restrained until the death of the admiral. The *speedy arrangement* upon which he determined was, to set off immediately for Ireland, and, by regaining his castle, defy legal authority, —if there could be found any that would be rash enough to attempt his person, when encircled by his lawless retainers.

As he descended from the chaise, at the handsomely furnished lodgings, in the west end of the metropolis, which he had engaged, his companion informed him, with a haughty air, that he would have the honour of paying his respects on the ensuing noon; while Rainscourt, with his usual indifference to money, dismissed the post-boys with a handsome gratuity, although there were not many guineas left in his purse; and then proceeded up to the drawing-room, on the first floor, where his wife and only daughter were anxiously awaiting his arrival.

Mrs Rainscourt, still a fine and elegant woman, had, in her youth, been remarkable for her great personal attractions; and, for two seasons, had been considered as the belle of the Irish metropolis. She was, at that period, a high-spirited and generous-minded girl, easily provoked, and as easily appeased,—proud of her beauty and her accomplishments, which her worldly-minded parents were in hopes would be bartered for a coronet. Rainscourt was also, at that time, one of the handsomest, if not the handsomest man in Ireland, with the advantage of polished manners, talent, and ancient birth. Received and courted in every society, he was as indefatigable in squandering

away his property, as the parents of Mrs Rainscourt were
in trying to obtain an advantageous establishment for their
daughter.   Rainscourt was proud and overbearing in disposition : vain, to excess, of his personal advantages, he
considered himself to be irresistible with the other sex.
He had seen and admired his future spouse ; but still, as
he required an alliance which would enable him to indulge
in his extravagance, and as her parents were aware that
Rainscourt was, or would soon be, a ruined man, in all
probability they would never have come in contact, but
have rolled in different orbits, more consonant to their views
and their happiness, had it not occurred that, at a large and
convivial party, Rainscourt's vanity had been piqued by his
companions, who told him that he never could obtain the
hand of Miss——, whose parents aspired to a higher connection.   Piqued at this remark, and flushed with the wine
that had been freely circulated, he offered to stake a
considerable sum that he would succeed before a certain
allotted time.   The wager was accepted.   Rainscourt
courted without affection ; and, by his assiduities and
feigned attachment, ultimately succeeded in persuading
the fond girl to destroy all the golden visions of her
parents, and resign herself to his arms, where he assured
her that competence and love would be found more than
commensurate to a coronet and neglect.

They eloped ;—all Dublin was in an uproar for three
days.   Rainscourt received the amount of his bet, and the
congratulations of his friends, and for a short time he and
his wife lived together without any serious fracas.   The
first that occurred proceeded from an anonymous letter,
evidently written by some envious and disappointed female,
acquainting Mrs Rainscourt with all the circumstances
attending the bet, to which she had been sacrificed.   This
mortifying news was received with showers of tears, and
some upbraiding : for Mrs Rainscourt really loved her
husband ; and although patched up by Rainscourt's pro-
testations, as to the falsehood of the accusation, it sunk deep
into her heart, and was but the forerunner of future misery.

Rainscourt soon became tired of a woman whom he had
never loved ; cursed his own vanity, that had induced him
to saddle himself with such an encumbrance as a wife ; and,
by alternate violence and moroseness, irritated her feelings,
and roused her spirit.   Neglect on his part produced
indifference on her side ; and as the means of gaiety and
expense melted away, so did all respect and esteem for each
other.

An extravagant man seldom makes a good husband : he
becomes embarrassed, and his circumstances prey upon his
mind, and sour his temper.   A woman who has, before
marriage, been the admiration of the metropolis, is not very
likely to prove a good wife.   She still sighs for the
adulation that she received, and which, from habit, has
become necessary to her, and would exact from the man for
whom she has given up the world, all the attention that she
has lost by the sacrifice.

Mr and Mrs Rainscourt were joined—but they were
not one.   Like many others in this world of error, their
marriage might be typified by a vial, of which one half has
been filled with oil, and the other with water, having a
cork in its mouth, which confined them, and forced them to
remain in contact, although they refused to unite.   The
fruit of this marriage was one daughter, now about six
years old.

" Well, Mr Rainscourt, all is well, I hope ; and may I
not kiss my daughter, and congratulate her upon being one
of the largest heiresses in the kingdom ? "

" You may, if you please, madam."

" May, if I please ?   Why, is it not so, Mr Rainscourt?"
replied the lady, startled at the moody brow of her husband,
as he threw himself on the sofa.

Now Rainscourt would not have so immediately answered
the question, but he was determined that his spouse should
participate in those pangs of disappointment which swelled
his own breast ; as a partner of all his joys, she was, of
course, fully entitled to an equal proportion of his cares.

" No, madam—it is not so."

"Surely you are trifling with me, Mr Rainscourt; is not the admiral dead?"

"Yes, madam; and his grandchild is alive."

"His grandchild!" cried the lady, in *alto*, pallid with vexation and disappointment. "Well, Mr Rainscourt, this is another specimen of your usual prudence and foresight. What man in his senses would not have ascertained such a fact, previous to squandering away his whole property, and leaving his daughter a beggar!"

"I think, madam, if the property has been squandered, as you term it, that you have assisted me in so doing; at all events, the property was my own; for I cannot exactly recollect that you increased it one shilling when I married you."

"Certainly, not much, Mr Rainscourt, except, indeed, the amount of the bet. I consider that as my marriage portion," replied the lady, with a sneer.

"Never made a worse bet in my life," replied the gentleman, throwing his legs upon the sofa.

"Perhaps not," replied his wife with offended seriousness; "but recollect, Mr Rainscourt, that *you* have no one to blame but yourself—*you* were not deceived. I might have been happy—might have met with sincerity and reciprocal affection. Your conduct towards me was an act of cruelty, which would have called forth some compunction in the breast of my bitterest enemy; and yet, unoffending, I was heartlessly sacrified to your vanity."

"Say, rather, to your own, which blinded you, or you would have been able to discriminate better."

Mrs Rainscourt burst into tears. Before her emotion could be controlled, her husband, who was hardened to these scenes of alternate anger and grief, either was, or pretended to be, in a sound sleep.

The little girl had nestled close to her mother at the ebullition of her feelings, and waited in silence until it was exhausted.

"Why, mamma, I thought you said we should be so happy now."

" Did I, my dear ? " replied Mrs Rainscourt, mournfully.

" Yes, you did, and told me that we should have a fine
house in London, and that we should not go back to the
old castle again.   I was sorry for that, though.   Where
shall we go now, mamma ? "

" God knows, my child ; you must ask your father."

"Papa's asleep, and I must not wake him.   I do hope
we shall go back to the castle."

" Then you'll have your wish, my love," replied Mr
Rainscourt, rousing up, " for I start this very evening."

" Are we to go with you, Mr Rainscourt ? " asked Mrs
Rainscourt, calmly, " or are we to be left here ? "

" As you please ; but I must be off, for that little
scoundrel, T——, threatened me with a visit to-morrow
morning as I got out of the chaise, and I am aware that he
will not come without a companion or two."

" T——!   What ! T——? your friend T——! that
you brought from Dublin with you, and who professes so
much admiration and esteem—your own factotum ? "

" Yes, my own factotum—snivelling little scoundrel.
But, however, there's no time to be lost.   You have some
jewels, my dear, and other articles of value ; you had better
pack them up, and consign them to me as soon as possible.
You may then take your choice,—go with me now, or
follow me in a day or two.   They cannot arrest *you*."

"I am aware of that, Mr Rainscourt," replied the
lady ; " but as I may not have the means of following, my
daughter and I will, if you please, become a part of your
travelling incumbrance, as well as the jewels and *other*
articles of value."

" Be it so," replied the gentleman, who perfectly understood her sarcastic meaning, but did not think it advisable
to retort at the moment ; "one post-chaise will carry
us all ; but we must leave town at twelve o'clock this
night.   If I recollect right, we are asked to a rout at Lady
G——'s ? "

" We are ; but pray, Mr Rainscourt, how am I to get

K. I.   I

ready so soon ?   The servants must be paid—all the bills
must be called in."

"If you wait until I can pay all the bills, you must wait
till eternity, perhaps.   Pack up everything of value that
is portable, without the knowledge of the servants; your
jewels you can have upon your own person, or in a pocket,
if you ever wear one.   Order the carriage—dress, and we
will both go to the rout.   I shall leave word with Roberts
to bring me any letters which may be sent, telling him
that the admiral is not dead yet, although hourly expected
—nothing has transpired to the contrary.   I can slip away
from the rout, and write the letter myself, which I will
send by a porter.   When I go home, and the chaise which
I shall order is at the door, I will put Emily in it, and
call for you at Lady G——'s.   The servants may suspect
something, but it will then be too late."

Danger will unite those who are at variance. Mrs R.
entered readily into the proposed arrangements, which
necessity imposed upon them, and in a few hours, father,
mother, and daughter were on their way to Ireland, leaving
the house rent, butchers, bakers, chandlers, and all other
bills, of no trifling sum total, to be paid at some more
favourable opportunity.   The servants indemnified themselves as well as they could, by seizing what was left,
and cursing the elopers; and the obsequious little gentleman in black vowed vengeance as he quitted the deserted
mansion, to which he had paid his promised visit in the
morning, with a particular friend or two, to enforce his
arguments with Mr Rainscourt.

Chapter XIX

Fal. Have you provided me here half a dozen sufficient men?
Shal. Marry have we, sir.
Fal. Let me see them, I beseech you.
Shal. Where's the roll! where's the roll!
—————Let them appear as I call.

SHAKESPEARE.

As the reader will have a more intimate acquaintance with them hereafter, I must now enter into some description of the characters of the captain and officers with whom our hero was fated to be a shipmate. To begin with the captain, who has already made his appearance in the course of these pages :—

Captain M—— was the son of a north-country gentleman—one of the numerous class still existing in this world, who have inherited large ideas and small fortunes. As usual, the latter were got rid of much sooner than the former. The consequence was, that although young M—— was an only son, it was considered advisable that he should be brought up to some profession. The naval service was selected by himself, and approved of by his father, who, although he had no money, had some interest,—that is to say, he had powerful and wealthy connections, who, for their own sakes, rather than have to support their young relation, would exert themselves to make him independent.

M—— rose to the rank of post-captain as fast as his friends could wish, and did credit to their patronage. Having once obtained for him the highest rank that the profession could offer, until he became an admiral from seniority, they thought that they had done enough; and had it not been that Captain M——, by his zeal and abilities, had secured a personal interest at the Board, he might have languished on half pay; but his services were appreciated, and he was too good an officer not to be employed. His father was dead, and the payment of debts which he had contracted, and the purchase of an annuity for his mother, had swallowed up almost all the prize-money which Captain M——, who had been very successful, had realised; but he was single from choice, and frugal from habit. His pay, and the interest of the small remains of prize-money in the funds, were more than adequate to his wants. He was enthusiastic in his profession, and had the bad taste to prefer a fine ship to a fine lady.

Having entered the service at a later period than was usual, he had the advantage of an excellent education, which, being naturally of a serious disposition, and fond of reading, he had very much improved by study. As an officer he was a perfect master of his profession, both in theory and practice, and was what is termed afloat, "all for the service." Indeed this feeling was so powerful in him, that, like Aaron's rod, it swallowed up all the rest. If there was any blemish in his character, it was in this point. Correct himself, he made no allowance for indiscretion; inflexibly severe, but always just, he in no instance ever spared himself, nor would he ever be persuaded to spare others. The rules and regulations of the service, as laid down by the Board of Admiralty, and the articles of war, were as rigidly observed by him, and exacted from others, as if they had been added to the Decalogue; and any deviation or neglect was sure to bring down reprimand or punishment upon the offender, whether it happened to be the senior lieutenant, or the smallest boy in the ship's company.

But, with all his severity, so determined was Captain M—— to be just, that he never would exercise the power without due reflection. On one occasion, in which the conduct of a sailor had been very offensive, the first lieutenant observed that summary punishment would have a very beneficial effect upon the ship's company in general. "Perhaps it might, Mr H——," replied he; "but it is against a rule which I have laid down, and from which I never deviate. Irritated as I am at this moment with the man's conduct, I may perhaps consider it in a more heinous light than it deserves, and be guilty of too great severity. I am liable to error,—subject, as others, to be led away by the feelings of the moment—and have therefore made a compact with myself never to punish until twenty-four hours after the offence has been committed; and so repeatedly, when at the time I have settled in my mind the quantum of punishment that the offender should receive, have I found, upon reflection, which delay has given time for, reasons to mitigate the severity, that I wish, for the benefit of the service, that the Admiralty would give a standing order to that effect."

Such was the character of Captain M——. It hardly need be added, after the events already narrated of this history, that he was a man of undaunted bravery. In his person, he was tall, and rather slight in figure. His features were regular; but there was a sternness in his countenance, and lines of deep thought on his brow, which rendered the expression unpleasing. It was only when he smiled that you would have pronounced him hand-some: then he was more than handsome,—he was fascinating.

Mr Bully, the first lieutenant (who was the second lieutenant in the ship in the action with the French frigate), was an officer who well understood his duty. He had the merit of implicitly obeying all orders; and, considering the well-known fact, that a first lieutenant has always sufficient cause to be put out of temper at least twenty times during the twelve hours, he was as good-tempered as a first lieutenant could possibly be. He had entered the service when very young, and, being of humble extraction, had not had any advantage of education. In person, he was short and thick-set, and having suffered severely from the smallpox during his infancy, was by no means prepossessing in his outward appearance.

The second lieutenant, whose name was Price, was a good-looking young man, who kept his watch and read Shakespeare. He was constantly attempting to quote his favourite author ; but, fortunately for those who were not fond of quotations, his memory was very defective.

Mr Courtenay, the third lieutenant, was a little bilious-looking personage, who, to use the master's phraseology, was never quite happy unless he was d—d miserable. He was full of misfortunes and grievances, and always complaining or laughing, at his real or imaginary disasters ; but his complaint would often end in a laugh, or his mirth terminate in a whine. You never could exactly say, whether he was in joke or in earnest. There was such a serio-comic humour about him, that one side of his countenance would express pleasure, while the other indicated vexation. There seemed to be perpetual war, in his composition, of good-humour *versus* bile, both of which were most unaccountably blended in the same temperament.

According to seniority, Mr Pearce, the master, is the next to be introduced to the reader ; in external appearance, a rough, hard-headed north-countryman ; but, with an unpromising exterior, he was a man of sense and feeling. He had every requisite for his situation : his nerves were like a chain-cable ; he was correct and zealous in his duty ; and a great favourite of the captain's, who was his countryman. He was about fifty years of age, a married man with a large family.

The surgeon, whose name was Macallan, was also most deservedly a great favourite with Captain M——; indeed there was a friendship between them, grown out of long acquaintance with each other's worth, inconsistent with, and unusual in, a service where the almost despotic power of the superior renders the intimacy of the inferior similar to the smoothing with your hand the paw of a lion, whose fangs, in a moment of caprice, may be darted into your flesh. He was a slight-made, spare man, of about thirty-five years of age, and had graduated and received his diploma at Edinburgh,—an unusual circumstance at that period, although the education in the service was so defective, that the medical officers were generally the best informed in the ship. But he was more than the above ;

he was a naturalist, a man of profound research, and well informed upon most points—of an amiable and gentle disposition, and a sincere Christian.

It would naturally be inferred, that those whose profession it is to investigate the human frame, and constantly have before their eyes the truth that we are fearfully and wonderfully made, would be more inclined than others to acknowledge the infinite wisdom and power. But this is too often found not to be the case, and it would appear as if the old scholium, that "too much familiarity breeds contempt," may be found to act upon the human mind even when in communion with the Deity. With what awe does the first acquaintance with death impress us! What a thrill passes through the living, as it bends over the inanimate body, from which the spirit has departed! The clay that returns to the dust from which it sprung,—the tenement that was lately endued with volition and life,— the frame, that exhibited a perfection of mechanism, deriding all human power, and confounding all human imagination, now an inanimate mass, rapidly decomposing, and soon to become a heap of corruption.

Strong as the feeling is, how evanescent it becomes, when once familiarised! It has no longer power over the senses, and the soldier and sailor pillow themselves on the corpse, with perfect indifference, if not with a jest. So it is with those who are accustomed to post-mortem arrangements, who wash, and lay out the body previous to interment.

Yet, although we acknowledge that habit will remove the first impressions of awe, how is it that the minute investigation upon which conviction ought to be founded, should too often have the contrary effect from that which it should produce? Is it because mystery, the parent of awe, is in a certain degree removed?

Faith, says the apostle, is the evidence of things not seen. There would be no merit in believing what is perfectly evident to the senses. Yet some would argue, that the evidence ought to be more clear and palpable. If so, would not the awe be also removed, and would religion gain by it ?   We have enough imparted to convince us that all is right; and is not that which is hidden or secret pur- posely intended to produce that awe, without which the proud mind of man would spurn at infinite wisdom ?

The above digression had nearly caused me to omit, that Macallan had one peculiar failing.   His language, from long study, had been borrowed from books, more than from men ; and when he entered upon his favourite science of natural history, his enthusiasm made him more pedantic in his style and pompous in his phraseology than ever.   But who is perfect ?

The purser, O'Keefe, was an elderly man, very careful of the pounds, shillings, and pence.   He was affected with an incurable deafness, which he never thought proper to acknowledge—but catching at a word or two in the sentence, would frame his answer accordingly, occasioning frequent mirth to his messmates, who he imagined were laughing with, and not at him.   For the present, I shall pass over the rest of the officers, with the exception of the boatswain, whose character was of a very peculiar nature.

He was a man who had long been considered as one of the best boatswains in the service, and had been applied for by Captain M——.   He used his cane with severity, but had always some jest at hand to soften down the smart of the blow, and was very active in his own person, setting an example to the men.   It had, however, happened, that about a year before he joined, Mr Hardsett had been induced by his wife to go with her to a conventicle, which the rising sect of methodists had established at the port where she resided ; and whether it was that his former life smote his conscience, or that the preacher was unusually powerful, he soon became one of the most zealous of his converts.   He read nothing but his Bible, which employed all his leisure hours, and he was continually quoting it in his conversation.   But he was not exactly a methodist, taking the cognomen in the worst or the best interpreta- tion ; he was an enthusiast and a fanatic—notwithstanding which, he contrived that his duty towards his Maker should not interfere with that of boatswain of the ship. Captain M—— regretted the man's bigotry; but as he never tried to make any converts, and did his duty in his situation, the captain did not attempt to interfere with his religious opinion,—the more so, as he was convinced that Hardsett was sincere.

The *Aspasia* was but a short time in harbour, for the captain was anxious to add to the laurels which he had already won; and having reported the ship ready for sea, received an order to proceed to the West India station. The frigate was unmoored, the blue-peter hoisted, and the fore-topsail loosened as the signal for departure; and after lying a short time with her anchor " shot stay apeak," Captain M—— came on board,—the anchor was run up to the bows, and once more the frigate started, like an armed knight in search of battle and adventure.

It was two o'clock in the afternoon, and the tenants of the gun-room had assembled to their repast. " Now all my misery is about to commence," cried Courtenay, as he took his seat at the gun-room table, on which the dinner was smoking in all the variety of pea-soup, Irish stew, and boiled mutton with caper sauce.

" Indeed!" said the master. " Pray, then, what is it that you have been grumbling about, ever since you have joined the ship?"

" Pshaw, they were only petty vexations, but now we are at sea. I shall be sea-sick. I am always obliged to throw off the accumulation of bile whenever I go out of harbour."

" I say, doctor," replied Pearce, " can you stop up the leak in that little gentleman's liver? He's not content to keep a hand-pump going to get rid of his bile when in harbour, but it seems that he requires the chain-pumps to be manned when he goes to sea."

" Chain-pumps!" exclaimed Courtenay shuddering, and drawing back his head with a grimace at the idea of such a forcible discharge, and then looking round at his mess-mates with one of his serio-comic faces.

"Pumps! ay," said Price; "you remember Shakespeare, in the 'Tempest'—he says—dear me,—I——"

"Come, Price," said Courtenay, "don't make me sick before my time,—it's unkind. You don't know what an analogy there is between spouting and sea-sickness. In both cases you throw up what is nauseous, because your head or your stomach is too weak to retain it. Spare me, then, a quotation, my dear fellow, till you see me in the agony of Nature aback,' and then one will be of service in assisting her efforts to 'box off.' I say, Billy Pitt, did you stow away the two jars of pickled cabbage in my cabin?"

We must here break off the conversation to introduce this personage to the reader. He was a black, who ran away, when quite a lad, from his master at Barbadoes, and entered on board of a man-of-war. Macallan, the surgeon, had taken a fancy to him, and he had been his servant for some years, following him into different ships. He was a very intelligent and singular character. Macallan had taught him to read and write, and he was not a little proud of his acquirements. He was excessively good-humoured, and a general favourite of the officers and ship's company, who used to amuse themselves with his peculiarities, and allow him a greater freedom than usual. But Billy's grand *forte*, in his own opinion, was as a lexicographer. He had a small Entick's dictionary, which he always carried in his jacket pocket, and nothing gave him so much pleasure as any one referring to him for the meaning of a hard word, which, although he could not always explain correctly, he certainly did most readily. Moreover, he was, as may be supposed, very fond of interlarding his conversation with high-sounding phraseology, without much regard as to the context.

Although Billy Pitt was the doctor's servant, Courtenay, who had taken a great fancy to him, used to employ him as his own, to which, as the doctor was not a man who required much attendance himself, and was very good-natured, no objection had been raised.

We must repeat the question—

"I say, Billy Pitt, did you stow away the two jars of pickled cabbage in my cabin ? "

" No, sar, I no hab 'em to stow. Woman say, that Mr Kartney not pay for the pickled onun—say quite incongrous send any more."

" Not pay for the onions ! No, to be sure I didn't, but I gave her a fresh order, which is the same thing." (Pearce laid down the potato which he was in the act of peeling, and stared at Courtenay with astonishment.)   " Well, to a London tradesman, it is, I can assure you."

" It may be, but I cannot conceive how.   If you owe me ten shillings, I can't consider borrowing ten more the same thing as paying the first."

"Pooh, you do not understand these things."

" I do not, most certainly," replied the master, resuming his potato.

" And so you haven't got them ? " resumed Courtenay to the servant.

" No, sar.   She say Massa Kartney owe nine shillings for onuns, and say I owe farteen for 'baccy, and not trust us any more.   I tell just as she say, sir.   Gentlemen never pay for anything.   She call me d——d nigger, and say, like massa like man.   I tell her not give any more *rhoromantade*, and walk out of shop."

" Well how cursed annoying ! Now I never set my mind upon anything but I'm disappointed.   One might as well be Sancho in the Isle of Barataria.   I think I'll go up to the captain, and ask him to heave-to, while I send for them. Do you think he would, master, eh ? " said Courtenay, in affected simplicity of interrogation.

" You had better try him," replied Pearce, laughing.

" Well, it would be very considerate of him, and pickled cabbage is the only thing that cures my sea-sickness." — (Perceiving Price about to speak)—" Stop now—it's no use—there's not a word about pickled cabbage in Shakespeare."

" I did not say that there was," retorted Price; " but

there's 'beef without mustard,' and that will be your case now."

"And there's 'Write me down an ass,'" replied Courtenay, who was not a little vexed at the loss of his favourite condiment.

"Did you hear what Courtenay said of you, O'Keefe?" continued Price, turning to the purser—

"Yes—yes—I know—hand him over a glass; but this is not a clane one. Steward, will you bring a clane wineglass?"

The rest laughed, while Courtenay proceeded.

"Why, O'Keefe, you hear better than ever. I say, doctor, you must put me in the sick-list—I'm not fit to take charge of a watch."

"If you'll prove that to me," replied Macallan, "I certainly will report you."

"Well, I'll prove it to you in five seconds. I'm just in that state, that if everything in the ship was to go overboard to the devil, I shouldn't care. Now, with such a feeling of indifference, a person is not fit to be trusted with the charge of a watch."

"That you're not fit to be trusted with the charge of a watch, as you state it yourself, I shall not deny," replied Macallan; "but I consider that to be a complaint for which you ought rather to be put *off* the list than on it."

"Ha! ha! ha! I say, Courtenay, you know what Shakespeare says, ''tis the curse of service,' that—that—"

"All hands, 'bout ship!" now resounded through the ship as it was repeated in the variety of basses of the boatswain and his mates, at either hatchway—one of the youngsters of the watch running down at the same time to acquaint the officers, in his shrill falsetto, with that which had been roared out loud enough to startle even the deaf purser. The first lieutenant, followed by the master, brushed by him, and was up the ladder before his supererogatory communication could be delivered.

"How cursed annoying!" cried Courtenay. "I was

just feeling a little better, and now I shall be worse than ever."

" You recollect in the 'Tempest,'" said Price, "where Shakespeare says——"

"Forecastle there !" roared out Captain M——, from the quarter-deck, in a voice that was distinctly heard below.

" By Jove you'd better skip for it, or you'll have what Captain M—— says. He's hailing your station," said Courtenay, laughing—a piece of advice immediately acted upon by Price, who was up the ladder and on the forecastle in a few seconds.—" And I must go up too. How cursed annoying to be stationed in the waist ! Nothing to do, except to stop my ears against the infernal stamp-and-go of the marines and after-guards, over my head; sweet music to a first lieutenant, but to me discord most horrible. I could *stamp* with vexation."

"Had you not better *go* first and *stamp* afterwards ? " observed the surgeon, drily.

" I think I had, indeed," replied Courtenay, as he bolted out of the gun-room door.—"Cursed annoying ! but the captain's such a bilious subject."

Chapter XX

This chair shall be my state, this dagger my sceptre, and this cushion my crown.

Henry IV. Part I.

WE must now descend to the steerage, where our hero is seated in the berth, in company with a dozen more (as they designated themselves, from the extreme heat of their domicile) *perspiring* young heroes, who were amusing themselves with crunching hard biscuits, and at the same time a due proportion of those little animals of the scaribee tribe, denominated weevils, who had located themselves in the *unleavened bread*, and which the midshipmen declared to be the only fresh meat which they had tasted for some time.

Captain M——'s character stood so high at the Admiralty, that the major part of the young *aspirants* who had been committed to his charge were of good family and connections. At that time few of the aristocracy or gentry ventured to send their sons into the navy ; whereas, at present, none but those classes can obtain admission.

A better school for training young officers could not have been selected ; and the midshipmen's berth of the *Aspasia* was as superior to those in other ships, as Captain M—— was himself to the generality of his contemporary captains in the service. But I cannot pay these young men the compliment to introduce them one by one, as I did the gun-room officers. It would be an anomaly unheard of. I shall, therefore, with every respect for them, describe them just as I want them. It was one bell after eight o'clock— a bottle of ship's rum, a black jack of putrid water, and a tin bread-basket, are on the table, which is lighted with a tallow candle of about thirteen to the pound.

"I say, Mr Jerry Sneak, what are you after there— what are you foraging for in that locker ?" said one of the oldsters of the berth to a half-starved, weak-looking object of a youngster, whose friends had sent him to sea with the hopes of improving his stamina.

"What for ?—why, for my supper if you must know. D'ye think I *look too fat ?* I stowed it away before I went on deck, that it might not fall into your ravenous maw."

"Mind your stops, my Jack of the Bonehouse, or I shall shy a biscuit at your head."

"Do, and prove your bravery ; it will be so very courageous. I suppose you'll expect to be gazetted for it."

The youngster who had been dignified with the above sobriquet, and who made these replies, was certainly a most miserable-looking object, and looked as if a top-gallant breeze would have blown him to atoms. But if his body was weak, his tongue was most powerful. He resorted to no other weapon, and used that skilfully. He was a species of Thersites, and no dread of punishment could control his railing. He offered no resistance, but bent down like the reed, and resumed his former position as soon as the storm was over. His keen and sarcastic remarks, although they occasionally subjected him to chastisement, to a certain degree served him as a defence, for he could always raise a laugh at the expense of the individual whom he attacked, with the formidable weapon which he had inherited direct from his mother.

The oldster before mentioned put his hand into the bread-basket, and seized a handful of the biscuit. "Now I'll bet you a glass of grog that you don't throw a biscuit at my head," cried Jerry, with a sneer.

"Done," replied the oldster, throwing the contents of his hand at Jerry with all his force.

"I'll just trouble you for that glass of grog, for you've lost," said the youngster, taking it up from the table where it stood before the oldster; "you've only thrown some pieces, and not a biscuit;" and following up his words with deeds, he swallowed down the whole contents of the tumbler, which he replaced very coolly before his opponent.

"Fair bet, and fairly lost," cried the rest of the berth, laughing.

"You scarecrow! you're not worth thrashing," said the oldster, angrily.

"Why, that's exactly what I have been trying to impress upon your memory ever since I have joined the ship. There's no credit to be gained by licking a half-starved wretch like I am; but there's Bruce, now" (pointing to one of the oldsters, between whom and his opponent a jealousy subsisted), "why don't you lick him? There would be some credit in that. But you know better than to try it."

"Do I?" retorted the oldster, forgetting himself in the heat of the moment.

"Yes, you do," replied Bruce, jumping up in defiance; and there was every appearance of a disturbance, much to the delight of Jerry, who, provided that they fought, was quite indifferent which party was the victor. But a fortunate interruption took place, by the appearance of the master-at-arms.

"Nine o'clock, gentlemen, if you please—the lights must be put out."

"Very well, master-at-arms," replied one of the oldsters.

The master-at-arms took his seat on a chest close to the door of the berth, aware that a second summons, if not a third, would be requisite, before his object was obtained. In a few minutes he again put his head into the berth. "Nine o'clock, gentlemen, if you please. I must report you to the first lieutenant."

"Very well, Byfield—it shall be out in a minute."

The master-at-arms resumed his station on the chest outside.

"Why, it's Saturday night," cried Bruce. "Sweethearts and wives, my boys, though I believe none of us are troubled with the latter. Forster, pass the rum."

"I'll pass the bottle, and you may make a bull of it, if you choose."

"Confound it, no more grog—and Saturday night. I must drink Auld lang syne, by Heavens."

The master-at-arms again made his appearance. "Gentlemen, you must put the light out."

"Stop one minute, Byfield. Let us see whether we can get any more rum."

The excuse appeared reasonable to the jack in office, and he disappeared.

"Boy, tell Billy Pitt I want him."

Billy Pitt had turned in, but was soon roused out of his hammock, and made his appearance at the berth door, with only his shirt on that he was sleeping in.

"You want me, Massa Bruce?"

"Billy, my beau, you know everything. We sent for you to tell us what's the meaning of a repartee?"

"Repartee, sir—repartee!—stop a bit—Eh—I tell you,

sir. Suppose you call me dam nigger—then I call you one dam dirty white-livered son of a b——; dat a repartee, sir."

"Capital, Billy—you shall be a bishop. But, Billy, has your master got any rum in his cabin?"

"Which massa, sir? Massa Courtenay, or Massa Doctor?"

"Oh! Courtenay, to be sure. The surgeon never has any."

"Yes, sar, I tink he have a little."

"Be quick, Billy, and fetch it. I will give it you back at the tub to-morrow."

"Suppose you forget, sir, you put me in very fine *predical-ament*. Massa Courtenay look dam blue—no, he not look blue, but he look dam yellow," replied Billy, showing his white teeth as he grinned.

"But I won't forget, Billy, upon my honour."

"Well, honour quite enough between two gentlemen. I go fetch the bottle."

Billy soon reappeared with a quart bottle of rum, just as three bells were struck. "By gad, I rattle the bottle as I take him out—wake Mr Courtenay—he say, dam black fellow he make everything adrift—cursed annoying, he say, and go to sleep again."

"Really, gentlemen, I cannot wait any longer," resumed the master-at-arms; "the lights must be reported, or I shall be in disgrace."

"Very true, Byfield; you are only doing your duty. Will you take a glass of grog?"

"If you please," replied Mr Byfield, taking off his hat. "Your health, gentlemen."

"Thank you," replied the midshipmen.

"Tank you, sir," replied also Billy Pitt.

"Well, Billy. What's the last word you read in your dictionary?"

"Last word? Let me see—Oh! commission, sar. You know dat word?"

"Commission! We all know what that is, Billy, and shall be glad to get it too, by-and-bye."

"Yes, sar; but there are two kind of commission. One you want, obliged to wait for; one I want, always have at once,—commission as agent, sar."

"Oh, I understand," replied Bruce; "five per cent. on the bottle, eh?"

"Five per cent. not make a tiff glass of grog, Massa Bruce."

"Well, then, Billy, you shall have ten per cent.," replied the midshipman, pouring him out a *north-wester.* "Will that do?"

The black had the politeness to drink the health of all the gentlemen of the berth separately, before he poured the liquor down his throat. "Massa Bruce, I tink doctor got a little rum in his cabin."

"Go and fetch it, Billy; you shall have it back to-morrow."

"Honour, Mr Bruce."

"Honour, Mr Pitt."

"Ten per cent., Massa Bruce," continued Billy, grinning.

"Ten per cent. is the bargain."

"I go see."

Another quart bottle made its appearance; and the agent having received his commission, made his bow, and returned to his hammock.

"I do—really—think—upon—my word—that that—black—scoundrel—would—sell—his—own—mother—for—a—stiff—glass—of—grog," observed a youngster, of the name of Prose, a cockney, who drawled out his words, which, "like a wounded snake, dragged their slow length along."

"The lights, gentlemen, if you please," resumed the master-at-arms, putting his head again into the door.

"Another commission," said Jerry: "a tax upon light. Billy Pitt has the best right to it."

A second glass of grog was poured out, and the bribe disappeared down Mr Byfield's gullet.

"Now we'll put the light out," said one of the oldsters, covering the candlestick with a hat.

"If you will put your candle into my lanthorn," observed the obsequious master-at-arms, "I can then report
the lights out. Of course you will allow it to remain
there ?"

The suggestion was adopted ; and the light was reported
out to the first lieutenant, at the very moment that it was
taken *out* of the lanthorn again, and replaced in the candlestick. The duplicate supply began to have its effect upon
our incipient heroes, who commenced talking *of their friends*.
Bruce, a fine, manly, honourable Scotchman, had the
peculiarity of always allying himself, when half drunk, to
the royal house who formerly sat upon the throne of
England : but, when quite intoxicated, he was so treason-
able as to declare himself the lawful King of Great
Britain. Glass after glass increased his propinquity to the
throne, till at last he seated himself on it, and the uproar
of the whole party rose to that height, that the first
lieutenant sent out, desiring the midshipmen immediately
to retire to their hammocks.

"Send me to bed! 'Proud man, dressed in a little
brief authority.' If the Lord's anointed had been respected,
he, with millions, would be now bending the knee to me.
Well, if I can't be King of all England, at least I'll be king
in this berth. Tell me," cried Bruce, seizing the unfortunate Prose by the collar, "am I not king ?"

"Why—according—to—the—best—of—my—belief,"
said Prose, "I—should—rather—be—inclined—to—think
—that—you—are—not—the—king."

"Am not, base slave!" cried Bruce, throwing him on
the deck, and putting his foot on his chest.

"No—if—I die for it—I don't care—but if you are—
not king—I must own—that—you are one of—my thirty
tyrants," drawled out Prose, half suffocated with the
pressure.

"I—do—declare," cried Jerry, imitating Prose's drawl,
"that—he—has squeezed—a pun—out—of you."

"Am not I king ?" resumed Bruce, seizing Jerry, who
had advanced within reach, to laugh at Prose.

" I feel that you ought to be," replied Jerry: "and I don't doubt your lineal descent : for you have all the dispositions of the race from which you claim descent. A boon, your gracious majesty," continued Jerry, bending on one knee.

" Thou shalt have it, my loyal subject," replied Bruce, who was delighted with the homage, " even (as Ahasuerus said to Esther) to the half of my kingdom."

" God forbid that I should deprive your majesty of that," replied Jerry, smiling at the idea of *halving nothing*. " It is only to request that I may not keep the middle watch to-night."

" Rise, Jerry, you shall not keep a night-watch for a fortnight."

" I humbly thank your most gracious majesty," replied the astute boy, who was a youngster of the watch of which Bruce was mate.

As the reader may be amused with the result of this promise, he must know, that Bruce, who did not recollect what had passed, when he perceived Jerry not to be on deck, sent down for him. The youngster, on his appearance, claimed his promise ; and his claim was allowed by Bruce, rather than he would acknowledge himself to have been intoxicated. Jerry, upon the strength of the agreement, continued, for more than the prescribed time, to sleep in every night-watch, until, aware that he was no longer safe, he thought of an expedient which would probably ensure him one night longer, and prevent a disagreeable interruption of his dreams. Prose, whose hammock was hung up next the hatchway, had a bad cold, and Jerry thought it prudent to shift his berth, that he might not be found.

" It's the draught from the hatchway that makes your cold so bad, Prose ; you'll never get well while you sleep there. I will give you my inside berth until it is better—it is really quite distressing to hear you cough."

" Well, now, Jerry, that's what I call very good-natured of you. I have not had such a friendly act done towards me since I joined the ship, and I do assure you, Jerry, that I shall not be ungrateful—I shall not forget it."

It happened that, on the very night that Prose exchanged berths with Jerry, Bruce made his calculation that the fortnight had elapsed three days back: and although he felt himself bound in honour to keep his promise, yet feeling rather sore at being over-reached, he now ordered the quarter-master to cut Jerry's hammock down by the head. This was supposed to be done, and poor Prose, who had just fallen asleep after keeping the previous watch, awoke with a stunning sensation, and found his feet up at the beams and his head on the deck; while Jerry, who had been awakened by the noise, was obliged to cram the sheets into his mouth, that his laughter might be unperceived.

"Well now, I do declare, this is too bad—I most certainly will complain to the captain, to-morrow morning —as sure as my name is Prose. Sentry, bring me a light, and assist me to get my hammock up again—I will not put up with this treatment—I do declare;" and so saying, Prose once more resumed his position in his precarious dormitory.

But, during our digression, the berth has become empty —some walking, and others, particularly his majesty, reeling to bed. So we shall close this chapter, from which the reader may perceive, that, even in the best regulated ships, there is more going on in a midshipmen's berth than a captain is acquainted with, or that comes between Heaven and his philosophy.

Chapter XXI

With leave, Bassanio, I am half yourself, and I must freely have the half of anything that this same paper brings you.

SHAKESPEARE.

THE castle which had been built by the ancestors of Mr Rainscourt, and which, in feudal times, had been one of strength and importance, was about two miles from the town of ——, in the county of Galway, on the west coast of Ireland : and, as Mr Rainscourt had correctly surmised, when he returned to it, no officer could be found who was bold enough to venture his life by an attempt at caption, surrounded as he was by a savage and devoted peasantry, who had no scruples at bloodshed. Immured within its walls, with little to interest, and no temptation to expend money, Mr and Mrs Rainscourt lived for nearly two years indulging their spleen and discontent in mutual upbraidings, — their feelings towards each other, from incessant irritation, being now rather those of hatred than any other term that could be applied. The jewels of Mrs Rainscourt, and every other article that could be dispensed with, had been sold, and the purse was empty. The good-will of the tenants of the mortgaged property had for some time supplied the ill-assorted couple with the necessaries of life ; every day added to their wants, to their hatred, and their despair.

They were seated at the table, having finished a dinner off some game which Mr Rainscourt had procured with his gun, and which had been their fare, with little variety, ever since the shooting season had commenced : when the old nurse, the only domestic they retained,—probably the only one who would remain with them without receiving wages,—made her appearance. "And sure there's a letter for the master : Barney, the post-boy, is just bringing it."

"Well, where is it ? " replied Rainscourt.

"He says that it's two thirteens that must be paid for it, and the dirty spalpeen of a post-master tould him not to give you the letter without the money for it in his fist."

"Tell Barney to step in here—have you two shillings, Mrs Rainscourt ? "

"Not one, Mr Rainscourt," replied the lady, gloomily.

The nurse reappeared with Barney.

"Well, Barney, where's the letter ? " said Mr Rainscourt ; "let me look at it."

" Sure, your honour, it's not me that's refusing it ye.
But the muster tould me—'Barney,' says he, 'if you
give his honour the letter without the two thirteens in
your fist, it's a good *bating* that I'll give ye when you
come back.'"

" Well, but, Barney, let me look at, and see by the post-
mark where it's from. I shall know, directly, whether I
will take it up or not."

" And suppose that your honour should wish to open
the letter! It's not for gentlemen like ye to be standing
against the temptation ;—and then, the two thirteens, your
honour."

" Well, Barney, since you won't trust me, and I have no
money, you must take the letter back. It might bring me
good news—I have had nothing but bad of late."

" And sure enough it might bring you good news.
Then, your honour shall take the letter and I'll take the
bating ;" and the good-natured lad pulled out the letter
from his pocket, and gave it to Rainscourt.

Rainscourt, who first wished to ascertain whether it was
one of his usual dunning correspondents, examined the
post-mark and handwriting of the superscription, that he
might return it unopened, and save poor Barney from the
beating which he had volunteered to receive for his sake ;
but the hand was unknown to him, and the post-mark was
so faint and illegible that he could not decipher it. He
looked into the sides of the letter, and the few words which
he could read whetted his curiosity.

" I'm afraid, Barney, that I must open it."

" Good luck to your honour, then, and may it prove so."

The letter was opened, and the contents threw a gleam
of pleasure, which had been rarely seen of late on the brow
of the reader. His wife had watched his countenance.
" Barney," cried Rainscourt, with delight, " call to-morrow,
and I'll give you a guinea."

"Sure your honour's in luck, and me too," replied Barney,
grinning, and backing out of the room. " I'll go take my
bating at once."

But, to explain the contents of this letter, we must narrate events of which we have lost sight in following up the naval career of our hero.

About three weeks after the death of Admiral De Courcy, the line-of-battle ship in which old Adams had sailed with our hero under his protection, returned into port. The vicar, who anxiously awaited her arrival, immediately proceeded there, that he might claim Willy in the capacity of his guardian. Having obtained the address of Captain M——, he called upon him, and opened his case by requesting that the boy might be permitted to come on shore. He was proceeding to narrate the change which had taken place in his ward's prospects, when he was interrupted by Captain M——, who, first detailing the death of old Adams, and the conduct of Willy, stated that he had sent the boy home in the prize for an outfit. It was with great feeling that Captain M—— was forced to add the apparent certainty, that the vessel, which had never been heard of, had foundered at sea.

Shocked at the intelligence, which was communicated at a moment when his heart was expanded at the idea of having been instrumental in repairing the injustice and neglect which had been shown towards his *protégé*, the vicar, not caring to mention to a stranger the family particulars upon which his request had been grounded, withdrew, without even giving his name or address. Three years afterwards, when, as we have narrated, our hero again made his appearance, Captain M—— had no clue to guide him, by which he might communicate the intelligence of his recovery, to one whom he naturally concluded did not make such inquiries without having some interest in our hero's welfare.

The vicar, in the meantime, although he had every reason to believe that Willy was no more, resorted to every means that his prudence could suggest to ascertain the positive fact. For many months the most strict inquiries were set afloat by his agents, whether a captured vessel had been wrecked on the French coast. The prisoners at

Verdun and other depôts were examined, rewards were
offered, by emissaries in France, for the discovery of the
boy, but without success.   Having waited two years, all
hope became extinct, and the letter now received by Mr
Rainscourt was from the vicar, acquainting him with the
circumstances, and surrendering up the property to him as
next of kin.

"Pray, Mr Rainscourt, may I ask the contents of a
letter, the perusal of which not only makes you so
generous, but implies that you expect to have the means of
being so ? "

When happy ourselves, especially when unexpectedly so,
we feel kindly disposed towards others.   For a moment
Rainscourt seemed to have forgotten all his differences
with his wife; and he as readily imparted to her his good
fortune as he had, on a previous occasion, his disappointment.

" My dear Clara, the grandchild is dead, and we have
possession of the property."

" My dear Clara ! ! "   Such an epithet had never been
used since the first week of their marriage.   Overcome by
the joyful intelligence, but more overcome by the kind
expression of her husband, which recalled the days when
she fondly loved, Mrs Rainscourt burst into tears, and
throwing herself down with her face on his knees, poured
out, in sobs, her gratitude to Heaven, and her revived
affection for her husband.

Their daughter Emily, now ten years old, astonished at
so unusual a scene, ran up, impelled as it were, by instinct,
and completed the family group, by clinging to her father.
Rainscourt, who was affected, kissed the brow of the child,
and congratulated her on becoming an heiress.

" I never knew before that money would do so much
good," observed the child, referring to the apparent
reconciliation of her parents.

Mrs Rainscourt rose from her position, and sat down at
the table, leaning her face upon her hands.   " I am afraid
that it has come too late," said she, mournfully, as she

recalled the years of indifference and hostility which had preceded.

Mrs Rainscourt was correct in her supposition. Respect and esteem had long departed, and without their aid, truant love was not to be reclaimed. The feeling of renewed attachment was as transient as it was sudden.

"I must be off to England immediately," observed the husband. "I presume that I shall have no difficulty in obtaining money from the bank when I show this letter. Old ——— will be ready enough to thrust his notes into my hands now."

"Shall we not go with you, Mr Rainscourt?"

"No; you had better remain here till I have arranged matters a little. I must settle with three cursed money-lenders, and take up the bonds from T———. Little scoundrel! he'll be civil enough."

"Well, Mr Rainscourt, it must, I suppose, be as you decide; but neither Emily nor I are very well equipped in our wardrobes, and you will not be exactly competent to execute our commissions."

"And therefore shall execute none."

"Do you, then, mean to leave us here in rags and beggary, while you are amusing yourself in London?" replied Mrs Rainscourt, with asperity. "With your altered circumstances, you will have no want of society, either male or *female*," continued the lady, with an emphasis upon the last word—"and a *wife* will probably be an encumbrance."

"Certainly not such a kind and affectionate one as you have proved, my dear," replied the gentleman, sarcastically; "nevertheless I must decline the pleasure of your company till I have time to look about me a little."

"Perhaps, Mr Rainscourt, now that you will be able to afford it, you will prefer a separate establishment? If so, I am willing to accede to any proposition you may be inclined to make."

"That's a very sensible remark of yours, my dear, and shall receive due consideration."

"The sooner the better, sir," replied the piqued lady, as Mr Rainscourt quitted the room.

"My dear child," said Mrs Rainscourt to her daughter, "you see how cruelly your father treats me. He is a bad man, and you must never pay attention to what he says."

"Papa told me just the same of you, mamma," replied the girl, "yesterday morning, when you were walking in the garden."

"Did he! The wretch, to set my own child against me!" cried Mrs Rainscourt, who had just been guilty of the very same offence which had raised her choler against her husband.

Chapter XXII

The Queen of night, whose vast command
Rules all the sea, and half the land;
And over moist and crazy brains,
In high spring-tides at midnight reigns.

Hudibras.

AMONG the millions who, on the allowed and appointed day, lay aside their worldly occupations to bow the knee to the Giver of all good, directing their orisons and their thoughts to one mercy-beaming power, like so many rays of light concentrated into one focus, I know no class of people in whose breasts the feeling of religion is more deeply implanted than the occupants of that glorious specimen of daring ingenuity—a man-of-war. It is through His works that the Almighty is most sincerely reverenced, through them that His infinite power is with deepest humility acknowledged. The most forcible arguments, the most pathetic eloquence from the pulpit, will not affect so powerfully the mind of man, as the investigation of a blade of grass, or the mechanism of the almost imperceptible insect. If, then, such is the effect upon mankind in general, how strong must be the impressions of those who occupy their business in the great waters! These men "see the works of the Lord, and His wonders in the deep." They behold Him in all His magnificence, in all His beauty, in all His wrath, in all His vastness, in all His variety. Unassisted by theory, they practically feel that God is great, and their worship, although dumb, is sincere.

I am aware that it is the idea of many that sailors have little or no religion : and their dissolute conduct, when thrown on shore, is certainly a strong argument in support of this opinion; but they must not be so partially judged. Those who are constantly mixed with the world, and exposed to its allurements, are subject to a continual struggle against their passions, which they are more enabled to restrain, as temptation so rapidly succeeds temptation that one destroys the other,—effacing it from their recollection before they have had time to mature their embryo guilt. But in our floating monasteries, where rigid discipline and active duties allow only the thoughts to ramble to that society which never has been intended to be abandoned, the passions are naturally impelled towards that world, whose temptations are so much increased by long and unnatural seclusion.

In the mountain lake, whose waters are daily increasing, all is unruffled till their own weight has forced its boundaries, and the roaring cataract sweeps everything before it. Such is the licentious and *impetuous* behaviour of the sailor on shore.

But on board he is a different being, and appears as if he were without sin and without guile. Let those, then, who turn away at his occasional intemperance, be careful how they judge. They may "thank God that they are not as that publican," and yet be less justified, when weighed in that balance, where, although Justice eyes the beam, Mercy is permitted to stand by, and throw into the scale her thousand little grains to counterpoise the mass of guilt.

Religion in a sailor (I mean by the term, a common seaman) is more of an active than a passive feeling. It does not consist in reflexion or self-examination. It is in externals that his respect to the Deity is manifest.

Witness the Sunday on board of a man-of-war. The
care with which the decks are washed, the hauling
taut, and neat coiling down of the ropes, the studied
cleanliness of person, most of which duties are performed
on other days, but on this day are executed with an
extra precision and attention on the part of the seamen,
because it *is Sunday*. Then the quiet decorum voluntarily
observed; the attention to divine service, which would
be a pattern to a congregation on shore; the little knots
of men collected, in the afternoon, between the guns,
listening to one who reads some serious book; or the
solitary quarter-master, poring over his thumbed Testa-
ment, as he communes with himself,—all prove that
sailors have a deep-rooted feeling of religion. I once
knew a first lieutenant receive a severe rebuke from a
ship's company. This officer, observing the men scattered
listlessly about the forecastle and waist of the frigate,
on a fine Sunday evening, ordered the fiddler up, that
they might dance. The ship's company thanked him for
his kindness, but stated that they had not been accustomed
to dance on that day, and requested that the music might
be sent below.

The Sunday on board of a man-of-war has another
advantage over the Sabbath on shore: it is hallowed
throughout. It commences with respect and reverence,
and it ends with the same. There is no alehouse to
resort to, where the men may become intoxicated; no
allurements of the senses to disturb the calm repose of
the mind, the practical veneration of the day, which
bestows upon it a moral beauty.

It was on the evening of such a day of serenity, after
the hammocks had been piped down and the watch
mustered, that Captain M—— was standing on the gangway of the *Aspasia*, in conversation with Macallan, the
surgeon. It was almost a calm; the sails were not *asleep*
with the light airs that occasionally distended them, but
flapped against the lofty masts with the motion communicated to the vessel by the undulating wave. The moon,

nearly at her full, was high in the heavens, steering for the zenith in all her beauty, without one envious cloud to obscure the refulgence of her beams, which were reflected upon the water in broad and wavering lines of silver.

The blue wave was of a deeper blue—so clear and so transparent that you fancied you could pierce through a fathomless perspective, and so refreshing, so void of all impurity, that it invited you to glide into its bosom.

"How clear the moon shines to-night! to-morrow, I think, will be full moon."

"It would be well," observed the surgeon in reply to the remark of the captain, "to request the officer of the watch not to permit the men to sleep on the upper-deck. We shall have many of them moon-blind."

"I have often heard that effect of the moon in the tropics mentioned, but have never seen it. In what manner does it affect the eyes?"

"The moon can act but in one way, sir," replied Macallan—"by attraction. The men who are affected, see perfectly well in broad daylight; but as soon as it is dusk, their powers of vision are gone altogether. At the usual time at which the hammocks are piped down, they will not be able to distinguish the numbers. I have had sixty men in one ship in the situation I have described."

"We ridicule the opinion of the ancients, relative to the powers of this planet," observed the captain; "but, at the same time, I have often heard more ascribed to her influence than the world in general are inclined to credit. That she regulates the tides is, I believe, the only point upon which there is now no scepticism."

"There has been scepticism even upon that, sir. Did you ever read a work entitled 'Theory of the Tides'? I can, however, state some other points, from observation, in which the moon has power."

"Over lunatics, I presume?"

"Most certainly; and why not, therefore, over those who are rational? We observe the effect more clearly in the lunatic, because his mind is in a state of feverish excitement; but if the moon can act upon the diseased brain, it must also have power, although less perceptible, over the mind which is in health. I believe that there is an ebb and flow of power in our mechanism, corresponding to the phases of the moon. I mean, that the blood flows more rapidly, and the powers of nature are more stimulated, at the flood and full, than at the ebb and neap, when a reaction takes place in proportion to the previous acceleration. Dr Mead has observed, that of those who are at the point of death, nine out of ten quit this world at the ebb of the tide. Does not this observation suggest the idea, that nature has relaxed her efforts during that period, after having been stimulated during the flood? Shakespeare, who was a true observer of nature, has not omitted this circumstance; speaking of the death of Falstaff, Mrs Quickly observes, 'It was just at the turn of the tide.'"

"Well, but, Mr Macallan, laying aside hypothesis, what have you ascertained, from actual observation, besides that which we term moon-blindness?"

"The effect of the moon upon fish, and other animal matter, hung up in its rays at night. If under the half-deck, they would remain perfectly sweet and eatable; but if exposed to the moon's rays, in the tropics, they will, in the course of one night, become putrid and unwholesome. They emit no smell; but when eaten will produce diarrhœa, almost as violent as if you had taken poison."

"I have heard that stated, also, by seamen," said the captain; "but have never witnessed it."

"A remarkable and corroborative instance occurred, when I was in the Bay of Annapolis," resumed the surgeon. "I was becalmed in a small vessel, and amused myself with fishing. I pulled up several herrings; but, to my astonishment, they were putrid and sodden an hour or two after they were dead. I observed the circumstance to one of the fishermen, who informed me that several hundred barrels, taken at a fishery a few miles off, had all been spoiled in the same manner. I asked the reason, and the answer was, 'that they had been spawned at the full of the moon.' How far the man was correct, I know not; but he stated that the circumstance had occurred before, and was well known to the older fishermen."

"Very singular," replied Captain M——. "We are too apt to reject the whole, because we have found a part to be erroneous. That the moon is not the Hecate formerly supposed, I believe; but she seems to have more power than is usually ascribed to her. Is that seven bells striking?"

"It is, sir; the time has slipped rapidly away. I shall wish you good-night."

"Good-night," replied Captain M——, who for some time after the departure of the surgeon, continued leaning over the rail of the entering-port, in silent contemplation of the glassy wave, until the working of his mind was expressed in the following apostrophe:—

"Yes—placid and beautiful as thou art, there is foul treachery in thy smile. Who knows but that, one day, thou mayest, in thy fury, demand as thy victim the form which thou so peaceably reflectest? Ever-craving epicure! thou must be fed with the healthy and the brave. The gluttonous earth preys indiscriminately upon the diseased carcasses of age, infancy, and manhood; but thou must be more daintily supplied. Health and vigour—prime of life, and joyous heart—high beating pulse, and energy of soul —active bodies, and more active minds—such is the food in which thou delightest: and with such dainty fare wilt thou ever be supplied, until the Power that created thee, with the other elements, shall order thee to pass away."

The bell struck eight, and its sharp peals, followed by the hoarse summoning of the watch below, by the boat-swain's mates, disturbed his reverie, and Captain M—— descended to his cabin.

And now, reader, I shall finish this chapter. You may, perhaps, imagine that I have the scene before me, and am describing from nature: if so, you are in error. I am seated in the after-cabin of a vessel, endowed with as liberal a share of motion as any in his Majesty's service: whilst I write I am holding on by the table, my legs

entwined in the lashings underneath, and I can barely
manage to keep my position before my manuscript. The
sea is high, the gale fresh, the sky dirty, and threatening
a continuance of what our transatlantic descendants would
term a pretty-considerable-tarnation-strong blast of wind.
The top-gallant-yards are on deck, the masts are struck,
the guns double-breeched, and the bulwarks creaking and
grinding in most detestable regularity of dissonance as the
vessel scuds and lurches through a cross and heavy sea.
The main-deck is afloat: and, from the careless fitting of
the half-ports at the dock-yard, and neglect of caulking in
the cants, my fore-cabin is in the same predicament. A
bubbling brook changing its course, ebbing and flowing as
it were with the rolling of the ship, is dashing with mimic
fury against the trunks secured on each side of the cabin.

I have just been summoned from my task, in consequence
of one of the battens which secured my little library having
given way to the immoderate weight of learning that
pressed upon it: and as my books have been washed to
and fro, I have snatched them from their first attempts at
natation. Smith's Wealth of Nations I picked up first, not
worth *a fig*; Don Juan I have just rescued from a second
shipwreck, with no other *Hey-day* (Haidee) to console him,
than the melancholy one extracted from me with a deep
sigh, as I received his shattered frame. Here's Burton's
Anatomy of Melancholy, in a very melancholy plight
indeed, and (what a fashionable watering-place my cabin
has turned to!) here's Burke's Peerage, with all the royal
family and aristocracy of the kingdom, taking a dip, and a
captain of a man-of-war, like another Sally Gunn, pulling
them out.

So, you perceive, my description has been been all
moonshine.

"My wishes have been fathers to my thoughts."

My bones are sore with rocking. Horace says, that he
had a soul of brass who first ventured to sea; I think a
body of iron very necessary to the outfit. My cot is

K.   I.   L

swinging and jerking up to the beams, as if the lively scoundrel was some metamorphosed imp mocking at me. " Sarve you right—what did you *list* for ? "—Very true— Why did I ?—Well, anxious as I am to close this chapter, and to close my eyes, I will tell you, reader, what it was that induced me to go to sea. It was not to escape the drudgery and confinement of a school, or the admonitions received at home. The battle of Trafalgar had been fought—I recollect the news being brought down by the dancing-master when I was at school; but although I knew that eighteen or twenty sail of the line had been captured, yet never having seen a vessel larger than a merchant ship at London Bridge, I had very imperfect ideas on the subject—except that it must have been a very glorious affair, as we had a whole holiday in consequence. But when I returned home, I witnessed the funeral procession of Lord Nelson; and, as the triumphal car upon which his earthly remains were borne disappeared from my aching eye, I felt that death could have no terrors, if followed by such a funeral; and I determined that I would be buried in the same manner. This is the fac ; but I am not now exactly of the same opinion. I had no idea at that time, that it was such a terrible roundabout way to St Paul's. Here I have been tossed about in every quarter of the globe, for between twenty and five-and-twenty years, and the dome is almost as distant as ever.

I mean to put up with the family vault; but I should like very much to have engraved on my coffin—' Many years Commissioner,' or ' Lord of the Admiralty,' or ' Governor of Greenwich Hospital,' ' Ambassador,' ' Privy Councillor,' or, in fact, anything but Captain : for, though acknowledged to be a good travelling name, it is a very insignificant title at the end of our journey. Moreover, as the author of Pelham says, "I wish somebody would adopt me."

Now that I have stated my wishes, I have only to add, that all communications on the subject, directed, *post-paid*, to X.Y.Z., at Messrs Colburn and Bentley's, New Burlington Street, will meet with due consideration.

Chapter XXIII

When his pockets were lined, why his life should be mended,
The laws he had broken he'd never break more.

Sea Song.

ON his return to London, M'Elvina immediately repaired
to the residence of his patron, that he might enter into the
necessary explanations relative to the capture of the vessel,
and the circumstances which had produced his release from
the penalties and imprisonment to which he had been
subjected by his lawless career. Previous, however, to
narrating the events which occurred upon his arrival, it
will be advisable to offer some remarks relative to
M'Elvina, which, when they have been suggested to the
reader, will serve to remove much of the apparent inconsistency of his character. That a person who, from his
earliest childhood, had been brought up to fraud and
deceit, should, of his own accord, and so suddenly, return
to honesty, may at first appear problematical. But let it
be remembered, that M'Elvina was not in the situation of
those who, having their choice of good and evil, had preferred the latter. From infancy he had been brought up
to, and had heard every encomium upon dishonesty, without
having one friend to point out to him the advantages of
pursuing another course. The same spirit of emulation
which would have made him strenuous in the right path,
urged him forward in his career of error. If, after his
discharge from the Philanthropic School, he had had time
to observe the advantages, in practice, of those maxims
which had only been incalculated in theory, it is not improbable that he might have reformed; this, however, was
prevented, by the injudicious conduct of his master.

But although the principles which had been instilled
were not sufficiently powerful, unassisted by reflection, to
resist the force of habit, the germ, smothered as it was for
the time, was not destroyed; and after M'Elvina's seven

years' servitude in a profession remarkable for candour and sincerity, and in which he had neither temptation nor opportunity to return to his evil courses, habit had been counteracted by habit.   The tares and wheat were of equal growth.   This is substantiated by the single fact of his inclination to be honest when he found the pocket-book. A confirmed rogue would never have thought of returning it, even if it had not been worth five shillings.   It is true, if it had contained hundreds, that, in his distressed circum- stances, the temptation might have been too strong ; but this remark by no means disproves the assertion, that he had the inclination to be honest.   " There is a tide in the affairs of men," and it was on this decision between retaining or returning the pocket-book that depended the future misery or welfare of M'Elvina.   Fortunately, the sum was not sufficient to turn the nicely-balanced scale, and the generosity of old Hornblow confirmed the victory on the side of virtue.

I do not mean to assert that, for some time subsequent to this transaction, M'Elvina was influenced by a religious, or even a moral feeling.   It was rather by interested motives that he was convinced ; but convinced he was ; and whether he was proud of his return to comparative virtue, or found it necessary to refresh his memory, his constant injunctions to others to be honest (upon the same principle that a man who tells a story repeatedly eventually believes it to be true) assisted to keep him stedfast in his good resolutions.

Upon the other points of his character it will be un- necessary to dilate.   For his gentlemanly appearance and address he was indebted to nature, who does not always choose to acknowledge the claims which aristocracy thinks proper to assert, and occasionally mocks the idea, by bestowing graces on a cottager which might be envied by the inhabitants of a palace.   Of M'Elvina it may with justice be asserted, that his faults were those of education —his courage, generosity, and many good qualities, were his own.

M'Elvina, who knew exactly at what hour of the day his patron would be abroad, took the precaution of not going to the house until the time at which he would be certain to find Susan, as usual, in the little parlour, alone, and occupied with her needle or her book. The street-door had just been opened by the maid to receive some articles of domestic use, which a tradesman had sent home; and M'Elvina, putting his finger to his lips to ensure the silence of the girl, who would have run to communicate the welcome intelligence of his arrival, stepped past her into the passage, and found the door of the little parlour. Gently admitting himself, he discovered Susan, whom he had not disturbed, sitting opposite to the window, with her back towards him. He crept in softly behind her chair. She was in deep thought; one hand rested on her cheek, and the other held the pen with which she had been arranging the accounts of the former week, to submit them, as usual, to her father on the Monday evening. Of whom and what she was thinking was, however, soon manifested to M'Elvina; for she commenced scribbling and drawing with her pen on the blotting-paper before her, until she at last wrote several times, as if she were practising to see how it would look as a signature:

" Susan M'Elvina."
" Susan M'Elvina."
" Susan M'Elvina."

Although delighted at this proof that he was occupying her thoughts, M'Elvina had the delicacy to retire unperceived, and Susan, as if recollecting herself, slightly coloured, as she twisted up the paper and threw it under the grate; in doing which, she perceived M'Elvina, who still remained at the door. A cry of surprise, a deep blush of pleasure over her pale face, and a hand frankly extended, which M'Elvina could with difficulty resist the impulse to raise to his lips, were followed up by the hasty interrogation of—" Why, your arm is in a sling? You did not say that you were hurt when you wrote from Plymouth?"

"It was not worth mentioning, Susan—it's almost well; but, tell me, how did your father bear the loss of the vessel?"

"Oh! pretty well! But, Captain M'Elvina, you could not have done me a greater favour, or my father a greater kindness. He has now wound up his affairs, and intends to retire from all speculation. He has purchased a house in the country, and I hope, when we go there, that I shall be more happy, and have better health, than I have had of late."

"And what is to become of me?" observed M'Elvina, gravely.

"Oh, I don't know—you are the best judge of that."

"Well, then, I will confess to you, Susan, that I am just as well pleased that all this has taken place as you are; for I am not sorry to give up a profession respecting which, between ourselves, I have lately had many scruples of conscience. I have not saved much, it is true; but I have enough to live upon, as long as I have no one to take care of except myself."

"You raise yourself in my opinion by saying so," replied Susan; "although it is painful to me to condemn a practice which impeaches my father. Your courage and talents may be better applied. Thank God, that it is all over."

"But, Susan, you said that you hoped to have better health. Have you not been well?"

"Not very ill," replied Susan; "but I have had a good deal of anxiety. The loss of the vessel,—your capture,—has affected my father, and, of course, has worried me."

The discourse was now interrupted by old Hornblow, who had returned home to his dinner. He received M'Elvina in the most friendly manner, and they sat down to table.

After dinner, M'Elvina entered into a minute detail of

all that had occurred,—and, as far as he was concerned, with a modesty which enhanced his meritorious conduct.

Susan listened to the narrative with intense interest : and as soon as it was over, retired to her room, leaving old Hornblow and M'Elvina over their bottle.

"Well, M'Elvina, what do you mean to do with yourself?" said the old man. "You know that Susan has at last persuaded me into retiring from business. I have just concluded the purchase of a little property near the seaside, about seven miles from the village of ——, in Norfolk—it adjoins the great Rainscourt estate. You know that part of the coast."

"Very well, sir ; there is a famous landing-place there, on the Rainscourt estate. It was formerly the property of Admiral De Courcy."

"Ah! we don't mean to smuggle any more—so that's no use. I should not have known that it was near the Rainscourt property, only they inserted it in the particulars of sale, as an advantage ; though I confess I do not see any particular advantage in a poor man living too near a rich one. But answer my question—What are you going to do with yourself? If I can assist you, M'Elvina, I will."

"I do not intend to go to sea any more."

"No! what then? I suppose you would like to marry, and settle on shore? Well, if I can assist you, M'Elvina, I will."

"You could, indeed, assist me there, sir."

"Oh! Susan, I suppose. Nay, don't colour up; I've seen it long enough, and if I had not meant that it should be so, I should have put an end to it before. You are an honest man, M'Elvina, and I know nobody to whom I would give my girl sooner than to you."

"You have, indeed, removed a weight from my mind, sir, and I hardly know how to express my thanks to you for your good wishes ; but I have yet to obtain your daughter's consent."

"I know you have ; you cannot expect that she will anticipate your wishes as I have done. But as I wish this business to be decided at once, I shall send her down to you, and I'll take a walk in the meantime. All I can say is, that if she says she has no mind to you, don't you believe her, for I know better."

"Susan!" said old Hornblow, going to the door.

"Yes, father."

"Come down, my dear, and stay with Captain M'Elvina. I am obliged to go out."

Old Hornblow reached down his hat, put on his spencer, and departed; while Susan, whose heart told her that so unusual a movement on her father's part was not without some good reason, descended to the parlour with a quickened pulse.

"Susan!" said M'Elvina, who had risen from his chair to receive her, as soon as he heard her footsteps, "I have much to say to you, and I must be as brief as I can, for my mind is in too agitated a state to bear with much temporising. Do me the favour to take a chair, and listen while I make you acquainted with what you do not know."

Susan trembled; and the colour flew from her cheeks, as she sat down on the chair which M'Elvina handed to her.

"Your father, Susan, took me by the hand, at the time that I was in great distress, in consequence of my having pleased him by an act of common honesty. You know how kind and considerate a patron he has been to me since, and I have now been in his employ some years. This evening he has overpowered me with a weight of gratitude, by allowing me to aspire to that which I most covet on earth, and has consented to my robbing him, if I can, of his greatest treasure. You cannot mistake what I mean. But, previous to my requesting an answer on a point in which my future happiness is involved, I have an act of justice to perform towards you, and of conscience towards myself, which must be fulfilled. It is to be candid, and not allow you to be entrapped into an alliance with a person of whose life you, at present, know but the fair side.

"First, let me state to you, Susan, that my parentage is

as obscure as it well can be; and, secondly, that the early part of my life was as vicious. I may, indeed, extenuate it when I enter into an explanation, and with great justice: but I have now only stated the facts generally. If you wish me to enter into particulars, much as I shall blush at the exposure, and painful as the task assigned will be, I shall not refuse, even at the risk of losing all I covet by the confession: for, much as my happiness is at stake, I have too sincere a regard for you to allow you to contract any engagement with me, without making this candid avowal. Now, Susan, answer me frankly—whether, in the first place, you wish me to discover the particulars of my early life; in the next place (if you decline hearing them), whether, after this general avowal, you will listen to any solicitations, on my part, to induce you to unite your future destiny with mine?"

"Captain M'Elvina, I thank you for your candour," replied Susan, "and will imitate you in my answer. Your obscure parentage cannot be a matter of consideration to one who has no descent to boast of. That you have not always been leading a creditable life, I am sorry for; more sorry because I am sure it must be a source of repentance and mortification to you; but I have not an idle curiosity to wish you to impart that which would not tend to my happiness to divulge. I did once hear an old gentlewoman, who had been conversant with the world, declare, that if every man was obliged to confess the secrets of his life before marriage, few young women would be persuaded to go up to the altar. I hope it is not true; but whether it is or not, it does not exactly bear upon the subject in agitation. I again thank you for your candour, and disclaim all wish to know any further. I believe I have now answered your question."

"Not yet, Susan,—you have not yet answered the latter part of it."

"What was it?—I don't recollect."

"It was," said M'Elvina, picking up the piece of twisted paper which Susan had thrown under the grate,—"whether you would listen to my entreaties to sign your name in future as on this paper?"

"Oh, M'Elvina," cried Susan,—"how unfair—how ungenerous. Now I detest you!"

"I'll not believe that. I have your own hand-writing to the contrary, and I'll appeal to your father."

"Nay, rather than that—you have set me an example of candour, and shall profit by it. Promise me, M'Elvina, always to treat me as you have this day,—and here is my hand."

"Who would not be *honest*, to be so rewarded?" replied M'Elvina, as he embraced the blushing girl.

"Ah,—all's right, I perceive," cried old Hornblow, who had opened the door unperceived. "Come, my children, take my blessing—long may you live happy and united."

Chapter XXIV

> He was a shrewd philosopher,
> And had read ev'ry text and gloss over.
> Whatever sceptic could inquire for,
> For every *why* he had a *wherefore:*
> He could reduce all things to acts,
> And knew their nature by abstracts.
>
> *Hudibras.*

CAPTAIN M—— was not unmindful of the promise which he had made to M'Elvina relative to our hero; and when he returned to the ship, he sent for Macallan the surgeon, and requested as a personal favour that he would superintend Willy's education, and direct his studies.

Macallan was too partial to Captain M—— to refuse, and fortunately had imbibed a strong regard for Willy, whose romantic history, early courage, and amiability of disposition, had made him a general favourite. Macallan, therefore, willingly undertook the tuition of a boy who combined energy of mind with docility of disposition and sweetness of temper. There could not have been selected a person better qualified than the surgeon for imparting that general knowledge so valuable in after-life; and, under his guidance, Willy soon proved that strong intellectual powers were among the other advantages which he had received from nature.

The *Aspasia* flew before the trade winds, and in a few weeks arrived at Barbadoes; where Captain M—— found orders left by the admiral of the station, directing him to survey a dangerous reef of rocks to the northward of Porto Rico, and to continue to cruise for some weeks in that quarter, after the service had been performed. In three days the frigate was revictualled and watered; and the officers had barely time to have their sea arrangements completed, before the frigate again expanded her canvas to a favourable breeze. In a few hours the island was left as far astern as to appear like the blue mist which so often deceives the expectant scanner of the horizon.

"You Billy Pitt! is all my linen come on board?"

"Yes, sar," replied Billy, who was in Courtenay's cabin; "I make bill out; just now cast up multerpication of whole."

"I'm afraid you very often use multiplication in your addition, Mr Billy."

"True bill, sar," replied Billy, coming out of the cabin, and handing a paper to Courtenay.

"What's this?—nineteen tarts! Why, you black thief, I never had any tarts."

"Please let me see, sar," said Billy, peering over his shoulder. "Yes, sar, all right—I count 'em. Tell washerwoman put plenty of tarch in collar."

"Shirts, you *nigger!*—why don't you learn to spell with that dictionary of yours?"

"Know how to spell very well, sar," replied Billy, haughtily; "that my way spell ' *tarts.*' "

" ' Fourteen tockin, seventeen toul.'—You do know how to spell to a T."

"Massa Courtenay, doctor not write same way you write."

" Well, Mr Billy."

" You not write same way me—ebery gentleman write different hand. Now, if ebery gentleman write his own way, why not ebery gentleman spell his own way? Dat my way to spell, sar," continued Billy, very much affronted.

" I can't argue with you now, Mr Billy—there's one bell after four striking, and I have hardly had a glass of wine, from your bothering me. Upon my soul it's excessively annoying."

" One bell, Mr Courtenay!" cried Jerry, at the gun-room door; " Mr Price will thank you to relieve him."

" I say, Mr Prose," continued Jerry, as he passed through the steerage to return on deck, " I'll just trouble you to hand your carcass up as soon as convenient."

" Directly, Jerry,—I—will—but my tea—is so hot."

" Well, then leave it, and I'll drink it for you," replied Jerry, ascending the ladder.

" Well, Mr J——, did you tell Mr Courtenay?" inquired Price.

" Yes, sir," replied Jerry.

" What did he say?"

" He said, ' pass the bottle,' sir," replied Jerry, touching his hat and not changing a muscle of his countenance, although delighted with the vexation that appeared in that of the tired lieutenant as he walked away forward.

For two or three days the frigate sailed between the islands, which reared their lofty crests abruptly from the ocean, like the embattlements of some vast castle which had been submerged to the water's edge. Her progress was slow, as she was only indebted to the land or sea breezes as they alternately blew, and was becalmed at the close of the day, during the pause between their relieving each other from their never-ceasing duty. Such was the situation of the *Aspasia* on the evening of the third day. The scene was one of those splendid panoramas which are only to be gazed upon in tropical climes. The sun was near setting; and as he passed through the horizontal streaks of vapour, fringed their narrow edges with a blaze of glory, strongly in contrast with the deep blue of the zenith, reflected by the still wave in every quarter, except where the descending orb poured down his volume of rays, which changed the sea into an element of molten gold. The frigate was lying motionless in the narrow channel between two of the islands, the high mountains of which, in deep and solemn shade, were reflected in lengthened shadows, extending to the vessel's sides, and, looking downwards, you beheld the "mountains bowed." Many of the officers were standing abaft admiring the beauty of the scene; but not giving vent to their feelings, from an inward consciousness of inability to do justice to it in their expressions.

Macallan first broke the silence. "Who would imagine, Courtenay, that, ere yonder sun shall rise again, a hurricane may exhaust its rage upon a spot so calm, so beautiful, as this, where all now seems to whisper peace?"

The remark was followed by a noise like that proceeding from a distant gun. "Is it pace you mane, doctor?" said one of the midshipmen, from the sister kingdom. "By the powers, there's 'war to the knife,' already. Look," continued he, pointing with his finger, in a direction under the land, "there's a battle between the whale and the thrasher."

The remark of the midshipman was correct, and the whole party congregated on the taffrail to witness the struggle which had already commenced. The blows of the thrasher, a large fish, of the same species as the whale, given with incredible force and noise on the back of the whale, were now answered by his more unwieldy antagonist, who lashed the sea with fury in his attempts to retaliate upon his more active assailant; and while the contention lasted, the water was in a foam.

In a few minutes, the whale plunged, and disappeared.

"He has had enough of it," observed the master; "but the thrasher will not let him off so easily. He must come up to breathe directly, and you'll find the thrasher yard-arm and yard-arm with him again."

As the master observed, the whale soon re-appeared, and the thrasher, who had closely pursued him, as if determined to make up for lost time, threw himself out of the water, and came down upon the whale, striking him with tremendous force upon the shoulder. The whale plunged so perpendicularly, that his broad tail was many feet upraised in the air, and the persecuted animal was seen no more.

"That last broadside settled him," said Courtenay.

"*Sunk* him too, I think," cried Jerry.

"Strange," observed Courtenay, addressing Macallan, "that there should be such an antipathy between the animals. The West Indians assert, that at the same time the thrasher attacks him above, the sword-fish pierces him underneath—if so, it must be very annoying."

"I have heard the same story, but have never myself seen the sword-fish," replied Macallan; "it is, however, very possible, as there is no animal in the creation that has so many enemies as the whale."

"A tax on greatness," observed Jerry; "I'm glad it goes by *bulk*. Mr Macallan," continued he, "you're a philosopher and I have heard you argue that whatever is, is right—will you explain to my consummate ignorance, upon what just grounds the thrasher attacks that un-offending mass of blubber?"

"I'll explain it to you," said Courtenay, laughing. "The whale, who has just come from the northward, finds himself in very comfortable quarters here, and has no wish to heave up his anchor, and proceed on his voyage round Cape Horn. The thrasher is the port-admiral of the station, and his blows are so many guns to enforce his orders to sail forthwith."

"Thank you, sir," answered Jerry, sarcastically, "for your very ingenious explanation, but I do not see why his guns should be shotted. Perhaps Mr Macallan will now oblige me by his ideas on the subject."

"How far these islands may be the Capua to the whale, which Mr Courtenay presumes, I cannot say," answered the surgeon, pompously; "but I have observed that all the cetaceous tribe are very much annoyed by vermin, which adhere to their skins. You often see the porpoises, and smaller fish of this class, throw themselves into the air, and fall flat on the water, to detach the barnacles and other parasitical insects, which distress them. May it not be, that the whale, being so enormous an animal, and not able to employ the same means of relief, receives it from the blows of the thrasher."

"Bravo, doctor! Why, then, the thrasher may be considered as a medical attendant to the whale; and, from the specimen we have witnessed of his humanity, a naval practitioner, I have no doubt," added Jerry.

"Very well, Mr Jerry; if ever you come under my hands, you shall smart for that."

"Very little chance, doctor; I'm such a miserable object, that even disease passes by me with contempt. If I ever am in your list, I presume it will be for a case of plethora," replied Jerry, spanning his thin waist.

"Young gentlemen, get down directly. What are you all doing there on the taffrail?" bawled out the first lieutenant, who had just come up the ladder.

"We've been looking at a sea-bully," said Jerry, in a tone of voice sufficiently loud to excite the merriment of those about him, without being heard by the first lieutenant.

"What's the joke?" observed Mr Bully, coming aft, as the midshipmen were dispersing.

"Some of Mr J——'s nonsense," replied the surgeon.

This answer not being satisfactory, the first lieutenant took it for granted, as people usually do, that the laugh was against himself, and his choler was raised against the offending party.

"Mr J——! Ay, that young man thinks of anything but his duty. There he is, playing with the captain's dog; and his watch, I'll answer for it, or he would not be on deck. Mr J——," continued the first lieutenant to Jerry, who was walking up and down to leeward, followed by a large Newfoundland dog, " is it your watch ? "

" Yes, sir," replied Jerry, touching his hat.

" Then why are you skylarking with that dog ? "

" I am not skylarking with the dog, sir. He follows me up and down. I believe he takes me for a *bone*."

" I am not surprised at it," replied the first lieutenant, laughing.

The surgeon, who remained abaft, was now accosted by Willy, who had been amusing himself, leaning over the side of a boat, which had been lowered down by the first lieutenant to examine the staying of the masts, and catching in a tin-pot the various minute objects of natural history which passed by, as the frigate glided slowly along.

" What shell is this, Mr Macallan, which I have picked up ? It floated on the surface of the water by means of these air-bladders, which are attached to it."

" That shell, Willy," replied Macallan, who, mounting his favourite hobby, immediately spouted his pompous truths, " is called by naturalists the Ianthina fragilis, perhaps the weakest and most delicate in its texture which exists, and yet the *only one* * which ventures to contend with the stormy ocean. The varieties of the nautili have the same property of floating on the surface of the water, but they seldom are found many miles from land. They are only coasters in comparison with this adventurous little navigator, which alone braves the Atlantic, and floats about in the same fathomless deep which is ranged by the devouring shark, and lashed by the stupendous whale. I have picked up these little sailors nearly one thousand miles from the land. Yet observe, it is his security—his tenement, of such thin texture to enable him to float with greater ease, would not be able to encounter the rippling of the wave upon the smoothest beach."

" What use are they of ? "

" Of no direct use that I know of, William ; but if it

---

* I am aware that there are two or three other pelagic shells, but, at the time of this narrative, they were not known.

has no other use than to induce you to reflect a little, it has not been made in vain.   All created things are not applicable to the wants or the enjoyment of man; but their examination will always tend to his improvement. When you analyse this little creature in its domicile, and see how wonderfully it is provided with all means necessary for its existence,—when you compare it with the thousand varieties upon the beach, in all of which you will perceive the same Master-hand visible, the same attention in providing for their wants, the same minute and endless beauty of colour and of form,—you cannot but acknowledge the vastness and the magnificence of the Maker.   In the same manner, the flowers and shrubs, which embellish, as they cover the earth, are not all so much for use, as they are for ornament.   What human ingenuity can approach to the perfection of the meanest effort of the Almighty hand? Has it not been pointed out in the Scriptures 'Consider the lilies of the field, how they grow; they toil not, neither do they spin: And yet I say unto you, That even Solomon, in all his glory, was not arrayed like one of these.'   Never debate in your mind, Willy, of what use are these things which God has made—for of what *use*, then, is man, the most endowed and the most perverse of all creation, except to show the goodness and the forbearance of the Almighty! You may, hereafter, be inclined to debate why noxious reptiles and ferocious beasts, that not only are useless to man, but a source of dread and of danger, have been created.   They have their inheritance upon earth, as well as man, and combine with the rest of animated nature to show the power, and the wisdom, and the endless variety of the Creator.   It is true that all animals were made for our use; but recollect, that when man fell from his perfect state, it was declared, 'In the sweat of thy brow thou shalt eat bread.'   Are trackless forests, and yet unexplored regions to remain without living creatures to enjoy them, until they shall be required by man?   And is man, in his fallen state, to possess all the earth and its advantages, without labour,—without fulfilling his destiny?   No.

K. I.   M

Ferocious and noxious animals disappear only before cultivation. It is part of the labour to which he has been sentenced, that he should rend them out as the ' thistle and the thorn ; ' or drive them to those regions, which are not yet required by him, and of which they may continue to have possession undisturbed."

Such was the language of Macallan to our hero, whose thirst for knowledge constantly made fresh demands upon the surgeon's fund of information ; and, pedantic as his language may appear, it contained important truths, which were treasured up by the retentive memory of his pupil.

Chapter XXV

How frail, how cowardly is woman's mind !
Yet when strong jealousy inflames the soul,
The weak will roar, and calms to tempests roll.
LEE's *Rival Queen*.

BUT we must now follow up the motions of Mr Rainscourt, who quitted the castle, and travelling with great diligence, once more trod the pavement of the metropolis, which he had quitted in equal haste, but under very different circumstances. The news of his good fortune had preceded him, and he received all that homage which is invariably shown to a man who has many creditors, and the means of satisfying all their demands. As he had prophesied, the little gentleman in black was as obsequious as could be desired, and threw out many indirect hints of the pleasure he should have in superintending Mr Rainscourt's future arrangements ; and, by way of reinstating himself in his good graces, acquainted him with a plan for reducing the amount of the demands that were made upon him. Rainscourt, who never forgave, so far acceded to the lawyer's wishes, as to permit him to take that part of the arrangements into his hands ; and, after Mr T—— had succeeded in bringing the usurers to reasonable terms—

when all had been duly signed and sealed, not only were his services declined for the future, but the servants were desired to show him the street door.

As his wife had remarked, Rainscourt found no difficulty in makings *friends* of all sorts, and of both sexes—and he had launched into a routine of gaiety and dissipation, in which he continued for several months, without allowing his wife and daughter to interrupt his amusements, or to enter his thoughts.

He had enclosed an order upon the banker at——, soon after his arrival in London, and he considered that he had done all that was requisite. Such was not, however, the opinion of his wife—to be immured in a lonely castle in Ireland, was neither her intention nor her taste. Finding that repeated letters were unanswered, in which she requested permission to join him, and pointed out the necessity that Emily, who was now nearly twelve years old, should have the advantages of tuition which his fortune could command, she packed up a slender wardrobe, and in a week arrived in London with Emily, and drove up to the door of the hotel, to which Rainscourt had directed that his letters should be addressed.

Rainscourt was not at home when she arrived ; announcing herself as his wife, she was shown upstairs into his apartments, a minute survey of which, with their contents, was immediately made; and the notes and letters, which were carelessly strewed upon the tables, and all of which she took the liberty to peruse, had the effect of throwing Mrs Rainscourt into a transport of jealousy and indignation. The minutes appeared hours, and the hours months, until he made his appearance, which he at last did, accompanied by two fashionable roués with whom he associated.

The waiters, who happened not to be in the way as he ascended the stairs, had not announced to him the arrival of his wife, who was sitting on the sofa in her bonnet and shawl, one hand full of notes and letters, the superscriptions of which were evidently in a female hand—and the other holding her handkerchief, as if prepared for a scene. One leg was crossed over the other, and the foot of the one that was above worked in the air, up and down, with the force of a piston of a steam-engine, indicative of the propelling power within,—when Rainscourt, whose voice was heard all the way upstairs, arrived at the landing-place, and, in answer to a question of one of his companions, replied—

"Go and see her! Not I—I'm quite tired of her—By Jove, I'd as soon see my wife;" and as he finished the sentence, entered the apartment, where the unexpected appearance of Mrs Rainscourt made him involuntarily exclaim, "Talk of the devil——"

"And she appears, sir," replied the lady, rising, and making a profound courtesy.

"Pooh, my dear," replied Rainscourt, embarrassed, and unwilling that a scene should take place before his companions—"I was only joking."

"Good morning, Rainscourt," said one of his friends— "I'm afraid that I shall be *de trop.*"

"And I'm off too, my dear fellow, for there's no saying how the joke may be taken," added the other, following his companion out of the room.

Emily ran up to her father, and took his hand; and Rainscourt, who was as much attached to his daughter as his selfish character would permit, kissed her forehead.

Both parties were for a short time silent. Both preferred to await the attack, rather than commence it; but in a trial of forbearance of this description, it may easily be supposed that the gentleman gained the victory. Mrs Rainscourt waited until she found that she must either give vent to her feelings by words, or that her whole frame would explode; and the action commenced on her side with a shower of tears, which ended in violent hysterics.

The first were unheeded by her husband, who always considered them as a kind of scaling her guns previous to an engagement; but the hysterics rather baffled him. In his own house, he would have rung for the servants

and left them to repair damages; but at an hotel, an
éclat was to be avoided, if possible.

"Emily, my dear, go to your mother—you know how
to help her."

"No, I do not, papa," said the child, crying; "but
Norah used to open her hands."

Rainscourt's eyes were naturally directed to the fingers
of his wife, in which he perceived a collection of notes
and letters. He thought it might be advisable to open
her hand, if it were only to recover these out of her
possession. What affection would not have induced him
to do, interest accomplished. He advanced to the sofa,
and attempted to open her clenched hands; but whether
Mrs Rainscourt's hysterics were only feigned, or of such
violence as to defy the strength of her husband, all his
efforts to extract the letters proved ineffectual, and, after
several unavailing attempts, he desisted from his exertions.

"What else is good for her, Emily?"

"Water, papa, thrown in her face—shall I ring for
some?"

"No, my dear—is there nothing else we can do?"

"Oh, yes, papa, unlace her stays."

Rainscourt, who was not very expert as a lady's-maid,
had some difficulty in arriving at the stays through the
folds of the gown *et cetera*, the more so as Mrs Rainscourt
was very violent in her movements, and he was not a
little irritated by sundry pricks which he received from
those indispensable articles of dress, which the fair sex
are necessitated to use, pointing out to us that there are
no roses without thorns. When he did arrive at the
desired encasement, he was just as much puzzled to find
an end to what appeared, like the Gordian knot, to have
neither beginning nor end. Giving way to the natural
impatience of his temper, he seized a penknife from the
table, to divide it *á l'Alexander*. Unfortunately, in his
hurry, instead of inserting the knife on the inside of the
lace, so as to cut *to* him, he cut down upon it, and not
meeting with the resistance which he expected, the point

of the knife entered with no trifling force into the back
of Mrs Rainscourt, who to his astonishment, immediately
started on her legs, crying out, "Would you murder me,
Mr Rainscourt?—help, help!"

"It was quite accidental, my dear," said Rainscourt,
in a soothing tone, for he was afraid of her bringing the
whole house about her ears. "I really am quite shocked
at my own awkwardness."

"It quite recovered you though, mamma," observed
Emily, with great simplicity, and for which remark, to
her astonishment, she was saluted with a smart box on
the ear.

"Why should you be shocked, Mr Rainscourt?" said
the lady, who, as her daughter had remarked, seemed
wonderfully recovered from the phle-*back*-omy which had
been administered,—"why should you be shocked at
stabbing me in the back? Have I not wherewithal in my
hand to stab me a thousand times in the heart? Look at
these letters, all of which I have read! You had, indeed,
reason to leave me in Galway; but I will submit to it no
longer. Mr Rainscourt, I insist upon an immediate separation."

"Why should we quarrel, then, my dear, when we are
both of one mind? Now do me the favour to sit down,
and talk the matter over quietly. What is it that you
require?"

"First, then, Mr Rainscourt, an acknowledgment on
your part, that I am a most injured, and most ill-treated
woman."

"Granted, my dear, if that will add to your happiness.
I certainly have never known your value."

"Don't sneer, sir, if you please. Secondly, a handsome
allowance, commensurate with your fortune."

"Granted, with pleasure, Mrs Rainscourt."

"Thirdly, Mr Rainscourt, an extra allowance for the
education and expenses of my daughter, who will remain
under my care."

"Granted also."

" Further, Mr Rainscourt, to keep up appearances, I wish one of the mansions on your different estates in England to be appropriated for our use. Your daughter ought to be known, and reside on the property of which she is the future heiress."

" A reasonable demand, which I accede to. Is there anything further ? "

" Nothing of moment ; but, for Emily's sake, I should wish that you should pay us an occasional visit, and, generally speaking, keep up appearances before the world."

" That I shall be most happy to do, my dear, and shall always speak of you, as I feel, with respect and esteem. Is there anything more, Mrs Rainscourt ? "

" There is not ; but I believe that if I had been ten times more exorbitant in my demands," replied the lady, with pique, " that you would have granted them—for the pleasure of getting rid of me."

" I would, indeed, my dear," replied Rainscourt ; " you may command me in anything, except my own person."

" I require no *other* partition, sir, than that of your fortune."

" And of that, my dear, you shall, as I have declared, have a liberal share. So now, Mrs Rainscourt, I think we can have no further occasion for disagreement. The property in Norfolk, where Admiral De Courcy resided, is a beautiful spot, and I request you will consider it as your head-quarters. Of course you will be your own mistress when you feel inclined to change the scene. And now, as all may be considered as settled, let us shake hands, and henceforward be—good friends."

Mrs Rainscourt gave her hand, and sealed the new contract ; but, ill-treated as she had been,—at variance with her husband for years,—and now convinced that she had been outraged in the tenderest point, still her heart leaned towards the father of her child. The hand that now was extended in earnest of future separation, reminded her of the day when she had offered it in pledge of future fidelity and love, and had listened with rapture to his reciprocal obligation. She covered her face with her handkerchief, which was soon moistened with her tears.

Such is woman ! To the last moment she cherishes her love, pure as an emanation from the Deity. In the happy days of confidence and truth, it sheds a halo round her existence ;—in those of sorrow and desertion, memory, guided by its resistless power, like the gnomon of the dial, marks but those hours which were sunny and serene.

However, Mrs Rainscourt soon found out that an unlimited credit upon the banker was no bad substitute for a worthless husband; and assisted by her pride, she enjoyed more real happiness and peace of mind than she had done for many years. During her stay in London, Rainscourt occasionally paid his respects, behaved with great kindness and propriety, and appeared not a little proud of the expanding beauty of his daughter. Mrs Rainscourt not only recovered her spirits, but her personal attractions; and their numerous acquaintance wondered what could possess Mr Rainscourt to be indifferent to so lively and so charming a woman. In a few weeks the mansion was ready to receive them, and Mrs Rainscourt, with Emily, and a numerous establishment, quitted the metropolis, to take up their abode in it for the ensuing summer.

Chapter XXVI

Pericles.—That's your superstition.
Sailor.—Pardon us, sir. With us at sea it still hath been observed, and we are strong in earnest.

SHAKESPEARE.

THE weather was fine, and the water smooth, on the morning when the *Aspasia* arrived at the reef, which, although well known to exist, had been very incorrectly laid down ; and Captain M—— thought it advisable to drop his anchor, in preference to laying off and on so near to dangers which might extend much farther than he was aware. The frigate was, therefore, brought up in eighteen fathoms, about two miles from that part of the reef which discovered itself above water.

The captain and master undertook the survey; but any officers, who volunteered their assistance, or midshipmen, who wished to profit by the opportunity of gaining a practical knowledge of maritime surveying, were permitted to join the party, another boat having been lowered down for their accommodation. Hector, the captain's Newfoundland dog, was flying about the decks, mad with delight, as he always was when a boat was lowered down, as he anticipated the pleasure of a swim. Captain M——, who had breakfasted, and whose boat was manned alongside, came on deck; when the dog fawning on him, he desired that his broad leather collar, with the ship's name in large brass letters riveted round it, should be taken off, that it might not be injured by the salt water. Jerry, who was on deck, and received the order, asked the captain for the key of the padlock which secured it, and Captain M—— handed him his bunch of keys, to which it had been affixed, and desiring him to take the collar off, and return the keys to him, descended again to his cabin.

Jerry soon dispossessed the dog of his collar, and, ripe for mischief, went down to the midshipmen's berth, where he found Prose alone, the rest being all on deck, or scattered about the ship. Prose was the person that he wanted, being the only one upon whom he could venture a practical joke, without incurring more risk than was agreeable. Jerry commenced by fixing the collar round his own neck, and said "I wish I could get *promotion*. Now if the situation of *captain's dog* was only vacant, I should like the rating amazingly. I should soon get fat then, and I think I should look well up in this collar."

"Why, Jerry, that collar certainly does look as if it was made for you; it's rather ornamental, I do declare."

"I wish I had a glass, to see how it looks. I would

try it on you, Prose, but you've such a bull neck, that it wouldn't go half round it."

"Bull neck, Jerry—why, I'll lay you sixpence that my neck's almost as small as yours ; and I'll lay you a shilling that the collar will go round my neck."

"Done ; now let's see—recollect the staple must go into the hole, or you lose," said Jerry, fixing the collar round Prose's neck, and pretending that the staple was not into the hole of the collar until he had inserted the padlock, turned and taken out the key.

"Well I do declare I've lost, Prose. I must go and get you the shilling," continued Jerry, making his escape out of the berth, and leaving Prose with the collar so tight under his chin, that he could scarcely open his mouth. Jerry arrived on the quarter-deck just as the captain was stepping into the boat, and he went up to him, and touching his hat, presented him with the bunch of keys.

"Oh, thank you, Mr Jerry ; I had forgotten them," said Captain M——, descending the side, and shoving off.

"Whose clothes are these hanging on the davit-guys ? " said Mr Bully, who had given order that no clothes were to be drying there after eight o'clock in the morning.

"I believe that they are Mr Prose's, sir, though I am not sure," answered Jerry, who knew very well that they were not, but wished that Prose should be sent for.

"Quarter-master, tell Mr Prose to come up to me directly."

Jerry immediately ran down to the berth.

"Well, now, Jerry, this is too bad, I do declare. Come, take it off again, that's a good fellow."

"Mr Prose," said the quarter-master, "the first lieutenant wants you on deck directly."

"There, now, Jerry, what a mess I might have been in. Where's the key?"

"I have not got it," replied Jerry; "the captain saw me on the quarter-deck, and took the bunch of keys away with him.'

"What! is the captain gone away? I do declare now, this is too bad," cried Prose, in a rage.

"Too bad!—why, man, don't be angry—it's a distinction. Between me and the first lieutenant, you are created a knight of the *Grand Cross*. I gave you the *collar*, and he has given you the *order*, which I recommend you to comply with, without you wish further elevation to the mast-head."

"Mr Prose, the first lieutenant wants you immediately," said the quarter-master, who had been despatched to him again.

"Why, how can I go up with a dog's collar round my neck?"

"I'm sorry, very sorry indeed, Prose. Never mind—say it was me."

"Say it was you! Why so it was you. I'd better say that I'm sick."

"Yes, that will do. What shall your complaint be?—a *lockjaw*? I'll go up and tell Mr Bully—shall I?"

"Do—tell him I'm not well."

Jerry went up accordingly. "Mr Prose is not well, sir—he has a sort of lock-jaw."

"I wish to God you had the same complaint, sir," replied the first lieutenant, who owed him one. "Macallan, is Mr Prose ill?"

"Not that I know of; he has not applied to me. I'll go down and see him before I go on shore."

Macallan came up laughing, but he recovered his seriousness before Bully perceived it.

"Well, doctor."

"Mr Prose is certainly not very fit to come on deck in his present state," said Macallan, who then descended the side, and the boat, which had been waiting for him, shoved off. But, this time, Jerry was caught in his own trap.

"Mr J——, where is the dog's collar?—it must be oiled and cleaned," said the first lieutenant.

"Shall I give it to the armourer, sir?" replied Jerry.

" No, bring it up to me."

Jerry went down, and returned in a few minutes. "I cannot find it, sir; I left it in the berth when I came on deck."

"That's just like your usual carelessness, Mr J——. Now go up to the mast-head, and stay there till I call you down."

Jerry, who did not like the turn which the joke had taken, moved up with a very reluctant step—at the rate of about one rattling in ten seconds.

"Come, sir, what are you about ?—*start-up*."

"I'm no *up-start*, sir," replied Jerry to the first lieutenant—a sarcasm which hit so hard, that Jerry was not called down till dark; and long after Prose had, by making interest with the captain's steward, obtained the keys, and released his neck from its enthralment.

The party in the second boat were landed on the reef, and while the rest were attending to the survey, Macallan was employed in examining the crevices of the rocks, and collecting the different objects of natural history which presented themselves.

The boat was sent on board, as it was not required until the afternoon, when the gun-room officers were to return to dinner.

The captain's gig remained on shore, and the coxswain was employed by Macallan in receiving from him the different shells, and varieties of coral, with which the rocks were covered.

"Take particular care of this specimen," said the surgeon, as he delivered a bunch of corallines into the hands of Marshall, the coxswain.

"I ax your pardon, Mr Macallan,—but what's the good of picking up all this rubbish ?"

"Rubbish ?" replied the surgeon, laughing—"why you don't know what it is. What do you think those are which I just gave you ?"

"Why, weeds are rubbish, and these be only pieces of sea-weed."

" They happen to be *animals*."

" *Hanimals!* " cried the coxswain, with an incredulous smile; " well, sir, I always took 'em to be *weggittables*. We live and larn, sure enough. Are cabbage and *hingions hanimals* too ? "

" No," replied the surgeon, much amused, " they are not, Marshall ; but these are. Now take them to the boat, and put them in a safe place, and then come back."

" I say, Bill, look ye here," said the coxswain to one of the sailors, who was lying down on the thwarts of the boat, holding up the coral to him in a contemptuous manner— " what the hell d'ye think this is ? Why, it's a hanimal ! "

" A what ? "

" I'll be blowed if the doctor don't say it's a hanimal ! "

" No more a hanimal than I am." replied the sailor, laying his head down again on the thwarts, and shutting his eyes.

In a few minutes Marshall returned to the surgeon, who, tired with clambering over the rocks, was sitting down to rest himself a little. " Well, Marshall, I hope you have not hurt what I gave into your charge."

" Hurt 'em !—why, sir, a'ter what you told me, I'd as soon have hurt a cat."

" What, you are superstitious on that point, as seamen generally are."

" Super—what, Mr Macallan ? I only knows, that they who ill-treats a cat, comes worst off. I've proof positive of that since I have been in the service. I could spin you a yarn."

" Well, now, Marshall, pray do. Come, sit down here —I am fond of proof positive. Now, let me hear what you have to say, and I'll listen without interrupting you.

The coxswain took his seat as Macallan desired, and, taking the quid of tobacco out of his cheek, and laying it down on the rock beside him, commenced as follows :—

" Well now, d'ye see, Mr Macallan, I'll just exactly tell you how it was, and then I leaves you to judge whether a cat's to be sarved in that way. It was when

I belonged to the *Survellanty* frigate, that we were laying in Cawsand Bay, awaiting for sailing orders. We hadn't dropped the anchor more than a week, and there was no liberty ashore. Well, sir, the purser found out that his steward was a bit of a rascal, and turns him adrift. The ship's company knew that long afore ; for it was not a few that he had cheated, and we were all glad to see him and his traps handed down the side. Now, sir, this here fellow had a black cat—but it warn't at all like other cats. When it was a kitten, they had cut off his tail close to its starn, and his ears had been shaved off just as close to his figure-head, and the hanimal used to set up on his hind legs and fight like a rabbit. It had quite lost its natur, as it were, and looked, for all the world, like a little imp of darkness. It always lived in the purser's steward's room, and we never seed him but when we went down for the biscuit and flour as was sarving out.

" Well, sir, when this rascal of a steward leaves the ship, he had no natural affection for his cat, and he leaves him on board, belonging to nobody ; and the steward as comes in his place turns him out of the steward's room ; so the poor jury rigged little devil had to take care of itself.

" We all tried to coax it into one berth or the other, but the poor brute wouldn't take to nobody. You know, sir, a cat doesn't like to change, so he wandered about the ship, mewing all day, and thieving all night. At last, he takes to the master's cabin, and makes a dirt there, and the master gets very savage, and swears that he'll kill him, if ever he comes athwart him.

" Now, sir, you knows it's the natur of cats always to make a dirt in the same place,—reason why, God only knows ; and so this poor black devil always returns to the master's cabin, and makes it, as it were, his head-quarters. At last the master, who was as even-tempered an officer as ever I sailed with, finds one day that his sextant case is all of a smudge : so being touched in a sore place, he gets into a great rage, and orders all the boys of the ship to catch the cat; and after much ado, the poor cat was catched, and brought aft into the gun-room. 'Now, then, P——,' said the master to the first lieutenant, ' will you help kill the dirty beast?'—and the first lieutenant, who cared more about his lower deck being clean than fifty human beings' lives, said he would; so they called the sargent o' marines, and orders him to bring up two ship's muskets and some ball cartridge, and they goes on deck with the cat in their arms.

"Well, sir, when the men saw the cat brought up on deck, and hears that he was to be hove overboard, they all congregates together upon the lee gangway, and gives their opinions on the subject,—and one says, ' Let's go and speak to the first lieutenant;' and another says, ' He'll put you on the black list;' and so they don't do nothing —all except Jenkins, the boatswain's mate, who calls to a waterman out of the main-deck port, and says, ' Water-man,' says he, ' when they heaves that cat overboard, do you pick him up, and I'll give you a shilling;' and the waterman says as how he would, for you see, sir, the men didn't know that the muskets had been ordered up to shoot the poor beast.

"Well, sir, the waterman laid off on his oars, and the men, knowing what Jenkins had done, were content. But when the sargent o' marines comes up, and loads the muskets with ball cartridges, then the men begins to grumble; howsomever, the master throws the cat over-board off the lee-quarter, and the waterman, as soon as he sees her splash in the water, backs astarn to take her into the boat, but the first lieutenant tells him to get out of the way, if he doesn't want a bullet through his boat—so he pulls ahead again. The master fires first, and hits the cat a clip on the neck, which turns her half over, and the first lieutenant fires his musket, and cuts the poor hanimal right in half by the backbone, and she sprawls a bit, and then goes down to the bottom. ' Capital shots both,' says the first lieutenant : ' he'll never take an observation of your sextant again, master;' and they both laughs heartily, and goes down the ladder to get their dinner.

"Well, sir, I never seed a ship's company in such a farmant, or such a nitty kicked up 'tween decks, in my life : it was almost as bad as a mutiny; but they piped to grog soon a'ter, and the men goes to their berths and talks the matter over more coolly, and they all agrees that no good would come to the ship a'ter that, and very melancholy they were, and couldn't forget it.

"Well, sir, our sailing orders comes down the next day, and the first cutter is sent on shore for the captain, and six men out of ten leaves the boat, and I'm sure that it warn't for desartion, but all along of that cat being hove overboard and butchered in that way—for three on 'em were messmates of mine—for you know, sir, we talks them matters over, and if they had had a mind to quit the sarvice, I should have know'd it. The captain was as savage as a bear with a sore head, and did nothing but growl for three days afterwards, and it was well to keep clear on him, for he snapped right and left, like a mad dog. I never seed him in such a humour afore, except once when he had a fortnight's foul wind.

"Well, sir, we had been out a week, when we falls in with a large frigate, and beats to quarters. We expected her to be a Frenchman; but as soon as she comes within gunshot, she hoists the private signal, and proves to be the *Semiramus*, and our senior officer. The next morning, cruising together, we sees a vessel inshore, and the *Semiramus* stands in on the larboard tack, and orders us by signal to keep away, and prevent his running along the coast. The vessel, finding that she couldn't go no way, comes to anchor under a battery of two guns—and then the commodore makes the signal for boats manned and armed, to cut her out.

"Well, sir, our first lieutenant was in his cot, on his beam-ends, with the rheumatiz, and couldn't go on sarvice ; so the second and third lieutenants, and master, and one of the midshipmen, had command of our four boats, and the commodore sent seven of his'n. The boats pulled in, and carried the vessel in good style, and there never was a man hurt. As many boats as could clap on her took her in tow, and out she came at the rate of four knots an hour. I was coxswain of the pinnace, which was under the charge of the master, and we were pulling on board, as all the boats weren't wanted to tow—and we were about three cables' length ahead of the vessel, when I sees her aground upon a rock, that nobody knows nothing about, on the starboard side of the entrance of the harbour; and I said that she were grounded to the master, who orders us to pull back to the vessel to assist 'em in getting her off again.

" Well, sir, we gets alongside of her, and finds that she was off again, having only grazed the rock, and the boats towed her out again with a rally. Now the Frenchmen were firing at us with muskets, for we had shut in the battery, and as we were almost out of the musket-shot, the balls only pitted in the water, without doing any harm —and I was a-standing with the master on the starn-sheets, my body being just between him and the beach where they were a-firing from. It seemed mortally impossible to hit him, except through me. Howsomever, a bullet passes between my arm—just here, and my side, and striked him dead upon the spot. There warn't another man hit out of nine boat's crews, and I'll leave you to guess whether the sailors didn't declare that he got his death all along of murdering the cat.

" Well, sir, the men thought, as he had *fired first*, that now all was over; only Jenkins, the boatswain's mate, said, ' That he warn't quite sure of that.' We parts company with the commodore the next day, and the day a'ter, as it turned out, we falls in with a French frigate. She had the heels of us, and kept us at long balls, but we hoped to cut her off from running into Brest, if a slant o' wind favoured us—and obligating her to fight, whether or no. Tom Collins, the first lieutenant, was still laid up in his cot with the rheumatiks, but when he hears of a French frigate, he gets up, and goes on deck; but when he gets there he tips us a faint, and falls down on the carronade slide, and his hat rolled off his head into the waist. He tried, but he was so weak that he couldn't get up on his sticks again.

"Well, sir, the captain goes up to him, and says something about zeal and all that, and tells him he must go down below again because he's quite incapable, and orders the men at the foremost carronades to take him to his cot. Now, sir, just as we were handing him down the ladder, for I was captain of the gun, a shot comes in at the second port and takes off his skull as he lays in our arms, and never hurts another man. He was dead in no time; and what was more cur'ous, it was the only shot that hit the frigate. The Frenchman got into Brest—so it was no action after all.

"So, you see, Mr Macallan, in two *scrummages* only two men were killed out of hundreds, and they were the two who had killed the cat! Now, that's what I calls proof positive, for I seed it all with my own eyes; and I should like to know whether you could do the same, with regard to that thing being a *hanimal?*"

"I will, Marshall; to-morrow you shall see that with your own eyes."

"To-morrow come never!"* muttered the coxswain, replacing the quid of tobacco in his cheek.

Chapter XXVII

And, lo! while he was expounding, in set terms, the most abstruse of his pious doctrines, the head of the tub whereon the good man stood gave way, and the preacher was lost from before the eyes of the whole congregation.
Life of the Rev. Mr Smith, S.S.

SEYMOUR, who was always the companion of Captain M——, whenever either instruction or amusement was to

---

* The phraseology of sailors has been so caricatured of late, that I am afraid my story will be considered as translated into English. Seamen, however, must decide which is correct.

be gained, now quitted the surveying party to join Macallan, who still continued seated on the rocks, reflecting upon the remarkable coincidence which the coxswain had narrated, sufficient in itself to confirm the superstitious ideas of the sailors for another century. His thoughts naturally reverted to the other point, in which sea-faring men are equally bigoted, the disastrous consequences of " sailing on a Friday ; " the origin of which superstition can easily be traced to early Catholicism, when out of respect for the day of universal redemption, they were directed by their pastors to await the " morrow's sun." " Thus," mentally exclaimed Macallan, " has religion degenerated into superstition ; and that which, from the purity of its origin, would have commanded our respect, is now only deserving of our contempt. It is by the motives that have produced them, that our actions must be weighed. That which once was an offering of religious veneration and love, is now a tribute to superstition and to fear. " Well, Seymour," said he, addressing his companion, " how do you like sur- veying ? "

" Not much ; the sun is hot, and the glare so powerful that I am almost blind. What a pity it is that we had not some trees here, to shade us from the heat. I should like to plant some for the benefit of those who may come after us."

" A correct feeling on your part, my boy ; but no trees would grow here at present—there is no soil."

" There is plenty of some sort or other, in the part where we have been surveying."

" Yes, the sand thrown up by the sea, and the particles of shells and rock, which have been triturated by the wave, or decomposed by the alternate action of the elements ; but there is no vegetable matter, without which there can be no vegetable produce. Observe, Willy—the skeleton of this earth is framed of rocks and mountains, which have been proudly rearing their heads into the clouds, or lying in dark majesty beneath the seas, since the creation of the world, when they were fixed by the Almighty architect, to remain till time shall be no more.   Over them, we find the wrecks of a former world—once as beautiful, as thickly peopled but more thoughtless and more wicked than the present—which was hurled into one general chaos, and its component, but incongruous parts, amalgamated in awful mockery by the deluge—that tremendous evidence of the wrath of Heaven.   But it has long passed away ; and o'er the relics of former creation, o'er the kneaded mass of man in his pride, of woman in her beauty, of arts in their splendour, of vice in her zenith, and of virtue in her tomb, we are standing upon another, teeming with life, and yielding forth her fruits in due season as before.   But, Willy, the supports of life are not to be found in primeval rocks or antediluvial remains.   It is from the superficial covering, the thin crust with which the earth is covered, composed of the remains of former existence, of the brescia of exhausted nature, that animal creation derives its support ; and it is the grand axiom of the universe, that *animal life can only be supported by animal remains*.   From the meanest insect that crawls upon the ground, to man in his perfection, life is supported and continued by animal and vegetable food ; and it is only the decayed matter returned to the earth, which enables the lofty cedar to extend its boughs, or the lowly violet to exhale its perfume.   This is a world of eternal reproduction and decay—one endless cycle of the living preying on the dead—a phœnix, yearly, daily, and hourly springing from its ashes, in renewed strength and beauty.   The blade of grass, which shoots from the soil, flowers, casts its seed, and dies, to make room for its off-spring, nourished by the relics of its parent, is a type of the never-changing law, controlling all nature, even to man himself, who must pass away to make room for the generation which is to come."

The boat, which, returning from the ship, appeared like a black speck on the water, indicated that the dinner hour was at hand ; and Price and the purser, who had come on shore with Macallan, now joined him and Willy, who were sitting down on the rocks at the water's edge.

" Well, Macallan," said Price, " it's a fine thing to be a philosopher. What is that which Milton says? Let me see !—sweet—something—divine philosophy—I forget the exact words. Well, what have you caught?"

" If you've caught nothing, doctor, you're better off than I am," said the purser, wiping his brow, " for I've caught a head-ache."

"I have been very well amused," replied Macallan.

" Ay, I suppose, like what's-his-name in the forest—you recollect ? "

" No, indeed I do not."

"Don't you? Bless my soul—you know, sermons in stones, and good in everything. I forget how the lines run. Don't you recollect, O'Keefe?" continued Price, speaking loud in the purser's ear.

" No, I never *collect*. I don't understand these things," replied the purser, taking his seat by Macallan, and addressing him—" I cannot think what pleasure there can be in poking about the rocks as you do."

" It serves to amuse me, O'Keefe."

" *Abuse* you, my dear fellow ! Indeed I never meant it —I beg your pardon—you mistook me."

"It was my fault. I did not speak sufficiently loud. Make no apology."

" Too *proud* to make an apology !—No, indeed—I only asked what amusement you could find ?—that's all."

"What amusement ?" replied Macallan, rising from his seat, annoyed at these repeated attacks from all quarters upon his favourite study. " Listen to me, and I will explain to you how investigation is the parent of both amusement and instruction. What is this rock that I am standing on? Has it remained here for ages to be dashed by the furious ocean ?—or has it lately sprung from the depths, from the silent labour of the indefatigable zoophites ? Look at its sides, behold the variety of marine vegetation with which it is loaded. Are they of the class of the ulvæ, confervæ, or fuci ?—to be welcomed as old acquaintance, or, hitherto unnoticed, to be added to the catalogue of

Nature's endless stores? And what are those corals, that, like mimic tenants of the forest, extend their graceful boughs? Look at the variety of shells which are adhering to its sides. Observe the patellæ—with what tenacity they cling to save themselves from being washed into the deep water, and being devoured by the fishes that are playing in its chasms! What a source of endless amusement, what a field for deep reflection, is there in the investigation of this *one little rock!* When you contemplate the instinct of the different species, the powers given to them, so adapted to their wants and their privations—is not the eye delighted, is not the mind enlarged, and are not the feelings harmonised? Study the works of the creation, and you turn a desert into a peopled city—a barren rock into a source of admiration and delight. Nay, search into Nature for a few minutes, and you rise a better man. Dive into——"

What the conclusion of the doctor's rhapsody may have been, is not known; for, stamping too energetically upon the sea-weed on the edge of the rock, his foot slipped, and he disappeared, with the perpendicular descent and velocity of a deep sea lead, into the water alongside of it.

Marshall, the coxswain, who had been astonished at his speech, to which he had listened with mouth open for want of comprehension, quite forgot the respect due to an officer, at his unexpected finale.

"Watch there, watch!" cried the man, and then threw himself down, and rolled in convulsions of laughter. Price and Willy, whose mirth was almost as excessive, did however run to his assistance, and caught him by the collar as he rose again to the surface, for it was considerably out of his depth; while the deaf purser, whose eyes had been fixed on the ground, in deep attention to catch the doctor's word, and whose ears were not sufficiently acute to hear the splash, looked up as they were going to his assistance, and asked, with surprise, "Where's the doctor?"

The sides of the rock were so slippery, that the united efforts of Price and Seymour (whose powers were much

enfeebled from extreme mirth) were not sufficient to haul
Macallan upon *terra firma*. "Marshall, come here directly,
sir, and help us," cried Willy,—an order which the coxswain, who was sufficiently recovered, immediately obeyed.

"Give me your hand, Mr Macallan," said the man, as
the surgeon was clinging to the sea-weed; "it's no use
holding on by them slippery *hanimals*. Now then, Mr
Price—all together."

"Ay, and as soon as you please," called out the malicious
boat-keeper of the gig—"I seed a large shark but a
minute ago."

"Quick—quick!" roared the surgeon, who already
imagined his leg encircled by the teeth of the ravenous
animal.

By their united efforts, Macallan was at last safely
landed—and, after much sputtering, blowing, and puffing,
was about to address the coxswain in no very amicable
manner, when the purser interrupted him.

"By the powers, doctor, but you took the right way
to have a close examination of all those fine things which
you were giving us a catalogue of; but now give us the
remainder of your speech—you gave us a practical illustra-
tion of diving."

"What sort of sensation was it, doctor?" said Price.
"You recollect Shakespeare—and 'O, methinks what
pain it was to drown'—Let me see—something——"

"Pray don't tax your memory, Price; it's something
like our country,—past all further taxation."

"That's the severest thing you've said since we've
sailed together. You're out of humour, doctor. Well,
you know what Shakespeare says: 'There never yet was
found a philosopher'—something about the toothache.
I forget the words."

These attacks did not at all tend to restore the equanimity
of the doctor's temper, which, it must be acknowledged,
had some excuse for being disturbed by the events of the
morning; but he proved himself a wise man, for he made
no further reply. The boat pulled in, and the party

returned on board; and when Macallan had divested himself of his uncomfortable attire, and joined his messmates at the dinner table, he had recovered his usual serenity of disposition, and joined himself in the laugh which had been created at his expense.

Chapter XXVIII

A man must serve his time to every trade
Save censure,—critics all are ready made.
Take hacknied jokes from Miller, got by rote,
With just enough of learning to misquote;
A mind well skill'd to find or forge a fault,
A turn for punning—call it Attic salt:
Fear not to lie, 'twill seem a lucky hit,
Shrink not from blasphemy, 'twill pass for wit;
Care not for feeling,—pass your proper jest,
And stand a critic! hated, yet caress'd.

BYRON.

THE survey was continued. One morning, after a fatiguing walk from point to point, occasionally crossing from one islet to the others in the boats, the party collected under a projecting rock, which screened them from the rays of the vertical sun, and the repast, which had been brought from the ship in the morning, was spread before them. The party consisted of Captain M——; Pearce, the master; the surgeon, who had accompanied them to explore the natural productions of the reef; and the confidential clerk of Captain M——, a man of the name of Collier, who had been many years in his service, and who was now employed in noting down the angles taken with the theodolite.

Tired with the labours of the morning, Captain M—— did not rise immediately after their meal had been despatched, but entered into conversation with the surgeon, who was looking over the memoranda which he had made relative to the natural history of the reef.

" Do you intend to write a book, Mr Macallan, that you have collected so many remarks ? "

" Indeed I do not, sir. I have no ambition to be an author."

The clerk, who was very taciturn in general, and seldom spoke unless on points connected with his duty, joined the conversation by addressing the surgeon.

" It's a service of danger, sir, and you must be prepared to meet the attacks both of authors and reviewers."

" Of reviewers I can imagine," replied Macallan ; " but why of authors ? "

" That depends very much whether you tread over beaten ground, or strike into a new path. In the latter case you will be pretty safe from both, as the authors will be *indifferent*, and the reviewers, in all probability, *incapable*."

" And why, if I enter upon a beaten track, which, I presume, infers a style of writing in which others have preceded me ? "

" Because, sir, when a new author makes his appearance, he is much in the same situation as a strange dog entering a kennel pre-occupied by many others. He is immediately attacked and worried by the rest, until, either by boldly defending himself, or pertinaciously refusing to quit, he eventually obtains a domiciliation, and becomes an acknowledged member of the fraternity."

" Why, Mr Collier," observed the captain, " you seem to be quite *au fait* as to literary arrangements."

" I ought to be, sir," replied the clerk, " for in the course of my life, I have attempted to become an author, and practised as a reviewer."

" Indeed ! And did you fail in your attempt at authorship ? "

" My work was never printed, sir, for no bookseller would undertake to publish it. I tried the whole town ; no man would give himself the trouble to look over the MS. It was said that the public taste was not that way, and that it would not do. At last I received a letter of

introduction from an old acquaintance to his nncle, who
was a literary character.　He certainly did read some parts
of my performance."

" And what then ? "

" Why, sir, he shook his head—told me with a sneer
that, as an author, I should never succeed ; but, he added,
with a sort of encouraging smile, that, from some parts of
the MS. which he had perused, he thought that he could
find employment for me in the reviewing line, if I chose
to undertake it.

" My pride was hurt, and I answered that I could not
agree with him, as I considered that it required the ability
to write a book yourself, to enable you to decide upon the
merits of others."

" Well, I must say that I agree with you," replied the
captain.　" Proceed in your story, for I am interested."

" My friend answered,—' By no means, my dear sir ; a
d——d bad author generally makes a *very good reviewer*.
Indeed, sir, to be candid with you, I never allow any
gentleman to review for me, unless he has met with a misfortune similar to yours.　It is one of the necessary
qualifications of a good reviewer that he should have failed
as an author ; for without the exacerbated feelings arising
from disappointment, he would not possess gall sufficient
for his task, and his conscience would stand in his way
when he was writing against it, if he were not spurred on
by the keen probes of envy.' "

" And he convinced you ? "

" My poverty did, sir, if he did not.　I worked many
months for him ; but I had better have earned my bread
as a common labourer."

" Reviews ought to pay well, too," observed Macallan ;
" they are periodicals in great demand."

" They are so," replied Captain M——; " and the
reasons are obvious.　Few people take the trouble to think
for themselves ; but, on the contrary, are very glad to find
others who will think for them.　Some cannot find time to
read—others will not find it.　A review removes all these

difficulties—gives the busy world an insight into what is going on in the literary world—and enables the lounger not to appear wholly ignorant of a work, the merits of which may happen to be discussed. But what is the consequence? That seven-eighths of the town are led by the nose by this or that periodical work, having wholly lost sight of the fact, that reviews are far from being gospel. Indeed, I do not know any set of men so likely to err as reviewers. In the first place, there is no class of people so irascible, so full of party feeling, so disgraced by envy, as authors : hatred, malice, and all uncharitableness seem to preside over science. Their political opinions step in, and increase the undue preponderance ; and, to crown all, they are more influenced by money, being proverbially more in want of it than others. How, then, is it to be expected that reviews can be impartial? I seldom read them myself, as I consider that it is better to know nothing than to be misled."

" And, if it is a fair question, Mr Collier," continued Captain M——, " in what manner were you employed?"

" I am almost ashamed to tell you, sir—I was a mere automaton, a machine, in the hands of others. A new publication was sent to me, with a private mark from my employer, directing the quantum of praise or censure which it was to incur. If the former were allotted to it, the best passages were selected ; if condemned to the latter, all the worst. The connecting parts of review were made up from a common-place book, in which, by turning to any subject, you found the general heads and extracts from the work of others, which you were directed to alter, so as to retain the ideas, but disguise the style, that it might appear original."

" Are you aware of the grounds of praise or abuse ?— for it appears that those who directed the censure did not read the publications."

" The grounds were various. Books printed by a bookseller, to whom my master had a dislike, were sure to be run down ; on the contrary, those published by his connections or friends were as much applauded.   Moreover, the influence of authors, who were afraid of a successful rival in their own line, often d——d a work."

" But you do not mean to say that all reviews are conducted with such want of principle ? "

" By no means.   There are many very impartial and clever critiques.   The misfortune is, that unless you read the work that is reviewed, you cannot distinguish one from the other."

" And pray what induced you to abandon this creditable employment ?"

" A quarrel, sir.   I had reviewed a work, with the private mark of approval, when it was found out to be a mistake, and I was desired to review it with censure.   I expected to be paid for the second review as well as for the first.   My employer thought proper to consider it all as one job, and refused—so we parted."

" Pretty tricks in trade, indeed!" replied Captain M——. " Why, Mr Collier, you appear to have belonged to a gang of literary bravos, whose pens, like stilettoes, were always ready to stab, in the dark, the unfortunate individuals who might be pointed out to them by interest or revenge."

" I acknowledge the justice of your remark, sir ; all that I can offer in my defence is, the excuse of the libeller to Cardinal Richelieu—' Il faut vivre, monsieur.'"

" And I answer you, with the cardinal—' Je ne vois pas la nécessité,'" replied Captain M——, with a smile, as he rose to resume his labours.

Chapter XXIX

He fell, and, deadly pale,
Groan'd out his soul.

MILTON.

" Do, mamma, come here," said Emily, as she was looking out of the window of an inn on the road, where they had stopped to take some refreshment—" do come, and see what a pretty lady is in the chariot which has stopped at the door."

Mrs Rainscourt complied with her daughter's request, and acknowledged the justice of the remark when she saw the expressive countenance of Susan (now Mrs M'Elvina), who was listening to the proposal of her husband that they should alight and partake of some refreshment. Susan consented, and was followed by old Hornblow, who, pulling out his watch from his white cassimere *femoralia*, which he had continued to wear ever since the day of the wedding, declared that they must stop to dine.

"This country air makes one confoundedly hungry," said the old man; "I declare I never had such an appetite in Cateaton Street. Susan, my dear, order something that won't take long in cooking—a beef-steak, if they have nothing down at the fire."

Mrs Rainscourt, who was as much prepossessed with the appearance of M'Elvina as with that of his wife, gave vent to her thoughts with "I wonder who they are!" Her maid, who was in the room, took this as a hint to obtain the gratification of her mistress's curiosity as well as her own, and proceeded accordingly on her voyage of discovery. In a few minutes she returned, having boarded the Abigail of Mrs M'Elvina just as she was coming to an anchor inside the bar; and, having made an interchange of intelligence, with a rapidity incredible to those who are not aware of the velocity of communication between this description of people, re-entered the parlour, to make a report to her commanding officer, precisely at the same moment that Susan's maid was delivering her cargo of intelligence to her own mistress.

"They are a new married couple, ma'am, and their name is M'Elvina," said the one.

"The lady is a Mrs Rainscourt, and the young lady is her daughter, and a great heiress," whispered the other.

"They have purchased the hunting box close to the —— Hall, and are going there now," said the first.

"They live at the great park, close to where you are going, ma'am," said the second.

"The old gentleman's name is Hornblow. He is the lady's father, and as rich as a Jew, they say," continued Mrs Rainscourt's maid.

"Mrs Rainscourt don't live with her husband, ma'am; by all accounts he's a bad 'un," continued the Abigail of Susan.

The publicity of the staircase of an hotel is very convenient for making an acquaintance; and it happened that, just after these communications had been made, Emily was ascending the stairs as Mrs M'Elvina was going down to join her husband and father at the dinner table. The smiling face and beaming eyes of Emily, who evidently lingered to be spoken to, were so engaging that she soon found her way into the room which the M'Elvinas were occupying.

Mrs Rainscourt was not sorry to find that she was to have for neighbours a couple whose appearance had so prepossessed her in their favour. As she expected that her society would be rather confined, she did not suffer to escape the favourable opportunity which presented itself of making their acquaintance. As they were returning to their vehicles, Emily ran to Mrs M'Elvina to wish her good-bye, and Mrs Rainscourt expressed her thanks for the notice they had taken of her daughter. A few minutes' conversation ended in "hoping to have the pleasure of making their acquaintance as soon as they were settled."

The carriages drove off, and we shall follow that of the M'Elvinas, which arrived at its destination late in the evening, without any accident.

The cottage-orné (as all middle-sized houses with verandas and French windows are now designated), which Hornblow had purchased, was, for a wonder, quite as complete as described in the particulars of sale. It had the sloping lawn in front; the three acres (more or less) of plantation and pleasure ground, tastefully laid out, and planted with thriving young trees; the capital walled gardens, stocked with the choicest fruit trees, in full bearing; abundant springs of the finest water; stabling for six horses; cow-house, cart-house, farm-yard, and *complete piggery*. The dimensions of the conservatory, and rooms in the interior of the house were quite correct; and the land attached to it was according to the "accompanying plan," and divided into parcels, designated by the rural terms of "Homestead," "Lob's-pound," "Eight-acre meadow," "Little-orchard field," etc. etc.

In short, it was a very eligible purchase, and a very pretty and retired domicile; and when our party arrived, the flowers seemed to yield a more grateful perfume, the trees appeared more umbrageous, and the verdure of the meadows of a more refreshing green, from the contrast with so many hours' travelling upon a dusty road, during a sultry day.

"Oh, how beautiful these roses are! Do look, my dear father."

"They are indeed," replied old Hornblow, delighted at the happy face of his daughter;—"but I should like some tea, Susan—I am not used to so much jumbling. I feel tired, and shall go to bed early."

Tea was accordingly prepared; soon after which, the old gentleman rose to retire.

"Well," said he, as he lighted his chamber candle, "I suppose I am settled here for life; but I hardly know what to do with myself. I must make acquaintance with all the flowers and all the trees: the budding of the spring will make me think of grandchildren; the tree, clothed in its beauty, of you; and the fall of the leaf, of myself. I must count the poultry, and look after the pigs, and see the cows milked. I was fond of the little parlour in Cateaton Street, because I had sat in it so long; and I suppose that I shall get fond of this place too, if I find enough to employ and amuse me. But you must be quick and give me a grandchild, Susan, and then I shall nurse him all day long. Good-night — God bless you, my dear, good-night."

"Good-night, my dear sir," replied Susan, who had coloured deeply at the request which he had made.

"Good-night, M'Elvina, my boy; this is the first night we pass under this roof; may we live many happy years in it;" and old Hornblow left the room, and ascended the stairs.

M'Elvina had encircled Susan's waist with his arm, and was probably about to utter some wish in unison with that of her father's, when the noise of a heavy fall sounded in their ears.

"Good Heaven!" cried Susan, "it is my father who has fallen down stairs."

M'Elvina rushed out; it was but too true. The stair-carpet had not yet been laid down, and his foot had slipped at the uppermost step. He was taken up senseless, and when medical advice was procured, his head and his spine were found to be seriously injured. In a few days, during which he never spoke, old Hornblow was no more.

Thus the old man, like the prophet of old, after all his toiling, was but permitted to see the promised land; and thus are our days cut short at the very moment of realising our most sanguine expectations.

Reader, let us look at home. Shall I, now thoughtlessly riding upon the agitated billow, with but one thin plank between me and death, and yet so busy with this futile work, be permitted to bring it to a close? The hand which guides the flowing pen may to-morrow be stiff, the head now teeming with its subject may be past all thought ere to-morrow's sun is set—ay, sooner! And you, reader, who may so far have had the courage to proceed in the volumes without throwing them away, shall you be permitted to finish your more trifling task?—or, before its close, be hurried from this transitory scene, where fiction ends, and the spirit, re-endowed, will be enabled to raise its eyes upon the lightning beams of unveiled truth?

Chapter XXX

And if you chance his shipp to borde,
This counsel I must give withall.
Ballad of Sir Andrew Barton, 1550.

Discretion
And hardy valour are the twins of honour,
And, nursed together, make a conqueror;
Divided, but a talker.
BEAUMONT *and* FLETCHER.

THE survey having been completed, Captain M——, in pursuance of the orders which he had received, weighed his anchor, and proceeded to cruise until the want of provisions and water should compel him to return into port. For many days the look-out men at the mast-heads were disappointed in their hopes of reporting a strange sail, the chase or capture of which would relieve the monotony of constant sky and water, until, one Sunday forenoon, as Captain M—— was performing divine service, the man at the mast-head hailed the deck with "A strange sail on the weather-bow!"

The puritan may be shocked to hear that the service was speedily, although decorously closed; but Captain M—— was aware, from the fidgetting of the ship's company upon the capstan bars, on which they were seated, that it would be impossible to regain their attention to the service, even if he had felt inclined to proceed; and he well knew, that any worship of God in which the mind and heart were not engaged, was but an idle ceremony, if not a solemn mockery. The hands were turned up— all sail was made—and in an hour, the stranger was to be seen with the naked eye from the fore-yard.

"What do you make of her, Mr Stewart?" said the first lieutenant to him, as he sat aloft with his glass directed towards the vessel.

"A merchant ship, sir, in ballast."

"What did he say, Jerry?" inquired Prose, who stood by him on the gangway.

K. I.   O

"A French vessel, deeply laden, Prose."

"Bravo, Jerry!" said Prose, rubbing his hands. "We shall get some prize-money, I do declare."

"To be sure we shall. It will give us twenty pounds at least for a midshipman's share, for her cargo must be sugar and coffee. Only, confound it, one has to wait so long for it. I'll sell mine, dog-cheap, if anyone will buy it. Will you, Prose?"

"Why, Jerry, I don't much like speculation; but, now, what would you really sell your chance for?"

"I'll take ten pounds for it. We're certain to come up with her."

"Ten pounds! No, Jerry, that is too much. I'll tell you what, I'll give you five pounds."

"Done," replied Jerry, who was aware that a vessel in ballast would not give him thirty shillings, if Captain M—— sent her in, which was very unlikely. "Where's the money?"

"Oh, you must trust to my honour; the first port we go into, I pledge you my word that you shall have it."

"I don't doubt your word, or your honour, the least, Prose; but still I should like to have the money in my hand. Could you not borrow it? Never mind—it's a bargain."

In two hours the frigate had neared the stranger so as to distinguish her water-line from the deck, and, on hoisting her ensign and pendant, the vessel bore down to her.

"She has hoisted English colours, sir," reported Stewart to the captain.

"What, Stewart! did you say that she had hoisted English colours?" inquired Prose, with an anxious face.

"Yes, you booby, I did."

"Well, now, I do declare," cried Prose, with dismay, "If I haven't lost five pounds."

The vessel ran under the stern of the frigate, and requested a boat to be sent on board, as she had intelligence to communicate. The boat returned, and acquainted

Captain M—— that the vessel had been boarded and plundered by a French privateer schooner, which had committed great depredation in that quarter, and that it was not above eight hours that she had left her, and made sail towards Porto Rico, taking out two merchants, who were passengers.

The boat was immediately hoisted up, and all sail made, in the direction of the island, which was not above fifteen leagues distant. As the day closed in, their eyes were gratified by the sight of the schooner, becalmed close in under the land. Perceiving the frigate in pursuit of her, and unable to escape, she came to an anchor in a small and shallow bay, within a cable's length of the beach. Captain M——, having run his ship as close in as the depth of water would permit, which was between two or three miles of her, so as to render her escape impossible, came to an anchor, signifying to his officers his determination to cut her out with his boats on the ensuing day.

The officers who were to be entrusted with the command of the boats, and the crews which were to be employed on the service, were selected, and mustered on the quarter-deck, previous to the hammocks being piped down, that the former might hold themselves in readiness, and that the latter might remain in their hammocks during the night. All was anxiety for the sun to rise again upon those who were about to venture in the lottery, where the prizes would be honour, and the blanks—death.

There were but few whose souls were of that decided brute composition that they could sleep through the whole of the tedious night. They woke and " swore a prayer or two, then slept again." The sun had not yet made his appearance above the horizon, although the eastern blush announced that the spinning earth would shortly whirl the *Aspasia* into his presence, when the pipes of the boatswain and his mates, with the summons of " All hands ahoy—up all hammocks ! " were obeyed with the alacrity so characteristic of English seamen, anticipating danger.

The hammocks were soon stowed, and the hands turned up. "Out boats!" The yard tackles and stays were hooked, and the larger boats from the booms descended with a heavy splash into the water, which they threw out on each side of them as they displaced it with their weight; while the cutters from the quarter-davits were already lowered down, and were being manned under the chains.

Broad daylight discovered the privateer, who, aware of their intentions, had employed the night in taking every precaution that skill could suggest to repel the expected attack. Secured with cables and hawsers, extending from each bow and quarter—her starboard broadside directed to seaward—her boarding netting triced up to the lower rigging—and booms, connected together, rigged out from the sides, to prevent them from laying her on board. There was no wind; the sea was smooth as glass; and the French colours, hoisted in defiance at each mast-head, hung listlessly down the spars, as if fainting for the beeeze which would expand them in their vigour. She was pierced for eight ports on a side; and the guns, which pointed through them, with the tompions out, ready to shower destruction upon her assailants, showed like the teeth of the snarling wolf, who stands at bay, awaiting the attack of his undaunted pursuers.

The boats had received their guns, which were fixed on slides, so as to enable them to be fired over the bows, without impeding the use of the oars; the ammunition and arm-chests had been placed in security abaft.

The sailors, with their cutlasses belted round their waists, and a pistol stuck in their girdles, or in a becket at the side of the boat, ready to their hands—the marines, in proportion to the number which each boat could carry, sitting in the stern-sheets, with their muskets between their legs, and their well pipeclayed belts for bayonet and cartouch box crossed over their old jackets, half dirt, half finery—all was ready for shoving off, when Captain M—— desired the officers whom he had appointed to the expedition to step down into his cabin. Bully, the first

lieutenant, was unwell, with an intermittent fever, and
Captain M——, at the request of Macallan, would not
accede to his anxiety to take the command.   Price,
Courtenay, Stewart, and three other midshipmen, were
those who had been selected for the dangerous service.

"Gentlemen," said Captain M——, as they stood round
the table in the fore cabin, waiting for his communication,
"I must call your attention to a few points, which it is my
wish that you should bear in remembrance, now that you
are about to proceed upon what will, in all likelihood,
prove to be an arduous service.   This vessel has already
done so much mischief, that I conceive it my duty to
capture her if possible : and although there is no service in
which, generally speaking, there is so great a sacrifice of
life, in proportion to the object to be obtained, as that
which is generally termed 'cutting out,' yet, rather than
she should escape, to the further injury of our trade,
I have determined to have recourse to the measure.

"But, gentlemen (and to you, Mr Price, as commanding
the expedition, I particularly address myself), recollect
that, even in this extreme case, without proper arrangement, we may not only purchase our victory too dear, but
may even sacrifice a number of lives without succeeding
in our attempt.   Of your courage I have not the least
doubt; but let it be remembered, that it is something
more than mere animal courage which I expect in the
behaviour of my officers.   If nothing more were required,
the command of these boats might be as safely entrusted
to any of the foremast men, who, like the bulldogs of our
country, will thrust their heads into the lion's jaw with
perfect indifference.

"What I require, and expect, and will have, from every
officer who looks for promotion from my recommendation,
is what I term—conduct : by which I would imply, that
coolness and presence of mind which enable him to
calculate chances in the midst of danger—to take advantage
of a favourable opportunity in the heat of an engagement
—and to restrain the impetuosity of those who have fallen

into the dangerous error of despising their enemy. Of such conduct the most favourable construction that can be put upon it is, that it is only preferable to indecision.

"In a service of this description, even with the greatest courage and prudence united, some loss must necessarily be expected to take place, and there is no providing against unforeseen accidents; but if I find that, by rash and injudicious behaviour, a greater sacrifice is made than there is a necessity for, depend upon it that I shall not fail to let that officer know the high value at which I estimate the life of a British sailor. With this caution I shall now give you my ideas as to what appears the most eligible plan of insuring success. I have made a rough sketch on this paper, which will assist my explanation."

Captain M—— then entered into the plan of attack, pointing out the precautions which should be taken, etc.; and concluded by observing, that they were by no means to consider themselves as fettered by what he had proposed, but merely to regard them as hints to guide their conduct, if found preferable to any others which might be suggested by the peculiarity of the service, and the measures adopted by the enemy. The officers returned on deck, and descended into their respective boats, where they found many of the younger midshipmen, who, although not selected for the service, had smuggled themselves into the boats, that they might be participators in the conflict. Captain M——, although he did not send them on the service, had no objection to their going, and therefore pretended not to see them when he looked over the side, and desired the boats to shove off. Directly the order was given, the remainder of the ship's company mounted the rigging, and saluted them with three cheers.

The boats' crews tossed their oars while the cheers were given, and returned the same number. The oars again descended into the water, and the armament pulled in for the shore.

Chapter XXXI

Conquest pursues, where courage leads the way.
GARTH.

THE glasses of Captain M——, and of the officers who remained on board of the frigate, were anxiously pointed towards the boats, which in less than half an hour had arrived within gun-shot of the privateer. "There is a gun from her," cried several of the men at the same moment, as the smoke boomed along the smooth water.

The shot dashed up the spray under the bows of the boats, and *ricochetting* over them, disappeared in the wave, about half a mile astern.

The boats, which, previously, had been pulling in all together, and without any particular order, now separated, and formed a line abreast, so that there was less chance of the shot taking effect, than where they were before, *en masse*.

"Very good, Mr Price," observed the captain, who had his eye fixed on them, through his glass.

The boats continued their advance towards the enemy, who fired her two long guns, both of which she had brought over to her starboard side, but, though well directed, the shot did not strike any of her assailants.

"There's grape, sir," said the master, as the sea was torn and ploughed up with it close to the launch, which, with the other boats, was now within a hundred yards of the privateer.

"The launch returns her fire," observed Captain M——.

"And there's blaze away from the pinnace and the barge," cried one of the men, who stood on the rattlings of the main rigging. "Hurrah, my lads! keep it up," continued the man, in his feeling of excitement, which, pervading Captain M——, as well as the rest of the crew, received no check, though not exactly in accordance with the strict routine of the service.

The combat now became warm; gun after gun from the privateer was rapidly fired at the boats, who were taking their stations, previous to a simultaneous rush to board.

The pinnace had pulled away towards the bow of the privateer; the barge had taken up a position on the quarter; the launch remained on her beam, firing round and grape from her eighteen-pounder carronade, with a rapidity that almost enabled her to return gun for gun to her superiorly-armed antagonist.

Both the cutters were under her stern, keeping up an incessant fire of musketry, with which they were now close enough to annoy the enemy.

" A gun from the rock close to the barge, sir ! " reported the signal man.

" I expected as much," observed Captain M—— to the officers standing near him.

" One of the cutters has winded, sir ; she's stretching out for the shore," cried the master.

" Bravo !—that's decided—and without waiting for orders.   Who commands that boat ? " inquired Captain M——.

" It's the first cutter—Mr Bruce, sir."

The cutter was on shore before the gun could be reloaded, and fired a second time.   The crew, with the officer at their head, were seen to clamber up the rock ! In a minute they returned, and jumping into the boat, pulled off to give their aid to the capture of the vessel.

" He has spiked the gun, I am certain," observed Captain M——.

Before the cutter could regain her station, the other boats were summoned by the bugle in the launch, and, with loud cheering, pulled up together to the attack.   The booms, which had been rigged out to prevent them from coming alongside, already shot through by the grape from the launch, offered but little resistance to the impetus with which the boats were forced against them; they either broke in two, or sank under water.

"There's *board*!—Hurrah!" cried all the men who remained in the *Aspasia*, cheering those who heard them not.

But I must transport the reader to the scene of slaughter; for if he remains on board of the *Aspasia*, he will distinguish nothing but fire and smoke. Don't be afraid, ladies, if I take you on board of the schooner—" these our actors are all air, thin air," raised by the magic pen for your amusement. Come, then, fearlessly, with me, and view the scene of mortal strife! The launch has boarded on the starboard gangway, and it is against her that the crew of the privateer have directed their main efforts.

The boarding nettings cannot be divided, and the men are thrown back wounded or dead, into the boat. The crew of the pinnace are attempting the bows with indifferent success. Some have already fallen a sacrifice to their valour—none have yet succeeded in gaining a footing on the deck, while the marines are resisting, with their bayonets, the thrusts of the boarding pikes which are protruded through the ports. Courtenay has not yet boarded in the barge, for, on pulling up on the quarter, he perceived that, on the larboard side of the vessel, the boarding nettings had either been neglected to be properly triced up, or had been cut away by the fire from the boats. He has pushed alongside, to take advantage of the opening, and the two cutters have followed him. They board with little resistance—the enemy are too busy repelling the attacks on the other side—and as his men pour upon the privateer's deck, the crews of the launch and pinnace, tired with their vain endeavours to divide the nettings, and rendered desperate by their loss, have run up the fore and main rigging above the nettings, and thrown themselves down, cutlass in hand, into the *mêlée* below, careless of the points of the weapons which may meet them in their descent. Now is the struggle for life or death.

Courtenay, who was daring as man could be, but not

of a very athletic frame, re-climbed from the main chains of
the vessel, into which he had already once fallen, from one
of his own seamen having inadvertently made use of his
shoulder as a step to assist his own ascent.   He was over-
taken by Robinson, the coxswain of the cutter, who sprang
up with all the ardour and activity of an English sailor who
" meant mischief," and, pleased with the energy of his
officer (forgetting, at the moment, the respect due to his
rank), called out to him, by the *sobriquet* with which he had
been christened by the men,—" Brave, *Little Bilious !* that's
your sort ! "

" What's that, sir ? " cried Courtenay, making a spring,
so as to stand on the plane sheer of the vessel at the same
moment with the coxswain, and seizing him by the collar,
—"I say, Robinson, what do you mean by calling me
' *Little Bilious* ' ? " continued the lieutenant, wholly regard-
less of the situation they were placed in.   The coxswain
looked at him with surprise, and at the same moment parried
off with his cutlass a thrust of a pike at Courtenay, which,
in all probability, would otherwise have prevented his
asking any more questions ; then, without making any
answer, sprang down into the midst of the affray.

" You, Robinson, come back," cried Courtenay, after
him—" D—d annoying—*Little Bilious*, indeed ! " continued
he, as, following the example of the coxswain, he proceeded to vent his bile, for the present, on the heads of
the Frenchmen.

In most instances of boarding, but more especially in
boarding small vessels, there is not much opportunity for
what is termed hand to hand fighting.   It is a rush for
the deck ; breast to breast, thigh to thigh, foot to foot,
man wedged against man, so pressed on by those behind,
that there is little possibility of using your cutlass, except
by driving your antagonist's teeth down his throat with the
hilt.   Gun-shot wounds, of course, take place throughout
the whole of the combat, but those from the sabre and the
cutlass are generally given and received before the close,
or after the resistance of one party has yielded to the pertina-

city and courage of the other.   The crews of the barge and
cutters having gained possession of the deck in the rear of
the enemy, the affair was decided much sooner than it otherwise would have been, for the French fought with
desperation, and were commanded by a most gallant and
enterprising captain.   In three minutes, the crew of the
privateer were either beaten below, or forced overboard,
and the colours hauled down from the mast-heads,
announced to Captain M—— and the rest of the *Aspasia's*
crew the welcome intelligence that the privateer was in the
possession of their gallant shipmates.

The hatches were secured, and the panting Englishmen,
for a few minutes, desisted from their exertions, that they
might recover their breath ; after which Price gave directions for the cables and hawsers to be cut, and the boats
to go a-head, and tow the vessel out.

" They are firing musketry from the shore ; they've
just hit one of our men," said the coxswain of the pinnace.

" Then cast off, and bring your gun to bear astern.   If
you do not hit them, at least they will not be so steady in
their aim.   As soon as we are out of musket-shot, pull out
to us."

The order was executed, whilst the other boats towed
the privateer towards the frigate.   In a few minutes they
were out of musket-shot ; the pinnace returned, and they
had leisure to examine into the loss which they had
sustained in the conflict.   The launch had suffered most ;
nine of her crew were either killed or wounded.   Three
seamen and four marines had suffered in the other boats.
Twenty-seven of the privateer's men were stretched on the
decks, either dead or unable to rise.   Those who had not
been severely hurt had escaped below with the rest of the
crew.

Price was standing at the wheel, his sabre not yet
sheathed, with Courtenay at his side, when his inveterate
habit returned, and he commenced—

" ' I do remember, when the fight was done,'——"

" So do I, and devilish glad that it's over," cried Jerry,

coming forward from the taffrail with a cutlass in hand, which, although he could wield, he could certainly not have done much execution with.

"Why, how came you here, Mr Jerry?" inquired Courtenay.

"Oh! Stewart brought me in his boat, with the hopes of getting rid of me; but I shall live to plague him yet."

"You are not hurt, Seymour, I hope?" said Price to our hero, who now joined the party, and whose clothes were stained with blood.

"No," replied Seymour, smiling. "It's not my blood—it's Stewart's. I have been binding up his head; he has a very deep cut on the forehead, and a musket ball in his neck; but I think neither of the wounds is of much consequence."

"Where is he?"

"In the cutter. I desired them to put the wounded man in her, out of the launch, and to pull on board at once. Was not I right?"

"Yes, most assuredly. I should have thought of it myself."

"Well, Jerry," said Seymour, laughing, "how many did you——"

"I did not count them; but if you meet with any chaps with deeper wounds than usual, put them down to me. Do you know, Mr Price, you are more indebted to me than you may imagine for the success of this affair?"

"How, Mr Jerry? I should like to know, that I may prove my gratitude; 'eleven out of the thirteen' you paid, I've no doubt."

"It was not altogether that—I frightened them more than I hurt them: for when they would have returned the blows from this stalwart arm," said Jerry, holding out the member in question, which was about the thickness of a large carrot, "I immediately turned edgeways to them, and was invisible. They thought that they had to deal with either a ghost or a magician, and, depend upon it, it unnerved them——"

"'Approach thou like,'—what is it?" resumed Price,
"something—'Hence, horrible shadow, unreal mockery,
hence!'"

"Pretty names to be called in reward of my services,"
cried Jerry. "I presume this is a specimen of the gratitude
you were talking about. Well, after all, to take a leaf out
of your book, Mr Price, I consider that the better part of
valour is discretion. Now, that fellow, Stewart, he
actually gave them his head to play with, and I am not
sorry that he has had it broken—for I calculate that I shall
be saved at least a dozen thrashings by some of his hot
blood being let out—'the King's poor cousin!'"

"By-the-bye, I quite forgot—where's Robinson, the
coxswain of the cutter?" demanded Courtenay.

"Between the guns forward — seriously hurt, poor
fellow, I am afraid," answered Seymour.

"I'm very sorry for that—I'll go and see him—I wish to
speak with him," replied Courtenay, walking forward.

Robinson was lying near the long brass gun, which was
pointed out of the foremost port, his head pillowed upon
the body of the French captain, who had fallen by his hand,
just before he had received his mortal wound. A musket
ball had entered his groin, and divided the iliac artery; he
was bleeding to death—nothing could save him. The cold
perspiration on his forehead, and the glassy appearance of
his eye, too plainly indicated that he had but a few minutes
to live. Courtenay, shocked at the condition of the poor
fellow, who was not only the most humorous, but one of
the ablest seamen in the ship, knelt down on one knee
beside him, and took his hand—

"How do you feel, Robinson? are you in much pain?"

"None at all, sir, thank ye," replied the man faintly;
"but the purser may chalk me down DD. as soon as he
pleases. I suppose he'll cheat government out of our day's
grub though," continued the man with a smile.

Courtenay, aware of the truth of the first observation,
thought it no kindness to attempt to deceive a dying man
with hopes of recovery in his last moments; he therefore

continued—"Can I be of any service to you, Robinson? Is there anything I can do when you are gone?"

"Nothing at all, sir. I've neither chick nor child, nor relation, that I know of. Yes, there is one thing, sir, but it's on the bloody side; the key of the mess chest is in my trousers' pocket—I wish you'd recollect to have it taken out and given to John Williams; you must wait till I'm dead, for I can't turn myself just now."

"It shall be attended to," replied Courtenay.

"And, Mr Courtenay, remember me to the captain."

"Is there anything else?" continued Courtenay, who perceived that the man was sinking rapidly.

"Nothing—nothing, sir," replied Robinson, very faintly. "Good-bye, God bless you, sir, I'm going fast now."

"But, Robinson," said Courtenay, in a low soothing voice, bending nearer to him, "tell me, my good fellow—I am not the least angry—tell me, why did you call me *Little Bilious?*"

The man turned his eyes up to him, and a smile played upon his features, as if he was pleased with the idea of disappointing the curiosity of his officer. He made no answer—his head fell back, and in a few seconds he had breathed his last.

"Poor fellow—he is gone!" said Courtenay, with a deep sigh, as he rose up from the body—"Never answered my question too—Well," continued he, as he walked slowly aft, "now that's what I consider to be most excessively annoying."

By this time, the privateer had been towed under the stern of the frigate, and a hawser was sent on board to secure her astern. Price and the other officers returned on board, where they were well received by Captain M——, who thanked them for their exertions. The wounded had been some time under the hands of Macallan, and fresh crews having been ordered into the boats, they returned to the privateer. The hatches were taken off, and the prisoners removed to the frigate.

The name of the prize was the *Estelle*, of two hundred

tons burthen, mounting fourteen guns, and having on board, at the commencement of the attack, her full complement of one hundred and twenty-five men.

Chapter XXXII

Many with trust, with doubt few are undone.
LORD BROOK.

Doubt wisely : in strange way
To stand inquiring right, is not to stray ;
To run wrong, is.

DONNE.

WHEN the hatches were taken off on board of the privateer, the prisoners, as they came up, were handed into the boats. Jerry stood at the hatchway, with his cutlass in his hand, making his sarcastic remarks upon them as they appeared. A short interval had elapsed, after it was supposed that everybody had come from below, when a tall, thin personage, in the dress of a landsman, crawled up the hatchway.

"Halloo!" cried Jerry ; "Mr Longtogs, who have we here ? Why he must be the *padre.* I say, mounseer, je very much suspecte, que vous êtes what they call a Father Confessor, n'est-ce pas ? Devilish good idea. A privateer with a parson ! What's your pay, mounseer ?—a tenth, of course. Little enough too for looking after the souls of such a set of d——d rascals. Well, mounseer, vous êtes prisonnier, without benefit of clergy ; so hop into that boat. Why, confound it, here's another !" continued Jerry, as a second made his appearance. "He's the clerk, of course, as he follows the parson. Come, Mont' Arrivo Jack ! What a cock-eye the rascal has ! "

During this elegant harangue, which was certainly meant for his own amusement more than for their edification, as Jerry had no idea but that they were belonging to the privateer, and of course could not comprehend him, both the parties looked at him, and at each other, with astonishment, until the first who had appeared addressed the latter with, " I say, Paul, did you ever see such a thing before ? D—n it, why he's like a sixpenny fife,—more noise than substance."

Jerry at once perceived his mistake, and recollected, that the master of the vessel which they had boarded had mentioned that two English merchants had been taken out of her by the privateer, with the hopes of ransom ; but, nettled with the remark which had been made, he retorted with—

" Well, I'd recommend you not to attempt to play upon me, that's all."

" No, I don't mean, for I should only make you squeak."

" You are the two gentlemen who were detained by the privateer, I presume," said Pearce, the master, who had come on board to superintend the necessary arrangements previous to her being sent in.

" We are, sir, and must introduce ourselves. My name is Mr Peter Capon—that of my friend, designated by that young gentleman as Cock-eye, is Mr Paul Contract. Will you oblige us with a boat to go on board of the frigate, that we may speak to the captain ? "

" Most certainly. Jump into the first cutter there. I am sorry you have been so unpleasantly situated, gentlemen. Why did not you come on deck before ? "

Peter did not state the real ground, which was to secure their property, which was below, from being plundered by the privateer's crew ; but, wishing to pay off Jerry for his impertinence, replied—

" Why, we did look up the hatchway several times, but there was something so awful, and, I may say, so un-English-like, in the appearance of that officer with his drawn sword, that we were afraid ; we could not imagine into whose hands the vessel had fallen—we thought it had been captured by the Yahoos."

" Houyhnhnms, more likely. You'll find I'm a bit of a horse," replied Jerry in a passion.

" By Jove, then, you're only fit for the hounds," observed

the gentleman with oblique vision; "I should order you——"

"Would you? Well now I'll order you, sir," replied the youngster, whose anger made him quite forget the presence of his commanding officer—"Have the goodness to step into that boat."

"And I shall order you, Mr J——," observed the master with asperity—"I order you to go into that boat, and take these gentlemen on board, and to hold your tongue."

"Ay, ay, sir. This way, sir," said Jerry to Mr Peter, making him a polite bow, and pointing to the boat at the gangway—"In that direction, sir, if you please," continued Jerry, bowing to Mr Paul, and pointing to the quarter of the vessel.

"And why in that direction, sir?" observed Paul, "I am going on board of the frigate."

"I know it, sir; it was considerate on my part: I was allowing for the angle of obliquity in your vision. You would have exactly fetched the boat."

The indignation of Mr Paul was now at its height; and Pearce, the master, who was much annoyed at Jerry's excessive impertinence, which he knew Captain M—— would never have overlooked, detained the boat for a minute, while he wrote a few lines to Price, requesting him to send the bearer of it to the mast-head, upon delivery, for his impertinent conduct. "Mr J——, take this on board, and deliver it from me to the commanding officer."

"Ay, ay, sir," replied Jerry. "Shove off there, forward."

Mr Peter looked Jerry earnestly in his face for some time, as they were pulling on board.

"Well now, d—n it, I like you, if it's only for your excessive impudence."

"A negative sort of commendation, but I believe it is the only one that he has," replied the other, in a surly tone.

"Highly flattered, sir," replied Jerry to Mr Peter,

"that you should perceive anything to induce you to like
me : but I am sorry I cannot return the compliment, for
I really cannot perceive anything to like you for. As for
your friend there, I can only say, that I detest all *crooked*
ways.—In bow forward !—way enough. Now, gentlemen,
with your permission, I'll show you the road," said the
youngster, climbing up the side.

Jerry, who had some suspicion that the note was not in
his favour, took the liberty, as it was neither sealed nor
wafered, of reading it under the half-deck, while Price
was showing the two gentlemen into the cabin. Not to
deliver a note on service was an offence for which Captain
M—— would have dismissed him from the ship ; but to
be perched up, like a monkey, at the mast-head, in the
afternoon, after having fought like a man in the morning,
was very much against the grain. At any other time he
would have cared little about it. He went upon deck
again, where he found Prose on the gangway—"Well,
Prose, my boy, how are you ? "

"Why, upon my soul, Jerry, I am tired to death.
Seven times have I been backward and forward to that
abominable privateer, and now my tea is ready, and I am
ordered to go again for these gentlemen's things."

"Well, that is hard. I will go for you, Prose, shall I ?
Where's the boat ? "

"All ready, alongside. Well now, it's very kind of
you, Jerry, I do declare."

Jerry laid hold of the man-ropes, and began to descend
the side—and then, as if recollecting himself of a sudden,
said, "Oh, by-the-bye, I had nearly forgot. Here's a note
from the master to Mr Price. Give it him, Prose."

"Yes, Jerry, I will," replied Prose, walking over to the
side of the quarter-deck where Price was carrying on the
duty, while Jerry made all the haste he could, and shoved
off in the boat.

"A note, sir, from Mr Pearce, the master."

"Hum," said Price, running it over. "Mr Prose, go
up to the mast-head, and stay there till I call you down."

" Sir ! " replied Prose, aghast.

" No reply, sir—up immediately."

" Why, sir, it was——"

" Another word, sir, and I'll keep you there all night," cried Price, walking forward, in furtherance of the duty he was carrying on.

" Well, now, I do declare !   What have I done ?" said Prose, with a whimpering voice, as he reluctantly ascended the main-rigging, not unperceived by Jerry, who was watching the result as he pulled on board of the privateer.

" Come on board for these gentlemen's clothes, sir," said Jerry, reporting himself to Mr Pearce, who, not a little surprised to see him, inquired—

" Did Mr Price receive my note ? "

" Yes, sir, he did."

" Why, I requested him to mast-head you ! "

" Many thanks, sir, for your kindness," replied the youngster, touching his hat.

Pearce, who was annoyed that his request should not have been complied with, stated his feelings on the subject to Price, when he returned to the ship in the evening.

Price declared that he had sent Prose to the mast-head, and had not called him down until eight o'clock.   The affair was thus explained, and Jerry was pardoned for the ingenuity of his *ruse de guerre*, while all the comfort that was received by the unfortunate Prose was being informed, on the ensuing morning, that it was all a mistake.

The prize being now ready, Captain M—— desired Courtenay to take charge of it, and select two of the midshipmen to accompany him.   His choice fell upon Seymour and Jerry : the latter being selected rather for his own amusement, than for his qualities as an officer.   The distance to Jamaica, to which island he was directed to proceed, and from thence with his crew to obtain a passage to Barbadoes, was not great, and Captain M—— did not like to have the frigate short-manned ; he was therefore not allowed to take more than ten seamen with him, five prisoners being sent on board, to assist in navigating the vessel.

Mr Capon and Mr Contract, at their own request, went as passengers.

In the afternoon, as soon as the provisions were on board, Courtenay received his written orders, and in a few hours the frigate was out of sight. They had barely time to stow away everything in its place, and make the necessary arrangements, when a heavy N.E. swell, and louring horizon, predicted a continuance of the fair wind, and plenty of it. So it proved; the wind increased rapidly, and the men found it difficult to reduce the canvas in sufficient time. Before dark, the wind blew with considerable force, not steadily, but in fitful gusts: and the sun, as he descended in the wave, warned them, by his red and fiery aspect, to prepare for an increase of the gale. The schooner flew before it, under her diminished sail, rolling gunwale-to in the deep trough, or lurching heavily as her weather quarter was borne up aloft by the culminating swell. All was secured for the night; the watch was set, and Seymour walked the deck, while Courtenay and the rest went below, and at an early hour retired to their beds.

Among other reasons for selecting our hero as one of his assistants, Courtenay was influenced by his perfect knowledge of the French language, which might prove useful in communicating with the French prisoners, who were sent on board to assist in working the vessel. Jerry had also boasted of his talent in that way, as he wished to go in the prize; and, although the reader, from the specimen which he has had, may not exactly give credit to his assertions, yet Courtenay, who had never heard him, believed that he was pretty well acquainted with the language.

But, soon after they had parted with the frigate, when Courtenay desired the French prisoners to lay hold of the ropes and assist in shortening sail, they all refused. Seymour was not on deck at the time; he had been desired

to superintend the arrangements below: and although he
had been informed of their conduct, he had not yet spoken
to the prisoners.   Two of them were sitting aft under the
lee of the weather-bulwark, as Seymour was walking the
deck to and fro.   They were in earnest conversation, when
Seymour stopped near to them, carelessly leaning over the
weather-quarter, watching the long following seas, when
he overhead one say to the other—"*Taisez-vous, peut-être
qu'il nous entend.*"   "*Nous verrons,*" replied the other—who
immediately rose, and addressed Seymour in French, relative
to the weather.   What he had previously heard induced
our hero to shake his head, and continue to look over the
weather-quarter, and as Seymour only answered in the
English negative to a further interrogation, the prisoners
did not think it worth while to remove out of his hearing,
but, satisfied with his not being able to comprehend them,
sat down again, and resumed their conversation.   The
lurching of the vessel was a sufficient reason for not walking the deck; but Seymour, to remove all suspicion, took
another turn or two, and then again held on by the ropes
close by the Frenchmen.   The wind blew too fresh to
permit him to catch more than an occasional sentence or
two of their conversation: but what he heard made him
more anxious to collect more.

   " *Ils ne sont que seize, avec ce petit misère,*" observed one,
"*et nous sommes—*"   Here the rest of the sentence was
lost.   Seymour reckoned up the English on board, and
found that with Billy Pitts, whom Macallan had allowed
Courtenay to take with him as his steward, they exactly
amounted to that number.   The latter epithet he considered, justly enough, to be bestowed upon his friend
Jerry.   A few minutes afterwards, he intercepted—
"They'll throw us overboard, if we do not succeed—
we'll throw them overboard, if we do."   "*Courage, mon
ami, il n'y aura pas de difficulté; nous sommes trop forts,*"
replied the other, as, terminating their conversation, they
rose and walked forward.

   It was evident to our hero that something was in

agitation; but at the same time it appeared perfectly incomprehensible, that six prisoners should have even formed the idea of attempting the recapture of a vessel manned with sixteen Englishmen, and that they should consider themselves *so strong* as to ensure success. Determined to report what he had heard to Courtenay, Seymour walked the remainder of his watch, was relieved, and went below to his hammock.

The wind had increased during the night; but as it was fair, and the sky clear, and the sun shone bright, the breeze was rather a matter of congratulation when they met at breakfast in the morning, although Peter and Paul complained of the violent motion of the vessel having taken away their appetite. Seymour reported to Courtenay the fragments of the conversation which he had overheard; and insane as appeared to be the idea of recapture, the latter agreed with him that it demanded caution on their parts: but as it would appear very opposite to the English character to take open measures against six prisoners, when they were so numerous, he contented himself with desiring all the arms and ammunition to be stowed in the cabin, and gave orders that the prisoners, as they refused to work, should not be allowed to come on deck after dusk, — and then gave the affair no further thought. Seymour was aware that, although it was his duty to report the circumstance, he had no right to press the matter upon Courtenay, who was to be supposed the best judge; still he was not satisfied. He had an unaccountable foreboding that all was not right. He turned the subject in his mind until dinner was announced by Billy Pitts, which put an end to his reverie.

The violent jerking motion of the vessel made it no easy task to retain a position at the table, which was securely lashed. As for placing on it the whole of the dinner at once, decanters, etc., that would have been certain destruction; a plate and spoon for their soup was all which Billy Pitts, who was major-domo, would trust them with. Paul, who was not the best sailor in the world,

had secured to himself the seat to windward, and it consequently fell to his lot to help the pea-soup, which was
placed at the weather-side of the table.   To save time and
breakage,—two important things in a sea-mess,—they all
held their own plates, which they thrust in towards the
tureen from the different quarters of the table to receive
their supply.   Paul having helped those nearest to him,
rose from his chair that he might see to fill the plates on
the other side of the tureen.   He was leaning over, his
centre of gravity being considerably beyond the perpendicular, when a heavy sea struck the vessel, and threw her
nearly on her beam ends, pitching Paul right over the
table to leeward.   With the tureen, which he did not
forget to take with him, he flew into Jerry's arms, and
they rolled together on the floor.   The contents of the
tureen were rapidly deposited in the open bosom of Jerry,
who disengaged himself from the embraces of his enemy
as fast as he could, amidst the laughter of his companions.

"Well, you asked for soup," observed Courtenay.

"Yes, and my friend has helped me very liberally,"
replied Jerry, who was not at all out of humour, except
when he was foiled with his own weapons.   In the meantime, Paul, who was a little stunned with the blow he had
received on his head, had continued on the floor rolling in
the pea-soup, and was just attempting to get on his legs.

"You've got it all to yourself there, Mr Paul.   As you
seem to like it, perhaps you would prefer a spoon," said
Jerry, offering him one at the same time.

"I say, Paul, what a capital harlequin you would make,"
observed Peter.

Paul, who had recovered his legs, and now clung on by
the table, looked an answer horribly asquint, as if he did
not admire the joke ; but he resumed his seat at the table.

The remainder of the dinner was brought down without
further accident occurring ; and by the time it was over,
as the bottle had to be passed round, and everybody was
obliged to drink off immediately, and put his wine-glass
inside his waistcoat to save it from perdition, they all were

very merry and happy before the repast had been concluded.   "There," said Jerry, stroking himself down
when he had finished his cheese, as if he were a Falstaff,
"a kitten might play with me now."

"More than one dare do with me," rejoined Peter,
"for I'm cursedly inclined to *shoot the cat*."

But as the second evening closed in, the sky was loaded
with heavy clouds,—the scud flew wildly past them,—
the sea increased to mountains high,—and the gale roared
through the rigging of the schooner, which was now
impelled before it under bare poles.   They were really
in danger.   The hatches were battened down fore and
aft—the ports were knocked out to allow the escape of
the water, which poured over in such volumes as would
otherwise have swamped the vessel—and Courtenay and
his crew remained on deck until dawn of day, when the
violence of the gale seemed to have abated.

Courtenay desired Seymour and Jerry to turn in, and
relieve him at eight o'clock.   Our hero and Jerry went
down into the cabin, where they found the two passengers,
who, although they had not come on deck during the
night, had not retired to bed.   Peter was sitting up to
windward on the locker, looking very pale and very sea-
sick.   Paul was on the cabin floor, with one hand holding
on by the leg of the table, and a bottle of brandy in the
other.   His prayer-book he had abandoned during a
fright, and it was washing about in the lee-scuppers.
Jerry was delighted, but put on a rueful face.

"Well," observed Paul, who was nearly frightened
out of his wits, "how is it now ?"

"Worse and worse," replied Jerry; "there's nine
inches water in the well."

"Oh, my God !" cried Paul, who was not very *au fait*
at nautical technicalities,—raising one eye up to heaven,
while the other appeared to rest upon the bottle of
brandy.

"But why don't you turn in ?" said Jerry; "we can go
to the bottom just as comfortably in bed as anywhere else."

"I agree with you," replied Peter, who had often been at sea, and knew very well that all was right, by the two midshipmen coming off deck. "My mother prophesied that I never should die in my bed; but I'm determined that I will."

"You had better turn in, Mr Paul," said Seymour, kindly; "I'll ring for the steward."

Billy Pitts made his appearance. "By gad, gentlemen, the d——d schooner under water."

"Under water!" cried Paul, with dismay. The bottle was applied to his mouth, as if he was determined to leave as little room as possible for the element which he expected instantaneously to be struggling in.

With the assistance of Billy, Paul was placed in one of the standing bed-places at the side of the cabin. Jerry put his brandy bottle at the side of his pillow,—kindly informing him that he would have an opportunity of taking a few more swigs before he went down, for the water was only up to her bends at present. Peter was already in the cot next to him, and Seymour and Jerry turned in, without taking off their clothes, in Courtenay's bed on the other side of the cabin. Before they had fallen asleep, they heard Paul cry out, "Peter! Peter!"

"Well, what do you want?"

"Do you think there are any hopes?"

Peter, who wished to frighten his companion, replied, gravely—"I am afraid not;—but, Paul, I've just been reflecting upon the subject. Here we are, two men considerably on the wrong side of forty. We have enjoyed our youth, which is the happiest period of our life. We are now fast descending the hill, to old age, decrepitude, and disease—what avails a few more years, allowing that we are spared this time? Don't you perceive the *comfort* of my observations?"

Paul groaned, and made no answer; but even the creaking of the timbers could not disguise the repeated cleck-cleck-cleck, as the brandy from the bottle gurgled down his throat.

Chapter XXXIII

Two striplings, lads more like to run
Than to commit such slaughter.

Cymbeline.

THE gales of wind in the tropical climates are violent
while they last, but are seldom of long duration. Such
was the case in the present instance: for it subsided in
a few hours after daylight; and the schooner, that had
been propelled before it, was now sheltered under the
lee of the island of St Domingo, and, with all her canvas
spread, was gliding through a tranquil sea. Again they
were collected round the dinner-table, to a more quiet
repast than they had hitherto enjoyed since they had
come on board. Paul had not quite recovered his spirits,
although, when he went on deck, just before the dinner
was announced, he was delighted at the sudden change
which had taken place; but the mirth of his companions
at his expense was not received in very good part.

After dinner, finding himself in a better humour, he
turned to Peter, and addressed him,—"I say, Peter, I
made no answer to your remarks last night, when we
expected to go down; but I have since had time deliber-
ately to weigh your arguments, and I should like you
to explain to me where the *comfort* was that you so
strenuously pointed out, for hang me if I can discover
it."

Seymour again had charge of the first watch; and,
notwithstanding that the orders for the prisoners to remain
below after dark had been communicated to them, he
observed that, on one pretence or other, they occasionally
came on deck, and repeatedly put their heads above the
hatchway. This conduct reminded him of the conversation
which he had overheard, and again it was the subject of his
thoughts. Captain M—— had one day observed to him,
that if there was no duty going on, he could not employ

himself in a more useful manner, when he was walking the
deck, than by placing himself, or the ship, in difficult
situations, and reflecting upon the most eligible means of
relief. "Depend upon it," observed Captain M——,
"the time will come, when you will find it of use to you;
and it will create for you a presence of mind, in a sudden
dilemma, which may be the salvation of yourself and the
ship you are in."

Seymour, remembering this injunction, reflected upon
what would be the most advisable steps to take, in case of
the French prisoners attempting a recapture during his
watch on deck.   That there were but six, it was very true;
but, at the same time, during the night-watches there were
but five English seamen, and the officer of the watch, on
deck.   Should the Frenchmen have the boldness to attempt
to regain possession of the vessel, there was no doubt that,
if the watch could be surprised, the hatches would be
secured over those below.   What should be the steps, in
such a case, that he ought to take?

Such were the cogitations of Seymour, when midnight
was reported, and Jerry was summoned to relieve the deck
—which he did not do, relying upon our hero's good-nature,
until past one bell. Up he came, with his ready apology
—"I really beg your pardon, my dear fellow, but I had
not a wink of sleep last night."

"Never mind, Jerry, I am not at all sleepy. I had been
thinking about these French prisoners—I cannot get their
conversation out of my head."

"Why, I did not like it myself, when I heard of it,"
replied Jerry. "I hope they won't attempt it in my
watch; it would not give them much trouble to launch me
over the quarter—I should skim away, 'flying light,' like
a lady's bonnet."

"What would you do, Jerry, if you perceived them
rushing aft to retake the vessel?" inquired Seymour, who
was aware of his ready invention.

"Skim up the rigging like a lamp-lighter, to be sure.
Not that it would be of much use, if they gained

the day—except to say a few prayers before I went astern."

"Well, that was my idea; but I thought that if one had a musket and ammunition up there, a diversion might be created in favour of those below—for the prisoners have no firearms."

"Very true," replied Jerry; "we might puzzle them not a little."

"Now, Jerry, suppose we were to take that precaution, for I do not like their manœuvres during my watch. It will do no harm, if it does no good. Suppose you fetch two muskets and cartouch-boxes from the cabin—I'll take one, and secure it in the fore-cross-trees, and you do the same at the main: for Courtenay is too proud to keep an armed watch."

Jerry agreed to the proposal, and brought up the muskets and ammunition. Seymour gave him a stout *fox* to lash the musket; and taking another himself, they both ascended the rigging at the same time, and were busy securing the muskets up and down at the head of the lower masts, when they heard a sudden rush upon deck, beneath them.

It was dark, though not so dark but they could distinguish what was going on, and they perceived that their thoughts had but anticipated the reality. "The French are up!" roared the man at the wheel, to rouse those below, as well as the watch, who were lying about the decks; but, to the astonishment of the youngsters aloft, as well as of the men on deck, not six but about twenty Frenchmen, armed with cutlasses, made their appearance. The hatches were over and secured in a minute; and the unarmed English on deck were then attacked by the superior force. It was with agonised feelings that Seymour and Jerry heard the scuffle which took place; it was short; and plunge after plunge into the water, alongside, announced the death of each separate victim. The man at the wheel struggled long—he was of an athletic frame—but, overpowered by numbers, he was launched over the taffrail.

The French, supposing that the remainder of the crew were below, placed sentries over the hatches, that they might not be forced, and then collected together abaft, altering the course of the vessel for St Domingo.

It will be necessary to explain the sudden appearance of so many Frenchmen. When the captain of the privateer was occupied, during the night previous to the attack, with several plans of defence, he also arranged one for the recapture of the vessel, in case of their being overpowered. With this in view, he had constructed a platform in the hold, on which a tier of casks was stowed, and under which there was sufficient space for fifteen or twenty men to lie concealed. When the privateer's men had been driven below, and the hatches secured over them, fifteen, armed with cutlasses, concealed themselves in this place, with the hopes of recapturing the vessel from the prize-master, after she should have parted company with the frigate. The prisoners, who had been sent on board to assist in navigating the schooner to Jamaica, had communicated with them, unperceived, after dark. As all the English were fatigued, from having been on deck during the previous night, the middle watch was proposed for the attempt, which had thus far been attended with success.

Seymour and Jerry remained quiet at the mast-heads; for although they did not attempt to communicate with each other, for fear of discovery, they both rightly judged that it would be best to remain till daylight; by which time, some plans would have been formed by the party below, which their situation would enable them materially to assist. Nearly four hours elapsed previous to the dawning of the day, during which interval Jerry had ample time to say some of those prayers which he spoke of, and which it was to be supposed that they both did not fail to offer up in their perilous situation.

As soon as the day began to break, Jerry, who had not yet loaded his musket, lest he might be heard, thought it time to prepare for action. He primed, and put in his cartridge, in the ramming down of which a slight ringing of the ramrod against the muzzle attracted the notice of one of the Frenchmen, who, looking up, after a short time, exclaimed :—

" *Diable ! c'est monsieur misère qui est là !* "

Jerry levelled with a steady aim, and the bullet passed through the broad chest of the Frenchman, who rolled upon the deck.

"Now, they may chant your *miserere*," cried the youngster.

A second shot from the fore-cross-trees laid another Frenchman alongside of his companion.

" *Comment ! diable ! nous serons abîmés par ces enfans-là ; il faut monter.*"

The muskets were again loaded, and again each boy brought down his bird, before the Frenchmen could decide upon their operations. It was a case of necessity that the youngsters should be attacked ; but it was a service of no little danger, and of certain destruction to one, who must fall a sacrifice, that the other might be able to secure the youngster before he had time to reload his musket. Two of the most daring flew to the main rigging, one ascending to windward, and the other to leeward. Seymour, who perceived their intentions, reserved his fire until he saw the one in the weather rigging fall by Jerry's musket ; he then levelled at the one to leeward, who dropped into the lee-chains, and from thence into the sea. Thus had six Frenchmen already fallen by the coolness and determination of two boys, one but fourteen, and the other not sixteen years old.

A short consultation ended in the Frenchmen resorting to the only measures likely to be attended with success. Leaving three to guard the hatchways, the remaining twelve, divided into four parties, began to mount both fore and main-rigging, to windward and to leeward, at the same time. The fate of Jerry and Seymour now appeared to be decided. They might each kill one man more, and then would have been hurled into the sea. But during the consultation, Seymour, who anticipated this movement, and

had a knife in his pocket, divided the lanyards of the lee top-mast-rigging, and running up the weather side with his musket and ammunition, as soon as he had gained the top-mast cross-trees, hauled up the lee rigging after him; thus gaining a position that would admit but one person mounting up to him at a time. He called to Jerry, pointing out what he had done, that he might do the same; but unfortunately Jerry had not a knife, and could not. He contented himself with climbing up to the top-mast cross-trees, to which he was followed by two of the Frenchmen. Jerry levelled his musket, and passed his bullet through the skull of one of his pursuers, whose heavy fall on the deck shook the schooner fore and aft : and then, aware that nothing more could be done, pitched his musket overboard, that they might not gain possession of it, and climbing, with a nimbleness suited to the occasion, up to the mast-head, descended by the top-gallant-stay to the fore-topmast cross-trees, and joined Seymour, in the presence of the exasperated Frenchmen, who now, unable to reach either of them, were at a nonplus. "I say, monsieur, no catchee, no habbee," cried Jerry, laughing, and putting his hand to his side from loss of breath.

But we must now acquaint the reader with what is going on below. The surprise of Courtenay, when he found the hatches down, and the deck in possession of the French, was removed, when the men who had been secured with him stated that, as they lay in their hammocks, they had been awakened by a large body of men running up the hatchway. He now perceived that there must have been men concealed in the hold of the vessel. The struggle on deck, the splashing in the water, all had been plainly heard below; they were aware of the fate of their shipmates, and did not expect to see daylight again, until they were handed up as prisoners in a French port.

The feelings of Courtenay were not enviable. He upbraided himself for having, by his want of prudence, lost the vessel, and sacrificed the lives of the two midship-

men and five seamen who had the watch on deck. The
party below consisted of Courtenay, Peter and Paul,
Billy Pitts, and five seamen ; and a consultation was held
as to their proceedings. To regain the vessel and avenge
the death of their shipmates, or to perish in the attempt,
was the determination of the lieutenant.

He was aware that the French had no firearms ; and,
amply supplied as they were, he would have cared little
for their numbers if once on deck ; but how to get on deck
was the problem. To set fire to the vessel, and rush up in
the flames,—to scuttle her,—or to blow her up, and all go
down together, were each proposed and agitated.

Peter's plan was considered as the most feasible. He
suggested, that one half of the cabin table, which was
divided in two, should be placed upon the other, so as to
raise it up to the combings of the skylight-hatch ; on the
upper table, to place a pound or two of powder, which,
from the ascending principle of explosion, would blow off
the skylight and grating without injuring the vessel below.
Then, with their muskets loaded and bayonets fixed, to
jump on the table, and from thence, if possible, gain the
deck.

This was agreed to, and the preparations were well
forward, when the report of Jerry's musket was heard—
another succeeded, and they were perplexed. Had the
Frenchmen firearms ?—and if so, what could they be firing
at ? The falling of the bodies on deck, and the indistinct
curses of the Frenchmen, puzzled them even more.
" What can it be ? " observed Courtenay.

" I recollect now," said Paul, " as I lay awake, I saw a
young *devilskin* pass my bed with a musket—I wondered
what it was for."

" Then, probably, he has gained the rigging with it, and
is safe," cried Courtenay, intuitively.   " Be quick !
Where's the powder ?   Take that candle further off."

The train was laid as the muskets continued to be discharged ; they removed from the cabin ;—it was fired, and
the skylight was blown up, killing the Frenchman who

guarded the hatchway, at the very moment that the Frenchmen were in the rigging, puzzled with the manœuvres of Seymour and the escape of Jerry.

Courtenay and his party rushed into the cabin, mounted the table, and were on deck before the smoke had cleared away; and the Frenchmen, who had not had time to descend the rigging, were at their mercy.

Mercy they were not entitled to. They had shown none to the unarmed English, whom they had wantonly thrown into the sea when they had overpowered them, and were now thirsting for the blood of the two boys. No mercy was shown to them. As they dropped one by one from the rigging wounded or dead, they were tossed into the wave, as an expiatory sacrifice to the manes of the murdered Englishmen. In a few minutes the carnage was over. Seymour and Jerry descended from their little *fortalice* aloft, and were warmly greeted by their friends as they reached the deck.

"Really, Mr Paul," said Jerry, shaking his proffered hand, "this is quite an unexpected pleasure."

"Well, I never thought that I could possibly like you," answered the other.

"Well," observed Jerry, "it has quite stopped my growth."

"But not your tongue, I hope," replied Peter; "that would be a pity. Now explain to us how it all happened."

Jerry entered into the detail with his accustomed humour, while Courtenay walked aft with Seymour, to have a more sober narrative of the transactions which we have described, and which afforded ample matter for conversation, until the prize was brought to an anchor in Port Royal harbour, where Courtenay and his crew were ordered a passage to Barbadoes, in a frigate that had orders to proceed there in a few days; and Mr Peter Capon and Mr Paul Contract went on shore, declaring that until a mail coach ran between there and England, they should never leave the island and again subject themselves to the charming vicissitudes of a seafaring existence.

Chapter XXXIV

For the execution of all form, observance, ceremony, subordination, and the
like, even though, while he compels obedience, he may get himself
privately laughed at, commend me to our governor, Don Fabricio.
Humours of Madrid.

IN a few days, Courtenay, with the prize crew of the
Aspasia, sailed for Barbadoes, in the frigate which had been
ordered to receive them for a passage.

The frigate was commanded by one of the most singular
characters in the service. He was a clever man, a thorough
sailor, and well acquainted with the details and technicalities of the profession—a spirited and enterprising
officer, but of the most arbitrary disposition. So well was
he acquainted with the regulations of the service, that he
could hedge himself in so as to ensure a compliance with
the most preposterous orders, or draw the officer who
resisted into a premunire which would risk his commission.

In a profession where one man is embarked with many,
isolated from the power whence he derives his own—
where his fiat must be received without a murmur by
hundreds who can reason as well as himself, it is absolutely requisite that he should be invested with an authority
amounting to despotism. True it is that he is held
responsible to his superiors for any undue exercise of this
authority; but amongst so many to whom it is confided,
there must be some who, from disposition, or the bad
example of those under whom they have served, will not
adhere to the limits which have been prescribed. This,
however, is no reason for reducing that authority, which,
as you govern wholly by opinion, is necessary for the
discipline which upholds the service; but it is a strong
reason for not delegating it to those who are not fit to be
entrusted.

Captain Bradshaw had many redeeming qualities.
Oppressor as he was, he admired a spirit of resistance in

an officer, when it was shown in a just cause, and, upon reflection, was invariably his friend, for he felt that his own natural temperament was increased by abject obedience. Raynal, I think it is, has said that " the pride of men in office arises as much from the servility of their inferiors or expectants, as from any other cause." In our service, they are all inferiors, and all expectants. Can it then be surprising that a captain occasionally becomes tyrannical? But Captain Bradshaw was not naturally tyrannical: he had become so, because, promoted at an early age, he had never been afterwards opposed; no one contradicted him; every one applauded his jokes, and magnified his mirth into wit. He would try by a court-martial an officer who had committed a slight error, and on the same day would open his purse and extend his patronage to another whom he knew not, but had been informed that he was deserving, and had no friends. To his seamen he was as lavish with his money as he was with the cat. He would give a man a new jacket one day, and cut it to pieces on his back with a rope's end on the next. Yet it was not exactly inconsistency—it was an eccentricity of character—not natural, but created by the service. The graft was of a worse quality than the parent stock, and the fruit was a compound of the two. The sailors, who are of the most forgiving temper in the world, and will pardon a hundred faults for one redeeming quality, declared that " he warn't a bad captain after all."

His violent and tyrannical disposition made him constantly at variance with his officers, and continual changes took place in his ship; but it was observed, that those who had left him from a spirited resistance, were kindly received, and benefited by his patronage, while those who submitted were neglected. Like a pretty but clever woman, who is aware that flattery is to be despised, and yet, from habit, cannot exist without it, so Captain Bradshaw exacted the servility which he had been accustomed to, yet rewarded not those by whom it was administered. All the midshipmen promoted on the station had to pass through the

ordeal of sailing with Captain Bradshaw, who generally
had a vacancy; and it certainly had a good effect upon
those young men who were inclined to presume upon their
newly acquired rank; for they were well-schooled before
they quitted his ship.

When Courtenay and his party went on board of the
frigate, the first lieutenant, master, and surgeon, indignant
at language which had been used to them by the captain,
refused to dine in the cabin, when they were invited by
the steward, who reported to Captain Bradshaw, that the
officers would not accept his invitation.

"Won't they, by G—d! I'll see that. Send my clerk
here."

The clerk made his appearance, with an abject bow.

"Mr Powell, sit down, and write as I dictate," said
Captain Bradshaw, who, walking up and down the fore-
cabin, composed a memorandum, in which, after a long
preamble, the first lieutenant, master, and surgeon, were
directed to dine with him every day, until further orders.
Captain Bradshaw, having signed it, sent for the first
lieutenant, and delivered it himself into his hands.

"Ferguson!—Bradly!" cried the first lieutenant, entering the gun-room, with the paper in his hand, "here's
something for all three of us,—a positive order to dine
with the skipper every day, until—he gets tired of our
company."

"I'll be hanged if I do," replied the surgeon. "I'll put
myself in the sick list."

"And if I am obliged to go, I'll not touch anything,"
rejoined the master. "There's an old proverb, 'you may
lead a horse to the pond, but you can't make him drink.'"

"Whatever we do," replied Roberts, the first lieutenant,
"we must act in concert; but I have been long enough in
the service to know that we must obey first, and remon-
strate afterwards. That this is an unusual order, I grant,
nor do I know by what regulations of the service it can be
enforced; but at the same time I consider that we run a
great risk in refusing to obey it. Only observe, in the

preamble, how artfully he inserts 'appearance of a conspiracy, tending to bring him into contempt;' and again, 'for the better discipline of his Majesty's service, which must invariably suffer when there is an appearance of want of cordiality between those to whom the men must look for an example.' Upon my soul he's devilish clever. I do believe he'd find out a reason for drawing out all our double teeth, if he was inclined, and prove it was all for the benefit of his Majesty's service. Well now, what's to be done ? "

" Why, what's your opinion, Roberts ? "

" Oh, mine is to go ; and if you will act with me, he won't allow us to dine with him a second time."

" Well, then, I agree," replied the surgeon.

" And so must I, then, I presume ; but, by heavens, it's downright tyranny and oppression."

" Never mind, listen to me. Let's all go, and all behave as ill as we can—be as unmannerly as bears—abuse everything—be as familiar as possible, and laugh in his face. He cannot touch us for it, if we do not go too far—and he'll not trouble us to come a second time."

Their plans were arranged ; and at three o'clock they were ushered into the cabin, with one of the midshipmen of the ship, and Jerry, who, as a stranger, had been honoured with an invitation.

Captain Bradshaw, whose property was equal to his liberality, piqued himself upon keeping a good table ; his cook was an *artiste*, and his wines were of the very best quality. After all, there was no great hardship in dining with him—but, "upon compulsion!" —No.

The officers bowed. The captain, satisfied with their obedience, intended, although he had brought them there by force, to do the honours of his table with the greatest urbanity.

" Roberts," said he, " do me the favour to take the foot of the table.—Doctor, here's a chair for you.—Mr Bradly, come round on this side. Now, then, steward, off covers,

and let us see what you have for us. Why, youngster,
does your captain starve you?"

"No, sir," replied Jerry, who knew what was going on;
"but he don't give me a dinner every day."

"Humph!" muttered the captain, who thought Mr
Jerry very free upon so short an acquaintance.

The soup was handed round; the first spoonful that
Roberts took in his mouth, he threw out on the snow-
white deck, crying out, as soon as his mouth was empty,
"O Lord!"

"Why, what's the matter?" inquired the captain.

"So cursed hot, I've burnt my tongue."

"Oh, that's all! steward, wipe up that mess," said the
captain, who was rather nice in his eating.

"Do you know Jemmy Cavan, sir, at Barbadoes?"
inquired the doctor.

"No, sir, I know no Jemmies," replied Captain Bradshaw, surprised at his familiar address.

"He's a devilish good fellow, sir, I can tell you. When
he gets you on shore, he'll make you dine with him every
day, whether or not. He'll take no denial."

"Now that's what I call a d—d good fellow: you don't
often meet a chap like him," observed the master.

Captain Bradshaw felt that he was indirectly called a
chap, which did not please him.

"Mr Bradly, will you take some mutton?"

"If you please," said the master.

"Roberts, I'll trouble you to carve the saddle of
mutton."

The first lieutenant cut out a slice, and taking it on
the fork, looked at it suspiciously, and then held his nose
over it.

"Why, what's the matter?"

"Rather high, sir, I'm afraid."

"Oh, I smell it here," said Jerry, who entered into the
joke.

"Indeed! steward, remove that dish; fortunately it is
not all our dinner. What will you take, Mr Bradly?"

"Why, really, I seldom touch anything but the joint. I hate your kickshaws, there's so much pawing about them. I'll wait, if you please; in the meantime, I'll drink a glass of wine with you, Captain Bradshaw."

"The devil you will!" was nearly out of the captain's mouth, at this reversal of the order of things; but he swallowed it down, and answered, in a surly tone, "With great pleasure, sir."

"Come, doctor, let you and I hob and nob," said the first lieutenant. They did so, and clicked their glasses together with such force as to break them both, and spill the wine upon the fine damask table-cloth. Jerry could contain himself no longer, but burst out into a roar of laughter, to the astonishment of Captain Bradshaw, who never had seen a midshipman thus conduct himself at his table before: but Jerry could not restrain his inclination for joining with the party, although he had no excuse for *his* behaviour.

"Bring some wine-glasses, steward; and you'll excuse me, gentlemen, but I will thank you not to try the strength of them again," said Captain Bradshaw, with a very majestic air.

"Now, Mr Ferguson, I shall be happy to take a glass of wine with you. What will you have? There's sherry and moselle."

"I prefer champagne, if you please," answered the surgeon, who knew that Captain Bradshaw did not produce it, except when strangers were at the table.

Captain Bradshaw restrained his indignation, and ordered champagne to be brought.

"I'll join you," cried the first lieutenant, shoving in his glass.

"Come, younker, let you and I have a glass cosy together," said Jerry to the midshipman, who, frightened at what was going on, moved his chair a little further from Jerry, and then looked, first at him and then at the captain.

"Oh, pray take a glass with the young gentleman," said Captain Bradshaw, with mock politeness.

"Come, steward, none of your half allowance, if you please," continued the impertinent Jerry. "Now, then, my cock, here's *towards* you, and 'better luck still.'"

Captain Bradshaw was astonished. "I say, youngster, did Captain M—— ever flog you?"

"No, sir," replied Jerry, demurely, perceiving that he had gone too far; "he always treats his officers like gentlemen."

"Then, I presume, sir, when they are on board of his ship, that they conduct themselves as gentlemen."

This hint made Jerry dumb for some time; the officers, however, continued as before. The surgeon dropped his plate, full of damascene tart, on the deck. The first lieutenant spilt his snuff on the table-cloth, and laid his snuff-box on the table, which he knew to be the captain's aversion; and the master requested a glass of grog, as the rotgut French wines had given him a pain in the bowels. Captain Bradshaw could hardly retain his seat upon the chair, upon which he fidgetted right and left. He perceived that his officers were behaving in a very unusual manner, and that it was with a view to his annoyance: yet it was impossible for him to take notice of breaking glasses, and finding fault with the cookery, which they took care to do, sending their plates away before they had eaten a mouthful, with apparent disgust; neither could he demand a court-martial for awkwardness or want of good manners at his own table. He began to think that he had better have left out the "*every day until further orders,*" in the memorandum, as rescinding it immediately would have been an acknowledgment of their having gained the victory; and as to their going on in this way, to put up with it was impossible.

The dinner was over, and the dessert placed on the table. Captain Bradshaw passed the bottles round, helping himself to Madeira. Roberts took claret, and as soon as he had tasted it, "I beg your pardon, Captain Bradshaw," said he, "but this wine is corked."

"Indeed!—take it away, steward, and bring another bottle."

Another was put on the table.

"I hope you'll find that better, Mr Roberts," said the captain, who really thought that what he stated had been the case.

"Yes," replied the first lieutenant; "for the description of wine, it's well enough."

"What do you mean, sir? Why, it's Château Margot, of the first growth."

"Excuse me, sir," replied the officer, with an incredulous smile; "they must have imposed upon you."

Captain Bradshaw, who was an excellent judge of wine, called for a glass, and pouring out the claret, tasted it. "I must differ from you, sir; and, moreover, I have no better."

"Then I'll trouble you to pass the port, doctor, for I really cannot drink that stuff."

"Do you drink port, Mr Bradly?" said the captain, with a countenance as black as a thunder-cloud.

"No, not to-day; I am not well in my inside: but I'll punish the port to-morrow."

"So will I," said the surgeon.

"And as I am not among the *privileged*," added Jerry, who had already forgotten the hint, "I'll take my whack to-day."

"Perhaps you may," observed the captain, drily.

The officers now began to be very noisy, arguing among themselves upon points of. service, and taking no notice whatever of the captain. The master, in explanation, drew a chart, with wine, upon the polished table, while the first lieutenant defended his opinion with pieces of biscuit, laid at different positions—during which two more glasses were demolished.

The captain rang, and ordered coffee in an angry tone. When the officers had taken it, he bowed stiffly, and wished them good evening.

There was one dish which was an object of abhorrence

to Captain Bradshaw. The first lieutenant, aware of it, as they rose to depart, said, "Captain Bradshaw, if it's not too great a liberty, we should like to have some *tripe*, to-morrow. We are all three very partial to it."

"So am I," rejoined Jerry.

Captain Bradshaw could hold out no longer. "Leave the cabin immediately, gentlemen. By heavens, you shall never put your legs under my table again."

"Are we not to dine here to-morrow, sir?" replied the first lieutenant, with affected surprise; "the order says, 'every day.'"

"Till further orders," roared the captain; "and now you have them, for I'll be d——d if ever you dine with me again."

The officers took their departure, restraining their mirth until they gained the gun-room; and Jerry was about to follow, when Captain Bradshaw caught him by the arm.

"Stop, my young gentleman, you've not had your 'whack' yet."

"I've had quite sufficient, sir, I thank you," replied Jerry; "an excellent dinner—many thanks to your hospitality."

"Yes, but I must now give you your dessert."

"I've had my dessert and coffee too, sir," said Jerry, trying to escape.

"But you have not had your *chasse-café*, and I cannot permit you to leave the cabin without it. Steward, desire a boatswain's mate to bring his cat, and a quarter-master to come here with seizings."

Jerry was now in a stew—the inflexible countenance of Captain Bradshaw showed that he was in earnest. However, he held his tongue until the operators appeared, hoping that the captain would think better of it.

"Seize this young gentleman up to the breach of the gun, quarter-master!"

"Will you oblige me, sir, by letting me know my offence?"

"No, sir."

"I do not belong to your ship," continued Jerry. "If I have done wrong, Captain M—— is well known to be a strict officer, and will pay every attention to your complaint."

"I will save him the trouble, sir."

Jerry was now seized up, and every arrangement made preparatory to punishment. "Well, sir," resumed Jerry, "it must be as you please; but I know what Captain M—— will say."

"What, sir?"

"That you were angry with your officers, whom you could not punish, and revenged yourself upon a poor boy."

"Would he?—Boatswain's mate, where's your cat?"

"Here, sir;—how many tails am I to use?"

"Oh, give him the whole nine."

"Why, your honour," replied the man, in a compassionate tone, "there's hardly room for them there."

Jerry, who, when his indignation was roused, cared little what he said, and defied consequences, now addressed the captain.

"Captain Bradshaw, before you commence, will you allow me to tell you what I will call you after the first lash?"

"What, sir?"

"What!" cried Jerry with scorn,—"Why, if you cut me to pieces, and turn me out of the service afterwards, I will call you a paltry coward, and your own conscience, when you are able to reflect, will tell you the same."

Captain Bradshaw started back with astonishment at such unheard-of language from a midshipman; but he was pleased with the undaunted spirit of the boy—perhaps he felt the truth of the observation. At all events, it saved Jerry. After a short pause, the captain said—

"Cast him loose; but observe, sir, never let me see your face again while you are in the ship!"

"No, nor any other part of me, if I can help it," replied Jerry, buttoning up his clothes, and making a precipitate escape by the cabin-door.

Chapter XXXV

The air no more was vital now,
But did a mortal poison grow.
The lungs, which used to fan the heart,
Served only now to fire each part;
What should refresh, increased the smart.
And now their very breath,
The chiefest sign of life, became the cause of death ! "
                              SPRAT, *Bishop of Rochester.*

THE *Aspasia* did not drop her anchor in Carlisle Bay until three weeks after the arrival of the frigate which brought up Courtenay and the prize crew; but she had not been idle, having three valuable prizes, which she had captured in company. Courtenay immediately repaired on board of his ship, to report to Captain M—— the circumstances which had occurred connected with the loss of his five men.

He was too honourable to attempt to disguise or palliate the facts: on the contrary, he laid all the blame upon himself, and enhanced the merits of the two midshipmen. Captain M——, who admired his ingenuous confession, contented himself with observing, that he trusted it would be a caution to him during his future career in the service. To Seymour and Jerry he said nothing, as he was afraid that the latter would presume upon commendation; but he treasured up their conduct in his memory, and determined to lose no opportunity that might offer to reward them.

Courtenay descended to the gun-room, where he was warmly greeted by his messmates, who crowded round him to listen to his detail of the attempt to re-capture.

"Well," observed Price, "it appears we have had a narrow chance of losing a messmate."

"Narrow chance lose two, sar," replied Billy Pitts; "you forgit, sar, I on board schooner!"

"Oh, Billy, are you there? How does the dictionary come on?"

"Come on well, sar; I made a *corundum* on Massa Doctor, when on board schooner."

" Made a what?—a corundum ! What can that be ? "

" It ought to be something devilish hard," observed Courtenay.

" Yes, sar, debblish hard find out. Now, sar,—Why Massa Macallan like a general ? "

" I'm sure I can't tell. We give it up, Billy."

" Then, sar, I tell you. Because he *feelossifer*."

" Bravo, Billy !—Why you'll write a book soon. By-the-bye, Macallan, I must not forget to thank you for the loan of that gentleman : he has made himself very useful, and behaved very well."

" Really, Massa Courtenay, I tought I not give you satisfaction."

" Why so, Billy ? "

" Because, sar, you nebber give me present—not one dollar."

" He has you there," said Price ; " you must fork out."

" Not a rap—the nigger had perquisites. I saw the English merchants give him a handful of dollars, before they left the vessel."

" Ah ! they real gentlemen, Massa Capon and Massa ——dam 'um name—I forgot."

" And what am I, then, you black thief ? "

" Oh ! you, sar, you very fine officer," replied Billy, quitting the gun-room.

Courtenay did not exactly like the answer—but there was nothing to lay hold of. As usual, when displeased, he referred to his snuff-box, muttering something, in which the word " annoying " could only be distinguished.

The breeze from the windsail blew some of the snuff out of the box into the eyes of Macallan.

" I wish to Heaven you would be more careful, Courtenay," cried the surgeon, in an angry tone, and stamping with the pain.

" I really beg your pardon," replied Courtenay, " snuffing's a vile habit,—I wish I could leave it off."

" So do your messmates," replied the surgeon ; " I cannot imagine what pleasure there can be in a practice in itself so nasty, independent of the destruction of the olfactory powers."

"It's exactly for that reason that I take snuff; I am convinced that I am a gainer by the loss of the power of smell."

"I consider it ungrateful, if not wicked, to say so," replied the surgeon, gravely. "The senses were given to us as a source of enjoyment."

"True, doctor," answered Courtenay, mimicking the language of Macallan; "and if I were a savage in the woods, there could not be a sense more valuable, or affording so much gratification, as the one in question. I should rise with the sun, and inhale the fragance of the shrubs and flowers, offered up in grateful incense to their Creator, and I should stretch myself under the branches of the forest tree, as evening closed, and enjoy the faint perfume with which they wooed the descending moisture after exhaustion from the solar heat. But in civilised society, where men and things are packed too closely together, the case is widely different: for one pleasant, you encounter twenty offensive smells; and of all the localities for villanous compounds, a ship is indubitably the worst. I therefore patronise 'baccy,' which, I presume, was intended for our use, or it would not have been created."

"But not for our abuse."

"Ah! there's the rock that we all split upon—and I, with others, must plead guilty. The greatest difficulty in this world is, to know when and where to stop. Even a philosopher like yourself cannot do it. You allow your hypothesis to whirl in your brain, until it forms a vortex which swallows up everything that comes within its influence. A modern philosopher, with his hypothesis, is like the man possessed with a devil in times of yore; and it is not to be cast out by any means that I know of."

"As you please," replied Macallan, laughing; "I only deprecated a bad habit."

"An hypothesis is only a habit,—a habit of looking

through a glass of one peculiar colour, which imparts its hue to all around it. We are but creatures of habit. Luxury is nothing more than contracting fresh habits, and having the means of administering to them—*ergo*, doctor, the more habits you have to gratify, the more luxuries you possess. You luxuriate in the contemplation of nature—Price in quoting, or trying to quote, Shakespeare—Billy Pitts in his dictionary—I in my snuff-box ; and surely we may all continue to enjoy our harmless propensities, without interfering with each other : although I must say, that those still-born quotations of our mess-mate Price are most tryingly annoying."

" And so is a pinch of snuff in the eye, I can assure you," replied Macallan.

" Granted ; but we must ' give and take,' doctor."

" In the present case, I don't care how much you take, provided you don't give," rejoined Macallan, recovering his good humour.

A messenger from Captain M——, who desired to speak with Macallan, put an end to the conversation.

" Mr Macallan," said Captain M——, when the surgeon came into the cabin to receive his commands, " I am sorry to find, from letters which I have received, that the yellow fever is raging in the other islands in a most alarming manner, and that it has been communicated to the squadron on the station. I am sorry to add, that I have received a letter from the governor here, informing me that it has made its appearance at the barracks.   I am afraid that we have little chance of escaping so general a visitation. As it is impossible to put to sea, even if my orders were not decisive to the contrary, are there not some precautions which ought to be taken ? "

" Certainly, sir. It will be prudent to fumigate the lower deck ; it has already been so well ventilated and whitewashed, that nothing else can be done ; we must hope for the best."

" I do so," replied Captain M—— ; " but my hope is mingled with anxious apprehensions, which I cannot control. We must do all we can, and leave the rest to Providence."

The fears of Captain M—— were but too well grounded. For some days, no symptoms of infection appeared on board of the *Aspasia*; but the ravages on shore, among the troops, were to such an extent, that the hospitals were filled, and those who were carried in might truly be said to have left hope behind. Rapid as was the mortality, it was still not rapid enough for the admittance of those who were attacked with the fatal disease; and as the bodies of fifteen or twenty were, each succeeding evening, borne unto the grave, the continual decrease of the military cortège which attended the last obsequies, told the sad tale, that those who, but a day or two before, had followed the corpses of others, were now carried on their own biers.

Other vessels on the station, which had put to sea from the different isles, with the disappointed expectation of avoiding the contagion, now came to an anchor in the bay, their crews so weakened by disease and death that they could with difficulty send up sufficient men to furl their sails. Boat after boat was sent on shore to the naval hospital, loaded with sufferers, until it became so crowded that no more could be received. Still the *Aspasia*, from the precautions which had been taken, in fumigating, and avoiding all unnecessary contact with the shipping and the shore, had for nearly a fortnight escaped the infection; but the miasma was at last wafted to the frigate, and in the course of one night, fifteen men, who were in health the preceding evening, before eight o'clock on the following morning were lying in their hammocks under the half-deck. Before the close of that day, the number of patients had increased to upwards of forty. The hospitals were so crowded that Captain M—— agreed with Macallan that it would be better that the men should remain on board.

The frigate was anchored with springs on her cable, so as always to be able to warp her stern to the breeze; the cabin bulk-heads on the main-deck, and the thwart-ship bulk-heads below, were removed, and the stern windows and ports thrown open, to admit a freer circulation of air than could have been obtained by riding with her head to the sullen breeze, which hardly deigned to fan the scorching cheeks of the numerous and exhausted patients. The numbers on the list daily increased, until every part of the ship was occupied with their hammocks, and the surgeon and his assistants had scarcely time to relieve one by excessive bleeding, and consign him to his hammock, before another, staggering and fainting under the rapid disease, presented himself with his arm bared, ready for the lancet. More blood was thrown into the stagnant water of the bay than would have sufficed to render ever verdant the laurels of many a well-fought action (for our laurels flourish not from the dew of Heaven, but must be watered with a sanguine stream)—and, alas, too soon, more bodies were consigned to the deep than would have been demanded from the frigate in the warmest proof of courage and perseverance in her country's cause.

It is a scene like this which appals the sailor's heart. It is not the range of hammocks on the main-deck, tenanted by pale forms, with their bandages steeped in gore; for such is the chance of war, and the blood has flowed from hearts boiling with ardour and devotion. If not past cure, the smiles and congratulations of their shipmates alleviate the anguish and fever of the wound: if past all medical relief, still the passage from this transitory world is soothed by the affectionate sympathy of their messmates, by the promise to execute their last wishes, by the knowledge that it was in their country's defence they nobly fell. 'Tis not the chance of wreck, or of being consigned, unshrouded, to the dark wave, by the treacherous leak, or overwhelming fury of the storm. 'Tis not the " thought-executing fire." Every and all of these they are prepared and are resigned to meet, as ills to which their devious track is heir. But when disease, in its most loathsome form and implacable nature, makes its appearance—when we contemplate, in perspective, our own fate in the unfortunate who is selected, like the struggling sheep, dragged from the hurdled crowd, to be pierced by the knife of the butcher—when the horror of infection becomes so strong that we hold aloof from administering the kind offices of relief to our dearest friends; and, eventually prostrated ourselves, find the same regard for self pervades the rest, and that there is no voluntary attendance — then the sight of the expiring wretch, in his last effort, turning his head over the side of his hammock, and throwing off the dreadful black vomit, harbinger of his doom—'tis horrible ! too horrible !

And the anxiety which we would in vain suppress—the reckless laugh of some, raised but to conceal their fear from human penetration—the intoxicating draught, poured down by others to dull the excited senses—the follies of years reviewed in one short minute—our life, how spent, —how much to answer for !—a world how overvalued—a God how much neglected !—the feeling that we ought to pray, the inclination that propels us to do so, checked by the mistaken yet indomitable pride which puts the question to our manhood, " Will ye pray in fear, when ye neglected it in fancied security ? " Down, stubborn knees ! Pride is but folly towards men—insanity towards God !

But why dwell upon such a scene ? Let it suffice to state, that seventy of the *Aspasia's* men fell victims to the baneful climate, and that many more, who did recover, were left in such a state of exhaustion, as to require their immediate return to their native shores. Except O'Keefe, the purser, all the officers whom I have introduced to the reader escaped. Three, from the midshipmen's berth, who had served their time, and who for many months had been drinking the toast of " A bloody war and sickly season," fell a sacrifice to their own thoughtless and selfish desire ; and the clerk, who anticipated promotion when he heard that the purser was attacked, died before him.

When all was over, Jerry observed to Prose, " Well,

Prose, ' it's an ill wind that blows nobody any good.' We have had not one single thrashing during the sickness; but I suppose, now that their courage is returned, we must prepare for both principal and interest."

"Well now, Jerry, I do declare that's very likely, but I never thought of it before."

The large convoys of merchantmen that came out, supplied the men that were required to man the disabled ships; and transports brought out cargoes from the depôts to fill up the skeleton ranks of the different companies. Among the various blessings left us in this life of suffering, is forgetfulness of past evils; and the yellow fever was in a short time no longer the theme of dread, or even of conversation.

"Well, Tom, what sort of a place is this here West Hinges?" inquired a soldier, who had been just landed from a transport, to an old acquaintance in the regiment, whom he encountered.

"Capital place, Bill," returned the other to his interrogation; "plenty to drink, and always a-dry."

But as I do not wish to swell my narrative, and have no doubt but the reader will be glad to leave this pestilential climate, I shall inform him, that for three years the *Aspasia* continued on the station, daily encountering the usual risks of battle, fire, and wreck; and that at the end of that period the health of Captain M—— was so much injured, by the climate and his own exertions, that he requested permission to quit the station.

Chapter XXXVI

Sir Bash. This idol of my heart is—my own wife!
Love. Your own wife?
Sir Bash. Yes, my own wife. 'Tis all over with me: I am undone.
The Way to keep Him.

"Show us something new." Such was the cry of men at the time of the Prophet, and such it will continue until all prophecies are accomplished, all revelations confirmed. Man is constant in nought but inconsistency. He is directed to take pattern from the industrious bee, and lay up the sweet treasures which have been prepared for his use; but he prefers the giddy flight of the butter-fly, pursuing his idle career from flower to flower, until, fatigued with the rapidity of his motions, he reposes for a time, and revolves in his mind where he shall bend his devious way in search of "something new."

This is the fatal propensity by which our first parents fell, and which, inherited by us, is the occasion of our follies and our crimes. "Were man but constant, he were perfect;" but that he cannot be. He is aware of the dangers, the hardships of travel—of the difference between offices performed by an interested and heartless world, and the sweet ministering of duty and affection. He feels that home, sweet home, is the heaven of such imperfect bliss as this world can bestow; yet, wander he must, that he may appreciate its value: and although he hails it with rapture, soon after his return it palls upon him, and he quits it again in search of variety. Thus is man convinced of the beauty of Virtue, and acknow-ledges the peace that is to be found in her abode; yet, propelled by the restless legacy of our first parents, he wanders into the entangled labyrinths of vice—until, satisfied that all is vexation, he retraces his steps in repentance and disgust. Thus he passes his existence in sinning, repenting, and sinning again, in search of "some-thing new."

When Mr Rainscourt was first separated from his wife, he felt himself released from a heavy burthen, which had oppressed him for years; or as if fetters, which had been long riveted, had been knocked off; and he congratulated himself upon his regained liberty. Plunging at once into the depths of vice and dissipation, he sought pleasure after pleasure, variety upon variety,—all that life could offer, or money purchase: and for a time thought himself happy. But there are drawbacks which cannot be surmounted; and he who wholly associates with the vicious, must, more than any other, be exposed to the effects of depravity.   He found man more than ever treacherous and ungrateful—woman more than ever   deceiving — indulgence,   cloying — debauchery, enervating—and his constitution and his spirits exhausted by excess.   Satiated with everything, disgusted with everybody, he sought for " something new."

For more than two years he had not seen, and had hardly bestowed a thought upon, his wife and daughter, who still continued to reside at the mansion at——.   Not knowing what to do with himself, it occurred to him that the country air might recruit his health; and he felt a degree of interest, if not for his wife, at least for his daughter.   He determined, therefore, to pay them a visit. The horses were ordered: and, to the astonishment of Mrs Rainscourt, to whom he had given no intimation of his whim, and who looked upon a visit from her husband, in her retirement, as a visionary idea, Rainscourt made his appearance, just as she was about to sit down to dinner, in company with the M'Elvinas, and the vicar, who had become one of her most intimate associates.

If Rainscourt was pleased with the improvement of Emily, who was now more than fourteen years old, how much more was he astonished at the appearance of his wife, who, to his eyes, seemed even handsomer, if possible, than on the day when he had led her to the altar.   For more than two years, content, if not perfect happiness, had been Mrs Rainscourt's lot.   She had recovered her health, her bloom, and her spirits, and not having had any source of irritation, her serenity of temper had been regained; and Mrs Rainscourt, to whose extreme beauty, from assuetude, he had before been blind, now appeared to him, after so long an absence, quite a different person from the one whom he had quitted with such indifference; and as he surveyed her, he seemed to feel that freshness of delight unknown to vitiated minds, except when successful in their search after " something new."

But Rainscourt was not altogether wrong in his idea that his wife was quite a different personage from the one which he had quitted. The vicar, who was acquainted with her situation, had not failed in his constant exertions for the improvement of mankind; he had, by frequent conversation, and inculcation of our Christian duties, gradually softened her into a charitable and forgiving temper; and, now that she had no opportunity of exercising them, she had been made acquainted with the passive forbearance and humility constituting a part of the duties of a wife.

She met her husband with kindness and respect—while his daughter, who flew into his arms, proved that she had not been prepossessed against him, as he anticipated.

Pleased with his reception, and with the company that he happened to meet, Rainscourt experienced sensations which had long been dormant; and it occurred to him, that an establishment, with such an elegant woman as Mrs Rainscourt at the head, and his daughter's beauty to grace it, would not only be more gratifying, but more reputable, than the course of life which he had lately pursued. He made himself excessively agreeable—was pleased with the benevolent demeanour of the vicar— thought Susan a lovely young woman, and M'Elvina a delightful companion; and, when he retired to the chamber prepared for his reception, wondered that he had never thought of paying them a visit before.

It had been the intention of Rainscourt to have trespassed upon his wife's hospitality for one night only, and then have taken his departure for some fashionable watering- place; but there seemed to be such an appearance of renewed friendship between him and Mrs Rainscourt, that an invitation was given by the vicar, for the whole party, on the ensuing day, to meet at the vicarage; and this was followed up by another from M'Elvina, for the day afterwards, at his cottage. This decided Mr Rains- court to remain there a day or two longer.

But when the time of his departure arrived, Rainscourt

was so pleased with his new acquaintance, so delighted with his daughter, and, to his astonishment, so charmed by his wife, that he could not tear himself away.

Women are proverbially sharp-sighted in all where the heart is concerned, and Mrs Rainscourt soon perceived that the admiration of her husband was not feigned. Gratified to find that she had not yet lost her attractions, and, either from a pardonable feeling of revenge at his desertion, or to prove to him that he was not aware of what he had rejected, she exerted all her powers to please ; she was not only amiable, but fascinating ; and after a sojourn of three weeks, which appeared but as many days, Rainscourt was reluctantly compelled to acknowledge to himself, that he was violently enamoured of his discarded wife.

He now felt that he should assume a higher station in society by being at the head of his own establishment, and that his consequence would be increased, by the heiress of so large a property residing under his protection ; and he thought that, if he could persuade Mrs Rainscourt to live with him again, he could be happy, and exercise with pleasure the duties of a father and a husband. Neither the vicar nor M'Elvina were ignorant of his feelings ; and the former, who recollected that those whom God has joined, no man should put asunder, had made up his mind to bring the affair, if possible, to a happy issue ; and Rainscourt, who perceived the influence which the vicar possessed over his wife, determined to request that he would act as a mediator.

The vicar was delighted when Rainscourt called upon him one morning, and unfolded his wishes. To reconcile those who had been at variance, to restore a husband to his wife, a father to a daughter, was the earnest desire of the good man's heart. He accepted the office with pleasure ; and in the course of the afternoon, while Rainscourt called upon the M'Elvinas, that he might be out of the way, proceeded upon his mission of peace and good-will.

Mrs Rainscourt, who was not surprised at the intelligence, listened to the vicar attentively, as he pointed out the necessity of forgiveness, if she hoped to be forgiven—of the conviction, in his own mind, that her husband was reformed—of the unpleasant remarks to which a woman who is separated from her husband must always be subjected — of the probability that the faults were not all on his side, and of the advantage her daughter would derive from their reunion : to which he entreated her to consent.

Mrs Rainscourt was moved to tears. The conflict between her former love and her outraged feelings—the remembrance of his long neglect, opposed to his present assiduities—the stormy life she had passed in his company, and her repose of mind since their separation—weighed and balanced against each other so exactly, that the scale would turn on neither side.

She refused to give any decided answer, but requested a day or two for reflection ; and the vicar, who recollected the adage, that, in an affair of the heart, " the woman who deliberates is lost," left her with a happy presage that his endeavours would be crowned with success. But Mrs Rainscourt would not permit her own heart to decide. It was a case in which she did not consider that a woman was likely to be a correct judge; and she had so long been on intimate terms with M'Elvina, that she resolved to lay the case before him, and be guided by his opinion.

The next day, Mrs Rainscourt went to the cottage alone, and having requested Susan to exclude all visitors, entered into a full detail of all the circumstances which had occurred previous to her separation from her husband, and the decision that she was now called upon to make, from his importunity.

Susan, who felt that she was unable to advise, in a case of such importance to Mrs Rainscourt's future happiness, immediately referred the matter to M'Elvina.

His answer was decided.

" I should be sorry, Mrs Rainscourt, to give an opinion

in opposition to that of the worthy vicar, did I not conceive that his slight knowledge of the world would, in this instance, tend to mislead both himself and you. Before Mr Rainscourt had remained here a week, I prophesied, as Susan will corroborate, that this proposal would be made. Aware of his general character, and of the grounds of your separation, I took some pains to ingratiate myself, that I might ascertain his real sentiments; and, with regret I express my conviction, that his prepossession in your favour, strong as it really is at present, will but prove transitory, and that possession would only subject you to future insults. He is *not* reformed; but, satiated with other enjoyments, and fascinated with your attractions, his feelings towards you are those of renewed inclination, and not arising from conviction, or remorse at his unprincipled career. You are happy at present—your refusal may, by stimulating his attentions, increase your happiness: but if you yield, it will only be a source of misery to you both. Such is my opinion. Do not let him know that I have influenced you, or it will interrupt an intimacy, which I shall follow up, I trust, to your advantage; therefore, give no answer at present, nor while he remains here: for I perceive that he is a violent man when thwarted in his wishes. Demand a fortnight's consideration after he is gone, and then you will be able to decide from reflection, without being biassed against your own judgment, by his working upon feelings which, to the honour of women, when the heart is concerned, spurn at the cold reasonings of prudence and worldly wisdom."

The advice of the man of the world prevailed over that of the man of God; and Rainscourt, after waiting in town, with impatience, for the answer, received a decided but kind refusal. He tore the letter into fragments, with indignation, and set off for Cheltenham, more violently in love with his wife than he was before her rejection of him.

Chapter XXXVII

Great Negative! how vainly would the wise
Inquire, define, distinguish, teach, devise,
Didst thou not stand to point their dull philosophies.
                          ROCHESTER's *Ode to " Nothing."*

SHOULD you feel half as tired with reading as I am with writing, I forgive you, with all my heart, if you throw down the book, and read no more. I have written too fast—I have quite *sprained* my imagination—for you must know that this is all *fiction*, every word of it. Yet I do not doubt but there are many who will find out who the characters are meant for, notwithstanding my assertion to the contrary. Well, be it so. It's a very awkward position to have to write a chapter of sixteen pages, without materials for more than two; at least I find it so. Some people have the power of spinning out a trifle of matter, covering a large surface with a grain of ore—like the goldbeater, who, out of a single guinea, will compose a score of books. I wish I could.

Is there nothing to give me an idea? I've racked my sensorium internally to no purpose. Let me look round the cabin for some external object to act as a fillip to an exhausted imagination. A little thing will do.—Well, here's an *ant*. That's quite enough. *Commençons.*

" Home-keeping youths have ever homely wits," they say; but much as travel by land may enlarge the mind, it never can be expanded to the utmost of its capabilities, until it has also peregrinated by water. I believe that not only the human intellect, but the instinct of brutes, is enlarged by going to sea.

The ant which attracted my attention is one of a nest in my cabin, whose labours I often superintend: and I defy any ants, in any part of the four continents, or wherever land may be, to show an equal knowledge of mechanical power. I do not mean to assert that there is originally a disproportion of intellect between one animal and another of the same species; but I consider that the instinct of animals is capable of expansion, as well as the reason of man. That ants on shore would, if it were required, be equally assisted by their instinct, I believe; but not being required, it is not brought into play: and, therefore, as I before observed, they have not the resources of which my little colony at present are in possession.

Now I will kill a cockroach for them; there is no difficulty in finding one, unfortunately for me, for they gnaw everything that I have. There never was a class of animals so indifferent to their fare, whether it be paper, or snuff, or soap, or cloth. Like Time, they devour everything. The scoundrels have nearly demolished two dozen antibilious pills. I hope they will remember Dr Vance as long as they live.

Well, here's one—a fine one. I throw his crushed carcass on the deck, and observe the ants have made their nest in the beams over my head, from which I infer, that the said beams are not quite so sound as they should be. An ant has passed by the carcass, and is off on a gallop to give notice. He meets two or three—stops a second—and passes on. Now the tide flows; it's not above a minute since I threw the cockroach down, and now it is surrounded by hundreds. What a bustle!—what running to and fro! They must be giving orders. See, there are fifty at least, who lay hold of each separate leg of the monster, who in bulk is equal to eight thousand of them. The body moves along with rapidity, and they have gained the side of the cabin. Now for the ascent. See how those who hold the lower legs have quitted them, and pass over to assist the others at the upper. As there is not room for all to lay hold of the creature's legs, those who cannot, fix their forceps round the bodies of the others, *double-banking* them, as we call it. Away they go, up the side of the ship—a steady pull, and all together. But now the work becomes more perilous, for they have to convey the body to their nest over my head, which is three feet from the side of the ship. How can they possibly carry that immense weight, walking with their heads downwards, and clinging with their feet to the beams? Observe how carefully they turn the corner—what bustle and confusion in making their arrangements! Now they start. They have brought the body head-and-stern with the ship, so that all the legs are exactly opposed to each other in the direction which they wish to proceed. One of the legs on the fore side is advanced to its full stretch, while all the others remain stationary. That leg stops, and the ants attached to it hold on with the rest, while another of the foremost legs is advanced. Thus they continue, until all the foremost are out, and the body of the animal is suspended by its legs at its full stretch. Now one of the hindmost legs closes in to the body, while all the others hold on—now another, and another, each in their turn; and by this skilful manœuvre they have contrived to advance the body nearly an inch along the ceiling. One of the foremost legs advances again, and they proceed as before.

Could your shore-going ants have managed this? I have often watched them, when a boy, because my grandmother used to make me do so; in later days, because I delighted in their industry and perseverance; but, alas! in neither case did I profit by their example.

"Now, Freddy," the old lady would say, giving her spectacles a preparatory wipe, as she basked in a summer evening's sun, after a five o'clock tea, "fetch a piece of bread and butter, and we will see the ants work. Lord bless the boy, if he hasn't thrown down a whole slice. Why do you waste good victuals in that way? Who do you think's to eat it, after it has been on the gravel? There, pinch a bit off and throw it down. Put the rest back upon the plate—it will do for the cat."

But these ants were no more to be compared to mine, than a common labourer is to the engineer who directs the mechanical powers which raise mountains from their foundation. My old grandmother would never let me escape until the bread and butter was in the hole, and, what was worse, I had then to listen to the moral inference which was drawn, and which took up more time than the ants did to draw the bread and butter—all about industry, and what not; a long story, partly her own, partly borrowed from Solomon; but it was labour in vain. I could not understand why, because ants like bread and butter, I must like my book. She was an excellent old woman; but nevertheless, many a time did I have a fellow-feeling with the boy in the caricature print, who is sitting with his old grandmother and the cat, and says, "I wish one of us three were dead. It an't I—and it an't you, pussy."

Well, she died at last, full of years and honour; and I was summoned from school to attend her funeral. My uncle was much affected, for she had been an excellent mother. She might have been so; but I, graceless boy, could not perceive her merits as a *grandmother*, and showed a great deal of fortitude upon the occasion. I recollect a circumstance attendant upon her funeral which, connected as it was with a subsequent one, has since been the occasion of serious reflection upon the trifling causes which will affect the human mind, when prostrate under affliction. My grandmother's remains were consigned to an old family vault, not far from the river. When the last ceremonies had been paid, and the coffin was being lowered into the deep receptacle of generations which had passed away, I looked down, and it was full of water, nearly up to the arch of the vault. Observing my surprise, and perceiving the cause, my uncle was much annoyed at the circumstance; but it was too late—the cords had been removed, and my grandmother had sunk to the bottom. My uncle interrogated the sexton after the funeral service was over.

"Why, sir, it's because it's high water now in the river; she will be all dry before the evening."

This made the matter worse. If she was all adry in the evening, she would be all afloat again in the morning. It was no longer a place of rest, and my uncle's grief was much increased by the idea.   For a long while afterwards, he appeared uncommonly thoughtful at spring tides.

But although his grief yielded to time, the impression was not to be effaced. Many years afterwards, a fair cousin was summoned from the world, before she had time to enter upon the duties imposed upon the sex, or be convinced, from painful experience, that to die is gain.   It was then I perceived that my uncle had contracted a sort of *post-mortem* hydrophobia. He fixed upon a church, on the top of a hill, and ordered a vault to be dug, at a great expense, out of the solid chalk, under the chancel of the church.   There it would not only be dry below, but even defended from the rain above.   It was finished—and (the last moisture to which she was ever to be subjected) the tears of affection were shed over her remains, by those who lost and loved her.   When the ceremony was over, my uncle appeared to look down into the vault with a degree of satisfaction.   "There," said he, "she will lie as dry as possible, till the end of time."   And I really believe that this conviction on his part went further to console him than even the aid of religion, or the ministering of affection. He often commented upon it, and as often as he did so, I thought of my old grandmother and the spring tides.

I had an odd dream the other night, about my own burial and subsequent state—which was so diametrically opposite to my uncle's ideas of comfort, that I will relate it here.

I was dead; but, either from politeness or affection, I knew not which, the spirit still lingered with the body, and had not yet taken its flight, although the tie between them had been dissolved.   I had been killed in action : and the first lieutenant of the ship, with mingled feelings of sorrow and delight—sorrow at my death, which was a tribute that I did not expect from him, and delight at his assumed promotion, for the combat had been brought to a successful issue—read the funeral service which consigned me and some twenty others, sewed up in hammocks, to the deep, into which we descended with one simultaneous rush.

I thought that we soon parted company from each other, and, all alone, I continued to sink, sink, sink, until at last I could sink no deeper. I was suspended, as it were; I had taken my exact position in the scale of gravity, and I lay floating upon the condensed and buoyant fluid, many hundred fathoms below the surface. I thought to myself, "Here then am I to lie in pickle, until I am awakened." It was quite dark, but by the spirit I saw as plain as if it were noonday; and I perceived objects in the water, which gradually increased in size. They were sharks, in search of prey. They attacked me furiously; and as they endeavoured to drag me out of my canvas cerements, I whirled round and round as their flat noses struck against my sides. At last they succeeded. In a moment, I was dismembered without the least pain, for pain had been left behind me in the world from which I had been released. One separated a leg, with his sharp teeth, and darted away north; another an arm, and steered south; each took his portion, and appeared to steer away in a different direction, as if he did not wish to be interrupted in his digestion.

"Help yourselves, gentlemen, help yourselves," mentally exclaimed I; "but if Mr Young is correct in his 'Night Thoughts,' where am I to fumble for my bones, when they are to be forthcoming?" Nothing was left but my head, and that, from superior gravity, continued to sink, gyrating in its descent, so as to make me feel quite giddy: but it had not gone far, before one, who had not received his portion, darted down upon it perpendicularly, and as the last fragment of me rolled down his enormous gullet, the spirit fled, and all was darkness and oblivion.

But I have digressed sadly from the concatenation of ideas. The ant made me think of my grandmother,—my grandmother of my uncle,—my uncle of my cousin,—and her death of my dream, for "We are such stuff as dreams are made of, and our little lives are rounded with a sleep." But I had not finished all I had to say relative to the inferior animals. When on board of a man-of-war, not only is their instinct expanded, but they almost change their nature from their immediate contact with human beings, and become tame in an incredibly short space of time. Man had dominion given unto him over the beasts of the field; the fiercest of the feline race will not attack, but avoid him, unless goaded on by the most imperious demands of hunger; and it is a well-known fact, that there is a power in the eye of man, to which all other animals quail. What then must it be to an animal who is brought on board, and is in immediate collision with hundreds, whose fearless eyes meet his in every direction in which he turns, and whose behaviour towards him corresponds with their undaunted looks? The animal is subdued at once. I remember a leopard which was permitted to run loose after he had been three days on board, although it was thought necessary to bring him in an iron cage. He had not been in the ship more than a fortnight, when I observed the captain of the after-guard rubbing the nose of the animal against the deck, for some offence which he had committed.

"Why, you have pretty well brought that gentleman to his bearings," observed I; "he's as tame as a puppy."

"Tame! why, sir, he knows better than to be otherwise. I wish the *Hemp'rer of Maroccy* would send us on board a *cock rhinoceros*—we'd tame him in a week."

And I believe the man was correct in his assertion.

The most remarkable change of habit that I ever witnessed, was in a wether sheep, on board of a frigate, during the last war. He was one of a stock which the captain had taken on board for a long cruise, and being the only survivor, during the time that the ship was refitting he had been allowed to run about the decks, and had become such a favourite with the ship's company, that the idea of his being killed, even when short of fresh provisions, never even entered into the head of the captain. Jack, for such was his cognomen, lived entirely with the men, being fed with biscuit from the different messes. He knew the meaning of the different pipes of the boatswain's mates, and always went below when they piped to breakfast, dinner, or supper. But amongst other particularities, he would chew tobacco, and drink grog. Is it to be wondered, therefore, that he was a favourite with the sailors? That he at first did this from obedience is possible; but, eventually, he was as fond of grog as any of the men; and when the pipe gave notice for serving it out, he would run aft to the tub, and wait his turn—for an extra half pint of water was, by general consent, thrown into the tub when the grog was mixed, that Jack might have his regular allowance. From habit, the animal knew exactly when his turn came. There were eighteen messes in the ship; and as they were called, by the purser's steward, or sergeant of marines, in rotation—first mess, second mess, etc.,—after the last mess was called Jack presented himself at the tub, and received his allowance.

Now, it sometimes occurred that a mess, when called, would miss its turn, by the man deputed to receive the liquor not being present: upon which occasion, the other messes were served in rotation, and the one who had not appeared to the call was obliged to wait till after all the rest; but a circumstance of this kind always created a great deal of mirth; for the sheep, who knew that it was his turn after the eighteenth, or last mess, would butt away any one who attempted to interfere; and if the party persevered in being served before Jack, he would become quite outrageous, flying at the offender, and butting him forward into the galley, and sometimes down the hatchway, before his anger could be appeased—from which it would appear that the animal was passionately fond of spirits. This I consider as great a change in the nature of a ruminating animal, as can well be imagined.

I could mention many instances of this kind, but I shall reserve them till I have grown older; then I will be as garrulous as Montaigne. As it is, I think I hear the reader say—"All this may be very true, but what has it to do with the novel?" Nothing, I grant; but it has a great deal to do with *making a book*—for I have completed a whole chapter out of nothing.

Chapter XXXVIII

——And with a flowing sail
Went bounding for the island of the free,
Towards which the impatient wind blew half a gale;
High dash'd the spray, the bows dipp'd in the sea.
                                        BYRON.

AFTER a run of six weeks, the *Aspasia* entered the Channel. The weather, which had been clear during the passage home, now altered its appearance; and a dark sky, thick fog, and mizzling cold rain, intimated their approach to the English shore. But, relaxed as they had been by three years' endurance of a tropical sun, it was nevertheless a source of congratulation, rather than complaint; for it was "regular November Channel weather," and was associated with their propinquity to those homes and firesides, which would be enhanced in value from the ordeal to be passed before they could be enjoyed.

"Hah!" exclaimed an old quarter-master, who had served the earlier part of his life in a coaster, as he buttoned his pea-jacket up to the throat; "this is what I calls something like; none of your d——d blue skies here."

Such is the power of affection, whether of person or of things, that even faults become a source of endearment.

As the short day closed, the *Aspasia*, which was running before the wind and slanting rain, which seemed to assist her speed with its gravity, hove-to, and tried for soundings.

"Well, Stewart, what's the news?" said one of the midshipmen, as he entered the berth; the drops of rain, which hung upon the rough exterior of his great-coat, glittering like small diamonds, from the reflection of the solitary candle, which made darkness but just visible.

"News," replied Stewart, taking off his hat with a jerk, so as to besprinkle the face of Prose with the water that had accumulated on the top of it, and laughing at his sudden start from the unexpected shower; "why, as the fellows roar out with the second edition of an evening paper 'great news, glorious news!'—and all comprised in a short sentence :—Soundings in seventy-four fathoms; grey sand and shells."

"Huzza!" answered the old master's mate.

"Now for three cheers—and then for the song."

The three cheers having been given with due emphasis, if not discretion, they all stood up round the table. "Now, my boys, keep time. Mr Prose, if you attempt to chime in with your confounded nasal twang, I'll give you a squeeze."

> " For England, when, with favouring gale,
>   Our gallant ship up Channel steer'd,
> And, scudding under easy sail,
>   The high blue western land appear'd,
> To heave the lead the seaman sprung,
> And to the watchful pilot sung,
>   By the deep *nine*."

The song, roared out in grand chorus by the midshipmen, was caught up, after the first verse, by the marines in their berth, close to them; and from them passed along the lower deck as it continued, so that the last stanzas were sung by nearly two hundred voices, sending forth a volume of sound, that penetrated every recess of the vessel, and entered into the responsive bosoms of all on board, not excepting the captain himself, who smiled, as he bent over the break of the gangway, at what he would have considered a breach of subordination in the ship's company, had not he felt that it arose from that warm attachment to their country which had created our naval pre-eminence.

The song ended with tumultuous cheering fore and aft, and not *until then* did the captain send down to request that the noise might be discontinued. As soon as it was over, the grog was loudly called for in the midshipmen's berth, and made its appearance.

"Here's to the white cliffs of England," cried one,

drinking off his full tumbler, and turning it upside down on the table.

"Here's to the land of Beauty."

"Here's to the Emerald Isle."

"And here's to the land of Cakes," cried Stewart, drinking off his tumbler, and throwing it over his shoulder.

"Six for one for skylarking," cried Prose.

"A hundred for one, you d——d cockney, for all I care."

"No—no—no," cried all the berth ; "not *one* for *one*."

"You shall have a song for it, my boys," cried Stewart, who immediately commenced, with great taste and execution, the beautiful air—

> "Should auld acquaintance be forgot,
> And days o' lang syne?"

"Well, I've not had my toast yet," said Jerry, when the applause at the end of the song had discontinued :— "Here's to the shady side of Pall-mall."

"And I suppose," said Stewart, giving Prose a slap on the back, which took his breath away, "that you are thinking of Wapping, blow you."

"I think I have had enough of wapping since I've been in this ship," answered Prose.

"Why, Prose, you're quite brilliant, I do declare," observed Jerry. "Like a flint, you only require a blow from Stewart's iron fist to emit sparks. Try him again, Stewart. He's like one of the dancing dervishes, in the Arabian Nights ; you must thrash him, to get a few farthings of wit out of him."

"I do wish that you would keep your advice to yourself, Jerry."

"My dear Prose, it's all for the honour of Middlesex that I wish you to shine. I'm convinced that there's a great deal of wit in that head of yours : but it's confined, like the kernel in a nut ; there's no obtaining it without breaking the shell. Try him again, Stewart."

"Come, Prose, I'll take your part, and try his own

receipt upon himself, I'll thrash him till he says something witty."

"I do like that, amazingly," replied Jerry. "Why, if I do say a good thing, you'll never find it out. I shall be thrashed to all eternity. Besides, I'm at too great a distance from you."

"What do you mean?"

"Why, I'm like some cows; I don't give down my milk without the calf is alongside of me. Now, if you were on this side of the table——"

"Which I am," replied Stewart, as he sprang over it, and seizing Jerry by the neck—"Now, Mr Jerry, say a good thing directly."

"Well, promise me to understand it. We are just in the reverse situation of England and Scotland, after the battle of Culloden."

"What do you mean by that, you wretch?" cried Stewart, whose wrath was kindled by the reference.

"Why, I'm in your clutches, just like Scotland was—a conquered country."

"You lie, you little blackguard," cried Stewart, pinching Jerry's neck till he forced his mouth open: "Scotland was never conquered."

"Well, then," continued Jerry, whose bile was up, as soon as Stewart relaxed his hold; "I'm like King Charles in the hands of the Scotch. How much was it that you sold him for?"

Jerry's shrivelled carcase sounded like a drum, from the blow which he received for this second insult to Stewart's idolised native land. As soon as he could recover his speech, "Well, haven't I been very witty? Are you content, or will you have some more? or will you try Prose, and see whether you can draw blood out of a turnip?"

Stewart, who seemed disinclined to have any more elegant extracts from Jerry, resumed his former seat by Prose, who appeared to be in deep reflection.

"Well, Prose, are you thinking of your friends in Cheapside?"

"And suppose I am, Stewart? We have the same feelings in the city that you have in the heather: and although I do not, like you, pretend to be allied to former kings, yet one may love one's father and mother, brothers and sisters, without being able to trace back to one's great great grandfather. I never disputed your high pretensions; why, then, interfere with my humble claims to the common feelings of humanity?"

"I am rebuked, Prose," replied Stewart; "you shall have my glass of grog for that speech, for you never made a better. Give me your hand, my good fellow."

"I am glad that you, at last, show some symptoms of reason," observed the still indignant Jerry, standing close to the door. "I have some hopes of your majesty yet, after such an extraordinary concession on your part. You must have great reason to be proud that you are able to trace your pedigree up to a border chieftain, who sallied forth on the foray, when the spurs were dished up for his dinner; or, in plain words, went a cattle-stealing, and robbing those who could not resist. It might then be considered a mark of prowess; but times are altered now: and if your celebrated ancestor lived in the present time, why," (continued Jerry, pointing his finger under his left ear) "he would receive what he well deserved, that's all."

"By Him that made me, get out of my reach, if you do not wish me to murder you!" cried Stewart, pale with rage.

"I took care of that," replied Jerry, "before I ventured to give my opinion; and now that I'm ready for a start, I'll give you a piece of advice. Trace your ancestors as far back as you can, as long as they have continued to be honest men,—if you don't stop there, you are a *fool*"—and Jerry very prudently made his escape at the conclusion of his sentence.

"The hour of retribution will come," cried Stewart after Jerry, as the latter sprang up the ladder; but it did not, for when they met next morning, it was to feast their eyes upon the chalky cliffs of the Isle of Wight, as the *Aspasia*

steered for the Needles.   There are two events on board
of a man-of-war, after which, injuries are forgotten,
apologies are offered and received, intended duels are
suppressed, hands are exchanged in friendship, and good-
will drives away long-cherished animosity.   One is, after
an action—another, upon the sight of native land, after a
protracted absence.

Jerry fearlessly ranged up alongside of Stewart, as he
looked over the gangway.

"We shall be at anchor by twelve o'clock."

"You may bless your stars for it," replied Stewart, with
a significant smile.

The *Aspasia* now ran through the Needles, and having
successively passed by Hurst Castle, Cowes, and the
entrance to Southampton Water, brought up at Spithead in
seven fathoms.   The sails were furled, the ship was moored,
the boat was manned and Captain M—— went on shore
to report himself to the port-admiral, and deliver his
despatches.   When the boat returned, it brought off letters
which had been awaiting the arrival of the ship.   One informed Jerry of the death of his father, and of his being
in possession of a fortune which enabled him to retire from
the service.   Another, from the Admiralty, announced the
promotion of Stewart to the rank of lieutenant; and one
from M'Elvina to our hero, inviting him to take up his
quarters at his house, as long as the service would permit,
stating that Captain M—— had been written to, to request
that he might be allowed leave of absence.

As soon as Captain M—— had received an answer from
the Admiralty, he returned on board, and acquainted his
officers that he had obtained leave to remain on shore for
some time, for the re-establishment of his health, and that
another captain would be appointed to the ship.   He
turned the hands up, and addressed the ship's company,
thanking them for their good behaviour while under his
command, and expressing his hopes, that upon his re-
appointment he should find them all alive and well.   The
first lieutenant, to his great surprise and delight, was pre-

sented with his rank as commander, which Captain M——
had solicited from the Admiralty. The men were dismissed,
and Captain M——, bidding farewell to his officers,
descended the side and shoved off. As soon as the boat
was clear of the frigate, the men, without orders, ran up,
and manning the shrouds, saluted him with three farewell
cheers. Captain M—— took off his hat to the compliment,
and, muffling up his face with his boat cloak to conceal his
emotion, the boat pulled for the shore.

Seymour, who was in the boat, followed his captain to
the inn ; who informed him, that he had obtained his discharge into a guardship, that his time might go on, and
leave of absence for two months, which he might spend
with his friend M'Elvina. Captain M—— then dismissed
him with a friendly shake of the hand, desiring him to
write frequently, and to draw upon his agent if he required
any pecuniary assistance.

Seymour's heart was full, and he could not answer his
kind protector. He returned on board, and bidding farewell to his messmates, the next evening he had arrived at
the cottage of M'Elvina.

That his reception was cordial, it is hardly necessary to
state. M'Elvina, whose marriage had not been blessed
with a family, felt towards our hero as if he was his own
child ; and Susan was delighted with the handsome
exterior and winning manners of the lad, whose boyish
days had often been the theme of her husband's conversation.

If the reader will take the trouble to reckon with his
fingers, he will find that William Seymour is now sixteen
years old. If he will not, he must take my word for it ;
and it may also be as well to inform him, that Miss
Rainscourt is more than fourteen. I am the more particular in mentioning these chronological facts, because in
the next chapter I intend to introduce the parties to each
other.

Chapter XXXIX

——A strong bull stands, threat'ning furious war ;
He flourishes his horns, looks sourly round,
And, hoarsely bellowing, traverses his ground.
BLACKMORE.

IT was on the second day after the arrival of Seymour, that
Emily, who was not aware of the addition to the party
at the cottage, proceeded on foot through the park and
fields adjacent, to pay Susan a visit. She was attended
by a man-servant, in livery, who carried some books,
which Mrs M'Elvina had expressed a desire to read.
When Emily had arrived at the last field, which was
rented by a farmer hard by, she was surprised to perceive
that it was occupied by an unpleasant tenant, to wit, a
large bull; who, on their approach, commenced pawing
the ground, and showing every symptom of hostility. She
quickened her pace, and as the animal approached, found
that she had gained much nearer to the stile before her
than to the one which she had just passed over, and,
frightened as she was, she determined to proceed. The
servant who accompanied her manifested more fear than
she did. As the bull approached, Emily, who had heard
what precautions should be taken in a similar exigence,
turned her face towards the animal, and walked backwards
to the stile. The domestic seemed determined to preserve
the exact station which his duty and respect required, and
kept himself behind his young mistress. As, however,
the bull advanced, and seemed inclined to charge upon
them, his fears would not permit him to remain in that
situation, and throwing down the books, he took to his
heels, and ran for a gap in the hedge. By this manœuvre
Emily was left to make any arrangement she pleased with
the infuriated animal.

But the bull had no quarrel with a lady, dressed in a
white muslin frock ; he had taken offence at the red plush
inexpressibles, which were a part of the family livery, and

immediately ran at the servant, passing Emily without notice. The terrified man threw himself in an agony of fright into the gap, but was so paralysed with fear that he had not strength to force his passage through. With his head and shoulders on the other side of the hedge, there he stuck on his hands and knees, offering a fair target to the bull, who flew at it with such violence, that he forced him several yards into the opposite field. Senseless and exhausted, he lay there more from fear than injury, while the roaring bull paced up and down the hedge, with his tail in the air, attempting in vain to force a passage in pursuit of the object of his detestation.

The mind of woman is often more powerful than her frame; and the one will bear up against circumstances in which the other will succumb. Thus it was with Emily, who reached the stile, clambered over it with difficulty, and obtaining the house of M'Elvina, which was but a few yards distant, felt that her powers failed her as soon as exertion was no longer required. With difficulty she perceived with her swimming eyes that there was a gentleman in the parlour; and faintly exclaiming, " Oh ! Mr M'Elvina ! " fell senseless into the arms of William Seymour.

Mr and Mrs M'Elvina were not at home: they had walked to the vicarage; and Seymour, who was very busy finishing a sketch of the *Aspasia* for his hostess, had declined accompanying them in their visit. His surprise at finding a young lady in his arms, may easily be imagined; but, great as was his surprise, his distress was greater, from the extreme novelty of the situation. It was not that he was unaccustomed to female society: on the contrary, his captain had introduced him everywhere in the different ports of the colonies in which they had anchored; and perhaps there is no better society, although limited, than is to be met with at the table of a colonial governor: but here it was quite different. He had been habituated to follow in the wake, as the lady governess made sail for the dining-room, the whole fleet forming two lines abreast in close order, and then coming to an anchor, in beautiful pre-

cision, to attack the dinner, which surrendered at discretion.
He had been habituated to the ball-room, where the ladies
glided over the chalked floor, like so many beautiful yachts
plying in Southampton Water on a fine day ; he had tried
his rate of sailing down the middle of a country dance with
some fair partner ; and tacked and wore as required to the
mazes of poussette and right and left.   This was all plain
sailing ; but the case was now quite different.   Here was
a strange sail, who had not even shown her number, taken
aback in stays, and on her beam-ends in a squall.

Seymour knew nothing about fainting.   Sometimes a
man had fits on board a ship (although invariably discharged when it was known); but the only remedy, in a
man-of-war, in such cases, was to lay the patient down
between the guns, and let him come-to at his own leisure.
It was impossible to act so in this case ; and Seymour, as
he bent over the beautiful pale countenance of Emily, felt
that he never could be tired of holding her in his arms.
However, as it was necessary that something should be
done, he laid her down on the sofa, and seizing the bell-
rope, pulled it violently for assistance.   The wire had been
previously slackened, and the force which Seymour used
brought down the rope without ringing the bell.   There
was but one in the room : and, not choosing to leave
Emily, he was again compelled to rely on his own resources.
What was good for her ?   Water ?   There was none in
the room, except what he had been painting with, and that
was desperately discoloured with the Indian ink.   Nevertheless, he snatched up his large brush which he used for
washing-in his skies, and commenced painting her face and
temples with the discoloured water ; but without producing
the desired effect of re-animation.

What next ?—Oh, salts and burnt feathers ; he had read
of them in a novel.   Salts he had none—burnt feathers were
to be procured.   There were two live birds, called
cardinals, belonging to Mrs M'Elvina, in a cage near the
window, and there was also a stuffed green parrot in a
glass case.   Seymour showed his usual presence of mind

in his decision.   The tails of the live birds would in all
probability grow again; that of the stuffed parrot never
could.   He put his hand into the cage, and, seizing the
fluttering proprietors, pulled out both their long tails, and
having secured the door of the cage, thrust the ends of the
feathers into the fire, and applied them, frizzing and
spluttering, to the nostrils of Emily.   But they were
replaced in the fire again and again, until they would emit
no more smoke, and Emily still continued in a state of
insensibility.   There was no help for it—the parrot, which
he knew Mrs M'Elvina was partial to, must be sacrificed.
A blow with the poker demolished the glass, and the
animal was wrenched off its perch, and the tail inserted
between the bars of the grate.   But burnt feathers were of
no use ; and Seymour, when he had burnt down the parrot's
tail to the stump, laid it upon the table in despair.

He now began to be seriously alarmed, and the beauty
of the object heightened his pity and commiseration.   His
anxiety increased to that degree that, losing his presence
of mind, and giving way to his feelings, he apostrophised
the inanimate form, and, hanging over it with the tender-
ness of a mother over her lifeless child, as a last resource,
kissed its lips again and again with almost frantic anxiety.
At the time of his most eager application of this last remedy,
M'Elvina and Susan entered the room, without his being
aware of their approach.

The parrot on the table, with his tail still burning like a
slow match, first caught their eyes : and as they advanced
further in, there was Seymour, to their astonishment, kissing a young lady to whom he had never been introduced, and
who appeared to be quite passive to his endearments.

" Seymour ! " cried M'Elvina,—" what is all this ? "

" I'm glad you've come ; I cannot bring her to.   I've
tried everything."

" So it appears.   Why, you've smothered her—she's
black in the face," replied M'Elvina, observing the marks
of the Indian ink upon Emily's cheek.

Susan, who immediately perceived the condition of

Emily, applied her salts, and desired M'Elvina to call the women. In a few minutes, whether it was that the remedies were more effectual, or nature had resumed her powers, Emily opened her eyes, and was carried upstairs into Mrs M'Elvina's room.

We must return to the servant, who, with no other injury than a severe contusion of the os coccygis, from the frontal bones of the bull, recovered his senses and his legs at the same moment, and never ceased exerting the latter, until he arrived at——Hall, where he stated, what indeed he really believed to be the case, that Miss Emily had been gored to death by the bull; asserting, at the same time, what was equally incorrect, that he had nearly been killed himself in attempting her rescue. The tidings were communicated to Mrs Rainscourt, who, frantic at the intelligence, without bonnet or shawl, flew down the park towards the fields, followed by all the servants of the establishment, armed with guns, pitchforks, and any other weapons that they could obtain, at the moment of hurry and trepidation. They arrived at the field—the bull was there, waiting for them at the stile, for he had observed them at a distance, and as he was now opposed to half-a-dozen pair of inexpressibles, instead of one, his wrath was proportionally increased. He pawed the ground, bellowed and made divers attempts to leap the stile, which, had he effected, it is probable that more serious mischief would have occurred. The whole party stood aghast, while Mrs Rainscourt screamed, and called for her child—her child; and attempted to recover her liberty, from the arms of those who held her, and rush into the field to her own destruction.

The farmer to whom the animal belonged had heard his bellowing on the first assault, and had come out to ascertain the cause. He was just in time to behold the footman pushed through the hedge, and to witness the escape of Emily into the house of M'Elvina. Intending to remove the animal, he returned to his dinner, when his resumed bellowing summoned him again, and perceiving the cause, he joined the party, and, addressing Mrs Rainscourt, "The young lady is all safe, ma'am, in the gentleman's house yonder. The brute's quiet enough; it's all along of them red breeches that angers him. A bull can't abide 'em, ma'am."

"Safe, do you say? Thank God. Oh! take me to her."

"This way, ma'am, then," said the farmer, leading her round the hedge to the cottage of M'Elvina, by a more circuitous way.

Susan had just called up M'Elvina, and Seymour was again left to himself in the parlour, when Mrs Rainscourt, bursting from those who conducted her, tottered in, and sunk exhausted on the sofa. Seymour, to whom the whole affair was a mystery, and who had been ruminating upon it, and upon the sweet lips which he had pressed, in utter astonishment cried out, "What! another?" Not choosing, in this instance, to trust to his own resources, he contented himself with again shoving the parrot's tail between the bars, and as he held it to his patient's nose, loudly called out for M'Elvina, who, summoned by his appeals, with many others, entered the room, and relieved him of his charge, who soon recovered, and joined her daughter in the room upstairs.

The carriage had been sent for to convey Mrs Rainscourt and her daughter home. When they came down into the parlour, previous to their departure, Seymour was formally introduced, and received the thanks of Mrs Rainscourt for the attention which he had paid to her daughter, and a general invitation to the Hall.

Emily, to whom Susan had communicated the panacea to which Seymour had ultimately resorted, blushed deeply as she smiled her adieus; and our hero, as the carriage whirled away, felt a sensation as new to him as that of Cymon, when ignited by the rays of beauty which flashed from the sleeping Iphigenia.

Chapter XL

Idiots only will be cozened twice.
DRYDEN.

SEYMOUR did not fail to profit by the invitation extended by Mrs Rainscourt, and soon became the inseparable companion of Emily. His attentions to her were a source of amusement to the M'Elvinas and her mother, who thought little of a flirtation between a midshipman of sixteen and a girl that was two years his junior. The two months' leave of absence having expired, Seymour was obliged to return to the guard-ship, on the books of which his name had been enrolled. It was with a heavy heart that he bade farewell to the M'Elvinas. He had kissed away the tears of separation from the cheeks of Emily, and their young love, unalloyed as that between a brother and sister, created an uneasy sensation in either heart which absence could not remove.

When our hero reported himself to the commanding officer of the guard-ship, he was astonished at his expressing a total ignorance of his belonging to her, and sent down for the clerk, to know if his name was on the books.

The clerk, a spare, middle-sized personage, remarkably spruce and neat in his attire, and apparently about forty years of age, made his appearance, with the open list under his arm, and, with a humble bow to the first lieutenant, laid it upon the capstern-head, and running over several pages, from the top to the bottom, with his finger, at last discovered our hero's name.

"It's all right, young gentleman," said the first lieutenant. "Take him down to the berth, Mr Skrimmage, and introduce him. You've brought your hammock, of course, and it is to be hoped that your chest has a good lock upon it; if not, I can tell you you'll not find all your clothes tally with your division list by to-morrow morning.

But we cannot help these things here. We are but a sort of a 'thoroughfare,' and every man must take care of himself."

Seymour thanked the first lieutenant for his caution, and descended with the clerk, who requested him to step into his private cabin, previous to being ushered into the gun-room, where the midshipmen's mess was held—and of which Mr Skrimmage filled the important post of caterer. "Mrs Skrimmage, my dear," said Seymour's conductor, "allow me to introduce to you Mr Seymour." The lady curtsied with great affectation, and an air of condescension, and requested our hero to take a chair— soon after which Mr Skrimmage commenced—"It is the custom, my dear sir, in this ship, for every gentleman who joins the midshipmen's berth to put down one guinea as entrance money, after which the subscription is restricted to the sum of five shillings per week, which is always paid in advance. You will therefore oblige me by the trifling sum of six-and-twenty shillings, previous to my introducing you to your new messmates. You will excuse my requesting the money to be paid now, which, I assure you, does not arise from any doubt of your honour; but the fact is, being the only member of the mess who can be considered as stationary, the unpleasant duty of caterer has devolved upon me, and I have lost so much money by young gentlemen leaving the ship in a hurry, and forgetting to settle their accounts, that it has now become a rule, which is never broken through."

As soon as Mr Skrimmage had finished his oration, which he delivered in the softest and most persuasive manner, Seymour laid down the sum required, and having waited, at the clerk's request, to see his name, and sum paid, entered in the mess-book by Mrs Skrimmage, he was shown into the gun-room, which he found crowded with between thirty and forty midshipmen, whose vociferations and laughter created such a din as to drown the voice of his conductor, who cried out, "Mr Seymour,

gentlemen, to join the mess," and then quitted the
noisy abode, which gave our hero the idea of bedlam
broke loose.

On one side of the gun-room a party of fifteen or
twenty were seated cross-legged on the deck in a circle,
stripped to their shirts, with their handkerchiefs laid up
like ropes in their hands.   A great-coat and a sleeve-
board, which they had borrowed from the marine tailor,
who was working on the main-deck, lay in the centre,
and they pretended to be at work with their needles on
the coat.   It was the game of goose, the whole amusement of which consisted in giving and receiving blows.
Every person in the circle had a name to which he was
obliged to answer immediately when it was called, in
default of which he was severely punished by all the
rest.   The names were distinguished by colours, as
Black Cap, Red Cap; and the elegant conversation,
commenced by the master tailor, ran as follows; observing that it was carried on with the greatest rapidity of
utterance.

"That's a false stitch—whose was it?"

"Black Cap."

"No, sir, not me, sir.

"Who, then, sir?"

"Red Cap."

"You lie, sir."

"Who then, sir?"

"Blue Cap, Blue Cap."

"You lie, sir."

"Who then, sir?"

"Yellow Cap, Yellow Cap."

Yellow Cap unfortunately did not give the lie in time,
for which he was severely punished, and the game then
continued.

But the part of the game which created the most mirth
was providing a goose for the tailors, which was accomplished by some of their confederates throwing into the
circle any bystander who was not on his guard, and who,

K. I.   T

immediately that he was thrown in, was thrashed and kicked by the whole circle until he could make his escape. An attempt of this kind was soon made upon Seymour, who, being well acquainted with the game, and perceiving the party rushing on him to push him in, dropped on his hands and knees, so that the other was caught in his own trap, by tumbling over Seymour into the circle himself, from which he at last escaped, as much mortified by the laugh raised against him as with the blows which he had received.

Seymour, who was ready to join in any fun, applied for work, and was admitted among the journeymen.

" What's your name ? "

" Dandy Grey Russet Cap," replied Seymour, selecting a colour which would give him ample time for answering to his call.

" Oh ! I'll be d——d but you're an old hand," observed one of the party, and the game continued with as much noise as ever.

But we must leave it, and return to Mr Skrimmage, who was a singular, if not solitary instance of a person in one of the lowest grades of the service having amassed a large fortune. He had served his time under an attorney, and from that situation, why or wherefore the deponent sayeth not, shipped on board a man-of-war in the capacity of a ship's clerk. The vessel which first received him on board was an old fifty-gun ship of two decks, a few of which remained in the service at that time, although they have long been dismissed and broken up. Being a dull sailer, and fit for nothing else, she was constantly employed in protecting large convoys of merchant vessels to America and the West Indies. Although other men-of-war occasionally assisted her in her employ, the captain of the fifty-gun ship, from long-standing, was invariably the senior officer, and the masters of the merchant vessels were obliged to go on board his ship to receive their convoy instructions, and a distinguishing pennant, which is always given without any fee.

But Skrimmage, who had never been accustomed to deliver up any paper without a fee when he was in his former profession, did not feel inclined to do so in his present. Make a direct charge he dare not—he, therefore, hit upon a *ruse de guerre* which effected his purpose. He borrowed from different parties seven or eight guineas, and when the masters of merchant vessels came on board for their instructions, he desired them to be shown down into his cabin, where he received them with great formality and very nicely dressed. The guineas were spread upon the desk, so that they might be easily reckoned.

"Sit down, captain; if you please, favour me with your name, and that of your ship." As he took these down, he carelessly observed, "I have delivered but seven copies of the instructions to-day as yet."

The captain, having nothing to do in the meantime, naturally cast his eyes round the cabin and was attracted by the guineas, the number of which exactly tallied with the number of instructions delivered. It naturally occurred to him that they were the clerk's perquisites of office.

"What is the fee, sir?"

"Whatever you please—some give a guinea, some two."

A guinea was deposited; and thus with his nest-eggs, Mr Skrimmage, without making a direct charge, contrived to pocket a hundred guineas, or more, for every convoy that was put under his captain's charge. After four years, during which he had saved a considerable sum, the ship was declared unserviceable, and broken up, and Mr Skrimmage was sent on board of the guard-ship, where his ready wit immediately pointed out to him the advantages which might be reaped by permanently belonging to her, as clerk of the ship, and caterer of the midshipmen's berth. After serving in her for eight years, he was offered his rank as purser, which he refused, upon the plea of being a married man, and preferring poverty with Mrs S——to rank and money without her. At this the reader will not be astonished when he is acquainted, that the situation which he held was, by his dexterous plans, rendered so lucrative, that in the course of twelve years, with principal and accumulating interest, he had amassed the sum of £15,000.

A guard-ship is a receiving-ship for officers and men, until they are enabled to join, or are drafted to their respective ships. The consequence is, that an incessant change is taking place,—a midshipman sometimes not remaining on board of her for more than three days before an opportunity offers of joining his ship. In fact, when we state that, during the war, upwards of one thousand midshipmen were received and sent away from a guard-ship, in the course of twelve months, we are considerably within the mark. Now, as Mr Skrimmage always received one guinea as entrance to the mess, and a week's subscription in advance, and, moreover, never spent even the latter, or had his accounts examined, it is easy to conceive what a profitable situation he had created for himself. Mrs Skrimmage, also, was a useful helpmate: she lived on board, at little expense, and, by her attentions to the dear little middies and their wearing apparel, who were sent on board to join some ship for the first time, added very considerably to his profits.

Her history was as follows. It had three eras:—she had been a lady's maid, in town; and, in this situation, acquiring a few of the practices of "high life," she had become something else on the town; and, finally, Mrs Skrimmage. With the view of awing his unruly associates into respect, Mr Skrimmage (as well as his wife) was particularly nice in his dress and his conversation, and affected the gentleman, as she did the lady: this generally answered pretty well; but sometimes unpleasant circumstances would occur, to which his interest compelled Mr Skrimmage to submit. It may be as well here to add, that, at the end of the war, Mr Skrimmage applied for his promotion for long service, and, obtaining it, added his purser's half-pay to the interest of his accumulated capital, and retired from active service.

The steward and his boy entering the gun-room with two enormous black tea-kettles, put an end to the boisterous amusement. It was the signal for tea.

"Hurra for Scaldchops!" cried the master tailor, rising from the game, which was now abandoned. A regiment of cups and saucers lined the two sides of the long table, and a general scramble ensued for seats.

"I say, Mr *Cribbage*," cried an old master's mate, to the caterer, who had entered shortly after the tea-kettles, and assumed his place at the end of the table, "what sort of stuff do you call this?"

"What do you mean to imply, sir?" replied Mr Skrimmage, with a pompous air.

"Mean to ply?—why I mean to ply, that there's d——d little tea in this here water; why, I've seen gin as dark a colour as this."

"Steward," said Mr Skrimmage, turning his head over his shoulder towards him, "have you not put the established allowance into the tea-pot?"

"Yes, sir," replied the steward; "a tea-spoonful for every gentleman, and one for coming up."

"You hear, gentlemen," said Mr Skrimmage.

"Hear?—yes, but we don't taste. I should like to see it sarved out," continued the master's mate.

"Sir," replied Mr Skrimmage, "I must take the liberty to observe to you, that that is a responsibility never entrusted to the steward. The established allowance is always portioned out by Mrs Skrimmage herself."

"D—n Mrs Skrimmage," said a voice from the other end of the table.

"What!" cried the indignant husband; "what did I hear? Who was that?"

"'Twas this young gentleman, Mr Caterer," said a malicious lad, pointing to one opposite.

"Me, sir!" replied the youngster, recollecting the game they had just been playing; "you lie, sir?"

"Who then, sir?"

"Black Cap—Black Cap," pointing to another.

" I d—n Mrs Skrimmage! You lie, sir."

" Who then, sir?"

" Red Cap—Red Cap."

" I d—n Mrs Skrimmage! You lie, sir."

And thus was the accusation bandied about the table, to the great amusement of the whole party, except the caterer, who regretted having taken any notice of what had been said.

" Really, gentlemen, this behaviour is such as cannot be tolerated," observed Mr Skrimmage, who invariably preferred the *suaviter in modo*. " As caterer of this berth——"

" It is your duty to give us something to eat," added one of the midshipmen.

" Gentlemen, you see what there is on the table; there are rules and regulations laid down, which cannot be deviated from, and——"

" And those are, to starve us. I've paid six-and-twenty shillings, and have not had six-and-twenty mouthfuls in the three days that I have been here. I should like to see your accounts, Mr Caterer."

" Bravo! let's have his accounts," roared out several of the party.

" Gentlemen, my accounts are ready for inspection, and will bear, I will venture to assert, the most minute investigation; but it must be from those who have a right to demand it, and I cannot consider that a person who has only been in the ship for three days has any pretence to examine them."

" But I have been in the ship three weeks," said another, " and have paid you one pound sixteen shillings. I have a right, and now I demand them—so let us have the accounts on the table, since we can get nothing else."

" The accounts—the accounts," were now vociferated for by such a threatening multitude of angry voices, that Mr Skrimmage turned pale with alarm, and thought it advisable to bend to the threatening storm.

" Steward, present the gentlemen's respects to Mrs

Skrimmage, and request that she will oblige them by
sending in the mess account-book. You understand—the
gentlemen's respects to Mrs Skrimmage."

"D—n Mrs Skrimmage," again cried out one of the
midshipmen, and the game of goose was renewed with
the phrase, until the steward returned with the book.

"Mrs Skrimmage's compliments to the gentlemen
of the gun-room mess, and she has great pleasure in
complying with their request; but, in consequence of
her late indisposition, the accounts are not made up further
than to the end of last month."

This was the plan upon which the wily clerk invariably
acted, as it put an end to all inquiry; but the indignation
of the midshipmen was not to be controlled, and as they
could not give it vent in one way, they did in another.

"Gentlemen," said one of the oldest of the fraternity,
imitating Mr Skrimmage's style, "I must request that
you will be pleased not to kick up such a d——d
row, because I wish to make a speech: and I request that
two of you will be pleased to stand sentries at the door,
permitting neither ingress nor egress, that I may ' spin my
yarn ' without interruption.

"Gentlemen, we have paid our mess money, and we
have nothing to eat. We have asked for the accounts,
and we are put off with 'indisposition.' Now, gentlemen,
as there can be no doubt of the caterer's honour, I propose
that we give him a receipt in full."

"And here's a pen to write it with," cried out another,
holding up the sleeve-board, with which they had been
playing the game.

"Then, gentlemen, are you all agreed—to cobb the
caterer?"

The shouts of assent frightened Mr Skrimmage, who
attempted to make his escape by the gun-room door, but
was prevented by the two sentries, who had been placed
there on purpose. He then requested to be heard—to
be allowed to explain; but it was useless. He was
dragged to the table, amidst an uproar of laughter and

shouting. "Extreme bad headaches"—"Mrs Skrimmage" —"nervous" — "ample satisfaction" — "conduct like gentlemen"—"complain to first lieutenant"—were the unconnected parts of his expostulation, which could be distinguished. He was extended across the table, face downwards; the lappels of his coat thrown up, and two dozen blows, with the sleeve-board, were administered with such force, that his shrieks were even louder than the laughter and vociferation of his assailants.

During the infliction, the noise within was so great, that they did not pay attention to that which was outside, but as soon as Mr Skrimmage had been put on his legs again, and the tumult had partially subsided, the voice of the master-at-arms requesting admittance, and the screaming of Mrs Skrimmage, were heard at the door, which continued locked and guarded. The door was opened, and in flew the lady.

"My Skrimmage! my Skrimmage!—what have the brutes been doing to you? Oh, the wretches!" continued the lady, panting for breath, and, turning to the midship-men, who had retreated from her;—"you shall all be turned out of the service—you shall—that you shall. We'll see—we'll write for a court-martial—ay, you may laugh, but we will. Contempt to a superior officer— clerk and caterer, indeed! The service has come to a pretty pass—you villains! You may grin—I'll tear the eyes out of some of you, that I will. Come, Mr Skrimmage, let us go on the quarter-deck, and see if the service is to be trifled with. Dirty scum, indeed—" and the lady stopped for want of breath occasioned by the rapidity of her utterance.

"Gentlemen," said the master-at-arms, as soon as he could obtain hearing,—"the first lieutenant wishes to know the reason why you are making such a noise?"

"Our compliments to Mr Phillips, and we have been settling the mess account, and taking the change out of the caterer."

"Yes," continued Mrs Skrimmage, "you villains, you

have, you paltry cheats—you blackguards—you warmin—
you scum of the earth—you grinning monkeys—you!—
don't put your tongue into your cheek at me, you—you
beast—you ill-looking imp, or I'll write the ten command-
ments on your face—I will—ay, that I will—cowardly
set of beggars—" (No more breath).

"I'll tell you what, marm," rejoined the old master's
mate, "if you don't clap a stopper on that jaw of yours,
by George, we'll *cobb* you."

"Cobb me!—you will, will you?—I should like to see
you. I dare you to cobb me, you wretches!"

"Cobb her, cobb her!" roared out all the midshipmen,
who were irritated at her language; and in a moment
she was seized by a dozen of them, who dragged her
to the table. Mrs Skrimmage struggled in vain, and
there appeared every chance of the threat being put in
force.

"Oh,—is this the way to treat a lady?—Skrimmage!
help, help!"

Skrimmage, who had been battered almost to stupefaction, roused by the call of his frightened wife, darted
to her, and throwing his arm round her waist,—"Spare
her, gentlemen, spare her, for mercy's sake, spare her,—
or," continued he, in a faltering voice, "if you will cobb
her, let it be *over all*."

The appeal in favour of modesty and humanity had its
due weight; and Mr and Mrs Skrimmage were permitted
to leave the gun-room without further molestation. The
lady, however, as soon as she had obtained the outside
of the gun-room door, forgetting her assumed gentility,
turned back, and shaking her fist at her persecutors,
made use of language, with a repetition of which we will
not offend our readers,—and then, arm-in-arm with her
husband, quitted the gun-room.

"Mrs Skrimmage's compliments to the gentlemen of
the gun-room mess," cried one of the midshipmen,
mimicking, which was followed by a roar of laughter,
when the quarter-master again made his appearance.

"Gentlemen, the first lieutenant says, that all those who are waiting for a passage round to Plymouth are to be on deck with their traps immediately. There's a frigate ordered round—she has the blue-peter up, and her top-sails are sheeted home."

This put an end to further mischief, as there were at least twenty of them whose respective ships were on that station. In the meantime, while they were getting ready, Mr Skrimmage, having restored the precision of his apparel, proceeded to the quarter-deck and made his complaint to the first lieutenant: but these complaints had been repeatedly made before, and Mr Phillips was tired of hearing them, and was aware that he deserved his fate. Mr Skrimmage was therefore silenced with the usual remark—"How can I punish these young men, if they are in the wrong, who slip through my fingers immediately?—the parties you complain of are now going down the side. *Why don't you give up the catership?*"

But this, for the reasons before stated, did not suit Mr Skrimmage, who returned below. For a day or two the mess was better supplied, from fear of a repetition of the dose; after that, it went on again as before.

END OF VOL. I.

TURNBULL AND SPEARS, PRINTERS, EDINBURGH.